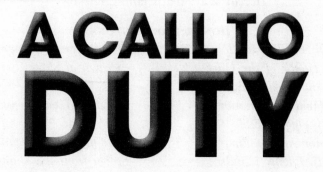

A CALL TO
DUTY

**For a complete listing of Baen titles by David Weber
and by Timothy Zahn, please go to www.baen.com**

A CALL TO DUTY

★ BOOK I OF ★
Manticore Ascendant

DAVID WEBER & TIMOTHY ZAHN

A Novel of the Honorverse

A Call to Duty: Book I of Manticore Ascendant

This is a work of fiction. All the characters and events portrayed in this book are fictional, and any resemblance to real people or incidents is purely coincidental.

Copyright © 2014 by Words of Weber, Inc. & Timothy Zahn

A Baen Books Original

Baen Publishing Enterprises
P.O. Box 1403
Riverdale, NY 10471
www.baen.com

ISBN: 978-1-4767-3684-6

Cover art by David Mattingly

First printing, October 2014

Distributed by Simon & Schuster
1230 Avenue of the Americas
New York, NY 10020

Library of Congress Cataloging-in-Publication Data

Weber, David, 1952–
   A Call to Duty : a Novel of the Honorverse / David Weber and Timothy Zahn.
       pages cm. — (Manticore Ascendant ; Book 1)
   ISBN 978-1-4767-3684-6 (hardback)
1. Science fiction. I. Zahn, Timothy. II. Title.
   PS3573.E217C35 2014
   813'.54—dc23
                                                            2014020010

10 9 8 7 6 5 4 3 2 1

Pages by Joy Freeman (www.pagesbyjoy.com)
Printed in the United States of America

For Anna, Diane, and Sharon.
Thanks for putting up with us.

FOREWORD

You may have noticed that this book has two authors' names on the cover: David Weber and Timothy Zahn. There really ought to be a third name on it, however, and that name is Thomas Pope.

When David decided to invite Tim to do an Honorverse series set in the early days of the Star Kingdom and dealing with the actual birth of the Royal Manticoran Navy, he wanted the books to do more than merely cover a time period which hadn't been fully explored in the Honor Harrington novels. He wanted them to have a different feel, as well, and he'd always really, really liked Tim's writing. The fact that Tim had done several short fiction pieces for the anthologies—including one which happened to be set in exactly the right time period—was icing on the cake. So after due consultation with Toni Weisskopff, the invitation was issued.

But, wait, you say! Did we not say that there should be three names on the cover? Indeed we did, because Tom Pope and BuNine have been assisting David in the expansion, indexing, and enrichment of (and other really neat labors of love for) the Honorverse for a long time now. In point of fact, it wouldn't be especially unfair to say that by this time, Tom knows at least as much about the nuts and bolts of the Honorverse as David does, since David spends lengthy periods of time discussing them with Tom on the phone and having the occasional "Ohh-hhhh, shiny!" moments along the way. So, especially since we were going to be dealing with the necessity of filling in David's existing notes about the Star Kingdom's early history, and the far cruder technology available at the time the RMN was created, it made perfectly good sense to him to bring Tom on board, as well. He's been the main keeper of the technology, plot analyst, concept suggester, continuity analyst, copy editor, and proofreader throughout the project, and in the process, his contribution is as much a part of this book's DNA as anything Tim or David might have contributed.

The only reason his name didn't appear on the cover of this first book was a marketing concern. Because there have been so many multi-author anthologies in the Honorverse, we felt some concern lest the appearance of three authors on the cover might have led people to assume that this was another anthology, and not a complete novel intended as the first of a series of complete novels. Some people don't read anthologies, and we were afraid they might pass this book by if that was what they thought it was. Since we happen to think it's a pretty darn good book, we would have considered that a tragedy. Of course, the crass commercialism of missed sales would never have entered our thinking, you understand.

However, when it comes to the second and any subsequent Travis Long novels, you will see all three authors listed on their covers. Hopefully by the time Book Two comes out, this first one will have thoroughly clued them in to the fact that they are looking at novels, not anthologies.

And that's enough about why there are only two names on the cover. If we keep on gabbing away at you'll never get the book read. So shoo! Go read!

We hope you have as good a time reading it as the three of us had writing it.

David Weber
Timothy Zahn

BOOK ONE

1529 PD

CHAPTER ONE

"MOM?" TRAVIS URIAH LONG CALLED toward the rear of the big, quiet house. "I'm going out now."

There was no answer. With a sigh, Travis finished putting on his coat, wondering whether it was even worth tracking his mother down.

Probably not. But that didn't mean he shouldn't try. Miracles did happen. Or so he'd been told.

He headed down the silent hallway, his footsteps unnaturally loud against the hardwood tiles. Even the dogs in the pen behind the house were strangely quiet.

Melisande Vellacott Long was back with the dogs, of course, where she always was. The reason the animals were quiet, Travis saw as he stepped out the back door, was that she'd just fed them. Heads down, tails wagging or bobbing or just hanging still, they were digging into their bowls.

"Mom, I'm going out now," he said, taking a step toward her.

"I know," his mother said, not turning around even for a moment from her precious dogs. "I heard you."

Then why didn't you say something? The frustrated words boiled against the back of Travis's throat. But he left them unsaid. Her dog-breeding business had had first claim on his mother's attention for as long as he could remember, certainly for the eleven years since her second husband, Travis's father, had died. Just because her youngest was about to graduate from high school was apparently no reason for those priorities to change.

3

In fact, it was probably just the opposite. With Travis poised to no longer be underfoot, she could dispense with even the pretense that she was providing any structure for his life.

"I'm not sure when I'll be home," he continued, some obscure need to press the emotional bruise driving him to try one final time.

"That's fine," she said. Stirring, she walked over to one of the more slobbery floppy-eared hounds and crouched down beside him. "Whenever."

"I was going to take the Flinx," he added. *Say something!* he pleaded silently. *Tell me to be in by midnight. Tell me I should take the ground car instead of the air car. Ask who I'm going out with. Anything!*

But she didn't ask. Anything.

"That's fine," she merely said, probing at a section of fur on the dog's neck.

Travis retraced his steps through the house and headed for the garage with a hollow ache in his stomach. Children, he remembered reading once, not only needed boundaries, but actually craved them. Boundaries were a comforting fence against the lurking dangers of absolute freedom. They were also proof that someone cared what happened to you.

Travis had never had such boundaries, at least not since his father died. But he'd always craved them.

His schoolmates and acquaintances hadn't seen it that way, of course. To them, chafing under what they universally saw as random and unfair parental rules and regulations, Travis's absolute freedom had looked like heaven on Manticore. Travis had played along, pretending he enjoyed the quiet chaos of his life even while his heart was torn from him a millimeter at a time.

Now, seventeen T-years old and supposedly ready to head out on his own, he still could feel a permanent emptiness inside him, a hunger for structure and order in a dark and unstructured universe. Maybe he'd never truly grown up.

Maybe he never would.

It was fifteen kilometers from Travis's house to the edge of Landing, and another five from the city limits to the neighborhood where Bassit Corcoran had said to meet him. As usual, most of the air car pilots out tonight flew their vehicles with breathtaking sloppiness, straying from their proper lanes and ignoring the speed limits and other safety regulations, at least until they reached the city limits. Travis, clenching his teeth and muttering uselessly at the worst of the offenders, obeyed the laws to the letter.

Bassit and two of his group were waiting at the designated corner as Travis brought the Flinx to a smooth landing beside the walkway. By the time he had everything shut down the three teens had crossed the street and gathered around him.

"Nice landing," Bassit said approvingly as Travis popped the door. "Your mom give you any static about bringing the air car?"

"Not a word," Travis said, reflexively pitching his voice to pretend that was a good thing.

One of the others shook his head. "Lucky dog," he muttered. "Guys like you might as well be—"

"Close it, Pinker," Bassit said.

He hadn't raised his voice, or otherwise leaned on the words in any way. But Pinker instantly shut up.

Travis felt a welcome warmth, compounded of admiration and a sense of acceptance, dissolving away the lump in his throat. Bassit was considered a bad influence by most of their teachers, and he got into trouble with one probably twice a week. Travis suspected most of the conflict came from the fact that Bassit knew what he wanted and wasn't shy about setting the goals and parameters necessary to get it.

Bassit would go far, Travis knew, out there in a murky and uncertain world. He counted himself fortunate that the other had even noticed him, let alone been willing to reach out and include him in his inner circle.

"So what are we doing tonight?" Travis asked, climbing out and closing the door behind him.

"Aampersand's is having a sale," Bassit said. "We wanted to check it out."

"A sale?" Travis looked around, frowning. Most of the shops in the neighborhood were still open, but there didn't seem to be a lot of cars or pedestrians in sight. Sales usually drew more people than this, especially sales at high-end jewelry places like Aampersand's.

"Yes, a sale," Bassit said, his tone making it clear that what they *weren't* doing was having an extended discussion about it. That was one of his rules: once he'd made up his mind about what the group was doing on a given evening, you either joined in or you went home.

And there wasn't anything for Travis to go home to.

"Okay, sure," he said. "What are you shopping for?"

"Everything," Bassit said. Pinker started to snicker, stopped at a quick glare from Bassit. "Jammy's girlfriend's got a birthday coming up, and we're going to help him pick out something nice for her." He laid his hand on Travis's shoulder. "Here's the thing. We've also got a reservation at Choy Renk, and we don't want to be late. So what I need you to do is stay here and be ready to take off just as soon as we get back."

"Sure," Travis said, a flicker of relief running through him. He wasn't all that crazy about looking at jewelry, and the reminder that other guys had girlfriends while he didn't would just sink his mood a little deeper. Better to let them stare at the diamonds and emeralds without him.

"Just make sure you're ready to go the second we're back," Bassit said, giving him a quick slap on the shoulder before withdrawing his hand and glancing at the others. "Gentlemen? Let's do this."

The three of them headed down the street. Travis watched them go, belatedly realizing he didn't know what time the restaurant reservation was for.

That could be a problem. A couple of months ago, when Pinker had been looking for something for *his* girlfriend, they'd all spent nearly an hour poring over the merchandise before he finally bought something. If Jammy showed the same thoroughness and indecision, it could be like pulling teeth to get him back outside again.

Travis smiled wryly. Maybe it would be like pulling teeth for *him* to get Jammy out. For Bassit, it would be a stroll down the walkway. When it was time to go, they would go, and whenever the reservation was for they would make it on time.

Assuming, of course, that Bassit remembered how Travis insisted on sticking to the speed limit. But Bassit wouldn't forget something like that.

Putting all of it out of his mind, Travis looked around. Businesswise, he'd once heard, this was one of the more volatile neighborhoods in the city, with old shops closing and new ones opening up on a regular basis. Certainly that had been the case lately. In the two months since he'd last been here one of the cafés had become a bakery, a flower shop had morphed into a collectables store, and a small upscale housewares shop—

He felt his breath catch in his throat. In the housewares shop's place was a recruiting station for the Royal Manticoran Navy. Behind the big plate-glass window a young woman in an RMN uniform was sitting behind a desk, reading her tablet.

A series of old and almost-forgotten memories ghosted across Travis's vision: his father, telling his five-year-old son stories of the years he'd spent in the Eris Navy. The stories had seemed exotic to Travis's young and impressionable ears, the stuff of adventure and derring-do.

Now, as he looked back with age and perspective, he realized there had probably been a lot more routine and boredom in the service than his father had let on. Still, there had surely been *some* adventure along with it.

More to the point, everything he'd read about militaries agreed that they were steeped in tradition, discipline, and order.

Order.

They probably wouldn't want him, he knew. He was hardly at the top of his class academically, his athletic skills were on a par with those of the mollusk family, and with Winterfall, the family barony, long since passed to his half-brother Gavin he had none of the political clout that was probably necessary to even get his foot in the door.

But Bassit and the others would be shopping for at least half an hour, probably longer. The recruiter was all alone, which meant no witnesses if she laughed in his face.

And really, there was no harm in asking.

The woman looked up as Travis pulled open the door.

"Good evening," she greeted him, smiling as she set aside her tablet and stood up. "I'm Lieutenant Blackstone of the Royal Manticoran Navy. How can I help you?"

"I just wanted some information," Travis said, his heart sinking as he walked hesitantly toward her. *Blackstone* was a noble name if he'd ever heard one, her eyes and voice were bright with intelligence, and even through her uniform he could see that she was very fit. All three of the probable strikes against him were there, and he hadn't even made it to the desk yet.

Still, he was here. He might as well see it through.

"Certainly," she said, gesturing him toward the guest chair in front of the desk. "You're looking for career opportunities, I assume?"

"I really don't know," Travis admitted. "This was kind of a spur-of-the-moment thing."

"Understood," Blackstone said. "Let me just say that whatever you're looking for, the RMN is the perfect place to start." Her voice, Travis noted, had changed subtly, as if she was now reading from an invisible script. "Career-wise, we have some of the best opportunities in the entire kingdom. Alternatively, if you decide the Navy isn't for you, you'll be out in five T-years, with the kind of training and technical skills that will shoot you right past the competition for any job or career you want. There's going to be plenty of opportunity in the civilian economy for decades still, rebuilding from the Plague, and someone with the skills and discipline of a Navy vet can expect to command top dollar. It's as close to a no-lose situation as you could ever imagine."

"Sounds pretty good," Travis said. Though now that he thought about it, wasn't there a faction in Parliament that was determined to shut down the Navy? If that happened, there wasn't going to be much left of careers *or* exotic training.

"Are you interested in the Academy?" Blackstone continued. "That's where the men and women in our officer track start their training."

"I don't know," Travis said, starting to relax a little. If she thought this was a joke, it didn't show in her face or voice. And that officer's uniform she was wearing definitely looked sharp. "I might be. What kind of requirements do you need to get in?"

"Nothing too horrendous," Blackstone assured him. "There's a vetting process, of course. Certain academic standards have to be met, and there are a few other credentials. Nothing too hard."

"Oh," Travis said, his brief hope fading away. There it was: academics. "I probably won't—"

And then, from somewhere down the street came the boom of a gunshot.

Travis spun around in his chair, a sudden horrible suspicion hammering into his gut and morphing into an even more horrifying certainty. Bassit—Jammy and his girlfriend's supposed birthday—that bulge he now belatedly remembered seeing beneath Pinker's floppy coat—

There was another boom, a double tap this time and somewhat deeper in pitch. Travis started to stand up—

"Stay there," Blackstone ordered, shoving down on his shoulder as she ran past him, a small but nasty-looking pistol gripped in her hand. She reached the door, slammed to a halt with her left shoulder against the jamb, and eased the door open.

There was another pair of deep booms, then another of the slightly higher-pitched ones as the first weapon answered. Travis jumped up, unable to sit still any longer, and raced over to join Blackstone.

"What's going on?" he breathed as he shoulder-landed against the wall at the other side of the door.

"Sounds like we've got a robbery going down," she said. Her eyes bored into Travis's face. "Friends of yours?"

Travis's tongue froze against the roof of his mouth. What was he supposed to say?

"I thought they were."

"Uh-huh." She turned back to the door as two more shots echoed. "Well, I hope you're not going to miss them, because one way or another they're going down. The cops will be here any minute, and if they're not gone by now, they're not going. What was your part of the job?"

Briefly, Travis thought about lying. But Blackstone had probably already figured it out.

"They told me we had early reservations at a restaurant," he said. "They said they were going to do some shopping and that I needed to be ready to head out as soon as they got back."

"Where was this supposed shopping? Aampersand's?"

"Yes."

Blackstone grunted. "Big mistake. Aampersand's apprentice goldsmith is a retired cop. Why you?"

"My mom has an air car," Travis said. "I guess they thought they could make a faster getaway in that than in a ground car."

"Were they right?"

Travis blinked. "What?"

"Would an air car have made for a better getaway?"

Travis stared at her profile, confusion coloring the fear swirling through his gut. What in the world kind of question was that? Was she trying to get him to incriminate himself? Hadn't he already more or less done that?

"I don't understand."

"Show me you can think," she said. "Show me you can reason. Tell me why they were wrong."

Some of Travis's confusion condensed into cautious and only half-believed hope. Was she saying she wasn't going to turn him in?

Apparently, she was.

He took a deep breath, forcing his mind away from what was happening to Bassit and the others and focusing on the logical problem Blackstone had presented.

"Because air cars are faster, but there aren't as many of them in the city," he said. "That makes them more easily identifiable."

"Good," Blackstone said approvingly. "And?"

Travis's throat tightened as he abruptly noticed that the gunfire had stopped. Whatever had happened was apparently over.

"And as soon as you get above rooftop level, you're visible for five kilometers in any direction," he went on. "The cops would have you in sight the whole time they were chasing you."

"What if you wove in and out between the buildings?"

That's illegal, was Travis's reflexive thought. But of course someone who'd just robbed a jewelry store would hardly be worried about traffic regulations.

"Well, if you didn't crash into something and kill yourself," he said slowly, trying to work it through, "you'd pop up as a red tag on every other air car's collision-avoidance system. Oh—right. The police could just follow the trail on their readouts and have their pick of where to force you down." He dared a wan smile. "They could also slap a dozen traffic violations on top of the armed robbery charge."

To his surprise, Blackstone actually smiled back.

"Very good. What else?"

In the distance, the sound of approaching police sirens could be heard. Again, Travis had to force his mind away from Bassit as he tried to come up with the answer Blackstone was looking for.

But this time, he came up dry.

"I don't know," he admitted.

"The most basic flaw there is," Blackstone said, turning a thoughtful gaze on him. "They picked the wrong person for the job."

Travis grimaced. "I guess they did."

"I'm not talking about your piloting skills," Blackstone assured him. "Or even your loyalty to people who don't deserve it. I'm talking about the fact that someone who's not in on the plan isn't exactly going to burn air when the gang comes charging up with guns smoking and pockets bulging with rings and bracelets."

She tilted her head to the side.

"Especially when that person comes equipped with an ethical core. You *do* have an ethical core, don't you, Mr.—?"

Travis braced himself.

"Long," he said. "Travis Uriah Long. I guess so." He tried another half-smile. "Is an ethical core one of the requirements you mentioned for naval officers?"

"If it was, the officer corps would be a lot smaller," Blackstone said dryly. "But if it's not a requirement, it's certainly a plus. Shall we go back inside and get started on the datawork?"

Outside, two police air cars appeared, their flashing lights strobing as they settled onto the street.

"I don't know," Travis said, feeling a fresh tightness in his chest as cops began streaming out of the vehicles, guns at the ready. Blackstone was right—if Bassit and the others weren't out of the neighborhood by now, they were done for.

And if they were still alive after all that shooting, they were going to talk.

"It can't hurt to try," Blackstone pressed. "The vetting process will take two to four weeks, and you can change your mind at any time."

And if part of their confession included such facts as the name of their intended getaway driver . . .

"How about regular Navy?" he asked. "Not officer, but regular crew. How long does that take?"

Blackstone's forehead wrinkled.

"Assuming there are no red flags in your record, we could ship you out to the Casey-Rosewood boot camp by the end of the week."

"You mean no flags other than armed robbery?"

"Pretty hard for anyone to link you up with that one," Blackstone said. "Especially given that you were in here with me when it went down. Are you sure you wouldn't rather go the academy route?"

"Positive," Travis said, wondering briefly what his mother would think of this sudden right-angle turn in his life. Or whether she would even notice. "You said there was datawork we had to do?"

"Yes." Blackstone took a final look outside and closed the door on the flashing police lights. "One other thing," she added as she holstered her gun. "Back when I told you to stay put, and you didn't? Bear in mind that once you're in the Navy you're going to have to learn how to obey orders."

Travis smiled, his first real smile of the day. For the first time in years, he could see some cautious hope beckoning from his future.

"I understand," he said. "I think I can manage."

CHAPTER TWO

I SEEK POLITICAL ASYLUM, the first man in the popular joke pleaded. *Take a transport to the House of Lords,* the second man retorted. *That's the finest political asylum in the world.*

There were days, Gavin Vellacott, Second Baron Winterfall, thought sourly as he strode along the busy corridor toward his office, that the joke was more fact than fiction, and not at all funny.

Today had been one of those days.

It had started with an Appropriations Committee meeting. Winterfall wasn't actually on that committee, but Countess Calvingdell had double-booked herself again and asked Winterfall to sit in for her. Then Earl Broken Cliff, the Secretary of Education, had double-downed with a snap straw vote that had forced Winterfall to go racing across the building with all the dignity of a low-range chicken, and for absolutely nothing.

Now, to close off the day, he'd returned to his desk to find a hand-delivered note from Earl Breakwater, Chancellor of the Exchequer, requesting Winterfall's presence at his earliest convenience.

And when the second-ranking member of His Majesty's government said *earliest convenience* he meant *now.*

Breakwater's secretary passed Winterfall through the outer office with her usual perfunctory smile. He crossed to the door, gave it a brisk two-knock, and pushed it open.

Two steps into the room he stopped short as his brain belatedly registered the fact that Breakwater wasn't alone. With him were Baroness Castle Rock, Earl Chillon, and Baroness Tweenriver. All of them political powerhouses; all of them far above Winterfall in rank or status or both; all of them gazing at the newcomer with utterly neutral expressions.

What the hell was going on?

"Come in, My Lord," Breakwater invited, waving to the empty chair beside Tweenriver. "Thank you for your time. I trust Jakob's vote was illuminating?"

"Not really, My Lord," Winterfall said, ungluing his feet and continuing on into the expansive office. Whatever was going on, he was determined to maintain an air of casual professionalism, as if he was invited to top-level political meetings all the time. "It broke along the same interest lines as always."

Chillon snorted. "*There's* a surprise," he rumbled.

"If there's one thing Parliament has going for it, it's consistency," Castle Rock agreed.

"The consistency of bull-headed stubbornness," Chillon countered scornfully. "Nothing ever changes except which group is plotting to stab which other group in the back in the name of protecting their own little turf and their own little collection of cronies. And nothing's ever *going* to change unless we can shake them up." He peered intently at Winterfall from beneath bushy white eyebrows. "*All* of them."

Winterfall didn't reply, pretending to be preoccupied with the complicated business of lowering himself into his chair. What was he supposed to say to a comment like that?

Fortunately, Breakwater was already moving into the conversational gap.

"Which is the purpose of this gathering, My Lord," he said. "The four of us—plus a few others—have come up with a new proposal we hope will break the permanent stalemate that Parliament seems to have settled into." He tilted his head slightly. "In a nutshell, Gavin—may I call you Gavin?"

"Of course, My Lord," Winterfall said, the unexpected familiarity again briefly throwing him off-balance until he realized it was probably meant to do precisely that. Certainly he had no illusions that Breakwater was offering any reciprocal intimacy.

"Thank you," Breakwater said. "In a nutshell, Gavin, we propose a complete restructuring of the Royal Manticoran Navy."

Winterfall felt a flicker of disappointment. From the buildup, not to mention the political firepower surrounding him, he'd expected something a little more groundshattering. As it was, plans and arguments involving the RMN's future littered the Star Kingdom's political landscape like the droppings that littered his mother's dog run.

"I see," he said.

"I doubt it," Chillon said. "Because we're not simply suggesting a variant of O'Dae's tired old scrap-the-battlecruisers plan."

"And we're *certainly* not going with Dapplelake's perennial hope that Parliament will throw the entire budget onto his desk and let him take his fleet out into the galaxy and fight someone," Breakwater said contemptuously. "No, we believe we've found a middle ground that actually takes political and economic realities into account."

That would be a first for Parliament. "Sounds interesting," Winterfall said aloud. "I'd like to hear more."

Breakwater looked at Castle Rock, and out of the corner of his eye Winterfall saw her give the Chancellor a small nod. Apparently, she was the one who'd been tasked with reading Winterfall's vocals and body language and deciding if he was the right person for the job.

Whatever the job was.

"I'm sure you know the RMN's history," Breakwater said, turning back to Winterfall. "From the four frigates that the Trust had waiting when the colony ship arrived, it grew to nineteen by the time of the first skirmish with the Free Brotherhood, seventeen years later, then to a total of thirty-four warships over the next forty years."

"And now here we sit with twenty-eight of the damn things," Chillon growled. "All of them draining funds from the treasury like giant blood leeches."

"And sucking off the workforce our civilian infrastructure needs a hell of a lot more than the Navy does," Breakwater threw in. "We've still got enormous holes from all the people we lost during the Plague, and even with the Trust's spadework before *Jason* got here, we're still playing catch-up with the rest of the galaxy as far as indigenous tech and industrial capacity are concerned. We don't just need the *money* it would take to put the fleet back into the kind of service Dapplelake is fantasizing about; we can't afford to waste that much trained, skilled manpower aboard ships that aren't contributing a damned thing to the economy."

"Especially those nine utterly useless battlecruisers," Castle Rock added.

"Exactly," Chillon said, nodding. "In service to nothing and no one except the officers and crew lazing around inside."

"Actually, two or three of them *are* officially in service," Tween-river murmured. "Depending on how you count."

"Irrelevant," Chillon said with a sniff. "Being in service doesn't mean they're actually *doing* anything." He jabbed a finger at Winterfall. "Case in point: Jakob's deadlocked vote this afternoon. If even a tenth of the RMN's budget was reallocated to Education, do you think there would be nearly so much acrimony on how to spend their funds?"

Actually, Winterfall knew, there probably would. For one thing, there were some serious philosophic differences dividing the members of the Education committee. Without a drastic change in the group's membership, that wasn't likely to change, extra money or no.

But of course that wasn't Chillon's point. His point was that, whatever the Star Kingdom's bank balance might be back in the Solarian League, that money was a long ways away, and a sizeable fraction was already earmarked for the ongoing Assisted Immigration project. The resources available right here and now were far more limited. And, as Breakwater and his allies were fond of pointing out, part of Parliament's job was to see that those resources were used as wisely and efficiently as possible.

Of course, for all of the budget hawks' focus on the Navy budget, it really wasn't that large a slice of the Exchequer's commitments. True, if the ships were all put back into full service, with the systems' damage they'd suffered during their hasty demobilization at the height of the Plague, it would cost a pretty penny. At present levels of spending, though, the burden was scarcely crushing, especially with the steady resurgence of the Star Kingdom's economy, thanks to the immigrants who'd flooded in to provide the necessary workers.

The charge that rebuilding the Navy's depleted manpower was in direct competition with the civilian economy's needs was a much more valid criticism, to Winterfall's thinking. And there wasn't much question that Dapplelake's ambitious manning totals would push naval manpower costs up into levels which could become burdensome. Especially if he was simultaneously spending money bringing the RMN's obsolescent vessels back up to acceptable levels of serviceability.

On the other hand...

"I'm not sure it would be a good idea to scrap the Navy entirely," he said cautiously, trying to read Breakwater's face. "The Free Brotherhood incident—"

"Don't be ridiculous," Chillon cut him off. "No one's suggesting a complete scrapping. But let's be realistic. The chances that anyone out there would bother with us are pretty damn small."

"As for the Free Brotherhood, that card was already decades out of date the first time Dapplelake played it," Breakwater added. "The dangers to the Star Kingdom aren't coming from outside, Gavin. They're coming from *inside*."

Winterfall felt his face go rigid. Was Breakwater actually suggesting—?

"Relax," Castle Rock soothed, an amused smile tweaking her lips. "We're not talking about treason or Enemies Domestic, as the Navy oath so quaintly puts it. We're referring to the ever-present threat of natural disasters to the transports, ore miners, and other ships that ply Star Kingdom space."

"Oh," Winterfall said, feeling relieved and foolish at the same time. He should have realized it was something like that.

And they were right about the risks of intersystem space travel. Only last month one of the ore miners in Manticore-B's Unicorn Asteroid Belt had lost its fusion bottle and disintegrated, taking its entire crew with it. A nasty incident, and sadly not an isolated one.

"Baroness Castle Rock is right," Breakwater said. "At this point in the Star Kingdom's history a navy bristling with battle-eager warships is the last thing we need." He grimaced. "It's the workforce— the *people*—putting our deep-space infrastructure back together that we really need. They're an absolutely vital national resource, and the Navy would be far more useful protecting *them* than defending all of us against imaginary interstellar foes. The bottom line is that what we need right now is an expansion of the Em-Pars fleet."

"Yes, that makes sense," Winterfall murmured. MPARS—the Manticoran Patrol and Rescue Service—was the group that patrolled the spacelanes around the twin suns of the Manticore System, focusing a lot of their attention on the asteroid belts where so much of the Star Kingdom's resource mining took place.

MPARS expansion was hardly a new idea—the Chancellor had raised such suggestions more than once during Winterfall's years in Parliament. So far none of the proposals had gained traction, not just from monetary considerations but even more so because of the scarcity of trained personnel and the only gradually accelerating resource flow.

And, of course, because of politics. Unlike the Royal Manticoran Navy, which was under the authority of Earl Dapplelake's Defense Ministry, MPARS was controlled by Breakwater's own Exchequer.

Distantly, Chillon's comment about turf-fighting flicked through Winterfall's mind.

"I imagine Dapplelake would argue that any new small ships the Star Kingdom gets should be warships," he murmured.

"Ah—but that's the point," Breakwater said. "They *will* be warships. The sloops we have in mind will be every bit as well-armed as the Navy's corvettes and frigates, ready to take on any external threat that might befall us."

"But under the Exchequer's authority."

Breakwater waved a hand in dismissal.

"An accident of history," he said. "That's simply the way MPARS was set up. It has nothing to do with me personally."

"The point is that the sloops will be designed for *in-system* defense, not the kind of extra-system war expedition that battlecruisers are best suited for," Castle Rock said. Her expression probably showed more scorn than she intended it to, but she was a long-standing member of the Parliamentary faction which distrusted Dapplelake and cast a leery eye toward the sort of foreign adventures they feared the Defense Minister might be tempted to use his Navy for. "In the unlikely event that another group of marauders like the Free Brotherhood ever tried anything, we could swarm them with at least the same number of missiles as we could now," she added.

"And when these new ships aren't fighting mythical bogeymen," Chillon said, "they'll be available to assist with any *real* trouble that might arise."

"I see," Winterfall said, feeling a small frown creasing his forehead. The idea made a certain amount of sense, as far as it went. But Breakwater and the others seemed to be ignoring the giant hexapuma in the room. "I understand how a fleet of smaller ships would save money in the long run," he continued.

"But at the moment, we don't have them. So we're still talking about building more ships, and I don't see where the extra money would come from."

"Indeed," Breakwater said with a nod. "As Chancellor I know more about the budget than anyone else on Manticore. You're absolutely right—the money simply isn't there. *Unless.*"

He let the word hang in the air a moment. Winterfall leaned forward a few centimeters...

"*Unless* these new ships are created from existing ones," Breakwater concluded.

Winterfall blinked. That was *not* the answer he'd expected.

"Excuse me?" he asked carefully.

This time, it wasn't just Castle Rock who smiled smugly. It was all of them.

"No, you heard right," Chillon assured him. "Tell me, have you ever heard of Martin Ashkenazy?"

Winterfall searched his memory. The name sounded vaguely familiar, but he couldn't place it.

"I don't think so."

Chillon's lip twitched. Disappointment?

"He's a mining ship designer, working with civilian spacecraft and mostly under governmental radar," he said. "He's also the grandson of one of the officers on the original *Triumph* battle-cruiser eighty-odd years ago. It turns out that he has copies of the diagrams and specs of that ship."

"And with a little prompting from us," Breakwater said, "he's concluded that each of those mothballed battlecruisers can be taken apart, reformed, rebuilt, and converted into a pair of corvette-sized ships."

"*What?*" The word blurted unasked-for from Winterfall's lips.

"And for a fraction of the cost of building those ships from scratch," Breakwater continued, graciously ignoring the disrespectful outburst.

"As we said: political *and* economic realities," Tweenriver added.

"So that's the plan," Breakwater said, his eyes boring into Winterfall's. "Your thoughts?"

"It's...very interesting," Winterfall managed, struggling to figure out how exactly this was going to work. He'd never seen a battlecruiser up close and personal, but he'd seen plenty of holos and vids, and no matter how he tried to visualize such deconstruction his mental image of the results came out looking hideously ugly, like spacegoing versions of the misshapen hunchbacked ogres of the Old Earth legends he used to read as a kid. An irreverent thought flashed through his mind: *Hans Christian Anderson's Ugly Ducklings—*

"Naturally, it won't be simply a matter of cutting the ship in half like a banana and sealing all the openings," Castle Rock said. "It'll take some serious refitting, rewiring and replumbing."

"But there are a lot of repeaters and redundancy centers—environment, energy, and others—scattered around each of the big ships that can form the center of the smaller ships' systems," Chillon added.

"We don't pretend to understand all of it," Tweenriver said. "But Ashkenazy is an expert, and he's convinced the theory is sound."

"I've also run the financial numbers," Breakwater said. "If he's right, we'll be able to create our new Home Guard without unduly straining the budget. And every penny we spend on it will be spent right here in the Star Kingdom, providing jobs and helping to build—rebuild—our infrastructure, not ordering ships from some well-heeled shipyard back in the League."

And the fact that some of your staunchest political allies happen to own the local shipyards where all that work will be done—and where all that money will be spent—is just an added bonus, isn't it, My Lord? Winterfall very carefully did not ask out loud.

"Granted, the new ships won't be sleek and beautiful," Tweenriver said. "But they'll be functional." She smiled. "I daresay aesthetics will be the last thing on the minds of a mining crew facing certain death as their rescuers arrive."

"Yes," Winterfall murmured. "A question, if I may?"

Breakwater waved a hand in invitation, and Winterfall braced himself.

"Why me?"

"Why not you?" Castle Rock asked.

It was, Winterfall knew, a reply designed to deflect the question. But for once, he wasn't going to be dissuaded. Not even by such people as these.

"I'm just a baron," he said doggedly. "My house and lands are miniscule, my political and economic positions are negligible, and all my friends are in pretty much the same state as I am. If my grandparents hadn't been one of the first fifty investors in the colony, no one in the Star Kingdom would ever even have heard of me."

"But they *did* make that investment, and you *are* in the Lords," Breakwater reminded him. "Accident of history or not, it still makes you one of the fifty most powerful men and women in the Star Kingdom." He pursed his lips. "Fifty-one, of course, counting King Michael."

"I understand that," Winterfall said. "Please don't misunderstand. I'm honored and flattered that you consider me worth inviting into your confidence. I simply don't see what additional assets I can bring to the table."

"You give yourself too little credit," Breakwater said calmly. "Where you see weaknesses, we see strengths. Your youth and circle of friends make you the ideal person to reach out to young peers of similar rank and position. Your political averageness helps allay any suspicions that your true motivation is to draw more power to yourself."

"Because, frankly, you're not destined to rise much higher than you already are," Chillon said. "No offense."

"None taken," Winterfall assured him. It was a conclusion he'd reluctantly come to years ago.

"There's also Clara Sumner's tacit recommendation," Tween-river said. "The countess wouldn't let just *anyone* sit in on an Appropriations meeting for her, you know. We trust Clara, and she obviously trusts you."

"And of course, there's your brother," Castle Rock added. "He'll add a nice touch of additional sincerity to your message of reform."

"Excuse me?" Winterfall frowned. His *brother*? What did his brother have to do with this?

"Your brother," Castle Rock repeated. "Sorry; your half-brother. Travis Long."

"Yes, I know who you mean," Winterfall said. "What about him?"

The others exchanged puzzled glances.

"He's just enlisted in the Navy," Castle Rock said.

"He *what*?" Winterfall demanded, feeling his eyes go wide in disbelief. "*Enlisted*?"

"Three weeks ago," Castle Rock said, staring at him in some confusion of her own. "He's already two weeks into boot camp." She threw a look at Breakwater. "You didn't know?"

"No, I didn't," Winterfall ground out. He'd talked with his

mother not two days ago, and she hadn't said a single word about Travis, let alone mentioned anything about any such sudden and seriously major decisions.

Unless his mother herself didn't know.

He felt his throat tighten. Four years ago, Travis had tried to talk to him about his growing isolation from his mother. Winterfall, in his usual hurry to finish up the perfunctory visit and return to his work, had brushed the concerns aside, assuming Travis was merely presenting with standard teenage angst, and had offered the boy the same half-baked aphorisms he himself had been given when he was that age.

Now, he wondered if maybe Travis *hadn't* been imagining things. Wondered, too, if he should have listened to his brother a little more closely.

"But it doesn't matter," he said, trying to filter the foreboding from his voice. He had no idea what RMN boot camp was like, and he frankly didn't know his half-brother very well. Even so, he had a pretty good idea that Travis and the rigors of boot camp wouldn't be especially compatible. "He's my brother, not me. Whatever he does or doesn't do, his actions don't impinge on my life and career. Nor do they affect how well I can assist in this undertaking."

He looked at Breakwater. "Assuming you still want me."

Once again, Breakwater looked at Castle Rock. Winterfall looked at her too late to catch her response; but when he turned back to Breakwater the other was smiling.

"Welcome aboard, My Lord," he said, inclining his head. "The Committee for Military Sanity is pleased to have you among us."

His smile faded.

"Let's just pray we can get the rest of the Lords to see the universe the same way we do. Before it's too late."

CHAPTER THREE

THE CASEY-ROSEWOOD INSTRUCTIONAL CENTER WAS THE RMN's all-purpose training base for enlisted and noncommissioned officers, with an entry-level boot camp at its southern end, a set of training schools in its northern and western quadrants, and the more esoteric advanced training facilities to the east.

And it was quickly apparent that the boot camp section of the complex had been designed and built solely for the purpose of killing naïve young recruits like Travis Uriah Long.

Travis's first three weeks there were a nightmare. Literally. They were a half-comatose, pulse-pounding, muscle-aching, walking, marching, being-continually-yelled-at nightmare.

The order and structure he'd always yearned for were there, just as he'd hoped. But it was a structure he could feel choking the life out of him. Morning began before the sun was even up, with a loud bugle call or an even more raucous banging of metal bars on metal trash can lids. Once the noise started, the thirty men and women in their respective ends of the barracks had exactly twenty seconds to scramble out of their bunks and stand at rigid attention along the central aisle, and heaven help the maggot who missed the deadline, or even made it in time but was the last one in position. The platoon commander, Gunner's Mate First Class Johnny Funk, knew more curses than Travis had ever heard, and had the volume and tone control an operatic singer would have envied.

By the end of the first week Travis probably would have quit if quitting had been an option. Several of the other boots, he gathered from the muttered curses and soft moans of aching muscles in the night, felt the same way.

But quitting wasn't possible. Not yet. They'd signed up for five T-years, and by God and by First Lord of the Admiralty Admiral Thomas P. Cazenestro, RMN (ret), they *would* put in those five years or die trying. Or so GM1 Funk said.

Funk had given them his full name the very first time he'd faced them, and had all but dared anyone to make jokes about it. A couple of the braver or more foolhardy boots had done so, though they were smart enough to offer their humor where neither Funk nor any of the other platoon commanders or drill instructors could overhear.

Such private triumphs were short-lived. GM1 Funk found out about every one of them, and the humorists' muscles had ached extra hard for the next few days from the dozens of additional workout reps the unamused platoon commander had put them through. No one made any such jokes now.

Which was hardly unexpected. People didn't make jokes about the devil incarnate, and by the end of the second week Travis was convinced that that was who GM1 Funk truly was. The man was up ahead of them every morning and was the last angry face they saw before staggering to the barracks and collapsing into comas in their bunks. His brain was an encyclopedia of the General Orders, the Manual of Arms, Uniform Code of Conduct, ship types, weapon types, ship systems, ship terminology, history, officer lists, and every other bit of information that anyone could possibly want. He could see a twitching lip two ranks away, could hear the smallest snicker *four* ranks away, and could almost literally draw blood with the serrated edge of his voice.

There was no possible way that Travis could ever become accustomed to such a hell. And yet, to his numbed disbelief, by the end of the third week he could feel himself actually doing so. The aches became fewer and less intense, he started being less overwhelmed by the flood of information Funk and the other instructors firehosed at them, and the rhythms and cadences of the marching were starting to stick in his brain stem, freeing his higher functions to drop into a neutral state that almost qualified as extra sleep.

By the end of the fourth week he knew all twenty-five men and fourteen women in his platoon better than he'd ever known anyone in his life. Better than he'd ever realized he *could* know anyone. He'd heard their stories and their histories; knew their strengths and quirks and weaknesses; knew which ones he could trust and which he couldn't and which he needed to steer wide of when they got that certain gleam in their eye, because when their latest scheme or infraction fell apart he didn't want to be anywhere inside GM1 Funk's blast radius.

By the end of the fifth week something in his brain abruptly clicked, and the patterns and relationships inherent in the mass of information being poured into the boots' brains suddenly made sense. From that point on, the classwork was under the same kind of control as the marching and pushups and obstacle course: not exactly easy, but no longer on the edge of hopeless. It was the point where Travis finally and truly began to believe that he not only could, but *would* get through this.

At the end of the sixth week, the whole thing was nearly snatched away.

☆   ☆   ☆

Predictably, it was because of Chomps.

Charlie Townsend had picked up the nickname *Chomps* early in the platoon's nickname-attaching process. He was from Sphinx, shorter and squatter than average, but immensely strong and invariably cheerful. Unfortunately, his cheerfulness bled over into the forbidden area of commander baiting, and he caused the platoon more than its fair share of midnight marches and snap inspections.

The man also had an enormous appetite. The son of assisted immigrants from the Kismet System, he had the super-active metabolism of someone whose ancestors had been genetically engineered for heavy-gravity environments. There weren't that many people on Sphinx, even now, but Sphinxians appeared to be overrepresented in the Navy. Four of the mess men were Sphinxians themselves, and at first they'd made sure to surreptitiously heap extra food on Chomps's meal trays, even though they were supposed to dole out exactly the same rations to everyone. That ended midway through the third week when some by-the-book officer wandered into eyeshot and ordered the servers back to proper procedure.

Chomps's countermove was to make sure he was the first one in the platoon to go through the mess line, wolf down his food, then slip back into line and collect a second meal before the last boot made it through and service was closed down. Again, the mess crew played along; again, some wandering rule-stickler caught on and ended the game.

For the next week, in the quietest part of the night, it was possible to hear the sound of soft stomach rumbling across the men's side of the barracks. The various meals were supposed to provide sufficient nutrition for anyone, even a Sphinxian, but Travis wasn't sure he bought that.

Chomps was absolutely sure *he* didn't buy it, and there was no doubt that he was losing weight. In fact, his face had begun to look almost gaunt as he suffered his deprivation in increasingly grouchy silence, his cheerful attitude fading like the charm of mess hall borscht.

And then, sometime late in the fourth week, he found the final card he could play.

If they wouldn't give him the food he needed, he would steal it.

Travis knew nothing about it at the time, of course. As he'd been learning about the rest of the platoon, they'd likewise been learning about him, and the last thing anyone planning mischief wanted was "Rule-stickler" Long hearing about it.

That was fine with Travis. He had enough stress on mind and body without dragging his ethics on a twenty-five-klick march of their own.

It was also why his first indication that something was up was as he walked past Chomps's locker shortly before lights-out one evening and caught the delicate aroma of chocolate chip cookies.

His first reflexive thought was that he was having an olfactory flashback to the cookies that had been racked at the dessert station at lunch that afternoon. But no—this aroma was very real.

And unfortunately, there was only one possible explanation for the presence of food in the barracks.

He moved slowly down the line of lockers, sniffing carefully, wondering who the thief was and what he, Travis, would do when he found him out. Food of any sort was absolutely forbidden in barracks, and the penalty for theft was even more severe. Those were the rules, and Travis had always tried his best to follow the rules.

The problem was that such obedience wasn't as straightforward as it used to be. Over the past few weeks he'd become aware that there were other rules in force in the Royal Manticoran Navy, rules that might not be in the manual but were just as binding.

And at the top of that unwritten list of unwritten rules was that you supported the men and women of your platoon. No matter what.

But this was *theft*. This wasn't just an infraction of a minor rule. This was a real, actual *crime*.

"Hey, Stickler."

Travis jerked and spun around. Chomps was standing at the end of the line of lockers, an unreadable expression on his face.

"Chomps," Travis managed in return.

"Anything wrong?" Chomps asked, his eyes steady on Travis. "You look like you just saw a ghost."

"Not *saw*," Travis corrected, his heart picking up its pace. His body had muscled up a lot in the past few weeks, but Chomps could still eat him for breakfast. "And not a ghost." Steeling himself, he pointed at Chomps's locker. "Cookies."

Chomps's lip twitched. Probably he was thinking about Travis's reputation for sticking to the rules. Maybe wondering what it would take to shut him up.

Then, to Travis's relief, he lowered his eyes and inclined his head.

"Cookies it is," he admitted. "I guess you hadn't noticed my stomach isn't keeping everyone awake anymore."

Travis felt a flush of annoyance with himself. As a matter of fact, he *hadn't* noticed the new level of peace and quiet in the barracks, and he really should have.

"Not much food value in cookies," he said, some obscure impulse driving him to argue the point.

"No, there isn't," Chomps agreed without rancor. "Usually, I just take *real* food." He nodded toward his locker. "I brought those back as a thank-you for my team."

An unpleasant shiver ran up Travis's back. There was a *team*?

"Ah," he said lamely. "I hadn't thought . . ."

"It's not like you could sneak into the kitchen all by yourself," Chomps pointed out. "You need a diversion, for starters, to get the right mess man looking the wrong way. You also need to know what's happening right after lunch—not a good idea to go on a twenty-five-klick hike with bags of sliced meat hanging under your armpits and breadsticks up your sleeves."

"Or the obstacle course," Travis murmured. "Which was what we were supposed to do today."

"Exactly," Chomps said, nodding. "Classwork can be tricky, too, depending on how aromatic the stuff is that you took. You don't want to be sitting in a small room watching an impeller systems deconstruction with salami in your shorts."

"No," Travis agreed, the memories of today's lunch flashing back to mind.

But now he was seeing the images with fresh eyes. Elaine Dunharrow—"Whistler"—bobbling her tray for several seconds before regaining control, with the mess man nearest the swinging door into the kitchen watching in fascinated and nervous anticipation of what would have been an ugly clean-up job. "Shofar" Liebowitz, talking earnestly with the next closest mess man. "Professor" Cyrene and "Betcha" Johnston, standing together in animated conversation right where their bodies would block the view of the door from the platoon commanders' table.

And a glimpse of a broad back disappearing through the kitchen door, a back Travis had assumed belonged to one of the Sphinxians in the mess crew.

"But the obstacle course is the worst," Chomps said, flashing one of the smiles that had been his normal expression before the mess hall started starving him. "I did that last week when Professor's intel went sideways. It wasn't pretty. He double-checks his facts now."

"So why are they still here?" Travis asked, waving again toward the locker. "No one was hungry during study time?"

"We couldn't coordinate with Whistler," Chomps said. "She's going to sneak over after lights-out for a little get-together in the shower room."

Travis winced. Sneaking out of barracks at night. Not the same level of crime as theft, but another serious rule violation.

Chomps caught the wince.

"I guess the question is what you're going to do now that you know," he said.

Travis exhaled, his brain feeling like it was running its own obstacle course. A crime...but whatever anyone said about the meals, Chomps really *did* need the additional food. A conspiracy...but the Sphinxian really *couldn't* do it alone. Loyalty to his platoon... but where did that loyalty become a crime in and of itself?

"I don't—"

And then, from the far side of the row of lockers came the sound of the outer door being slammed open.

"Ten-*hut!*" Funk barked.

Travis snapped reflexively to attention, his heart suddenly in his throat.

"Long?" Funk shouted over the sound of boots scrambling madly off their bunks or chairs. *"Long!"*

There was nothing for it.

"Sir, here, Sir!" Travis called back, wondering if he dared take a step or two away from the locker toward the PC's voice. You weren't supposed to move a single muscle when at attention, but if Funk came back here and smelled the cookies...

It was just as well he didn't try to take that step. Barely half a second later Funk came storming into view around the end of the lockers, moving faster than usual for this time of night. Whatever the reason for this unexpected visit, it must be important. Maybe important enough that he wouldn't pause long enough to inhale?

"Get dressed," Funk growled, his eyes taking in Travis's undershirt and bare feet. "You're wanted at—" He broke off, his eyes narrowing as his nostrils flared. "What am I smelling?" he demanded, his voice suddenly cold and dark. "Is that *cookies*, Recruit Long?"

Chomps's face had gone pale. But there was nothing to be gained by feigning ignorance.

"Sir, yes, Sir," Travis said.

Funk turned his gaze onto Chomps, a knowing expression on his face.

"And how exactly did cookies get into this barracks?" he asked, his voice purring with grim anticipation.

Travis took a deep breath. The crime was laid bare, and payment had to be made. But the rule of loyalty to a comrade in need also had to be upheld.

And in that split-second, Travis could think of only one way to satisfy both ethical requirements.

"Sir, I brought them in, Sir," he said.

Funk's head snapped back around, his eyes turning from Chomps just in time to miss the Sphinxian's own suddenly widened eyes.

"*You* brought them in, Recruit Long?" he demanded.

Too late, Travis wondered if this might not have been a good idea.

"Sir, yes, Sir," he said.

"Really," Funk said. "Travis Uriah 'Rule-stickler' Long. You broke into the mess hall and stole a pile of chocolate chip cookies."

"Sir, yes, Sir," Travis said. "Sir, I was hungry, Sir."

"Uh-huh." Funk folded his arms across his chest. "How'd you do it?"

Travis's mouth went dry as he saw the trap laid invitingly in front of him. As Chomps had already pointed out, it was impossible to pull off such a stunt alone. Travis had admitted to the crime; Funk was now fishing for the identities of his confederates.

And he would have them, too, Travis knew. Even if he used the same vague descriptions that Chomps had just given him, Funk would be able to compare notes with the other PCs and piece it together.

Unless Travis, Chomps, and Funk were all wrong about one crucial fact.

"Sir, I went in the side door after lunch, Sir," he said, his mind racing to stay ahead of his mouth.

"Which side door?"

"Sir, the north door, by all the trash cans, Sir," Travis said.

Funk snorted.

"The door that's always locked?" he asked pointedly.

"Sir, the blond mess man always props the door open when he bring out his bags of trash, and he always pauses to take a look at the western sky before he goes back in, Sir," Travis said. "Sir, I slipped in while he wasn't looking, Sir."

"What about the rest of the mess men?" Funk countered, clearly not buying it for a second. "You just tango your way past them?"

"Sir, the others were all in the dining area cleaning up, Sir," Travis said. "Sir, I put on an apron and kept my back to anyone who came in, Sir."

"Mm," Funk said. So far, Travis thought uneasily, he seemed more intrigued than angry. Travis wasn't sure what to make of that, but it couldn't be good. "Lucky for you we cancelled that twenty-five-klick hike that was supposed to happen after lunch."

So now he was fishing for Travis's intel source. Fortunately, Travis already had the answer for this one.

"Sir, yes, Sir," he said. "Sir, I noticed you had a second roll at lunch, Sir. Sir, you never do that when there's a strenuous activity planned, Sir."

Just visible at the edge of Travis's peripheral vision, Chomps's lower jaw had been dropping ever lower as the conversation progressed. Fortunately, Funk seemed to have eyes only for Travis.

"You're a very clever maggot, Recruit Long," Funk said, his voice still unnaturally calm. "Good thing we were already on our way to see the CO." He jerked his head toward the barracks door. "Get dressed. Now."

☆　　☆　　☆

Travis had seen Colonel Jean Massingill exactly twice since his arrival at Casey-Rosewood. The first time had been when she addressed and welcomed the new recruits, the second had been when he spotted her getting into an air car on the far side of the obstacle course. On neither occasion had she seemed particularly intimidating.

She was more than making up for that now. And the most unnerving part of it was that, unlike Funk's standard procedure, she never once raised her voice.

"I presume Gunner's Mate Funk has already told you what the penalty for food theft was in early wet navies," she said, her voice calm, her face composed, her eyes seeing far enough through Travis's face to set the back of his skull on fire. "The thief was flogged around the deck."

She stopped, apparently expecting some sort of response.

"Ma'am, yes, Ma'am," Travis said, his mind going completely blank on anything else.

"What was it, some whim?" she suggested. "Some spur-of-the-moment craving for chocolate?"

"Ma'am, I was hungry, Ma'am," Travis said. The excuse sounded even less plausible now than it had when he'd trotted it out a few minutes ago for Funk. But he still didn't have anything better to offer.

"Or was it perhaps a return to your old ways?"

Travis blinked.

"Ma'am?"

"Ma'am what?" Funk growled.

"Ma'am, I don't understand, Ma'am."

"Really." Massingill picked up her tablet. "That's not what Bassit Corcoran testified in court this morning. He says you were part of a gang that attempted to rob a jewelry store in Landing two months ago."

Travis felt the blood drain from his face. So Bassit had survived the abortive robbery attempt after all. Before Travis's arrival at

Casey-Rosewood he hadn't had the nerve to hunt for information
on Bassit's fate, and afterward he'd been so busy he'd nearly
forgotten about the other teen.

But Bassit clearly hadn't forgotten him. And whether he'd
named Travis in an attempt to cut a deal or whether it was pure
spite, the bottom line was that the whole ugly incident had now
come home to roost.

And with that, he had no doubt, his five-year enlistment was
at an end.

"The colonel's waiting," Funk prompted darkly.

"Ma'am, I was briefly associated with Mr. Corcoran, Ma'am,"
Travis said, trying to keep his voice from shaking. Suddenly, and
almost to his surprise, he realized just how much he wanted to
continue this path he'd started. How much he genuinely wanted
to serve the Star Kingdom alongside the men and women of his
platoon. Now, between Bassit and Chomps, between naïveté and
impulsive self-sacrifice, he was going to lose it all. "Ma'am, on
that particular night, without my knowledge, he attempted the
robbery you spoke of, Ma'am. Ma'am, I was not on the scene at
the time, but was in fact speaking with a Navy recruiter, Ma'am."

"Mm." If Massingill was impressed, she didn't show it. "Corcoran
further stated that the robbery was your idea. That you were the
mastermind behind the plan."

Travis stared at her. Bassit had said *that*?

Of course he had. Because from Travis's new perspective on
life, he now realized that what he'd taken to be Bassit's proud
refusal to compromise his beliefs and goals was really nothing
more than a self-centered refusal to follow any rules but his own,
and to put his own skin ahead of anything else.

One of the first rules of any society was that actions had consequences. If there was any single rule Bassit would try his best
to lie his way out of, that would be it.

"Ma'am, no, Ma'am," Travis said. "I was not involved in any
way in the robbery."

"Because you were talking to a recruiter at the time."

"Ma'am, yes, Ma'am."

"Joining the RMN," Massingill said. "Where you could come
to boot camp and steal cookies."

Travis felt his throat tighten. Again, what could he say?

"Ma'am, yes, Ma'am."

"Mm," she murmured again. "He also said you were a travesty of a human being. Rather exotic phrase for a common punk thief. Some private joke between you?"

Travis winced. He'd hoped that hated high school nickname had been left behind. One final gift from his false friend.

"Ma'am, no, Ma'am."

For a long moment Massingill continued to impale him with her eyes. Then, she nodded microscopically toward the door.

"Wait in the outer office," she ordered. "Gunner's Mate Funk will join you shortly."

"Ma'am, yes, Ma'am." Executing a crisp about-face, Travis strode back across the office.

So that was it, he told himself bleakly as he opened the door and stepped into Massingill's outer office. The only question now was how hard the colonel would bring the hammer down on him on his way out.

And how much it would hurt.

CHAPTER FOUR

MASSINGILL WAITED UNTIL THE DOOR had closed behind Long. Then, keying her outer-office monitor camera, she nodded to Funk.

"At ease, Gunner's Mate," she said. "Let's hear your side of this."

"My side, Ma'am?" Funk asked, frowning as he dropped into parade rest.

"As in why you don't think Long stole the cookies," Massingill said, watching the monitor out of the corner of her eye. There wasn't anything valuable out there, nor was any confidential data readily accessible on any of the computers. But Long didn't know that. And a habitual or even a semi-hardened thief ought to at least look around on general, reflexive principles, with the hope of nabbing a consolation prize on his way out.

But Long was doing nothing of the sort. He'd planted himself beside the office door in parade rest and was standing with his face and eyes pointed rigidly forward.

And those eyes looked like they were stifling back tears.

"I never said he didn't steal the cookies, Ma'am," Funk protested. "At this point I don't know anything other than that he confessed to the crime."

"I'm aware of that," Massingill said. "I'm also aware that in describing the incident you went out of your way to use words like *he stated* and *I was told*. That doesn't sound to me like someone who believes what he's hearing."

Funk's lip twitched.

"No, Ma'am, I don't," he said reluctantly. "He spins a good

yarn, but I doubt anyone could pull off something like that all by himself. And I *know* those cookies weren't meant for Long."

"A payoff for something?"

"More likely extra fodder for a Sphinxian gullet," Funk said. "Recruit Charles Townsend. He's been trying to scam himself extra food ever since he hit dirt here."

Massingill felt her lip twist as the gunner's mate's tone registered. So Funk didn't think too much of Training Command's brainstorm either, did he?

"And someone thoughtfully stole a few cookies for him?" she asked.

"More than a few, Ma'am," Funk said. "That memo from Mess Division two days ago pretty well shows the pilferage has been going on for at least a couple of weeks."

"And you don't think Long's smart enough to pull off a long-term crime?"

"Oh, he's smart enough," Funk said. "But he's also the ethical, rule-following type. If he's involved at all, he's on the fringe. More likely he just stumbled into it and went all heroic to cover for the real thieves."

"Perhaps," Massingill said. On the monitor, Long was still waiting at parade rest. Waiting for whatever fate the future had in store for him.

That fate wasn't entirely in Massingill's hands. Luckily for him, part of it was.

"Very well," she said. "Return him to the barracks. The Provost Marshal is sending an air car to take him in for testimony tomorrow at oh-nine-hundred—make sure he's ready. Assuming the King's Prosecutor has the brains to see through Corcoran's B.S. and sends him back, write him up for tonight's incident and give him ten hours' extra duty."

"Yes, Ma'am." Funk sounded a bit . . . conflicted, Massingill noted. The standard book punishment for food theft was considerably stiffer than that, and the gunner's mate wasn't generally in favor of shorting his recruits on something like that. In this case, though . . .

"You can also confiscate the cookies if they're still there," Massingill went on. "Which I'm not really expecting. Dismissed."

"Yes, Ma'am." Spinning around in an about-face that was twice as crisp as Long's had been, Funk strode to the door and left the office. Massingill watched the monitor as he collected Long and the two of them left the office suite and headed out into the night.

And then, muttering an ancient French curse she'd once heard and memorized just because she liked the sound of it, she dug into her bottom desk drawer and pulled out a half-full bottle of scotch.

Damn them all, she thought sourly as she poured herself a tall drink. Damn the ineffectual nobles and careerists running the RMN. Damn the mid-rank officers, many of whom just seemed to be coasting along for the ride. And *especially* damn the particular set of idiots in Parliament—and the serving officers prepared to go along with them—who seemed to think the military's job was to serve as a petri dish for their own pet social experiments.

Especially insane social experiments like this one.

The directive that had come down from Captain Alexander Caldecott two months ago had been as explicit as it had been top secret, and Massingill wondered exactly how top-secret it actually was. Caldecott was a staff weenie of the worst possible variety: someone who'd never held a line commission, never exercised executive authority over an actual operational unit, but who figured he knew exactly how those Neanderthal line officers *ought* to be doing their jobs. Worse, he had the sort of exalted family connections—in his case, to the Baron of Yellow Oak—which made him dangerous to cross. Worse still, his cousin the Baron—and Caldecott himself, for that matter—had a touching, childlike faith in academic analyses formed by men and women with even less experience with a real military than he possessed himself. And, worst of all, his current slot in the Bureau of Personnel was that of Recruit Training Syllabus Officer, which put him in a position to display the truly profound depths of his idiocy.

Allow all the boots the exact same amount of food. That was the order. Even for the Sphinxians, and never mind that their heavier musculature—not to mention the enhanced metabolisms of so many of the more recent immigrants—demanded more than the average number of calories. You *didn't* reduce a recruit's caloric intake below the level of sustainability, which was what it amounted to in the Sphinxians' case, at the same time that you deliberately stressed that recruit's body to the point of exhaustion. You just didn't, and Massingill had protested the order when it came down.

Without success. It was possible that Caldecott, whose family had settled on Manticore, not Sphinx, and who therefore had less personal experience with genies in general, had been unaware of the consequences of the heavy-grav genetic modifications. Not that his ignorance made it any better. He damned well should have realized, and if he'd been a quarter as smart as he clearly thought he was, he would have done at least a little research before he imposed his brilliance on Massingill's hapless recruits.

Unfortunately, he hadn't. Or perhaps he had, and if that was the case, the colonel wanted a few moments alone with him in a suitably dark alley.

The theory behind the aforesaid brilliance was that each platoon would notice the problem and rally around its members, those with fewer needs voluntarily giving up food to those who needed more. The directive had waxed eloquent about how this would be an ideal way to cement each unit, and how this would be so much better than the traditional approach of grinding the boots into the dirt and creating unity from a universal hatred of their platoon commanders and drill instructors. Some no doubt ivory-tower type—Massingill hadn't bothered to link through to the referenced study so she didn't know for sure—had concluded that this would create better cohesion and be less damaging to the boots' tender psyches, and Caldecott had bought into it.

Unfortunately, the geniuses had failed to appreciate three minor points. One, *no one* in boot camp felt like he or she was getting enough to eat, especially under such a grueling physical regimen, which left them disinclined to share the nourishment their weary bodies craved. Two, the Sphinxians—and especially the genetically modified ones—genuinely *weren't* getting enough to eat. And three, the other obvious approach to hunger was to simply steal the damn food.

On one level, Massingill had to admit the scheme had worked like a champ. Travis Uriah Long, an apparently staunch and ethical rule-follower, had either stolen food for a hungry mate by himself, or else had lied about it to protect the true thieves in his platoon. Unit cohesion, all right, in spades.

The Uniform Code of Conduct listed the required punishment for Long's crime. But Massingill had final say in enforcement, and there was no way she was going to throw the full book at the kid for this. Not when Caldecott had effectively undercut the whole basis for the punishment with this lunatic social experiment. Not when the crime's motivation had been to aid a starving comrade in the most effective way the idiot behind that experiment had allowed him. Especially not when there was no way to prove Long had even committed the crime, and every indication that he was merely protecting more of his comrades.

They were cohesive, all right. They were a cohesive band of thieves.

Massingill sipped broodingly at her scotch. Ten T-years ago, when she and her husband Alvis had been lured away from the Solarian League to help train the Star Kingdom's recently formed Royal Manticoran Marine Corps, the recruiters had been all aglow with praise and promises.

And for a while things had gone reasonably well. There were other Marine vets who'd been drawn into the process, not all of them from the League, not all of them capable of finding their butts with a high-image satellite. The Manticorans who'd been in the original Fleet Marine Forces before the reorganization also had their own ideas of how to do things, most of which ranged from quaint to flat-out wrong. But the work had been interesting, the newer recruits had been sufficiently malleable, and the promotions had kept coming. Their Assisted Immigration debt had been paid off, and she and Alvis had settled in for what they'd expected to be the long haul.

But over the past couple of years their enthusiasm had been slowly but steadily fading. Alvis had been promised work on a pair of ambitious refitting projects, but both of those had now stalled out, and without them Alvis's extensive engineering and yard-dog experience was being wasted. Massingill herself had been moved into the CO slot at Casey-Rosewood, only to find that the politics here were even worse than in the main fleet, thanks to the meddling of idiots like Caldecott whose political connections put them into position to do real damage.

Abruptly, she knocked back the rest of her drink. The social experiments, she knew, would continue as long as there were Caldecotts to conduct them. But this particular experiment was going to end. Right now.

She pulled out her uni-link and keyed it to all-base memo mode.

"To all mess personnel," she said. "All previous restrictions on meal portions are hereby rescinded. Recruits, commanders, instructors, and officers can from this point on have as much food as they damn well want. Any questions on this order will be directed to me."

She keyed off with a snort. That wouldn't sit well with Caldecott or his fellow political upper-echelon officers. God only knew where the idiots who actually sat in Parliament were going to go in the end—there'd been pressure for years to turn the Navy into little more than an extension of Breakwater's MPARS fleet, and in the meantime they were willing to allow idiocies like Caldecott's scheme. They weren't going to be very happy if someone *called* them on their idiocy, and young as the Star Kingdom's aristocratic hierarchy was, its denizens had already learned how to game the system when somebody pissed them off.

Well, let them. Let First Lord Cazenestro kick her out of Casey-Rosewood, if he wanted. She and Alvis could find civilian jobs and leave this mess behind them.

Because a star nation could have a battle fleet, a system patrol-and-rescue force, or a stage for social experimentation. It couldn't have all three.

There were dangerous people out there. Far more of them than the Manticorans seemed to realize. So far the Star Kingdom had escaped their notice, but that would change. Sooner or later, that would change.

She could only hope King Michael and his schizophrenic Parliament decided what they wanted from their Navy before that happened.

☆   ☆   ☆

It had been close to lights-out when Travis was taken to see Colonel Massingill, and most of the rest of the boots were already in their racks by the time a glowering Funk dropped him off and stalked out again. Trying to ignore the eyes he could feel silently watching him through the darkness, Travis headed to his locker to begin his own nighttime prep.

There he discovered that Chomps had left him a cookie.

Possibly as a thank-you. More likely as a going-away present.

Because the most reasonable assumption was that Travis wouldn't be coming back after the courtroom hearing Funk had said he would be attending in the morning. And even if the court let him go, there was no guarantee that RMN justice would follow suit. The regs said that food theft carried a penalty of up to three nights in the brig and fifty hours of extra duty, which was pretty bad all by itself.

But those same regs also gave the CO a lot of say in meting out that punishment. If Massingill decided to make an example of him, he could find himself dishonorably discharged by lunchtime.

His first indication that things might not be as bad as he feared came at breakfast. He and the others arrived in the mess hall to find a new sign informing the boots that there was no longer a limit on portion sizes.

That morning, Travis noted, Chomps went through the line three times.

The next surprise came when Funk pulled him out of class at oh-eight-thirty and took him to an unoccupied room in the HQ building. The boots hadn't yet been issued dress uniforms, presumably on the sensible theory that it was still possible to wash out of training and the RMN didn't want to bother passing out clothing that would never be worn. But sometime during the night, someone had apparently issued such a uniform for Travis. Funk glowered at the wall until Travis had finished changing, then escorted him to the landing area and waited with him until the Provost Marshal's air car arrived to collect him.

He and his escort had to wait outside the hearing room for nearly an hour before they were finally summoned inside. To Travis's relief, it was a closed hearing, with only the attorneys and judge present. No need for the awkwardness of having to face Bassit or the others of his gang.

The questioning was as tough as Travis had expected, with the defense attorney doing everything she could to malign, intimidate, or undermine his story. But everything about that evening had been laser-etched onto Travis's memory, and he answered each question truthfully and with the same stoic expressionlessness that he'd learned to present to Funk and Casey-Rosewood's drill instructors.

He was just finishing up when an unexpected witness—unexpected to Travis, anyway—arrived: his RMN recruiter, Lieutenant Blackstone, resplendent in her gold-trimmed black officer's uniform. Her cool, no-nonsense testimony seemed to deliver the final blow to the defense's efforts to paint Travis as the gang's criminal mastermind. When she was finished, the judge apparently decided he didn't even need to review the testimony. He dismissed the pending charges against Travis, thanked him and Blackstone for their time, and ordered them back to their duties.

It added up to nothing more than a lost half-day of class, which Travis's escort made very clear he would have to make up. But Travis didn't care. He'd been cleared of all charges, and that unpleasant chapter in his life was now officially over.

As a bonus, he now knew that Lieutenant Blackstone's first name was Anne.

His return to Casey-Rosewood was without fanfare. The staff sergeant who checked him in handed him his fatigues and pointed him to the head, accepting his dress uniform without comment after Travis had changed. He rejoined his platoon in the middle of a presentation on fusion bottle physics, and with that the morning's adventure was over.

Later, in the barracks, Chomps asked about the meeting with Massingill and the morning in court, and thanked him for whatever he'd done that had gotten the mess hall's food policy changed. Travis's protestations that he'd done absolutely nothing were summarily brushed aside, and Chomps declared himself to be Travis's friend for life.

Fortunately, no one else in the platoon seemed inclined to shower Travis with the embarrassment of undeserved praise. In fact, from all outward appearances, it seemed the rest of them had barely even noticed Travis's two absences, let alone cared where he might have been.

And yet, over the next few days Travis noticed some subtle changes in the atmosphere around him. The half-sneering, half-sarcastic tone that had always accompanied Travis's nickname *Stickler* faded away, with the nickname now sounding simply ironic or, occasionally, even friendly. The boots sometimes still got impatient at Travis's insistence on following procedure without cutting corners, but there wasn't nearly as much of the earlier contempt or under-the-breath derision. A few of them even tried, at least for a while, to follow procedure more closely themselves.

But even as Travis almost began to relax, he noticed that the word *travesty* was creeping into casual conversation.

He never figured out whether or not the word was aimed at him and his hated nickname. He never seriously tried to find out, either. If it was a dig at him, his best bet was to ignore it.

If it was just a word the platoon had picked up by overhearing something Funk had said, then Travis likewise didn't want to draw attention to himself.

Besides, right now all that mattered was that he was back on track to becoming part of the RMN. If the cost of that was some annoying wordplay, it was a price he was willing to pay.

☆   ☆   ☆

Four weeks later, it was suddenly over.

The boots were run through the graduation drill and marches for the last time. They were issued their dress uniforms, and taught how to wear them.

And on a bright, crisp morning, in front of Colonel Massingill and a dozen other men and women Travis didn't recognize, the boots were officially inducted into the Royal Manticoran Navy.

It was over. Or rather, it was just beginning.

The spacers—not *boots* anymore, but *Spacers Third Class*— scattered from the barracks and drill fields at the southern end of Casey-Rosewood to their new assignments in the equally unadorned barracks and more specialized training school classrooms of the base's northern and western ends. Travis was assigned to Impeller Tech training, and there was soon a running gag among the new spacers that if a failed impeller node got stuck in place he could simply scold it into doing its job properly.

But somehow, the jokes no longer mattered. Travis had made it. He was in the Royal Manticoran Navy, and his future lay ahead of him.

Whatever that future was, he was determined to make the most of it.

CHAPTER FIVE

WINTERFALL HADN'T SEEN KING MICHAEL in person very often, and most of those occasions had been formal or ceremonial, where the Star Kingdom's monarch had been dressed in his full garb of state. Seeing him dressed in a simple business suit, seated in an ordinary chair in the palace conference room, was something of a shock.

Still, even outfitted like an ordinary Manticoran citizen, there was something in Michael's eyes and the way he quietly dominated the room that underlined the dignity and authority lurking just beneath the surface. He had his mother's very dark complexion but his grandfather's chin, coupled with the broad shoulders of his father's family, and there was something... solid about him. He was a man, Winterfall had often thought, who wore the kingship well. A man who, as the cliché went, could be said to have been born to the position.

Which was surely one of the great ironies of history, given that Michael hadn't been born to anything of the sort. He'd been a full twenty-seven T-years old when the Manticore Colony, Ltd., had reorganized its corporate-management system into the Star Kingdom of Manticore, with Michael's grandfather Roger as its first monarch and his family designated the House of Winton.

The stories from those first heady years spoke of how Roger's daughter Elizabeth—who would be crowned herself upon her father's death four years later—had taken to the responsibilities like a duck to water. Michael, unfortunately, hadn't been nearly so enthusiastic. His interests and talents lay in other directions, and while he'd accepted the throne without complaint it was clear that he hadn't particularly wanted it. Still, in the eight years since his ascension to the throne he'd proved himself an able enough monarch.

Able, but not really inspiring. Nowhere in those eight years had he done anything dramatic or memorable. Certainly he'd made no decisions or taken any actions that could legitimately be said to have changed the course of Manticoran history.

Today, Winterfall mused, the King had the chance to do exactly that.

Michael listened in silence as Breakwater laid out the plan. The Exchequer finished, and for another moment the King continued his silence. Then, he stirred and looked at the three men seated across the table from Breakwater and the rest of the Committee for Military Sanity.

"James?" the monarch invited. "Or would you prefer First Lord Cazenestro went first?"

"No, I think an overall summary would be in order here," Defense Minister James Mantegna, Earl Dapplelake, said. "With all due respect to Chancellor Breakwater, I don't think I've ever heard a more ridiculous suggestion. Cutting up a battlecruiser to make a pair of sloops? That's insane. If you want more frigates or corvettes to patrol the system, it makes more sense to build them from scratch."

"Does it?" Breakwater countered. "How much does it cost to import a ship's fusion plant from the Solarian League these days? How much for an impeller ring?" He pointed at the tablet in front of him. "I've run the numbers. They're not cheap."

"Then—" Dapplelake broke off, and Winterfall saw a flicker of annoyance cross his face.

Small wonder. The obvious retort to Breakwater's numbers would be to suggest that they simply build a few new hulls and cannibalize the mothballed battlecruisers for impellers and fusion plants to put inside them.

But Dapplelake didn't dare bring up that option. Stripping the battlecruisers for parts would destroy them as effectively as cutting them up, and the Defense Minister was firmly committed to keeping his Navy at its current strength.

"Then?" Breakwater prompted.

"Then let's learn how to build our own fusion plants and impellers," Dapplelake said. "In fact, let's learn how to build our own ships."

"To what end?" Breakwater scoffed. "A merchant fleet? Nonsense— the League and Havenite ships that come calling are more than capable of handling all the interstellar trade we need."

"Countess Acton might disagree," First Lord of the Admiralty Admiral Cazenestro put in mildly. "Her company already has one merchantman plying the local circuit, and she's making noises about building two more over the next ten years."

"I'd also take issue with your assumption that our trade *should* be handled by foreign carriers," Admiral Carlton Locatelli added. "It seems to me that a properly forward-thinking people would want to seize that future for themselves. For that matter," he said, giving Breakwater a less than warm look, "I keep hearing people talk about what a drag on the civilian economy the Navy is. If we were building our own ships—and those merchant vessels Earl Dapplelake and First Lord Cazenestro mentioned—we'd be building up our industrial base, as well. Surely that's a factor worth weighing, wouldn't you say, My Lord?"

"I think we're straying a bit from the point," Breakwater said. "The issue before us today isn't a Manticoran merchant marine, but—"

"Excuse me, My Lord, but this is very much the point," Locatelli interrupted, his voice firm. "Your whole proposal rests on the need for more patrol and rescue ships for the asteroid-mining regions. Very well, then. Instead of the short-term solution of wrecking a group of perfectly good ships, shouldn't our focus be on the long-term building of the Star Kingdom's future?"

"The future is also not the issue," Breakwater insisted. "Making grandiose plans for tomorrow at the cost of today is folly, pure and simple. If the Star Kingdom needs to develop a merchant marine, it will do so when the time is right. In the meantime, these so-called *perfectly good* ships of yours are sitting in permanent orbit and draining resources that could be going to our schools, our infrastructure, the whole Gryphon expansion project—"

"Our infrastructure is doing just fine," Dapplelake cut him off. "So is Gryphon. And I'd consider it a personal favor if you'd retire Broken Cliff's tired old smokescreen argument about schools and education. Whatever problems our education system is having, extra money and people alone won't solve them."

"And since you bring up Gryphon," Cazenestro added, "let's not forget how much that world owes to the men and women of the RMN. Without them, the planet would be even farther from a self-sustaining population base than it is now."

Breakwater snorted.

"If I were you, My Lord, I wouldn't bring up the whole navy-in-a-box affair. Buying all those Solarian ships and crews was where the financial drain began, and the reason why we're in this situation to begin with."

"Excuse me, My Lord, but those ships and their crews are the *reason* we're able to sit here discussing it instead of living in the midst of a shattered economy trying desperately to rebuild," Locatelli said severely. "Without them, the Brotherhood would have broken us down to nothing."

"That assumes the Brotherhood would ever have come to Manticore in the first place," Breakwater retorted. "To the best of my knowledge, that's never been confirmed."

"Fine," Locatelli said. "Ignore history, if you wish. Let's move on to current events, starting with Gustav Anderman and his ambitions of empire."

"Please," Breakwater said contemptuously. "Anderman is a lunatic, and everyone knows it."

"He may well be a lunatic," Locatelli said. "But he's also conquered Nimbalkar and Tomlinson. That speaks volumes about his resources and tactical skill. And if reports from the region are to be believed, he's got his eye on several other nearby systems."

"One: he's a long way away," Breakwater said, ticking off fingers. "Nearly four months even for a warship. Two: we don't have anything he could possibly want, so don't start with any *imminent threat* nonsense. And three: his so-called empire will implode ten minutes after his death as his generals and admirals start fighting over the territory. Read your history, Admiral—empires and kingdoms started by rogue mercenaries always end that way."

Winterfall stole a look at Michael. The King was watching the verbal tennis match with an expression that seemed to be a mixture of impatience and resignation. He'd probably presided over hundreds of such battles over the years, Winterfall realized suddenly: the behind-the-scenes power struggles and scrappy negotiation sessions that the public never saw.

Maybe Michael was tired of it all. At seventy-two T-years he was still reasonably young and healthy. But political stress took its toll, especially on those who didn't especially enjoy the game.

Or maybe the impatience and resignation were because he knew Breakwater and Dapplelake well enough to also know how this particular battle was going to end.

"—dual impeller ring design makes it easy to split the ships in half," Breakwater was saying. Apparently, he'd managed to drag the conversation back to the original issue during the few seconds Winterfall had been lost in contemplation. "In fact, I'd go so far to say—and let me point out that Martin Ashkenazy agrees completely with me on this—that the original *Victory*'s designers deliberately built the ship with an eye toward cutting it into two independent sections if necessary."

"With all due respect, that's ridiculous," Cazenestro said scornfully. "You're also mixing apples and oranges. Of course a battlecruiser's forward and aft sections are designed to operate independently. In a battle, a near-miss or ruptured sidewall could easily knock out one part of a ship, and without redundant systems the wedge would go down and the ship would be dead. But redundancy in itself is a far cry from suggesting that a ship could be simply be cut in half and both sections go sailing off on their merry way."

"In general, you may be right," Breakwater said, and Winterfall could hear a hint of anticipation in his voice as he prepared to play his trump card. "But the *Triumph* class has one small but vital difference from the rest of your fleet: unlike your other warships, they have two *separate* reactors, one for each impeller ring, which of course means one in each half of the ship. That reactor and its placement are at the heart of Ashkenazy's conclusion as to the designers' original intentions."

"Yes, you've made Mr. Ashkenazy's position abundantly clear," Dapplelake said. "As well as your own." His eyes swept across the other four men and women on Breakwater's side of the table. "But I can't help noticing that your so-called Committee for Military Sanity seems to be more of a Committee of the Incessantly Voiceless. Don't any of them have anything to add?"

And then, to Winterfall's dismay, the minister's roving gaze came to a halt on him.

"Lord Winterfall," he said with a sort of ironic civility. "What's *your* opinion on all this?" He gave a little snort. "Or were you

brought aboard merely to be an extra warm body and not actually think?"

Winterfall froze. Breakwater's strategy—in fact, his explicit
order—had been for the Chancellor to carry the ball on this
one. He was to present the plan to the King and RMN leaders
while the rest of the group maintained a solid but silent wall of
endorsement. For his own part, Winterfall had been more than
happy to let Breakwater handle their side of the conversation
while he himself observed from the sidelines.

But now he'd been asked a direct question by a senior member
of the government. He had no choice but to answer.

And that answer, he knew, had better be good.

"I do have an opinion, My Lord," he said, inclining his head
politely to Dapplelake. Peripherally, he saw that Breakwater and
the others had turned to face him, but the angle wasn't good
enough for him to make out any of their expressions. Probably
just as well. "I fully expect that, no matter what any of us say
here today, the Royal Manticoran Navy is going to lose one or
more of its mothballed battlecruisers. The only real questions are
how many, and when."

Dapplelake was staring at him as if he'd suddenly changed
color. Apparently, whatever response the defense minister had
been expecting to his abrupt question, that hadn't been it.

"Excuse me?" he asked, his tone ominous.

"I said—"

"What do you mean, *when*?" Locatelli put in. Of the three
men on that side of the table, he seemed the least taken aback
at one of Breakwater's human props suddenly developing a voice.

"I mean this project will go through," Winterfall said, a surge
of adrenaline rushing through him. He'd seldom been in any
sort of spotlight, and never one this intense. To his surprise, he
found it strangely exhilarating. "The necessary votes are there
already, and more will be forthcoming if Parliament perceives
that you're stonewalling on the issue."

"Yes, well, the King will have a great deal of the final say on
this," Dapplelake huffed, giving Michael a quick nod of respect.
"And he knows that there are too many potential dangers out
there for us to completely—"

"You sound as if you have a suggestion, My Lord," Michael
spoke up calmly. "Perhaps you'd be willing to share it with us?"

Winterfall braced himself, feeling another jolt of adrenaline as the spotlight cranked up to its highest possible level. The King himself had asked him a question....

"Yes, Your Majesty, I do," he said with all the respect he could muster. "The most efficient way to carry out the Committee's plan would be to dismantle all nine battlecruisers at the same time. By that I mean a team would cut one of them in half, then move on to the next while a different crew—"

"Your Majesty—" Dapplelake began urgently.

Michael silenced him with a gesture. "Continue," he said.

Winterfall worked a quick dab of moisture into his mouth. "As I said, Your Majesty, that kind of assembly-line procedure would make the most sense economically. It would tie up the orbiting dock and the work crews for the minimum amount of time while putting the rescue sloops into service at the maximum rate."

"Is that your suggestion, then?" Michael asked.

"Not exactly, Your Majesty," Winterfall said, a small part of his mind noting that the King seemed to already be ahead of him, with his questions and comments merely there to shepherd Winterfall along. "Any new technology or procedure should be approached with caution, especially something as radical and untested as this. My suggestion would be that we do the conversion on only *one* of the battlecruisers, carrying it completely through the process before touching any of the others."

"That seems reasonable," Breakwater put in, sounding eminently satisfied with Winterfall's answer.

Winterfall braced himself. The Chancellor's gratified tone was about to change.

"I also recommend, Your Majesty," he continued, "that the finished sloops be in service for a minimum of five T-years before any action is taken on the other battlecruisers."

Even two seats away, Winterfall had no trouble hearing Breakwater's sudden intake of breath. But Michael's own gaze didn't even twitch. "Five years," the King repeated. "You think we'd need that many?"

"Perhaps three?" Winterfall backpedaled hastily. Was that a microscopic smile touching the corners of the King's lips? "Yes—three, Your Majesty. That should be a sufficient trial run."

"Ridiculous," the Chancellor bit out. "Three to five *years*? Come now—any problems or design flaws would surely become evident within a year at the most. Any delay beyond that would do nothing but scatter the work teams and make it harder to bring them back together."

"Or those years will give the planners and techs time to come up with better alternatives," Dapplelake said. He still didn't look happy, Winterfall noted, but he looked less unhappy than he had during Breakwater's earlier presentation. "Understand, Your Majesty, that I and the RMN are still completely opposed to this whole venture." He flashed an appraising look at Breakwater, as if he could tell just by observation how many votes the Committee had tucked under its belt. Maybe he could. "But if it has to be done," he concluded reluctantly, "this does seem the most reasonable way to go about it."

"I concur," the King said. "First Lord Cazenestro, you're to draw up a schedule and a framework for this operation at your earliest convenience." He cocked an eyebrow. "Such convenience to be within the next three months," he added, a bit more sternly. "When you've finished, I'll examine it and, if necessary, we'll convene again to make whatever alterations are necessary. I trust that will be satisfactory?"

Cazenestro seemed to collapse a bit on himself. "Most satisfactory, Your Majesty. I'll get started immediately."

"Thank you." The King looked around the table, holding each person briefly with his eyes. "And thank you all for your time." He lifted a hand in dismissal.

And with that, the meeting was over.

The five Committee members had been passed through the gate and were heading for their cars when Breakwater finally broke the silence.

"Interesting meeting," he commented.

"*Interesting* isn't exactly the word I would have used," Chillon growled, glaring past Breakwater at Winterfall. "What the *hell* was that all about?"

"I was asked a question," Winterfall reminded him stiffly, determined not to wilt under the earl's scowl. No less a person than King Michael himself had stated his approval of Winterfall's ideas. "What was I supposed to do, tell him I was just there as window dressing?"

"You were *supposed* to defer to Chancellor Breakwater," Chillon shot back.

"Leave the boy alone, Ross," Tweenriver advised coolly. "I doubt you'd have done any better when you were his age."

"Age has nothing to do with it," Chillon snapped. "The point is that this young pup's flapping gums have now undercut our entire proposal."

"Not at all," Breakwater told him. "What this young pup has done is given us victory."

"So victory now comes in three-year installments?" Castle Rock asked sourly.

"Victory comes wherever and however one can find it," Breakwater said. "Or didn't you notice that Baron Winterfall was able to slide a bald-faced bluff straight through Dapplelake's wall? We don't have nearly the votes to force this through. Not yet. Possibly not ever."

"But three *years*?" Castle Rock protested.

"Only between the first and second conversions," Breakwater assured her. "Once the first pair of sloops have proven themselves, the others can be created with the assembly-line efficiency Lord Winterfall suggested." He favored Winterfall with a smile. "That was an amazing performance, young man, especially given the whole ambush nature of Dapplelake's question. You may have more of a future in this profession than I thought."

"I'm not sure I'd go *that* far, My Lord," Winterfall said modestly even as his cheeks warmed with the compliment. "It was mainly the same speech I've been giving to the younger MPs you asked me to talk to."

"Including the five-year hesitation step?" Castle Rock muttered.

"People don't like change," Winterfall said. "I thought building in a delay would help soothe any fears that we were rushing into this." He drew himself up. "Besides, it makes sense."

"More to the point, it got us what we wanted," Breakwater said, his tone saying that the subject was closed. "Let's get back to work. We'll want our own timetable ready in case Dapplelake tries to pull a delaying action on us." He looked at Winterfall. "Perhaps, My Lord, you'd have time to assist me on that."

"Yes, My Lord," Winterfall said, inclining his head. "I would be honored."

☆   ☆   ☆

Only later—much later—would it occur to Winterfall to wonder if perhaps the whole thing had been a setup. If perhaps Dapplelake and the King had heard about his conversations with the younger Lords and had maneuvered him into offering a compromise suggestion onto the official record. After all, a low-level baron with no appreciable political or economic power had nothing to lose should the proposal go down in flames.

But such thoughts were fleeting, and Winterfall didn't spend much time with them. Breakwater himself had said it: he had a future in Star Kingdom politics.

Whatever that future was, Winterfall was determined to make the most of it.

CHAPTER SIX

LIFE IN THE GREAT NORTHWEST, as the Casey-Rosewood training school sector was informally called, was much easier physically than boot camp had been. The endless hours of marching and hikes were gone, though there were still enough weekly formations to ensure that the spacers didn't forget what they'd learned. The calisthenics and twenty-five-klick hikes were also less frequent, with most of the physical exercise requirements being filled by more intensive unarmed combat training. Where and how such techniques would ever be used in a modern navy, Travis noted, was never really explained. Those particular workouts ushered in their own set of bruises and sore muscles, but in general they were far less of an annoyance than the permanent muscle aches of boot camp.

Which was just as well, given that the brain pummeling had just begun.

Travis had always known, in a vague civilian sort of way, that impeller nodes and ring systems were complicated pieces of machinery. But until he began studying them he'd had no idea how insanely complex they truly were.

The mechanics were bad enough, with thousands of components built to the specifications of a physics that could be mathematically defined but not—at least to Travis—intuitively understood. The electronics driving the multiton tangle of components were even worse, with critical timings in the attosecond range and multiple, delicately balanced redundancies. Casimir cells running on plasma coming directly from the ship's fusion plant drove the creation of the wedge, the nodes heterodyning between each other and the wedge planes themselves, the process eventually reaching a threshold where it began to extract much of its power directly from the Alpha hyperspace band.

Even sitting in a nice safe lab at Casey-Rosewood, with the forces and energies involved merely a computer simulation, Travis found the procedure to be both awesome and terrifying.

The impeller system's software, naturally, was its own special brand of nightmare.

For the first few weeks Travis trudged back to the barracks every evening with either a massive headache or a sort of information overload haze. His dreams alternated between nightmares and some of the most bizarre traveling excursions he'd ever experienced. Most of the latter involved looming cliffs or creatures that chattered exactly like the node computerized analysis readouts. Way too many of them involved showing up for a test or demo in his underwear.

They were two months into the training when, as had also happened in boot camp, his brain abruptly seemed to find a private handle on the flood of information. After that, even though the deluge didn't let up, he was able to stay with it. He began to handle the disassembly and assembly exercises with more confidence, and his test scores began to edge up. Best of all, the nightmares mostly went away.

With his new abilities and confidence he was able to relax a bit, and instead of being completely buried in his own struggles was able to open up his horizons and pay some attention to the struggles of his fellow students.

To discover that at least half of them were cheating.

It was so stunning a revelation that at first he refused to believe it. It took him three weeks' worth of surreptitious observation during tests and quizzes before he reluctantly concluded that his earlier discovery hadn't been an aberration.

He wrestled with the situation for another week, trying to reconcile the ethics of such fraud with the unspoken rule of loyalty to one's unit.

Unfortunately, there really wasn't a choice. This wasn't stealing a few bites of food to help a starving comrade. The impellers were an absolutely vital aspect of ship operation, and a single error or lapse in observation could literally spell the difference between life and death for hundreds of men and women. Every detail of their training was vital, and a spacer who cheated was by definition not properly learning those details. Travis owed it to the crews of the ships on which these spacers would eventually serve to make sure his class could be trusted to do their jobs right.

And so, with reluctance and heart-pounding trepidation, an hour before lights-out one evening he made his way to the office of the Impeller Tech Division's senior officer, Lieutenant William Cyrus.

☆   ☆   ☆

Only to find that, for all intents and purposes, Cyrus didn't care.

The lieutenant *said* he cared, of course. He made all the right noises, and made all the right promises.

But nothing happened. Not the next day, not the day after that, not the week after that.

He went to Cyrus again, and again, and again. But it was the same each time. The lieutenant thanked Travis for pointing out the problem, promised to fix it, and sent Travis on his way.

And after that, nothing. Except more cheating.

Apparently, despite what it said in the Casey-Rosewood manual, cheating was simply part of the routine.

It was two days after his latest attempt, as he was finishing dinner and mentally mapping out his strategy for the evening's studying, when he had an unexpected visitor.

"Hey, Stickler," Chomps said genially, dropping down onto the mess hall bench beside him. The whole bench shook as he did so—clearly, the Sphinxian had gained back all the weight he'd lost in boot camp. "How's it going?"

"Not bad," Travis said. "You?"

"Can't complain," Chomps said with a grin. "Not allowed, you know. Got a minute?"

"Sure," Travis said, frowning. He hadn't seen Chomps except in passing since their graduation from boot camp, when Travis had been sent to impeller school and Chomps had disappeared into gunner's mate training. Odd that Chomps was suddenly seeking him out now. "Is there a problem?"

"I don't know," Chomps said, standing up again. "Finish up, and let's go find out."

Two minutes later, they were outside the mess hall, heading through the thinning crowd of other spacers heading back toward their own barracks.

"We going to pass in review?" Travis asked jokingly as he spotted the empty parade ground directly ahead.

"Why, you need the practice?" a familiar voice asked from just behind Travis.

Travis turned his head, feeling his whole body stiffen with reflexive reaction. Striding along just behind them was none other than Gunner's Mate First Class Johnny Funk.

"Sir, no, Sir," he said.

"Relax, Spacer Long," Funk said with a little snort. "And lose the *sir*—this isn't boot camp."

"Yes, Gunner's Mate," Travis said, a kaleidoscope of horrible images from boot camp flashing across his eyes. He'd always assumed his deep and multilayered fear of Funk would fade away once he was out from under the other's authority. Clearly, he'd been wrong.

"I said *relax*, Spacer," Funk said, probably as soothingly as was possible for the man. "We're just here to talk to you."

Travis gave Chomps a sideways look. *We?*

"I hear you've been trying to light a fire under Lieutenant Cyrus about cheating in the impeller school," Funk continued.

"Yes, Gunner's Mate, I am," Travis said, feeling his stomach tightening around his still undigested dinner. *Relax,* Funk had said. Right. Like he was going to relax *now.* "Uh...may I ask—?"

"His yeoman's a friend of mine," Funk said. "Here's the question. Are you pressing this because cheating is against the rules, or because it's a detriment to the future competence of the cheaters?"

"I don't see how you can separate the two," Travis said stiffly. "Competence is the whole reason the rule is there to begin with."

"Yeah." Funk gave a little sigh. "Look. You're a good kid, Long, and you've got potential. But you don't get how the real world works. So I'm going to tell you."

"I'm not sure you understand the scope of the problem, Gunner's Mate," Travis said. "This isn't just some isolated incidence. I have evidence that at least eight of the students in my class—"

"Yes, Long, I *do* understand the problem, thank you," Funk cut him off irritably. "Shut up and listen."

"Yes, Gunner's Mate," Travis said between clenched teeth. "Listening."

"Here's the deal," Funk said, taking a couple of longer steps to come up to Travis's side. "This—" he gestured around them, a sweeping wave of his hand "—is the classroom." He raised his hand and pointed to the sky. "Out *there* is the real world."

"Yes, Gunner's Mate," Travis said cautiously. "I was under the impression that the real world was what we were being taught."

"That would be nice," Funk said. "But it isn't. Even in a properly run Navy classroom, there's a big gap between how things *should* work and how they *do* work. Once you're assigned to a ship, you'll find out how all this theory really shakes out. And it isn't always the way you were taught. Maybe it never is."

"Yes, Gunner's Mate," Travis said, peering closely at Funk's face. If this was a joke, Funk was hiding it well. "That sounds rather . . . inefficient."

"Do you recall anyone promising that life would be efficient, Spacer Long?"

"No. But—"

"Then back off and let the cheaters be," Funk said. "They're getting enough of the basics. That's all they'll need when their future petty officers start their *real* training. The sooner they graduate out of here, the sooner that happens."

Travis clenched his teeth. But this wasn't just about grades and graduating. Couldn't Funk see that? Ignoring such a fundamental tenet as academic honesty eroded the entire structure of discipline and respect for authority. If the spacers got away with it here—worse, if they recognized that their misconduct was known and simply being ignored—it would seep into every aspect of their attitude. Part of the oath he'd taken flashed to mind: *enemies domestic . . .*

"But—"

"But why don't we teach them the real-world in the first place?" Funk gave a little shrug. "Because the book assumes Navy ships are all bright and sparkly and have all the gear they're supposed to have. Sadly, they don't."

"Yes, Gunner's Mate," Travis said uncertainly. He'd read articles about how the Navy didn't have all the equipment it was supposed to. But most of the reporters involved with those stories had framed it as a tactic by First Lord Cazenestro to squeeze more funding out of Parliament.

He looked questioningly at Chomps. The Sphinxian grimaced, but shrugged.

"I don't like it any more than you do," Chomps admitted. "But Gunner's Mate Funk is right. That's the way things are, and not just in impellers. The big question is whether you're going to be able to put your rule-stickling on hold enough to ignore it."

"Because if you can't," Funk said, "and if you keep at this, you're just going to piss off Lieutenant Cyrus. Trust me: pissing off officers isn't a smart idea."

"And don't worry—the cheaters will do all right once they're finally on their ships," Chomps assured him. "They'll take a little longer to get up to speed, but they'll make it."

"We'll straighten them out," Funk promised. "Trust me. So. Any other questions?"

Travis thought about it. He had plenty more questions. But it was clear that none of them were going to be answered. Not to his satisfaction, anyway.

"No, Gunner's Mate."

"Good," Funk said briskly. "You two probably have some studying to do. You'd better get to it."

"Yes, Gunner's Mate," Chomps said. "Thank you for your time."

"No problem." Funk peered closely at Travis. "And don't worry, Long. You said half your class was cheating. That means half the class *isn't* cheating. Try to focus on that half." Giving each of them a brisk nod, Funk angled off at the next walkway and headed back toward the boot camp section of the base.

"So what am I supposed to do?" Travis asked bitterly. "Just ignore it?"

"Ignore it, or else join in," Chomps said. "Sorry—lost my head. Seriously, it's going to be all right. You just focus on getting through the training, graduating, and getting assigned to a ship. It'll work out. Really." He tapped Travis's arm with the backs of his massive fingers. "I've got to get back to the barracks—big test tomorrow. Hang in there, okay?"

"Sure." Travis hesitated. "Thanks for—you know. I guess I needed to hear that. Even if I didn't want to."

"No problem," Chomps said. "I know it's a travesty, but—sorry; couldn't resist."

"Yeah, I'll bet," Travis growled.

"Oh, come on," Chomps cajoled. "Look, I'll make it up to you. Next week we're going to be watching a combat simulation. Why don't you come by and watch?"

"Sounds exciting," Travis said without much enthusiasm.

"No, really, it is," Chomps assured him. "Got to be better than the vid lectures you're getting in impeller class. Besides, they'll be doing missile simulations—you can tell them if they programmed the missile impellers right."

"I'm sure they really need my input."

"Even officers need to be kept honest," Chomps pointed out. "In fact, *especially* officers need to be kept honest. I'll let you know when we get our schedule."

"Sure," Travis said.

"Okay." Chomps tapped him on the arm again. "Hang in there, Stickler."

Travis thought about it on the walk back to his barracks. He thought about it some more during the next few days, especially as he watched the cheaters taking tests with their hidden formula cards and glow-etched crib notes.

He thought about it even more during four agonizing hours as he sweated over a particularly nasty electronics problem set, and then completely nosedived the subsequent quiz. Especially when the three highest scores on that quiz went to some of the cheaters.

But ultimately, all of his thought and analysis was just so much mental gymnastics. He simply couldn't cheat. It was against Casey-Rosewood policy, and it was against his own personal ethics. No matter what anyone else did. No matter what it did to his own grades or standing in the class.

Maybe that made him more noble than the others. Maybe it just made him more neurotic and stupid.

Or maybe it made the RMN not the organization he'd thought it would be.

He hoped that wasn't the case. Hoped it desperately. Because he'd signed his name to a promise that he would give five T-years of his life to this Navy.

And by God, by First Lord of the Admiralty Cazenestro, and by Gunner's Mate First Class Johnny Funk himself, Travis would do whatever it took to fulfill that promise.

☆   ☆   ☆

Captain Horace "Race" Kiselev had always liked his nickname. *Race.* It resonated with adventure and action, the sort of name worthy of the heroic characters Kiselev had always admired in his impressionable book- and vid-filled youth.

Still, he'd always had the sneaking suspicion that the sobriquet had been awarded with more irony than conviction. As much as Kiselev admired the action heroes of fiction, he knew down deep that he wasn't anything like them. Academics were more his forte. Academics, and the dogged and painstaking attention to detail that made for a good administrator.

Or, in the case of HMS *Mars* and her fellow mothballed battlecruisers, a good nurse.

Because that was really what he was. He and the fifty spacers in his crew were the caretakers of the RMN's six mothballed warships, parked in orbit and abandoned during the plague years when the Navy ran out of money and personnel to crew them. Kiselev's job was to oversee his people as they traveled the circuit of the evacuated ships, checking for vacuum welding, stress and tidal-force microdamage, and all the other problems that could befall spacecraft that had lain empty for so long in the hostile environment of space. Especially ships that had been mothballed as hastily and haphazardly as these had been.

But it wasn't just an extended wake for vessels long past any hope of utility. As the RMN slowly rebuilt its manpower, there were increased rumblings that Parliament might start bringing the remaining heavy cruisers and battlecruisers out of their forced retirement and returning them to active service.

That was the hope that continued to drive Kiselev and his people. The hope that one day someone would come with orders to restart the quiet fusion engines, to flood the empty decks with air and heat, to refill the fluid reservoirs, and to reactivate the electronics.

And when those orders came, Kiselev had privately promised himself, *Mars* would be the first ship that would be brought back to life.

Because *Mars* was their home. It hadn't made sense to create a new space station just for the caretaker crew, not with six perfectly serviceable ships sitting out here. So *Mars* had been nursed back to partial life, her fusion plant turning out enough power to keep the spin section running and supplied with the necessities of life. Kiselev had spent the past five years living aboard her, first as the caretaker unit's XO, then as its CO.

And finally, the day of new orders had arrived. Admiral Carlton Locatelli, commanding officer of the Star Kingdom's System Command, had personally come to *Mars* to deliver them.

Only the orders weren't the ones Kiselev had hoped for. Not

in his wildest nightmares had he ever expected to receive orders like these.

Kiselev's beloved *Mars* wasn't going to be brought back to life. She was going to die.

To be murdered.

"I don't understand, Sir," Kiselev said, his heart sinking, his stomach tying itself in a succession of ever-tighter knots. "She's being *dismantled*?"

"Only partially," Admiral Locatelli assured him, offering Kiselev his tablet. "She's going to be cut in half and turned into two new sloops."

Kiselev sent a hooded glance at the image on the tablet. One glance was all he wanted.

"That's ridiculous," he insisted, turning his eyes resolutely away. "Whose stupid idea was this, anyway?"

"You can blame it on Breakwater, if it makes you feel any better," Locatelli said. "He's the one who started the ball rolling. Just be thankful he didn't get to mulch all nine of the battlecruisers at the same time. That was his original wish list."

Kiselev mouthed a silent curse. The Chancellor would have done it, too. He would have taken the battlecruisers apart, and in the process emasculated the Star Kingdom.

"He should be charged with treason," he bit out. "In fact, he should have been charged a long time ago. If he'd given us the funds we needed to keep *Mars* and the others running like they should, they could have *been* the precious patrol ships he claims to want."

Locatelli smiled faintly as he pointed at Kiselev's chest.

"Preacher," he said. He tapped his own chest. "Choir."

"Yes, Sir, I know," Kiselev said, feeling slightly ashamed of himself. He was an officer of the RMN, and he shouldn't be venting his frustration this way. Not to a superior officer. "My apologies, Admiral." He braced himself. Horrible or not, he had a duty to see what they were planning to do to his ship. "May I see that, Sir?"

Silently, Locatelli handed him the tablet. Kiselev took it and forced himself to look.

It was as bad as he'd expected. It was certainly as insane.

The first sloop was to be created from *Mars*'s stern section, making the cut through the hull just behind the spin section, leaving the aft fusion plant and impeller ring intact. The aft endcap would be removed, taking with it the aft laser and autocannon, with the various conduits, flowlines, power and sensor cables rerouted or repositioned to accommodate the shorter length. The work stations and living quarters would also have to be drastically rearranged, he knew, with those details presumably on a set of schematics lower in the stack. A truncated neck and small forward endcap were to be added to the stub, with the heavy armored hull plating removed, presumably to save mass. A pair of autocannon jutted from the endcap, with a pair of missile box launchers attached midway down the neck. "Box launchers?" Kiselev asked scornfully.

"A concession to us," Locatelli explained. "First Lord Cazenestro insisted the sloops be armed. I doubt Breakwater ever expects the weapons to actually be used."

Kiselev grunted and keyed to the next page. The forward sloop was just as ridiculous looking as the aft one, though with a slightly different flavor of insanity. Again, the cut here was to be made in front of *Mars*'s spin section, with the forward part of the ship left mostly intact, except for the large middle section where the hull plating was again to be cut away. The forward autocannon were intact, but the amidships autocannon and missile tubes had vanished with that section of hull. Two more of the box launchers had been installed behind the endcap. Apparently, box launchers were Breakwater's idea of a consolation prize.

"And he thinks this is actually going to be cheaper than building a pair of corvettes from the keels up?" he asked.

"So he says," Locatelli said, gesturing toward the tablet. "And he has numbers to back him up, supposedly from a professional ship designer named Martin Ashkenazy."

"Then Ashkenazy's even more incompetent than Breakwater," Kiselev growled, scrolling down the document and finding Ashkenazy's bottom-line estimates. "These estimates can't possibly be right."

"I agree," Locatelli said, his voice darkening. "So do our own engineering experts. But Ashkenazy had answers for everything, and in the end Parliament gave him the go-ahead."

"It's insane," Kiselev insisted. "Ashkenazy can't be this much of a fool."

"A fool?" Locatelli shook his head. "Consider. Ashkenazy now has at least a year's worth of steady work ahead of him, probably two or three, with all the prestige and comfortable funding that comes from a Parliament-sanctioned project. Breakwater gets what he wants: a small but immediate reduction in RMN monetary outflow, at least on paper, which fits his long-term philosophy of having more to spend on his own pet projects. Not to mention that the sloops will be transferred out of the Navy and straight into MPARS. Under the circumstances, I hardly think either of them would be motivated to honestly look for flaws in their proposal."

"I suppose not, Sir," Kiselev said with a sigh. It was still criminally insane, and it was going to hurt like hell to watch his ship being slowly tortured to death.

But he was an officer of the RMN. He had his orders, and he would obey them.

"Do we have a timetable yet?"

"The final details are being worked out," Locatelli said. "But you won't be the one dealing with it. You're being transferred to Casey-Rosewood as the new CO of the Northwest Sector training school."

Kiselev felt his mouth drop open. No—that had to be a mistake. Aside from a short stint teaching electronic warfare at the Academy three years ago, every minute of the past five years had been spent aboard *Mars*. This was *his* ship; and if she was to be destroyed, it was his right and responsibility to oversee that destruction.

"Sir, I respectfully request—"

"Save your breath, Captain," Locatelli said. "It's already been decided at the highest levels that your particular talents will best serve the RMN at Casey-Rosewood."

"Yes, Sir, I'll just bet that was what they were thinking," Kiselev ground out. "I don't suppose there were any suggestions that I might take this personally, and therefore might not put the necessary effort into the operation?"

"Rest assured that no such thoughts were ever voiced," Locatelli said, his tone studiously neutral.

Which wasn't to say Dapplelake or Cazenestro or Breakwater hadn't thought it, of course. Not only were they going to take his ship away from him, but they were going to bring his professionalism into question in the bargain. Snakelike butt-coverers, the whole lot of them.

"Yes, Sir," he said stiffly.

"If it makes you feel any better, I opposed the decision," Locatelli said. "That's just between you and me, of course."

"Yes, Sir," Kiselev said again. That was Locatelli, all right—a man by, for, and from the RMN, without a single political bone in his body. "Thank you, Sir."

"I'm just sorry I couldn't carry the day," Locatelli said ruefully. "What's the old quote? If it has to be done, a real man shoots his own dog himself."

Kiselev winced. No political bones, but not always the most tactful of men, either.

"Something like that, Sir."

"Yes," Locatelli said. "At any rate, you're to report to Casey-Rosewood at oh-nine-hundred next Tuesday for a preliminary briefing from Colonel Massingill. The two of you will have some flexibility as to when your permanent transfer will take place."

"Yes, Sir," Kiselev said. "I assume my replacement will be aboard before I leave?"

"Yes, assuming Breakwater gets his rear in gear and confirms one of the people the First Lord has put forward," Locatelli said. "Not sure why he was allowed veto power over that decision, since the transfer to MPARS isn't going to happen until after the conversion. But it is what it is. At any rate, you'll still be in command here until he or she is approved and on board." He pursed his lips. "Well. I'm sorry to have been the bearer of bad news. If there are no further questions, I'll be on my way."

"No questions, Sir," Kiselev said. No questions that Locatelli could answer, anyway.

"Very good," Locatelli said, his voice all brisk and businesslike again. "I'll be sure to check in with you again after you settle into Casey-Rosewood and see how you're doing." He cocked an eyebrow. "Oh, and one other matter I don't believe I mentioned. Along with your new assignment, you'll be receiving a promotion." He offered his hand. "Congratulations, Commodore Kiselev."

Swallowing, Kiselev took the other's hand and shook it.

"Thank you, Sir."

"No thanks needed," Locatelli assured him. "It's long overdue. Good luck, Commodore, and I'll see you again in a few weeks."

With a nod, the admiral turned and left Kiselev's office.

The office that had been Kiselev's official working home for the past three years. The office, and the home, that would soon be torn up and mangled, all at the egomaniacal whim of an ignorant, pennypinching civilian. And there was nothing Kiselev could do about it.

But maybe there was someone else who could.

Circling his desk, he sat down in his swivel chair and keyed his com system. On a real ship, the odd thought struck him, he would have a yeoman or communications officer to do this for him. Maybe at Casey-Rosewood he would, as well. But for right now, he was perfectly comfortable doing such things for himself.

The com ran through its protocols and self-checks and aimed its laser at the nearest System Command relay satellite.

"This is Captain—this is *Commodore* Kiselev, aboard HMS *Mars*," he said into the mike.

"System Command communications," a brisk feminine voice came back promptly. "How may I direct your call, Commodore?"

Kiselev smiled tightly. So his promotion had already popped up in the system, without the mid-rank delay that could be embarrassing to a newly minted officer and disconcerting to the subordinates who hadn't yet received an official notice. Leave it to Locatelli to get even the small details right.

"Patch me through to *Defiant*," he ordered.

"Direct or message?"

"Message," Kiselev said. He wasn't exactly sure where *Defiant* was at the moment, and even a few of seconds' time delay made direct conversations awkward.

Besides, there was no guarantee the recipient would even remember his old division CO. Best to post a message that would give him time to sort it out before responding.

"Recipient?"

Kiselev took a deep breath. "Commander Edward Winton," he said. "That's Commander *Prince* Edward Winton."

CHAPTER SEVEN

"MISSILE TRACE, THIRTY-FIVE HUNDRED GEES," THE young woman at the missile room's sensor repeater station said briskly. "Estimated impact—"

"How many traces?" the senior grade lieutenant supervising the exercise interrupted.

"I'm sorry, Sir," the woman apologized. "Two traces. I was going to—"

"Apologies waste time, Midshipwoman," the supervisor cut her off again. "Start over, and get it right."

"Yes, Sir," the woman said, a hint of clenched jaw in her voice. "Missile trace, two: thirty-five hundred gees, estimated time to impact eighty-three seconds."

"Copy two inbound, three five hundred gees, impact eight three seconds," one of her fellow students called an acknowledgment from the command station. "Tracking good?"

"Tracking good," the woman confirmed.

"Midshipwoman Jones?" the supervisor invited. "You should be joining the conversation about now."

"Yes, Sir," another woman said from the fire-control station. "Autocannon prepped and ready, Sir."

"Missile capacitors charged," a second man added from the missile station. "Still waiting for targeting parameters."

"Hang on," the student commander said, fiddling with his board.

Peering at the big display that showed the scene inside the simulator, trying to stay beneath Fire Control Specialist First Class

69

Matayoshi's direct line of sight, Travis felt a mixture of envy and frustration. Envy, because this kind of simulation looked a lot more interesting than his own impeller class schedule. Frustration, because the Academy students in there clearly hadn't properly learned the procedures for this kind of action.

What made it even more annoying was that the bits of procedure they were muffing weren't even part of Travis's curriculum. This was officer territory, a tactical scenario that enlisted personnel like Travis, Chomps, and most of the rest of Chomps's fellow students sitting silently in the observation room around them would never even get to play via simulation, let alone experience for real. The only reason Travis knew anything at all about it was that he'd happened on the listing once while looking up something else and had read it through because it had looked interesting.

Apparently, the officers-in-training hadn't found it nearly so intriguing. More than once as the simulation progressed Travis had caught himself muttering the proper wording under his breath, as if the observation room's intercom went both ways.

Each time, he'd clamped his jaw firmly shut. Matayoshi and his assistant, Fire Control Tech Third Class Lorelei Osterman, had been extremely leery about having an outsider join the class for their observation, and it had only been through some fast talking on Chomps's part—which had included the fact that, as an impeller-track student, Travis might someday be handling these same missiles—that the two petty officers had reluctantly allowed Travis to stay. But they'd made it clear he was to keep his mouth shut.

Still, lapses in the students' procedure apart, it was a fascinating exercise, every bit as intense as his reading had implied it would be.

Not that anyone in there was ever likely to run into this kind of situation in the real world. If history was anything to go by, there would be little need for the RMN to ever shoot at anything out there, and even less likelihood that anything would shoot back. Far more important to the RMN was good old-fashioned tech training.

Because a mistuned compensator could kill the entire ship's crew faster than an enemy warship could ever hope to achieve. Ditto for a balky impeller node, a field-cracked fusion bottle, a ruptured coolant line, or damage to any of a hundred other critical systems. Simulator battles were undeniably fun, but there was little point in learning how to fight if the crew managed to blow up their own ship on the way to battle.

Which was why the cheating problem nagged so hard at him. Funk had warned him to drop it, and Travis was really, really trying to do that. But the cheating continued, and at some point he was pretty sure he would break down and once again bring the topic to Lieutenant Cyrus's attention.

"Missile trace: one," the woman at the sensors called. "Ten thousand gees, estimated time to impact one hundred twenty seconds."

"Copy one inbound," the man at the command station acknowledged.

Travis frowned, looking at the repeater tactical readout beside the main display. This latest attack had been launched from Bogey Two, which at five hundred thousand kilometers was the more distant of the two opponents. The missile was coming in at the higher of the two standard missile accelerations, instead of using the lower setting of the two missiles coming from Bogey One.

Except that this latest attack was stupid. At ten thousand gravities the missile's wedge would burn itself out in barely sixty seconds, with over three hundred thousand kilometers still separating it from its target. At its six-thousand-kilometers-per-second terminal velocity, it would take nearly a minute to cross that remaining distance, and it would be following a purely ballistic vector the entire way.

The autocannon would have no trouble intercepting it well outside of kill range. Travis could practically climb out on the hull with a hunting rifle and shoot the damn thing down manually. On the surface, it looked like a colossally idiotic waste of an expensive weapon.

But surely the people who programmed these simulations didn't make such obvious mistakes. There had to be something going on beneath the surface, some lurking threat or subtle trap.

Only Travis couldn't figure out what that trap might be. The missile was tracking along just as it should, coming in on a vector that would take it across the forward edge of the starboard sidewall. The controller in Bogey Two would undoubtedly try to twitch that vector a bit before the missile's wedge burned out, but that would still leave it running helplessly into the autocannon's blaze of metal shrapnel.

"Don't know why they have to use *our* simulator in the first place," Chomps muttered toward Travis's ear. "If the Academy can't afford to build one of their own, they should fire a couple of admirals or cut back on the fancy shellfish parties—"

A sudden, muted klaxon cut off his grousing. "Got a malfunction," Jones called tautly from her autocannon station, hunching over her board.

"Well, *fix* it," the supervisor said.

"I'm *trying*," Jones snapped, her hands fumbling with the settings. "They're not responding."

"Should we pitch wedge?" the student at the sensor station asked, looking at the supervisor.

"I don't know," the supervisor countered. "Should you?"

"There's no time," the commander ground out. "Jones—"

"Got it," Jones cut him off. The red section of the status grid returned to green—

The klaxon cut off, its raucous noise replaced with hardly a missed beat by the equally disagreeable chatter of the autocannon. But at least that particular noise meant the ship and crew were still alive.

At least for the moment. Travis shifted his attention back to the remaining missile—

And felt his mouth drop open. The missile was no longer following its burn-out vector toward the starboard sidewall. Instead, it had inexplicably and impossibly changed course, weaving a convoluted wiggle toward a point clear of the sidewall and straight down the ship's throat.

The command midshipman apparently spotted it the same time Travis did.

"Jones!" he barked.

"I see it," she snarled. "What the *hell*—?"

She never finished the sentence. An instant later every display, status grid, and control board flared pure white and then went dark.

"Congratulations, Midshipmen," the supervisor said into the stunned silence. "You're all dead."

For a couple of seconds the image remained, the midshipmen staring in disbelief or chagrin at their boards or their own simulation displays, the supervisor busily and calmly making notes on his tablet. Then, Matayoshi reached to a wall control board and tapped a switch. The display blanked and the speaker went silent, leaving only the repeater tactical readout still operating.

"Well, spacers," the petty officer said. "What have we learned today?"

"I don't understand, Sir," one of the students, Geoffrey Smith said, sounding bewildered. "That missile was dead. It was, wasn't it, Kelderman?"

"That's what the sensors said," one of the other students confirmed. "Its wedge had burned out." She sent a puzzled frown at Matayoshi. "Unless Bogey Two shut off the wedge before it burned out and then turned it back on?"

"They can't," Travis murmured to Chomps.

"You say something, Long?" Matayoshi demanded.

Travis winced. He thought he'd spoken too softly for Matayoshi to hear. Clearly, he'd been wrong.

"My apologies, Fire Control Specialist Matayoshi," he said.

"I didn't ask for an apology, Long," Matayoshi growled. "I asked what you said."

Travis braced himself.

"I was just telling Spacer Townsend that it's not possible to turn a missile wedge off and then on again. Missiles have only two settings, and both of them run the wedge until the impellers are gone."

"Why is that?"

"Trying to shut down a missile's wedge en route would start a feedback loop that would burn the impellers out right there and then," Travis said.

"What if the impellers were shielded?" Smith asked.

"Shielded how?" Travis countered. "And against what? Themselves?"

"Spacer Long is right," Matayoshi said. "But only as far as he goes. You're all thinking inside the lines, and an enemy's lines may be in different places than yours are. They could have different tech or battle doctrine, and either of those can throw off your assumptions. So. If you can't just shut off a missile wedge, what else could it have been?"

The students looked at each other. "It wasn't shielding another missile," Kelderman said slowly. "We would have seen the edge on the gravitics display. So..."

"Two separate wedges?" Chomps suggested hesitantly. "One lighting up after the other burned out?"

"No," Travis said. "That's impossible."

"Is it?" Matayoshi asked, a sly twinkle in his eye.

"No, he's right—it makes sense," Smith said. Out of the corner of his eye, Travis saw Kelderman step to the wall control and start cycling through the different pages on the sensor display history. "Warships have two impeller rings," Smith continued. "Why not a missile?"

"Because it's too small—" Travis began.

"Son of a bitch," Kelderman said. She looked guiltily at Matayoshi. "Sorry, Petty Officer."

"I've heard worse," Matayoshi assured her. "You find something?"

"Yes." Kelderman gestured to the display. "Townsend was right. There were two separate wedges on that missile."

"That's impossible," Travis repeated.

"Take a look," Matayoshi offered, waving at the display. "It's right there. Read and weep."

"It's a simulation, Fire Control Specialist," Travis pointed out stiffly. "You could put flying dragons into a simulation if you wanted to. But that wouldn't make it right."

"You have a problem with an exercise that stretches people's minds, Spacer Long? You want life in the Navy to be easy and predictable?"

The observation room had gone very quiet. Matayoshi was glaring at Travis, the twinkle long since vanished from his eye. Osterman was studying Travis with a less hostile but hardly friendly expression. Chomps looked interested and slightly amused by the direction the conversation had taken. Everyone else looked like they were desperately hoping Matayoshi would forget any of them were there.

"I don't see how it serves proper training to suggest that the impossible can happen, Fire Control Specialist," Travis said as calmly as he could. "I think that would encourage us to waste time and energy looking in useless directions instead of concentrating on the possible. Unlikely or unexpected, but still possible."

"Quite a speech, Spacer Long," Matayoshi said stiffly. "Been practicing it?"

"He just has a knack," Chomps muttered.

"You don't think impossible problems are a proper teaching method?" Matayoshi demanded, ignoring Chomps's comment.

"That depends, Fire Control Specialist," Travis said feeling sweat breaking out on his forehead. What had started out as an objection on purely technical grounds had somehow morphed into a debate on Casey-Rosewood's teaching doctrine. "If students are being graded on how they react to a situation, either individually or a team, that would certainly be legitimate. But if they're being graded on how they deal with an impossible scenario, I would question the propriety."

"I see." For a long moment Matayoshi stared at him. "In that case, Spacer Third Class Long, since we clearly have an impasse here, I suggest you take it to higher authority. Lieutenant Cyrus should still be in his office. Report to him immediately and explain the situation."

Travis winced. Once again, he'd managed to step right into it. "Yes, Fire Control Specialist."

"And be sure you tell him *exactly* why a two-stage missile is impossible," Matayoshi added. "Osterman, kindly escort Spacer Long out of my sight."

"Yes, Sir."

"As for the rest of you," Matayoshi added, turning back to the silent spacers, "we'll be heading back to class and running through the exercise minute by minute. As we do, you'll tell me exactly where everyone in there screwed up."

☆   ☆   ☆

Cyrus hadn't seen Spacer Travis Long, or endured any of his pedantic complaints, for over two weeks. He hadn't missed those visits, either.

Still, dealing with student questions was part of his job, and at least Long knew how to get to his point quickly and coherently. He'd handled Long's previous complaints with professionalism, and he had no doubt he could do the same this particular evening.

Until, that was, he learned the topic of Long's latest tirade.

"No," Cyrus said flatly, years of practice enabling him to hold onto his temper. "There is *no* physical reason such a missile couldn't be built. None."

"I believe there is, Sir," Long said, his voice respectful but firm. "Two impeller rings at such close proximity can't avoid bleeding control flickers and capillary fields between them. The fact that the secondary set isn't yet active doesn't matter—it'll still be misaligned when it *does* light up."

"Then you shield the second set," Cyrus bit out. "You put something between the two rings to keep that from happening."

"You *can't*, sir," Long insisted doggedly. "It's a quantum tunneling effect. No known material or counterfield can block or suppress it. You'd need a good hundred meters of distance between the rings, which would either require an acceleration-resistant pylon that's physically impossible to construct with any known material, or else a much thicker pillar that will jump the costs with every square centimeter of cross-section that you add. The missile would end up as big as a corvette and as expensive as a destroyer. Either way, it would *not* show up on sensors as a normal missile. Not the way it did on the simulation."

Cyrus ground his teeth. The dual-stage missile had been his hobby and his obsession for nearly seven years, and he'd been nagging at the Navy to pick up the project for the last five of those years. Bad enough when some unimaginative tech told him the thing was impossible; but for a snot-nosed spacer third class to lecture him was the final straw. "Well, maybe you should write the definitive paper on impeller node interactions and instabilities," he ground out.

"Actually, it's already been written, sir," Long said. "About twenty years ago. A monograph by the Solarian League physicist—"

"Then you need to write the definitive *Manticoran* one," Cyrus snapped. "Fifty pages, minimum, on my desk by Friday."

He had the satisfaction of seeing Long's eyes widen in shock and disbelief. "Sir?" the kid breathed.

"Dismissed, Spacer Long." Swiveling his chair halfway around, Cyrus picked up his tablet and punched up a random report.

Then watched out of the corner of his eye as Long squared his shoulders, executed a passable about-face, and left the office.

Cyrus dropped the tablet back on his desk with a muttered curse. The kid was gone now, but he'd be back. He'd be back with yet more complaints, arguments, or lectures. Not to mention the fifty-page analysis that Cyrus had ordered in the ill-advised heat of the moment.

And since the report would be on record, he would now have to read it. Every damn word of it.

And suddenly, Cyrus decided he was tired of Spacer Long.

He picked up his uni-link, turning it over in his hands while he worked out a plan. Stockmann, he decided. The petty officer was probably as tired of hearing Long's voice in impeller class as Cyrus was of hearing that voice in his office. Besides, Stockmann owed Cyrus a favor.

On second thought, this probably shouldn't go over the airwaves.

He tucked the uni-link away. Tomorrow after lunch, he decided. He'd grab Stockmann right after lunch and lay it out for him.

And if all went well, by the beginning of next week Long would be out of his hair. Forever.

☆　　☆　　☆

The room behind the plain wooden door was referred to by the palace staff as the Royal Sanctum, and as a boy Edward Winton could remember spending hours wondering what his grandmother Queen Elizabeth was doing in that mysterious chamber. Not until he reached the age of twenty-one T-years did she allow him inside, where he discovered somewhat to his disappointment that the Sanctum was merely a private office where she went whenever she wanted to concentrate on work without the nuisance of calls or visitors. By the time Edward's father Michael ascended the throne the Sanctum had long since lost its original air of mystique.

Still, as Edward had worked his way up through the ranks of the Royal Manticoran Navy the idea of having a place all to yourself took on a greater allure than any of his childhood imaginings could ever have achieved.

He'd been waiting in the Sanctum for nearly an hour, alternating his attention between the paintings on the walls and the workload on his tablet, when the King finally arrived.

"Ah—there you are," Michael huffed as he strode into the room, closing the door behind him.

"Didn't you get the message that I'd wait for you here?" Edward asked, standing up as he ran a critical eye over his father's face.

What he saw shocked him. He'd known that eight years of kingship had been hard on the other, but he hadn't realized just how much punishment those eight years had delivered. Michael's face was deeply lined, the skin sagging, the eyes tired and with an air of lost-child about them. Below the weary face was a weary body, shoulders slumped, legs slightly stiffened, feet shuffling across the deep carpet.

"I never trust messages to adequately foretell the future," Michael said, giving his son a quick handshake. "Especially when the sender is not his own master. You're looking good, Edward."

"You're looking kingly, Dad," Edward replied, suppressing the reflexive surge of annoyance. Twenty-two T-years in the Navy, and he was still getting oblique grief from his father over that decision.

"In other words, I look like flash-frozen hell?" Michael suggested with a small smile.

"I didn't say that."

"You didn't have to. Let's sit, shall we?" Carefully, or so it seemed to Edward, the King sat down on the couch. Edward sat down beside him. "So what brings you to Landing?" Michael continued. "No—let me guess. Breakwater's Ugly Duckling project?"

Edward blinked. "His *what*?"

"Sorry," Michael said with another smile, a more genuine one this time. "One of the many private nicknames floating around Parliament and the RMN. I'm surprised you hadn't heard that one."

"Sorry—no nicknames have reached us out there yet."

"Too bad," Michael said. "Some of them are quite imaginative. My personal favorite is *sloop du jour*. All rather beside the point, I suppose. That *is* why you're here, isn't it?"

"Yes," Edward confirmed. Once upon a time, he remembered, his father had been better at small talk and not so blunt and focused. Part of the price of kingship? "A former colleague asked if I would talk to you about it."

"Not much to talk about, I'm afraid," Michael said. "I think it's a mistake, too. But there's nothing I can do to stop it."

"Are you sure?" Edward pressed. "You *are* the King. That has to count for something."

"It counts for a great deal," Michael said ruefully. "Or it counts for nothing at all, depending on the situation. This is one of the latter. I spent all the political capital I could and still came up short. For whatever reason, this idea has fired Parliament's imagination, and there's no way to quench that flame. The best I can do—the best we *have* done—is to keep the project focused on a single battlecruiser until we see how it turns out."

Edward snorted.

"*That* one's just common sense," he said, "which appears to be in short supply these days. Just because we haven't had a battle in a hundred years doesn't mean the Navy hasn't been vital to our defense. We may never know how many groups like the Brotherhood took a look at *Victory* and *Vanguard* and *Invincible* and decided to go after easier prey."

"I agree," Michael said. "The problem is that we *won't* ever know that, and a lack of data never wins debates. Meanwhile, there are many other worthy groups and causes clamoring for money and people, and even with the immigration program it's going to be a long time before we have enough warm bodies to satisfy all our needs."

"In that case, why not just leave *Mars* and the other battle-cruisers where they are?" Edward asked. "They're not costing a damn thing sitting out in orbit except for whatever it takes to run the caretaker crew."

"You're missing the political nuances," Michael said heavily. "On the surface is the fact that the new sloops will be in MPARS under the Exchequer's jurisdiction. Slightly deeper than that is the fact that many of the people working on the project are Breakwater's friends and colleagues. Getting government money is always good for one's prestige."

"And for the future trading of favors."

"The chief form of political currency," Michael agreed. "But there's one more layer to Breakwater's thinking. I think he suspects that the Navy is quietly stripping those battlecruisers of the parts and equipment necessary for keeping the other ships flying. I think the *Mars* plan is the first step in his attempt to cut off that supply."

Edward felt a curse bubbling at his lips. Like cutting the last bit of fat off a starving man in order to make him starve that much faster.

"I always knew he was a bastard," he said. "I never realized just how big a bastard he was."

"He doesn't like the Navy," Michael said. "Never has. And frankly, I can understand his point of view. The RMN costs money and people, and at the moment has no real use."

"At the moment, maybe," Edward said. "What Breakwater fails to appreciate is that a military is like a counter-grav backpack. If you ever need one, and don't have it, you're dead."

"Agreed," Michael said. "And we *will* need it someday. The situation at New Berlin shows that there are still powerful and potentially unfriendly forces out there." He sighed. "You know, Edward, sometimes I think the board made a serious mistake in recasting Manticore as a kingdom. There's something about titles and a division of the citizenry between nobles and commoners that affects people's brains. A rich and well-connected man or woman has a certain level of power, but they're still just peo-ple. You make that *Earl* Rich Man or *Countess* Well-Connected Woman, and suddenly everyone sees them differently."

"Including themselves."

"Especially themselves," Michael said ruefully. "And make a man king...well, that's even more problematic."

"I suppose," Edward said carefully, an odd tingle running

through him. It was no secret in the family that his father had never particularly liked being king. But that was a far cry from wishing the Star Kingdom had never been born. "So you're thinking we ought to go back to Manticore, Limited?"

"I'll admit sometimes I'm tempted." Michael shook his head. "But going backwards never works. Even if I could figure out another way to guarantee the rights of the original colonists over the newer immigrants, I doubt the general population would go along with such a drastic change. Certainly all the barons, earls, and countesses have become comfortable with their titles and their lands." He smiled. "Though I would guess you're familiar with that aspect."

"A bit," Edward said, smiling back, freshly aware of the commander's insignia on his uniform collar. Yes, he knew plenty of men and women in the RMN who were madly in love with their ranks and titles. Some of them were even decent officers. "So that's it?"

"Unless you can come up with a brilliant plan of your own," Michael said.

"I'll work on it," Edward promised, gazing into his father's face. So very, very tired... "Is there anything I can do for you, Dad?"

"I don't think so, Edward," Michael said, reaching over and squeezing his son's arm. "You have your life, and I have mine."

A life, Edward knew soberly, which would someday be his. *King Edward...* "I suppose so."

"And now, if you'll forgive me, I have to get back to work," Michael said, standing up. "Thank you for coming by."

"I'm glad I did," Edward said, standing up, too. "By the way, is there any chance you can send me a copy of Breakwater's full proposal?"

"Certainly," Michael said, his forehead wrinkling. "I thought copies had been made public."

"The basics have been, but not the technical details of the transformation," Edward told him. "I'd like to see the whole thing, if I may."

"I'll send it right away," his father promised. "I'll warn you, though, that it's pretty long."

"That's all right," Edward assured him. "We have a fair amount of free time on our hands for reading these days."

"I expect you do," Michael said. He reached out his hand.

"Let's try to get together more often, shall we? I know your sister would like that."

"We'll make it the whole family next time," Edward promised, taking the proffered hand and squeezing it. Suddenly, for no particular reason, he flashed back to a scene from when he was thirteen years old, sitting silently and listening as his father and grandmother discussed the future of the Star Kingdom and the tasks that lay ahead. For a moment he puzzled at the image, wondering why that particular memory had popped up.

And then it clicked. Grandma Elizabeth had been seventy-two T-years old at the time, the same age as his father was now.

Elizabeth had looked old, but she'd also looked bright and fresh, ready and eager to take on the challenges before her. Michael just looked old. Old, and burdened.

"I'll see you soon, Dad," he promised. He held his father's hand another moment before reluctantly releasing it. "I promise."

"Take care, Edward," Michael said. He took a deep breath.

And suddenly, the years and age lines seemed to fall away from his face. He straightened, the weight of his office visibly falling from his shoulders.

Edward caught his breath. What in the name of—?

His father smiled, a faint, knowing thing . . . and then Edward understood.

Michael, father of Edward, could be himself in front of his son. Michael, King of Manticore, could not. He had a role to play, and whether he liked that role or not he was determined to play it to the best of his ability.

"You take care, too, Dad," Edward said softly. "See you again soon."

☆   ☆   ☆

It was raining when Travis left the classroom building, his head spinning with the latest cubic meter's worth of information that had been poured into his skull. And there was going to be a test on that very material right after dinner.

Still, it could be worse. If he only took a half portion and wolfed it down, then used the rest of the time to study—

His train of thought came to an abrupt halt. Standing five meters directly in front of him was Gunner's Mate Funk. The petty officer was staring woodenly at Travis, apparently oblivious to the rain water pouring off his hat.

"Gunner's Mate," Travis said, stopping as quickly as he safely could on the wet pavement.

"Come with me," Funk said. Turning, he strode away.

Travis's first, hopeful thought was that they were headed for the mess hall. They passed it by without slowing. His second was that they were going to the Base Exchange. It, too, was soon behind them. Travis kept walking, his eyes on the back of Funk's neck, the hairs on the back of his own neck starting to tingle unpleasantly. The only structure in this direction was the picnic shelter overlooking the base's game yard. A yard that was, not surprisingly given the downpour, currently deserted.

But the shelter wasn't. As Funk led the way toward it, Travis could see a shadowy figure standing rigidly in the center of the shelter with his back toward them.

I'm going to die. I'm going to die, and then they're going to bury me in the sand in the high-jump pit. Quickly, guiltily, Travis chased the ridiculous thought from his mind.

But if he wasn't here to be quietly murdered, what *was* he here for?

Funk led the way up the shelter's pair of short steps, and as Travis came up the steps behind him the third man finally turned to face them. He was middle aged, his hair a short-cropped gray-ing blond, his forehead and cheeks lined, his expression neutral. Now, close up, Travis could also see that he was wearing the insignia of a senior chief petty officer.

"Senior Chief," Funk greeted the man, his tone formal. "Spacer Third Travis Long, as requested."

"Spacer Long," the man said, just as formally. "I'm Senior Chief Dierken. You're in a purple-gilled mess of trouble, Spacer."

Travis felt his heart seize up. He flicked a glance at Funk, but the other was watching him with the same hard expression that Dierken was.

"You were told to stay clear of Lieutenant Cyrus," Dierken continued. "Why the hell didn't you listen?"

"Uh..." Travis's brain seemed to shrivel under Dierken's glare. "I didn't—"

"No one ever does," the senior chief cut him off brusquely. "No matter. Too late now, anyway. You've rattled the wrong cage, Long, and your life's about to change. Drastically.

"Sit down, shut up, and listen."

CHAPTER EIGHT

IN SOME WAYS, Commodore Kiselev mused, his return to academia felt like coming home.

In other ways, it felt like exile.

He scowled out the window of his new office in the Casey-Rosewood HQ building. A *real* window, not a viewscreen, with grass and trees and blue sky on the other side. His office didn't face any of the main pedestrian routes, but there was a lesser-used walkway in sight and every minute or two someone went striding briskly past. Occasionally, an air car cut across the corner of his view, heading over the top of the building on its way to the landing area or rising over the roof as it headed out again. It was certainly tolerable, even reasonably pleasant.

But it wasn't like being aboard a ship. It didn't even feel, really, like being a proper Naval officer.

It felt like being a *civilian*.

He sighed, a long, frustrated sound that he would never have given vent to in front of anyone else. He still missed *Mars*, and he was still angry at what was being done to her.

But the past few weeks had turned the red-hot fury in his heart into a cooler ache in the pit of his stomach. He'd done everything he could to save his ship, and his efforts had failed. Time to let her go. His job now was to usher new spacers through this second stage of their training and prepare them for life in the Royal Manticoran Navy.

Assuming that the Navy still existed by the time they were ready for their assignments.

He gave the view one last look, then turned back to his desk and terminal. If the RMN was going to fade away, there was nothing he could do to stop it. But let it never be said that Commodore Horace Kiselev had been part of its demise. He would do his job; and the first part of that job was to familiarize himself with everyone under his command.

He'd spent the entire day yesterday going through the officer and instructor files. Today, it was time to look at the students themselves.

Pulling up the first of the files, he began to read.

It was just before four in the afternoon when he reached the file of Spacer Third Class Travis Uriah Long.

Up to now Kiselev had been skimming the reports. Not anymore. This one he read carefully, all the way through. Then he reread two other files, read Long's again, and followed three of the attached links.

When he had finished, he sent out a summons for Lieutenant William Cyrus to report to his office.

He was checking a section of the Uniform Code of Conduct when the yeoman ushered Cyrus into the office.

The other strode to Kiselev's desk and came to attention.

"Lieutenant William Cyrus reporting as ordered, Sir," he announced formally.

"At ease, Lieutenant," Kiselev said, studying the other's face. It seemed open and guileless, the face of a man with no strains on his conscience. "I've been reading over the personnel files," he continued. "I like what I see."

"Thank you, Sir," Cyrus said briskly. "We have a good team here."

"So it seems," Kiselev said. "Tell me about Spacer Third Class Travis Long."

Cyrus had his expression under good control, as befitted a man who'd had to deal with all kinds of superiors through the course of his career. But the control wasn't perfect. "Sir?" he asked, his tone suddenly cautious, his face tightening just enough for Kiselev to see.

"It says here that Long was caught cheating on a test," Kiselev said, waving toward the terminal, "and that he was subsequently transferred from your impeller track to the gravitics track. In fact, from the date stamps, it looks like he was *immediately* transferred to gravitics. Is that correct?"

"Yes, Sir," Cyrus said. "As you can see, it was on a quiz—"

"Cheating is a serious offense, Lieutenant, punishable by summary dishonorable discharge," Kiselev cut him off. "So why didn't you go ahead and file formal charges? Why was he simply transferred to a different track?"

"We, uh, were still trying to ascertain the circumstances when he put in for a transfer to gravitics. It was thought that a fresh start—someone must have thought it would be good for him, because the transfer went through immediately."

"And you didn't challenge it?" Kiselev asked. "You and your witness? I assume you *did* have a witness to this alleged cheating?"

Cyrus's throat worked.

"Ah . . . the suspicion was brought to my attention by one of Long's instructors, Sir."

"The suspicion," Kiselev said. "Not any actual cheating? Just the *suspicion* of cheating?"

Cyrus was starting to take on the look of a cornered animal.

"Someone apparently thought it was advisable to transfer him to a track—"

"Yes, you already said that," Kiselev said. "Would you like to know what *I* think, Lieutenant? *I* think that Long's allegations of cheating in the impeller unit threatened your own record, so you trumped up this charge as an excuse to get him out of your hair. And if that got the kid bounced on his butt with a DD in his permanent record to hang over his head for the rest of his life, that was just too damned bad, wasn't it?"

"Sir, I—there were no allegations of cheating," Cyrus protested. "I mean, he had suspicions, but never offered any specifics."

"Didn't he?" Kiselev countered. "Or did you simply refuse to listen?"

"He had no specifics, Sir," Cyrus insisted.

"That's interesting." Kiselev gestured to the terminal again. "Because he filed quite a number of specifics onto the Provost Marshal's records folder. Including names, times, *and* methods."

Cyrus's mouth twitched. Apparently, he hadn't realized Long had done that.

"I—Sir, I had no idea—"

"Of course you didn't," Kiselev said. "Because the regs call for all such accusations to be dual-filed that way, except hardly anyone ever does. I gather Long is a strict rule-follower?"

Cyrus seemed to gather himself. "Sir, none of those accusations are provable," he said flatly. "And even if they were . . . Sir, half the damn class is involved. And you know as well as I do that they'll all need to be retrained anyway once they're aboard their ships."

"That's your defense, Lieutenant?" Cyrus asked coldly. "That everyone does it, and that it doesn't matter anyway?"

Cyrus's jaw wrinkled with a momentary clenching of his teeth.

"Sir, Spacer Long is a royal pain in the butt. He's disruptive, argues every little damn thing, and irritates everyone around him. I just . . . it seemed better to let the transfer go through without a fuss. Let him irritate someone else for a change."

"Someone who wouldn't put impossible situations into mid-shipman simulations?" Kiselev suggested. "Oh, yes, that's in here, too," he added as Cyrus paled. "So is the link to your many attempts to get BuEng and BuOrd interested in your dual-stage missile idea. Though to be fair, Long didn't know about those. I dug up that connection myself."

"Sir—"

"Bottom line, Lieutenant Cyrus," Kiselev said, dropping his voice into the cryogenic temperature range. "Did Spacer Long cheat, or didn't he?"

Cyrus's throat worked again.

"No, Sir."

Kiselev let the words hang in the air for a long moment.

"Thank you, Lieutenant," he said at last. "We'll be talking again later. Dismissed."

He stared at the closed door for a long time after Cyrus left, simmering with anger and frustration. And wondering what he was going to do about this.

Because the hell of it was that, on one level, Cyrus was right. The bright-eyed students here *would* have to be retrained once their theoretical schooling slammed head-on into the real world. The dirty little secret was that the training school's main purpose was merely to give them the basic background they would need to build on once they reached their ships, along with the intellectual techniques required to assimilate new information. The rest of the bookwork was essentially meaningless, especially here in the RMN's declining days, when more equipment and techniques were cobbled together than were taken shiny out of the box. Exposing the students' cheating to the light would merely kick out a bunch of perfectly adequate spacers and open the RMN to a scandal it couldn't afford.

Worse yet were the specific students who would be thrown out. The Navy might be in its twilight days, but that hadn't stopped the rich and powerful from sending their sons and daughters to try to grab some glory and command rank for themselves before the end. The Academy was always the first choice, of course, but when the midshipman slots were filled the next choice was Casey-Rosewood and the hoped-for petty officer track. The names on Long's list of offenders weren't the biggest on Manticore, but they were big enough, and their high and noble families would not take kindly to having those names smeared across the center of a scandal.

And the last thing the Navy needed was more names on its enemies list.

Which meant that for the good of the Service, Kiselev was going to have to sweep this one under the rug. No punishment for the students, no overt punishment for Cyrus.

And Spacer Long would be left hanging in the wind.

Kiselev scowled at his terminal. Maybe, but maybe not. Long had been in the center of his impeller class—a decent enough showing, considering that most of those above him were habitual cheaters, but on paper hardly spectacular. In contrast, in the gravitics track where Cyrus had sent him he was second of eleven students. A much better showing, probably helped along by Lieutenant Krauss's practice of allowing her students to use notes during tests. Her argument, delineated in full in her file, was that a lot of on-board gravitic work was done via ship's computer, where relevant formulas were always available, and therefore those formulas didn't need to be memorized. A reasonable enough teaching philosophy, Kiselev had concluded, which also had the benefit of making most cheating superfluous. Long would rise or fall there on his own, and it looked like he was rising just fine.

And really, gravitics was as just good a specialty as impellers. All Long had lost in this whole deal had been a little pride and a little face, and most of that had been between him and a handful of others, since Cyrus had needed to keep the details of his plot private.

Besides, deep down, Kiselev could sympathize with Cyrus's motivation. Strict rule-followers tended to be staid, petty, and colorless, usually with little humor and no imagination. They were the invisible ones, plugging along at their jobs and keeping things running, but seldom attracting the attention of anyone higher than their division head. They stayed strictly on the lines, never daring anything new or deviating from the precise rule of regulations and orders. Long would do his years in the Navy, collect an unimpressive list of unenthusiastic commendations, and be promoted on schedule until he reached the end of his career. At that point, he would retire to sit in the shade with his grandchildren, as colorless at the end of his life as he'd been at the beginning of it.

Assuming he ever *had* grandchildren. That personality type didn't exactly draw husband-seeking women.

So Spacer Long was set. Which left just one loose end Kiselev still needed to tie up.

Senior Chief Dierken responded to the summons faster even than Lieutenant Cyrus had. Almost, Kiselev mused, as if he'd been expecting the call.

"Good to see you, Senior Chief," Kiselev said after the official greetings were out of the way. "It's been a while."

"Three years two months, Sir." Dierken grinned lopsidedly. "And no, I had to look it up. Congratulations on your promotion, by the way."

"Thank you." Kiselev raised his eyebrows. "Tell me about Spacer Third Class Travis Long."

"Off the record, Sir?"

"Extremely," Kiselev assured him.

"Lieutenant Cyrus was planning to kick Long out of the service," Dierken said. "He trumped up a cheating charge—"

"I know all that," Kiselev said. "Skip to the part where your signature's on Long's transfer orders."

Dierken gave a small shrug.

"I heard through the grapevine that Long was being set up for a fall. A couple of people I trust said he was good Navy material but hadn't yet learned how and when to keep his mouth shut."

"And so you arranged to get him transferred out of impellers before Cyrus could drop a brick on him?"

"The Navy takes care of its own, Sir," Dierken said. "I figured that Cyrus was at least smart enough to recognize a fait accompli and not push his case. Especially since the charges were one hundred percent soap bubble to begin with."

Kiselev smiled faintly.

"*Soap bubble?*" he chided. "Language, Senior Chief, language."

"Yes, Sir, I know," Dierken said with a wry smile. "Ever since Eleanor started asking our pastor's wife in for Sunday afternoon tea, I've had to work on editing my language."

"It's good practice," Kiselev said. "So how much of Long's career have you mapped out?"

"*Me*, Sir?" Dierken said with feigned astonishment. "Surely you're not serious. You know I don't screw with people's lives."

"Unless they're part of your division?"

"Well, yes," Dierken conceded. "In that case I screw with them completely. All I know is that it looks like Long is slated to be assigned to *Vanguard* after graduation."

Kiselev smiled humorlessly. *Vanguard*. Commanded by Captain Robert Davison, one of the most lackluster commanders in the Navy.

"He and Davison should get along swimmingly," he murmured.

"I'm sure he will, Sir," Dierken agreed dryly. "How he'll get along with everyone else, of course, is an entirely different question. I'm told *Vanguard*'s crew can be a troublesome bunch."

Kiselev nodded. An environment like that would definitely be a pain in Long's butt.

But he'd make it through. Rule-followers were stiff and annoying, but they were usually survivors. If only because they kept things running while everyone else was goofing off.

"Speaking of troublesome . . . ?" Dierken said.

"Yes," Kiselev said. "Unfortunately, there's really nothing I can do about Lieutenant Cyrus. The spacers Long caught cheating are well-connected, and I can't stir up anything on Cyrus without dragging Long and everyone else into the stewpot along with him."

"That's kind of what I figured, Sir," Dierken said. "That's okay. All I wanted to do here was keep a promising kid in the Navy. Lieutenant Cyrus's fate is out of my hands. Wouldn't want it there anyway."

"Things tend to balance out," Kiselev said. "Thank you. You and Eleanor should come by the house sometime, now that I'm permanently back on Manticore."

"Thank you, Sir, I'd like that," Dierken said. "I'll have her call Juliana and find a time for us to all get together."

"I'll look forward to it," Kiselev said. "Dismissed, Senior Chief."

"Yes, Sir." Stiffening to attention, Dierken turned and left the room.

Kiselev leaned back in his seat, turning to once again stare out his window. So that was that. He would deal with Cyrus by *not* dealing with him, by letting matters stand as they were. It wasn't ideal—hell, it was about as far from ideal as it was possible to get.

But it was the best solution for a difficult situation. What was best for the Navy came before what was best for any individual member of it.

With a sigh, he turned back to his terminal. Next file down was that of Spacer Third Class Susanne Loomis. With a brief but fervent hope that this one had done a better job of keeping a low profile, he began to read.

☆　　☆　　☆

"Gill?" the foreman's voice came over the earphone. "You awake in there?"

Gill—*Alvis* to his wife, *Senior Chief Petty Officer Alvis Massingill* to the people who signed off on his pay packets, *Gill* to everyone else—rolled his eyes. It was the third time in as many hours that the foreman had called with the same prompt in the exact same words. "Still awake," he promised. "Why? Is there some reason I need to be?"

"Just get ready," the foreman growled. "Should be any time now."

"Right," Gill said.

Though to be honest, he'd been tempted to take a nap more than once during the hours he'd been stuck here in *Mars*'s 05-098/187-13-P inspection passageway. He didn't know what was holding up the show out there, and probably didn't want to.

But it didn't bode well for the future. The *sloop-de-do* project already had a scheduled completion time of over ten months, and if they couldn't even get it started on time the reality was likely to far outpace the projection.

"Okay, here we go," the foreman said. "Starting the cut...now."

There was the brief sizzle of a plasma torch on metal, the noise cutting off as the foreman killed his mike. Flicking on his light, Gill switched on the hand-held monitor linked to the twenty temperature sensors he'd spent his first hour in here placing against the dull metal of the inner hull.

And with that horrendously complicated task completed, it was back to waiting.

Waiting, and brooding.

This was criminal. It really was. Not just because the Manticorans were wrecking a perfectly good battlecruiser, but also because the whole thing was going to cost way more than Chancellor Breakwater's numbers indicated. That should have been obvious to anyone with a working brain. It had certainly been obvious to Gill himself.

But had First Lord of the Admiralty Cazenestro asked *him* to testify before Parliament? Of course not. Cazenestro and Defense Minister Earl Dapplelake had called in several other yard dogs, but not Alvis Massingill. Not a man who'd worked on ships both here and in the Solarian League. Not a man who probably had more wide-ranging experience with ship types and design than anyone else in the entire Star Kingdom.

At the time, he'd wondered why Cazenestro had ignored him. He still did. Maybe it was because his wife was CO of Casey-Rosewood, and they thought Parliament would assume Gill was too close to the RMN's upper echelon to be a credible witness. Or maybe it was *because* he and Jean were immigrants from the League, and not Manticoran home-grown. He'd run into occasional prejudice among descendants of the First Settlers—most of it subtle, but definitely there. Maybe Parliament, with all its earls and countesses and barons, was more susceptible to that sort of bias.

But regardless of the reasons, the writing was on the wall. Both he and Jean had become disillusioned with the Navy.

Maybe it was time to move on.

The monitor beeped. "Gill," he announced into his mike. "I'm starting to feel the torch at this end."

"Acknowledged," the foreman came back, again with the torch's hiss in the background. "Let me know right away if the heat starts affecting the conduits."

"Acknowledged," Gill said.

Still, if there was one thing he'd learned in life it was that hasty decisions tended to be bad ones. He and Jean had secure positions here, and more importantly were accumulating benefits that would be lost if they left too soon. Another four or five years, and they should be able to get at least a partial retirement. That would be enough time to watch Parliament destroy *Mars.* Maybe enough time to watch them wreck their other battlecruisers, too, if that was the direction they decided to go.

Maybe even enough time to watch them destroy their entire Navy.

Only time would tell.

BOOK TWO

1532 PD

CHAPTER NINE

"YOU SEE IT?" Spacer First Class Travis Long called down the curved service tube behind the U-shaped console that was the heart of HMS *Vanguard*'s gravitics data collection center. "Chief? You see it?"

"Patience, son, patience," the lazy voice of Chief Gravitics Tech Randall Craddock drifted back. Craddock was only thirty-five T-years old, barely fifteen years older than Travis and less than ten years older than some of the other spacers and petty officers in his division. But he nevertheless insisted on calling all five of them *son* or *kiddo* anyway.

Spacer First Class Bonnie Esterle's theory was that he was quoting from some space-going drama or comedy, something so obscure that none of the rest of them had ever heard of it. The more widespread consensus was that as Craddock's hair went prematurely gray the brain beneath it was going prematurely senile.

Travis scowled as he looked at his chrono. *Vanguard*'s entire gravitic system had now been off-line for nearly thirteen minutes. Captain Davison's standing orders were very specific: no ship's sensor array was to be down for more than five minutes at a time.

Unfortunately, this was one of many situations where the violation couldn't be helped. On paper, the massive battlecruiser had two independent sets of gravitic sensor electronics, either of which could operate the array and pull in and analyze data on distant gravitational fields. In hard cold reality, though, both sets were rarely functional at any given time.

In fact, more often than not, one of the duals was down because it was being raided for parts to keep the other one running.

The lack of proper readiness was bad enough. What made it all the more frustrating was that a casualty report was supposed to be filed by the chief when any system was down for more than five minutes. Not only had Craddock never filed any such CASREP, as far as Travis could tell, but the chief had studiously ignored Travis's occasional gentle reminders of that regulation.

It wasn't just Craddock, either. *No* one around *Vanguard*, either above or below the chief, seemed to care about those clearly defined operational details.

Which was not only wrong, but dangerous as well. *Vanguard* was part of the ready reserve, and needed to be able to come to full action status in no more than ninety minutes. If Captain Davison didn't know which of *Vanguard*'s systems were functional and which weren't, how could he hope to bring the ship to action in an emergency?

"There it is," Craddock called. "It's a jump-burn, all right. Looks like we're going to need two quads and a hex."

Travis scowled some more. Terrific. "We've got a hex," he called back, "but only one quad."

"You sure?"

"Positive," Travis said. "We used one in the surge sump, remember?"

"No one told me that was our second to last," Craddock grumbled. "Fine. Better get Gadgets on it. Here—catch."

From around the curve of the tube a fist-sized chunk of electronics appeared. It bounced gently off the bulkhead, the impact sending it into a slow spin, then bounced again off the back of the nearest console. Two bounces later, it reached Travis. "Got it," Travis said, plucking it out of the air.

"And hurry back with the other stuff," Craddock ordered. "I can get started on the rest while she builds me a new quad."

"Right." Getting a grip on the nearest handhold, Travis gave himself a tug that sent him floating past the edge of the console bank and into the deserted monitor area itself. He caught hold of the back of one of the stations as he passed, giving himself more speed and a change of direction toward the open hatchway. He didn't manage to hit the opening dead center, but he got through without brushing against the sides.

He was pretty sure he would never really *enjoy* maneuvering in the zero-gee that held sway everywhere aboard *Vanguard* except the rotating spin section amidships. But after almost three years aboard he was at least becoming reasonably competent at it.

Esterle and Gravitics Tech First Class Amber Bowen were waiting for him in the small machine/electronics shop that they shared with the electronic warfare and hydroponics divisions. Esterle was playing her usual game of drifting slowly in a vertical circle around her center of mass as she and Bowen chatted, a maneuver which nearly always induced her conversational partner to match the movement, usually unconsciously, in order to keep them facing each other in what would be a normal position if they'd been groundside or in the ship's spin section. Sure enough, Bowen had matched Esterle's rotation, though in Bowen's case Travis had never been able to figure out whether she was unconsciously reacting to Esterle's game or had figured it out and was simply bored enough to play it back at her.

Both women looked over as he came through the hatchway. "Let me guess," Bowen said, waving toward the quad in Travis's hand. "Chief wants a rebuild."

"Chief wants, and we need," Travis confirmed, grabbing a handhold and bringing himself to a stop beside them. He was nearly forty-five degrees off their shared vertical, and he had to resist the urge to realign himself to match them. "Number-two Doppler analyzer."

"The Doppler's out *again*?" Bowen growled, taking the quad and peering at it. "Great. This is one I've already patched."

"You can do it, Ma'am," Esterle said encouragingly.

"Thank you for your confidence, Spacer Esterle," Bowen said dryly. She turned the quad over in her fingers, and then pushed off toward one of the work stations. "I'll see what I can do. Chief need anything else?"

"Another quad and a hex," Travis told her, giving himself a shove toward the wall of parts drawers.

"I think we're out of hexes," Bowen warned from behind him.

Travis wrinkled his nose. Yet another screw-up from the Logistics Department. Craddock, he knew, had requisitioned more hexes nearly six weeks ago. Clearly, they hadn't arrived, and the chief was *not* going to happy about that. "Great."

"No, we're okay—there are a couple left," Esterle said. There was the soft slap of a hand on handhold, and she floated past him. "I'll get it."

Only instead of heading toward the relay/transfer section of the wall, she was aiming for the bin where the higher-voltage parts were kept. Frowning, Travis changed direction to follow.

Esterle was pulling open a drawer labeled *Asymptotic Half-Link Routers* when he caught up with her. "Since when do we store hexes in the A-hale drawer?" he asked.

"Since Atherton caught that little greaseball from hydroponics— his words, not mine—filching some of our equipment."

"Atherton caught him in the act? Did he report him to the bosun?"

"It wasn't *quite* in the act," Esterle hedged. "But he's pretty sure it was him. Anyway, Atherton's not likely to go to the bosun any- time soon. Not after what happened the last time they chatted."

Travis nodded. He didn't know the details of that legendary conversation, but he did know that Spacer First Class Tully Ath- erton had emerged from it as Spacer *Second* Class Tully Atherton. "He still needs to report theft."

"He has other ways of dealing with it." Digging beneath the jumble of A-HLs, she pulled out a hex. "Here you go."

"So is this one of ours, or one of theirs?" Travis asked, gin- gerly taking it.

"Well, it *should* be one of ours," Esterle said. "A replacement for the one hydroponics made off with."

"Assuming it *was* made off with."

"Atherton keeps ridiculously close track of our stuff," Esterle reminded him. "We're definitely missing a few items." She shrugged. "He just got them back, that's all."

"Right," Travis murmured. Stealing parts was a serious offense, and *Vanguard*'s bosun, Master Chief Dovnar, had made it abun- dantly clear what he would do to anyone he caught doing that.

But Atherton hadn't *exactly* stolen anything. The hidden hex was still officially in the shop, where anyone could theoretically find and use it. The fact that no one would look for it in an A- HL drawer was mostly beside the point.

"You going to report him?" Esterle asked quietly.

Travis started. He hadn't realized his mental conflict had been so visible. "He's sure someone from hydroponics took our stuff?"

"Yes," Esterle said. "Why? Does that make a difference?"

Travis pursed his lips. It didn't, really. Or at least it shouldn't.

But hydroponics wasn't exactly a critical part of *Vanguard*'s official war footing. Not when the ship was parked in permanent high orbit over Manticore, with fresh fruit and vegetables just a shuttle trip away.

The gravitics division, on the other hand, *was* vital. They maintained the sensors that could spot the telltale hyper footprint whenever a ship entered Manticoran space, as well as being the long-range detectors that could track and identify ships already moving through the system.

Besides, parts *did* get misfiled on occasion. In fact, they got misfiled all the time.

He felt his stomach tighten. Reasonable, logical . . . and one hundred percent rationalization.

"I won't report him," he told Esterle. "But he needs to put everything back where it's supposed to be."

She was silent a moment. "Okay," she said at last. "No problem. I'll tell him."

Which, Travis was pretty sure, really meant she would tell Atherton to make sure Rule-Stickler Travesty Long didn't find out about any future attempts to make sure their equipment didn't develop legs.

So what was Travis accomplishing by trying to stick to the regs?

"If you really feel like filing complaints today, you might consider the com division," Esterle suggested as she shoved off the drawers and headed toward the cable bin. "There's supposed to be a line between here and the monitor station so that you can call for parts or tools instead of having to scamper back personally every time the chief needs something."

"I know," Travis said. "I've already filed one."

She blinked a frown at him as she stopped in front of a co-ax bin. "Seriously?"

"Seriously," Travis assured her.

"Good for you." She rummaged beneath one of the neat coils of cable and pulled out a hidden quad. "So what happened?"

"About what you'd expect," Travis said, taking the quad from her. "Com agreed it was their line, but said it was running along our bulkhead and through aft fire control's junction box, so that made it either our problem or AFC's."

"And AFC of course said it was ours?"

"*And* Chief Craddock said it was theirs." Travis turned back to Bowen. "How does it look?"

"Don't know yet," Bowen said. She had the quad partially disassembled, with the pieces neatly lined up on one of the tac strips beside the tool rack. "I'll know one way or another in half an hour."

"You might as well head back," Esterle said. "Leave the chief alone too long and he's likely to fall asleep. Embarrassing if some officer got lost and happened to wander by."

"Like *that's* going to happen," Bowen added. "Go on, Long. I'll have Esterle deliver if I get it working."

☆   ☆   ☆

Twenty-five minutes later, as Craddock and Travis were running their check on the other newly installed components, Esterle arrived with the quad in her hand and a self-satisfied look on her face. Craddock took it with a grunted thanks and headed back into the crawlspace.

"I told you she could fix it," Esterle said, peering down the passageway after the chief. "Anything else I can do while I'm here?"

Travis peered into the crawlspace, making sure Esterle couldn't see his face and this newest moral dilemma.

Yes, Esterle had assured them Bowen could rebuild the quad. The problem was that the quad she'd just handed him wasn't the same one he'd given Bowen. The other had had a scratch on the casing where a screwdriver had missed its mark. This one didn't have that scratch.

Probably it was just another of Atherton's private stash. But if it wasn't . . .

Travis exhaled slowly. He had no proof, he reminded himself firmly, or even a solid hint that anything illegal had happened. Quads were probably the most common single component present in *Vanguard*'s electronics, used everywhere from the automatic cooking systems in the galley to the cryogenic cooling system for the battlecruiser's heavy axial laser. And while regulations frowned on different divisions swapping parts and equipment, it wasn't considered an actionable offense.

"Long?" Esterle prompted. "Wake up, buddy. You need anything else?"

"No," Travis said. "You can head back. We're fine."

☆   ☆   ☆

"We are gathered here today," Breakwater intoned toward the cameras, "to inaugurate the latest addition to the Manticoran Patrol and Rescue Service, and to celebrate a new era in the ongoing saga that truly *is* the Star Kingdom of Manticore."

Floating at the far end of the group crowded into the bridge of the brand-new sloop HMS *Phobos*, positioned as far from the cameras as it was possible to be, Winterfall gripped the handhold beside him, trying to look as serious, noble, and historical as everyone else.

Trying with even more fervor not to throw up.

He'd done some research on the whole zero-gee thing in the two days since Breakwater had announced that *Phobos* was finally ready and informed Winterfall that he would be joining the rest of the Committee for the commissioning ceremony. He'd read about the effects of free-fall, both physiological and psychological, and had assumed he was adequately prepared.

He hadn't been. Not even close.

He clenched his teeth, silently telling his stomach and inner ear that he was not, in fact, falling helplessly to his death, but was hundreds of kilometers above Manticore and as safe as if he was in his own home.

His inner ear didn't believe him. His stomach certainly didn't.

Across the bridge, Breakwater was still droning on about *Phobos* and the new era the sloop was ushering in for MPARS and how much safer the Star Kingdom's citizens were now. After the Exchequer would come Defense Minister Dapplelake, and First Lord Cazenestro would probably have a few words to say, as well.

Winterfall could only hope that the rest of the assembled dignitaries weren't also planning to give speeches. If they were, this was going to be a long afternoon, because practically everyone who'd had a hand in the project was here, King Michael himself being the sole exception.

He focused across *Phobos*'s bridge, at Dapplelake standing—hovering, rather—straight and tall beside Cazenestro and Locatelli. It was easy to understand why Breakwater had wanted all of his people present. After all, this was the culmination of the Committee for Military Sanity's sole reason for existence, not to mention a personal triumph for Breakwater himself. The Chancellor had succeeded in performing the remarkable mathematical feat of subtracting one ship from Dapplelake's RMN and adding *two* ships to his own MPARS.

Breakwater's motives were clear. What bothered Winterfall was the fact that Dapplelake had also sent him a personal note requesting his presence.

Which was odd. Not to mention suspicious.

Because the Defense Minister wasn't just being a good loser. Not Dapplelake. He was a man who knew his enemies, never forgave them, and never, ever turned his back on them.

Winterfall's impromptu speech at that first meeting with King Michael had apparently tipped the balance in Breakwater's favor. That had to have put Winterfall's name on Dapplelake's enemies' list.

And yet, Dapplelake had wanted him here.

Was there something going behind the scenes? Some problem with *Phobos*, maybe? Or could it be something more long-term, something that Dapplelake expected might happen during the sloops' probationary period?

Maybe it was simpler. The price tag and completion time for two sloops had been way higher than Breakwater's conservative projections, higher even than Dapplelake's own experts' more somber and realistic numbers. Neither Dapplelake nor Cazenestro had said anything about it, but it was possible they were simply holding that particular big gun in reserve for use at a more advantageous time. In that case, maybe the Defense Minister had wanted Winterfall here to make sure all of them were on record as the instigators of this particular financial fiasco.

Winterfall squared his shoulders, his rebellious stomach momentarily forgotten. If Dapplelake thought he could take them all down, he was sadly mistaken. What Breakwater and the others did was up to them; but Winterfall, at least, was not going to simply curl up and slink away for the minister's convenience.

He'd had a taste of power and prestige. People knew who he was, and not just the men and women in the Lords who informed him which way he was supposed to vote on a particular bill. He was *somebody*.

And he was damned if he would give all of that up without a fight.

Breakwater was introducing *Phobos*'s new captain and executive officer. Again reminding his stomach to behave, Winterfall returned his attention to the proceedings.

☆   ☆   ☆

The speeches and posturing were finally over, and the last of *Phobos*'s guest dignitaries had shuttled back to Manticore.

Time to get the show on the road.

Commander Sophia Ouvrard gave a quick look at the displays as she strapped herself into her command station. Her XO, Lieutenant Commander Armand Creutz, seemed to have everything set and ready to go, from the impellers to *Phobos*'s galley and everything in between. All that was lacking was an official order; and once Ouvrard spoke those magic words the sloop and her one hundred thirty-member crew would be on their way to Manticore-B and the Unicorn Asteroid Belt that was to be their new home for the next eight months.

Ouvrard scowled as she gave the displays a second, more careful look. *Phobos*'s systems had all been checked out, and the sloop had successfully carried out preliminary maneuvers around Manticore. On paper, at least, she seemed good to go.

But official checkmarks meant zip, especially with a ship as bizarrely designed as this one. Over thirty equipment anomalies had already been logged, none of them fatal but all of them troubling to one degree or another. The fact that *Phobos*'s sister sloop, *Deimos*, was still being worked on without an official expected completion date was another source of concern, especially since the two ships had originally been scheduled to be launched together.

But at the end of the day, none of that apparently mattered. The Defense Minister, Parliament, and the King had all decreed that *Phobos* was ready to be put into service. And for the moment, at least, *Phobos* in service meant she was under the care and authority of Commander Sophia Ouvrard.

It was an honor and, in these waning days of the RMN, an increasingly rare privilege. With the Navy slowly hemorrhaging ships, and with all eight of the remaining battlecruisers poised to go to the same chopping block that had claimed *Mars*, command positions were evaporating like the morning mist. Ouvrard would never get a chance like this again, and even though it had meant switching from the Navy to MPARS, she had no regrets for that decision. She had a ship, now—her very own ship—and come quirks or flaws, high water or hell itself, she and *Phobos* were going to make a name for themselves.

"Station reports?" she called.

"All divisions report ready," Creutz confirmed. "Crew and equipment showing green."

Ouvrard grimaced. Her crew. One hundred and thirty officers and enlisted, the full complement the designers had calculated for a ship this size. Many of them had already been MPARS personnel, but nearly half of them, like Ouvrard herself, had been pulled from the RMN's ranks.

Meanwhile, virtually every Navy ship was running light, with anywhere up to a third of their personnel simply not there.

It was one more poke in the eye from Chancellor Breakwater. He didn't give a mouse's rear if the Navy went begging as long as he got the manpower he wanted.

There had, she knew, been talk of taking some of the money that had theoretically been saved by this conversion and shifting it over to Casey-Rosewood and the Academy to try to bolster the ranks. *Mars*'s former captain, in fact, had been sent to Casey-Rosewood to help with that buildup.

Personally, Ouvrard would believe it when she saw it.

Though if she was feeling cynical she might also note that a fully-crewed battlecruiser was supposed to have around five hundred officers and crew, while *Phobos* and *Deimos* combined would have just over half that number. Converting all the battlecruisers would double the total number of ships, but would simultaneously halve the total number of crew. If the conversions themselves didn't put the Navy out of business, maybe the diminishing numbers of needed spacers would.

Maybe that was the whole idea. Either way, taking the opportunity to move over to MPARS had clearly been her best career move.

Still, she was going to miss the Navy.

"Captain?" Creutz prompted.

Ouvrard drew herself up in her station. *Captain.* "Take us out of orbit, XO," she ordered. "Lay in a course for Manticore-B and the Gamma Sector of the Unicorn Belt."

☆　　☆　　☆

"Another glorious day in the Royal Manticoran Navy," Tully Atherton intoned with obvious satisfaction as he set his dinner tray down beside Travis's and worked his ample Sphinxian butt onto the bench. "A taste of paradise—" he sniffed experimentally "—with just a hint of lubricating oil thrown in for flavor."

"You're in a good mood tonight," Esterle commented as she turned her slab of beef over with her fork to check its underside. Travis still hadn't figured out what she was hoping—or fearing—to find, but her quirks did make meal times more entertaining. "You win the jousting tournament or something?"

"Sadly, the finals had to be postponed," Atherton said. "Kelly's entry got swiped."

"You're kidding," Esterle said, frowning. "Who swipes a cleaning remote?"

"His chief," Atherton said dryly. "They had to get something out of one of the feed lines for Laser One and Kelly's was closest to hand. Of course, they had to rip off the lance mounts to get it in. No, I was talking about the fact that the Star Kingdom's first new ship since *Casey* has just taken off into the wild black... and it's MPARS's, not ours."

Across the table, Spacer First Class Stacy Yarrow gave a snort. "You mean that *Phobos* nightmare? If *that's* what they're calling a ship these days, MPARS can have it."

"It has impellers, a hull, and a crew," Atherton pointed out. "I think that's the legal definition of a ship."

"It's a corpse," Yarrow said flatly. "Half a corpse, and the writing's on the wall. Breakwater's going to take us all out, piece by piece, ship by ship. You wait—they'll be ordering *Vanguard* savaged next."

"Easy, girl," Atherton soothed. "There's enough risk of indigestion with this slop without encouraging it."

"He's right," Esterle agreed, checking the underside of her potato slab. "Don't worry, they'll never take us down. Not while Captain Davison and XO Bertinelli are standing tall and vigilant on the bridge."

"Only because Davison wants to retire in peace, and Bertinelli wants a ship of his very own while the Navy still has some," Yarrow grumbled.

"I didn't say they were standing on the line for *us*," Esterle said. "It still adds up to job security."

"Well, *that's* different," Craddock's voice came from behind them.

Travis turned to see the chief walking toward them, his gait a little tentative in the half-gee that was maintained in this part of *Vanguard*'s spin section. He must have just come from the zero-gee core of the ship, and didn't quite have his grav legs yet.

"What's different, Chief?" Atherton asked.

"Esterle using the word *job*," Craddock said, eyeing Atherton suspiciously. Officers and petty officers tended to use that look with Atherton, Travis had noted, ever since his run-in with the bosun and his subsequent demotion. Travis didn't know if Craddock's look had any specifics to it, or whether it was just there on general principles. "Didn't know any of you knew the meaning of the term."

"I've read about it," Esterle offered. "Never thought it sounded like something a nice girl should get involved in."

"Well, you're getting involved in it tomorrow," Craddock said. "*All* of you."

There was a quick mutual exchange of glances around the table. "The new vane has come in?" Yarrow asked.

"It's in, it's tractored to the hull, and it's being checked over as we speak," Craddock confirmed. "And tomorrow you sorry excuses for RMN spacers are going to go EVA and swap it out with that useless Two-Three."

"That's great," Esterle said with a distinct lack of enthusiasm. "I don't suppose we're also getting the collation and analysis gear that'll actually make a full array useful?"

"Hey, be thankful we got this much," Craddock said sourly. "Aft Weapons is still waiting on that replacement autocannon they've been promised for the past eight months."

"Bully for Aft Weapons," Atherton said. "I presume it's pure coincidence that we're getting a new vane at the same time they're busy sweeping up the debris from the *Mars* project and looking for parts they didn't use?"

"I didn't ask, and I suggest you do likewise," Craddock said. "Like Esterle says, we still have a lot on our wish list, and looking less than falling-over-drunk with gratitude is likely to put us behind Aft Weapons and Data Tracking on BuEng's priority list. Hell, we might even end up behind the wardroom ice cream machine. So be grateful."

"Oh, we're grateful, Chief," Yarrow assured him. "Don't we look grateful?"

"You look ecstatically grateful," Craddock said acidly. "Just make sure you're looking grateful in airlock five at oh-eight-hundred tomorrow ready to suit up and go for a walk." Still moving carefully, he headed off toward the petty officers' mess.

"I guess a new vane's *something*," Esterle said. "Personally, I'd rather have a second analyzer up and running."

"Glass half full, Esterle," Yarrow advised.

"Maybe it's a sign of things to come," Atherton offered hopefully. "Maybe they really *did* free up enough money with the *Mars* thing to start making up the equipment shortfalls everywhere else."

Yarrow snorted. "That's not what *I* heard," she said. "I heard *Phobos* and *Deimos* are on their way to costing more than if they'd just built a couple of new corvettes from the keel up. And that includes having to buy new impeller rings from the League."

"I guess we'll see when the dust settles," Atherton said. He speared a bite of beef, popped it into his mouth, then waved the empty fork at Travis. "You're being awfully quiet, Long," he said around the mouthful. "Treecat got your tongue?"

"I was thinking that Esterle's right about another analyzer being a higher priority than a new vane," Travis said. "I was also wondering what the chief meant by us being behind the wardroom ice cream machine."

"Oh, it's nothing," Yarrow said with a sniff. "One of the control components burned out, that's all. But you know how officers like their little perks."

"Ah." Travis looked at Esterle. She was studiously attacking her meal, and seemed to be making a point of not looking back at him. "It wouldn't have been a quad, would it?"

"I didn't ask," Yarrow said, peering closely at him. "Why? Is it important?"

"Probably not," Travis murmured. *No proof,* he reminded himself. *No proof.* "Just curious."

CHAPTER TEN

THE TEAM WAS ASSEMBLED precisely at oh-eight-hundred the next morning. Forty minutes later, they were in their EVA suits and had done all the proper equipment checks, and the power systems to the section of hull where they would be working had been tagged off. Fifteen minutes after that, having double-checked everything himself, Craddock declared them ready to move out.

Only to discover that the new vane wasn't ready for deployment. Apparently, there was some snag in the sampler module and the electronics techs were still working on it.

Craddock's immediate and profanity-sprinkled argument was that *his* people were the gravitics techs, and that if anyone should be working on the vane it was them. But the complaint fell on deliberately deaf ears. The electronics techs were as bored with the daily routine as everyone else aboard *Vanguard*, and working on a gravitics vane was a big step up from swapping out hexes and quads and rebuilding balky interface circuits. Besides which, their CPO pointed out, the vane had been delivered to *them*, and until they released it to Gravitics it was theirs to play with.

The bosun ruled in favor of Electronics. Neither division's lieutenant was interested in getting involved, which was pretty much how Travis had guessed that approach would end up. Captain Davison liked things to run smoothly aboard his ship, and a report on two divisions arguing over who got to do a particular job didn't fit with his definition of *smooth*.

In the end, Travis and the others unsuited, the power circuits were untagged, and they went back to swapping out hexes and quads and trying to coax life back into dead circuit modules.

The performance was repeated the following morning, and the morning after that: Electronics first declaring the vane to be ready, then rescinding their pronouncement as they discovered some new glitch. Finally, on the fourth morning, they ran out of excuses and reluctantly declared the vane fit for duty.

The vane, all eleven by seven meters of it, had come across from the *Mars* refit area locked onto a cargo shuttle and then been tractored to the hull near the array. It took the gravitics team an hour to decouple the tractor units and confirm the vane's physical integrity. After that came a series of tests until Craddock was satisfied that Electronics was right about its fitness. Then, with their thruster packs augmented by larger payload versions, they drifted the vane toward the waiting array.

Travis hadn't done much EVA work in his time aboard *Vanguard*, mainly because there was little that Gravitics normally had to do out on the hull and casual joywalks were strongly discouraged. But the handful of times he'd been outside had been some of his best memories of shipboard life. There was a sense of openness and freedom—and yes, of comfortable solitude—that was hard to come by inside.

The downside, of course, was that *Vanguard* felt that much more cramped, noisy, and odoriferous when he came back in. But on balance, it was still worth it.

"Watch your end, Yarrow," Craddock's voice came from the speaker behind Travis's right ear. "Atherton, clear your safety line—it's trying to dance with your foot. Easy . . . okay, you've got it. Okay, we'll hold it here. Long, Esterle—go start pulling out the old one."

"Right," Travis said. Privately, he thought it would have been more efficient to come out and remove the ailing vane before hauling the new one all the way out here. But this was established RMN procedure, and there was presumably a good reason for it. Setting his boot against one of the safety-line anchor rings—regulations frowned on using thrusters more than necessary—he gave himself a gentle push and floated after Esterle toward the three vanes of the forward-ventral gravitic array jutting out from the hull. Number Two-Three was on the end closest to them, which fortunately meant the job wouldn't require them to squeeze between two of the vanes. Travis had checked the schematics when they'd first been told about this job, and those gaps had looked pretty cozy. Out here, close up and in person, they looked even cozier.

"You take that end," Esterle said, pointing Travis toward the near end of the vane as she gave herself a nudge toward the far end. "Race you to the middle."

"You're on," Travis said, rolling his eyes. Esterle could get competitive over the most ridiculous things.

So could everyone else. "I got ten bucks on Esterle," Atherton called.

"You're covered," Yarrow said. "Come on, Long, *hustle*."

Travis grimaced. The regs frowned on rushing EVA jobs even more than they did on overuse of thrusters.

But Craddock wasn't saying anything. In fact, there was every chance that he'd already silently signaled his own entry into the wager.

Regardless, Yarrow had ten dollars on him. For her sake alone he had to give it a try. Feeling slightly disgusted, both at the wager and at his own willingness to go along with the game, he caught one toe on another anchor ring and gave himself a fresh push. Esterle had farther to go to her end of the vane, but with her head start she had already arrived at the array. Drawing a wrench from her hip kit, she reached out a hand to catch the vane's edge to bring herself to a halt.

Travis was looking down, searching for another anchor ring, when the universe lit up like a strobe light in front of him.

He jerked his eyes back up, his helmet speaker erupting with a babble of exclamations, startled curses and a single short, gasping scream. Esterle was hurling away from *Vanguard*, her suit sheathed in a fading coronal haze. Over the babble Craddock's voice cut through like a plasma torch—"Emergency—Dutchman!" he bellowed. "Forward starboard, tracking thirty degrees bow-ventral. I say again: Dutchman, thirty degrees bow-ventral."

Travis blinked away the last of the afterimage, his teeth snapping together as someone behind him hauled him up short by his safety line before he could make the same deadly contact with the inexplicably powered array. Only then did he belatedly realize that Esterle's own safety line was gone, apparently vaporized by the same jolt that had sent her flying. Already she was barely visible as she flew into the darkness, her body spinning slowly, her suit's lights extinguished.

And without pausing to think it through, possibly the first

time in his life he'd ever done something like that, Travis pulled himself down into a crouch, snapped off his own safety line, and shoved himself off the hull after her.

"Long!" Craddock barked. "What the *hell* are you doing?"

Travis didn't bother to answer. His full attention was on the body falling toward the distant starscape, tweaking his intercept vector with short bursts from his thruster as he sped toward her. A new set of voices had entered the uproar coming from his helmet speaker as a rescue team acknowledged the accident and prepped a shuttle for launch.

The one voice Travis *didn't* hear was Esterle's. He could only hope the ominous silence was simply a matter of the electrical discharge having fried her com along with her safety line.

It seemed to take forever, but it was probably no more than three minutes before he floated up behind her. Steeling himself, he reached out and closed his hand around her arm.

And instantly lost his grip as she gave a violent convulsion. "It's okay—it's okay," he shouted, even knowing that she probably couldn't hear him. Her spin had now taken her arm out of his reach; grabbing a leg instead, he pulled himself around her and climbed up her suit until he was facing her.

Facing, but not seeing anything. Her back was to *Vanguard*'s distant lights, and the star glow wasn't nearly strong enough to penetrate her helmet's tinting. "It's okay, Esterle," he called again, remembering this time to press his faceplate against hers before he spoke. The book said physical contact would allow enough sound transference for two spacers to communicate if their coms were out. "It's me, Long. You hear me? Esterle?"

"Oh, God," a faint voice came back, tense and torn and ragged. Bracing himself for the worst, Travis fumbled with his sleeve controls and flicked on his helmet light.

And caught his breath. Her face, like her voice, was almost unrecognizable. She was staring past him at the stars, her eyes wide, her cheeks pinched, her throat working. Like she was staring hell straight in the face...

He cursed under his breath. The book also warned about spacer agoraphobia, but he'd never realized Esterle had it. Maybe she hadn't realized it, either. "Hey!" he snapped, shaking her shoulders. "Esterle! Look at me. Damn it, Esterle, *look at me!*"

She started, her eyes lowering from the distant stars to his face as if only just noticing he was there. Her arms, which had been hanging out limply from her body, abruptly came to life, her hands gripping his arms hard enough for him to feel through the material and air pressure. "Long?" she gasped. "Oh, God—"

"It's all right," he said as soothingly as he could. "Just keep your eyes on me. You got that? They're sending a boat; but until it gets here, keep your eyes on me. You got that, Spacer?"

A hint of life seemed to come back into the panicked eyes. "Got it," she said, her voice edging back toward normal. "What happened? There was a flash—oh, God. What did I *do*?"

"You didn't do anything," Travis assured her grimly. She was still gripping his arms, but he managed to get a hand to the diagnostic epaulet on his left shoulder and pull out the line and jack. "The array was *supposed* to be tagged out," he continued, working the jack around and into the readout socket on Esterle's own epaulet. "I guess someone missed the order. Are you all right?"

"I think so," Esterle said, her gaze unfocusing a bit as she apparently ran a mental inventory. "But it's getting hot in here. I think my life support must be fried."

"Oh, it's fried, all right," Travis confirmed grimly, running his eye down the analysis scrolling along the display at the right side of his helmet. "So are your com, your thruster controls, all your readouts—you probably already knew that one—and your locator. Oh, and the surge got your safety line, too."

"I didn't know they were conductive."

"I guess if you throw out enough voltage, *anything* can be conductive."

"I guess so." Abruptly, her grip on his arms tightened. "Wait a minute. Are *you* all right? I didn't even ask—"

"No, no, I'm fine," Travis assured her. "I just figured that if you weren't going to stick around and work, why should I?"

"Yeah, I'll bet that's what you thought," she said, a shiver running through her. "I just—"

"Eyes on me," Travis said tartly. "Come on, Esterle—we're the only two people in the universe."

"Right." She smiled uncertainly. "Are you asking me out or something?"

Travis's mouth went suddenly dry. "We *are* out," he managed, fighting to keep his tone light. "But okay—let's say we were looking to have dinner together. Where do you like to go?"

"I don't know," Esterle said. "No, wait, yes I do. There's this little Italian place in southeast Landing I like."

"Okay, that's probably too far to walk," Travis said. In the distance behind her, he saw a small set of lights detach themselves from *Vanguard* and head their way. "But I'm sure we can borrow a car. So what's your favorite dish there?"

"Well, I usually order either the parmigiana or else the spaghetti and Italian sausage..."

They were discussing appetizers, and the relative merits of fried zucchini versus stuffed mushrooms, when the rescue boat arrived.

☆   ☆   ☆

Travis's testimony in front of Commander Bertinelli's board of inquiry lasted an hour. Which was, a distant part of his mind noted, roughly three times longer than the actual incident.

"Thank you, Spacer Long," Bertinelli said gravely when the last question had been asked and answered. "We'll call you back if we need anything more. Dismissed."

"Yes, Sir." Travis hesitated. "A question, Sir, if I may?"

Bertinelli's forehead creased, but he gave a small flick his fingertips. "Go ahead."

"Will your report be available to those of us aboard *Vanguard*, Sir?" Travis asked. "Or will it just be going to System Command and the Defense Minister?"

"Why do you ask?" Bertinelli asked evenly.

"I'd like to know what happened, Sir," Travis said. "Whatever mistakes were made need to be—"

"You want someone punished, Spacer Long? Is that it?"

"No, Sir, I'm not looking for punishment," Travis said hastily. "I just want any problems with procedure to be corrected so something like this doesn't happen again."

"The procedures are fine," Bertinelli said stiffly. "There were a few small lapses in communication, that's all. Someone thought the tagged power circuit was an inadvertent holdover from the previous day, while the test that had been scheduled for three days after the vane *should* have been installed never had its date and time reset. The proper procedures, properly followed, would have covered both problems."

"Yes, Sir, I understand," Travis said, thoroughly confused now. "But if the procedures were adequate, then the people involved must not have followed them correctly."

"And back we go to punishment," Bertinelli growled. "You think anyone who makes a mistake, no matter how small or innocent, should be demoted or spend a night in the brig? *Do you, Spacer Long?*"

"I—" Travis broke off, trying desperately to figure out what he was supposed to say. Questions like that one weren't in the book.

"Or shall we look a bit farther from carelessness to *deliberate* violations of regulations?" Bertinelli went on darkly. "Or were you unaware of proper procedure during a Dutchman?"

Travis felt his throat tighten. *That* one, unfortunately, *was* in the book. "No, Sir. I mean, yes, Sir, I was aware of them."

"And yet you chose to charge off after Spacer Esterle," Bertinelli said. "Never mind you could have been just as quickly and easily lost as she was."

Travis winced. Except that his suit's beacon was working, and Esterle's wasn't. He'd made that point in his testimony, in fact.

Still, he could see Bertinelli's point, and the reason for that particular rule. If he'd missed Esterle, the rescue boat would have had two drifters to retrieve instead of one. "I thought it would make the rescue easier, Sir."

"Your job in that situation isn't to *think*, Spacer Long," Bertinelli ground out. "Your job is to follow procedure. If and when modifications are called for, someone with more experience and authority than you will inform you of that fact. Is that clear?"

"Yes, Sir," Travis said between clenched teeth.

"Good." Bertinelli eyed him a moment longer, then lowered his eyes to his tablet. "Fortunately for everyone, in this case the damage and injuries were minor. A set of reprimands for the parties involved, I think, followed by some refresher work and extra drill should take care of the problem."

Or in other words, *Vanguard*'s senior officers were going to downplay the whole mess and try to sweep it under the rug. Never mind that someone could have died, or that the whole gravitics array could have been fried by grounding it to the hull through Esterle's suit—

"Unless you have other questions," Bertinelli continued, in a tone that suggested Travis had better not, "we're done here. Dismissed."

"Yes, Sir." Executing an about-face, Travis strode out of the XO's office.

Atherton was waiting for him in the passageway. "How'd it go?" he asked, falling into step as Travis headed for the lift.

"About like you'd expect," Travis growled. "They're going to pretend the whole thing never happened and tape it over by assigning some procedural refresher work to the systems people who screwed up."

"They'd better add some repair work to the mix, then," Atherton said. "You know that all-ship notice that's supposed to go out every fifteen minutes when there are spacers on the hull? Turns out the guy who was testing the array didn't hear it because the intercom speaker in that compartment wasn't working."

Travis snorted. "Great."

"Isn't it?" Atherton said. "Speaking of people and things not working, Esterle's about to head out, and she wanted to see you before she left."

Travis's heartbeat picked up. "She said that?"

"Yeah, and if you want to catch her you'd better hustle," Atherton said. "Shuttle's leaving in ten."

He found Esterle waiting at the shuttle hatchway, one finger hooked around a handhold to keep from drifting with the air currents. Her forehead, wrinkled with thought or concern, smoothed out as Travis came around the corner. "There you are," she said as he floated to a landing at the handhold beside her. "I didn't think you were going to get out of Bertinelli's inquisition in time."

"There was a lot to talk about," Travis said, looking her up and down. It was the first time he'd seen her since they were taken off the rescue boat and hustled to different sections of sickbay. There were no bandages he could see, or any bulges in her fatigues that might be splints or immobilization casts. "How are you feeling?"

"Pretty good, actually," she said. "I figured I'd at least come out of it with a few electrical burns, but I didn't even get scorched. Turns out those suits are really good at siphoning current along the outside layers."

"Frying a few sets of electronics along the way."

"Well, there *is* that," Esterle conceded. "I hope they're not going to take the repair work out of my pay."

"If anyone's on the hook for that, it won't be you," Travis assured her. Her voice sounded fine, too, with none of the slurring or changes in tone that might indicate brain or neural damage.

Maybe Bertinelli hadn't been as far off the mark as Travis had thought when he described the incident as minor. "So I heard you're going on a couple months' leave?"

She lowered her eyes. "Not leave," she corrected quietly. "I'm being transferred groundside. Yeoman or tech work, probably, at either Casey-Rosewood or the Academy. They—" she swallowed "—don't think I should be in space anymore."

"Oh," Travis said, feeling suddenly off-balance. With his full focus on Esterle's physical well-being, he hadn't even considered the possibility that she might have sustained psychological trauma from the incident. "Did they think that, or did—? No, never mind."

"Or did *I* think it?" She smiled faintly. "Go ahead, you can say it."

"I didn't mean anything," Travis hastened to assure her.

"I know," she said. "It's okay. I didn't really know it myself. Not until—" She stopped, a shiver running through her.

"I'm sorry," Travis said. "I'm—we're going to miss you."

"I'll miss you, too." Esterle glanced around. "*Vanguard*, not so much. Maybe someday Parliament will give the Navy the money it needs to make these ships something to be proud of again. Until then—" She brought her eyes back to him. "Anyway, I wanted to thank you before I left. For, you know. Everything."

"You're welcome," Travis said, wondering if he dared reach over and hug her. Out in the open like this, with the shuttle prep crew floating around... "I just wish I could have done more."

"You did what I needed," she assured him. "You're a good friend, Travis."

She hesitated, and for a second Travis thought she was going to offer him a hug. But all she did was reach out and briefly squeeze his arm. "Take it easy, Long. I'll see you around."

And with that, she grabbed hold of the handhold and pulled herself through the hatchway into the shuttle.

Three minutes later, she and the shuttle were gone.

All the way back to the gravitics duty station Travis found himself replaying that last scene through his head. *Friend*. *Take it easy*.

No hug.

Basically, the story of his life.

With the whole thing still buzzing around his brain, he was a meter into the duty station before he realized that the entire division was present, crammed into the compartment literally from deck to ceiling.

His first, self-conscious thought was that they'd assembled to honor him for his part in Esterle's rescue. A second later, to his relief, he realized that they weren't facing him, but were instead gathered around Craddock, who seemed to be running through a long list of assignments. Craddock glanced over as Travis came into view—"And Long will be helping Bowen," he said. "Okay, you've got your jobs. Get busy."

Like a 3-D version of a parade-ground maneuver, the entire crowd turned in unison and surged for the hatchway. With a quick foot-grab on one of the deck handholds, Travis managed to get himself out of the way before the flow ran over him. "What's going on?" he asked as Bowen started past.

"We're getting *Vanguard* ready to fly," she said, grabbing his arm to bring herself to a halt. The extra momentum threatened to drag both of them off the deck, but Travis managed to maintain his foot grip. "Can you believe it? We're actually being *deployed*."

"Where?" Travis asked, struggling to wrap his brain around this sudden new development. *Vanguard* had been sitting in Manticore orbit so long that it was a standing joke to refer to her as *Rearguard*.

"Manticore-B," Bowen said. There was an excitement in her voice that Travis had never heard there before. "Unicorn Belt. We've been transferred to Gryphon Fleet."

"What, all two ships of it?"

"Don't be snide," Bowen admonished. "At least it's *something*. Better than just something, really—we're probably going to end up as the new flagship."

With some admiral or commodore coming aboard, no doubt. Briefly, Travis wondered how Captain Davison was going to react to having someone new watching over his shoulder.

"We'll be starting with a month of work-up exercises and maybe some gunnery practice," Bowen continued. "Oh, and get this— we're going to get to do a real hyperspace jump along the way."

Travis felt his eyes go wide. *Vanguard* was actually going into hyper? "That's great."

"Don't get *too* enthusiastic," Bowen warned. "It's only a little jump, you know, just from Manticore-A to Manticore-B. It's not like we're going to Haven or something. There's also this thing called the wall-crossing ceremony for hyperspace first-timers that you're not going to find very pleasant."

A knot started to form in Travis's stomach. He'd heard about the crossing-the-wall thing, but no one had ever gone into any detail. "What kind of unpleasant *is* it?"

"Let's just say it's not painful, but you'd better plan to leave your dignity at the lock," Bowen said. "But forget that. Everyone who's ever done hyper has been through it, we all survived, and you will, too. The point is that we get to fly, we get to see something besides Manticore—" she waved her free hand around her "—and we get to use our gravitics for something besides test runs."

"Sounds good," Travis said.

And to his mild surprise, it actually did. Any change in routine was something to look forward to; but to actually take *Vanguard* out into the sky was something he'd almost stopped hoping for and had certainly stopped expecting. "How soon do we leave? We're on ready-ninety status, right?"

"Yeah, right," Bowen said scornfully. The rest of the crowd had finished their mass exit, and she gave a quick shove off his arm to send her floating across the compartment toward the tool rack. "Even the Admiralty knows there's no chance we can prep that fast. No, they've given the captain seventy-two hours." She snagged a tool belt and tossed it over her shoulder toward him. "And if we don't have the Number One Sample Counter taken apart, cleaned, and rebuilt within the first five of those hours Craddock will have our hides. Let's get to it."

☆　☆　☆

It was much later, in the stillness of that last minute before falling asleep, that Travis wondered if the deployment could have been deliberately engineered in hopes of distracting *Vanguard*'s crew from the gravitics array fiasco.

But he chased the thought away. Surely First Lord Cazenestro and System Command wouldn't go to such a ridiculous extreme as that.

Surely they wouldn't.

CHAPTER ELEVEN

RAFE HANFORD HAD BEEN an asteroid miner for over half his life. He'd started as a crewman on one of the big mining ships, and had eventually reached the point where he was able to talk a group of investors into letting him captain a small ship of his own.

On balance, he'd done a good job of repaying their trust as well as their bank accounts. Over the years he'd become something of a specialist in working off the beaten path, poking around the emptier sectors of Manticore-B's Unicorn Belt in search of ore concentrations too small for the big boys to bother with but large enough for a small-ship operation like his to turn into a modest profit.

Overall, he liked both the work and his jauntily maverick approach to it. It was quiet out here in the sparselies, his sensors and his instincts were good enough to find enough ore to keep himself and his small crew in business, and he didn't have to answer to anyone except his investors.

There were times, though, when all that solitude had its drawbacks.

Times like now.

"Well, it's not the impeller ring," Katerina Shankweiler said, frowning at the engineering status board. "That's the good news. The bad news is that the burble's probably coming from the fusion plant. Probably some glitch in the containment bottle."

Hanford gazed at the board, tugging absently at his lower lip. Of all things that could go wrong on a ship, the fusion plant was the worst. Everything else could be fixed or cobbled together or run at half-limp speed if necessary. And indeed most everything else aboard *had* gone through one or more of those kluges over the years.

But the fusion plant was different. If that went, everything except emergency power and the survival suits went with it. "Can we make it back to civilization?" he asked.

"Depends on what you mean by civilization," Shankweiler said. "If you mean Unicorn One, not a chance. If you mean one of Tilliotson's mining factory groups, maybe. We'd probably do better to blast out a mayday and see if there's another independent nearby."

Hanford scowled. Like everything else plying the spacelanes, belter ships were required to supplement their com lasers with omnidirectional radios for precisely this kind of situation, and it was one piece of ship's equipment that he made sure was always in good working order.

But a mayday broadcast wasn't something you did on a whim. The administrators on Unicorn One and their Star Kingdom overseers down on Gryphon took a dim view of stirring up the rest of the belters unless such stirring was genuinely and urgently called for. "What about that new patrol ship?" he asked. "That—what the hell is it, anyway, a sloop or something? It's supposed to be stooging around these three sectors, right?"

"Yes—HMS *Phobos*," Shankweiler confirmed, kicking herself off the monitor console and floating over to the navigation board. "Let's see if we can pick up her beacon."

She puttered at the board a moment. Hanford studied the position plot, trying to come up with a workable Plan A, a contingency Plan B, and a last-ditch Plan C. Hopefully, this time he wouldn't also need a Plan D. There'd been occasions when he had.

"There she is," Shankweiler said. "Pretty far...and of course, she's also moving away from us. Damn." She looked over her shoulder at Hanford. "So what's Plan A?"

"We head for Unicorn One," Hanford told her. "Low acceleration, just kind of ease our way along."

"I already told you we'll never make the station."

"Maybe not, but that'll at least get us closer to the main travel lanes," he said. "More chance that way of getting in range of someone who can reach us if we need help. We'll keep an eye on the burble, and if it amps another twenty percent we'll shut it down and go on emergency power."

"I don't think the batteries will last nearly as long as you think they will," Shankweiler warned.

"As long as they last long enough for you to fix the bottle, that's all we need," Hanford said. "It *will* be easier with the system shut down, right?"

"You mean nearly impossible instead of totally impossible?" she suggested dryly. "I guess when you put it *that* way—"

"You can do it," Hanford assured her, floating over to the helm and strapping himself in. "Let's get this floating parts store turned around, and I'll get us on an arc for Unicorn One."

"You want me to tell the others?" Shankweiler asked.

For a moment, Hanford was tempted. He'd never liked delivering bad news, and the possibility that the twenty-five of them might be facing a horrific death was about as bad as news ever got. And Shankweiler had the kind of smile that always made things look and sound better.

But no. *Rafe's Scavenger* was *his* ship, not hers. If there was doom to be proclaimed, it was his job to proclaim it. "I'll tell them," he said. "You get your tail back over to the plant and see if you can figure out what the problem is."

"Will do," Shankweiler said. "Good luck."

"That's *my* line," Hanford corrected. "*You're* the one who'll be working on the fusion plant."

"Yeah, but *you're* the one who'll be telling Gratz he may soon be down to bottled air and cold hash."

Hanford grimaced. She had a point. "There's that," he conceded. "You just fix the damn plant. For both our sakes."

☆   ☆   ☆

As with many other life experiences, Travis reflected, getting HMS *Vanguard* out of orbit and into *real* space sounded much more exciting than it actually was.

The preliminaries were certainly frantic enough. Along with getting the replacement gravitic vane into place—which, thankfully, went off without a hitch this time—there were three shuttleloads of new equipment that had to be installed elsewhere on the ship, plus *four* shuttleloads of fresh food that needed to be brought aboard and stowed now that such supplies would no longer be a quick jaunt away. Captain Davison's seventy-two hours were a mad scramble from one end of the ship to the other, with the official duty roster more fiction than reality. On two separate occasions

Travis dragged himself into the mess for a break long after he was supposed to go off duty, only to find a sizeable percentage of other bleary-eyed spacers already there, sipping coffee in an attempt to revive flagging brain cells.

The actual departure from orbit, once it actually happened, was a definite anticlimax. The announcement came over the all-ship speaker system, and *Vanguard* was on her way.

It probably looked better on the bridge, Travis thought as he floated behind Senior Chief Gravitics Specialist Inzinga in the Combat Information Center. The bridge had their big visual displays, after all, whereas CIC's more modest monitors mainly showed false-color images or the more subtle constructs from the radar and lidar sensors.

It was the gravitic readout that most interested him, though, and he gazed in fascination at the flickering lines and curves on Inzinga's monitors, curves that formed the gravitational profile of the Manticore-A system. Back at Casey-Rosewood, after he'd been summarily switched to gravitics training, he'd tried to get into the Specialist track. But he'd been a late arrival, and the Navy had needed more techs than system operators, so that was where he'd been put.

But there were ways to get them to change their minds about such things. Ever since coming aboard *Vanguard* Travis had made a point of spending at least two hours a day studying the manuals and prep work for the Gravitics Specialist rating. Another three to six months, he estimated, and he'd be ready to request a proficiency test. If he passed, and if the RMN could find a slot for him, he might be able to graduate from digging into the guts of the gravitics system to facing this set of monitors and keeping the bridge informed of large masses or moving ships.

Not only was it a quieter, more peaceful job, but system operators never had to explain to a CPO why something hadn't gotten fixed because they'd run out of spare parts. That aspect alone would make the upgrade worthwhile.

Still, the bridge was where all the most interesting jobs were. That was where the monitors were, and where the captain, XO, tactics officer, and astrogator all hung out. Travis had visited the bridge exactly once, right when he'd come aboard, but the memory still lingered. *That* was where he wanted to be someday.

But the bridge was a long way up the ladder, especially for

a noncom, and that ladder was a hard climb. It required hard work, competence, and dedication.

Or there was that other ladder, the one no one officially talked about. The one that simply required having friends and patrons in high places.

It absolutely didn't involve having enemies in those same positions.

He felt his stomach knot up. Even now, three years later, he still found himself wondering if he should have handled that cheating accusation differently. The whole idea had been absurd, but he'd been so stunned by the charge that he'd found it impossible to do anything except stammer protestations. The deal Lieutenant Cyrus had offered, to quietly transfer from impellers to gravitics, had sounded a whole lot better than standing before a review board, and in his mind-numbed state he'd grabbed it.

Would standing for review have been better? Cyrus had warned that if the board convicted him he would be out on his ear, whereas a small note listing the suspicion of cheating would probably never be noticed by anyone, especially since the suspicion was unproved. So far, that seemed to be the case. Certainly neither Craddock nor the bosun had even hinted that they were aware of it.

But the men and women who selected personnel for bridge and CIC assignments were likely to be more thorough in their reading. Would they see it as a minor glitch, or would it doom his chances of advancement?

He didn't know. In fact, given the back-room nature of all such discussions, he would probably never know.

"Having fun?" Craddock's voice came from the side.

Travis jerked, his reflexive twitch bouncing his knee off the back of Inzinga's seat and starting him drifting away. "Yes, Chief, I am," he said, grabbing the seat's upper handhold and bringing himself to a stop. "I've been studying the operator's manual—"

"Yes, I know," Craddock said, glancing around as he floated into the compartment. "I presume you know this is a restricted area?"

"It's all right, Chief," Inzinga said. "I said he could watch."

"Yeah," Craddock said. "And *I* said he was supposed to hit his rack. Or did you somehow miss that order?"

"I'm sorry, Chief—I didn't realize it was an order," Travis apologized. "But I wasn't all that tired, and I wanted to see what the gravitics looked like with *Vanguard* in flight."

"That's nice," Craddock growled. "And now that you know it *was* an order?"

Travis felt his cheeks warm. "Yes, Chief," he said. "Permission to go back to the machine shop first and get my multitool?"

"Fine," Craddock said. "But I don't want to catch you turning a single bolt with it. The rest of the work can wait until next shift. Now get moving." He peered at Inzinga's displays for a moment, as if wondering what Travis found so fascinating, then shoved himself off the other's chair and disappeared through the hatchway.

"You heard the chief," Inzinga said. "Get some sleep. Something's bound to fall apart and need fixing tomorrow."

"Yes, Senior Chief." Travis gave the gravitics displays a final look of his own and pushed off toward the hatchway.

Someday, he promised himself. *Someday.*

The machine shop was, as expected, deserted. Travis collected his multitool from the tack strip where he'd left it and made his way back across the compartment.

He was nearly to the hatchway when a young female lieutenant suddenly loomed in the opening in front of him. "Finally," she said. "You a gravitics tech?"

"Yes, Ma'am," Travis said, flailing a bit. "Spacer First Class Travis Long."

"About time one of you showed," she growled. "I was starting to think you guys were running bureaucrat hours. Grab a tool kit and come with me."

Travis felt his mouth go suddenly dry. "Ah..."

"Is there a problem, Spacer Long?"

"Ah...I'm off—I've been ordered to report to my quarters, Ma'am," Travis changed course just in time. Somehow, he sensed that the words *off duty* wouldn't be smart to say right now.

Apparently, the word *quarters* wasn't much of an improvement. The lieutenant's expression didn't change, but suddenly Travis could almost see frost forming in the air between them. "Ordered by your chief?" she asked, her tone deceptively calm.

"Yes, Ma'am," Travis said. "Chief Gravitics Tech—"

"You see these?" the woman asked, inclining her head toward her insignia. "These say my orders supersede his orders. Now *get your tool kit.*"

"Yes, Ma'am," Travis said, kicking off toward the rack of kits.

Belatedly, now, he remembered where he'd seen her before. She'd come in twice during the past fifty hours, telling Craddock to get someone on some problem Travis hadn't quite overheard the details of. Both times Craddock had promised to get someone over to wherever she needed help and then sent her on her way. Both times, judging from her current glowering expression, he hadn't bothered to follow up on his promise.

Apparently, she'd gotten tired of taking *yes* for an answer.

Neither of them said a word as she led the way through the maze of passageways to one of *Vanguard*'s thousand-plus junction boxes. Waiting there was a young woman in a tech jumpsuit, looking equal parts tired and annoyed. "Here we go," the lieutenant said brightly as she caught a handhold and braked to a halt. "You two know each other? Never mind. Spacer Second Class Suzanne Marx from Communications, this is Spacer Long from Gravitics. I'm Lieutenant Donnelly. Lieutenant Lisa Donnelly, in case one of you is planning to write me up later."

She pointed to the junction box. "You see this box? This box is interfering with the telemetry subsystem for one of my aft missile guidance systems. Half of the cables coming in are owned by Gravitics; the other half and the box itself are Communications property. I can't seem to get either of your chiefs to take responsibility for the area, and I'm tired of asking." She leveled a forefinger each at Marx and Travis. "You two are techs. They're your systems. Fix the damn thing." She folded her arms across her chest. "Now."

Travis looked at Marx. It was clear she was thinking along the same lines he was: not only was this not how things in the RMN were supposed to be done, but Donnelly was probably skating at the edge of an actionable offense by cutting through protocol this way.

It was also abundantly clear that Marx was just as reluctant as Travis was to point any of that out.

He took a careful breath. "You have a key?" he asked.

Marx's lip twitched, but she nodded. "Yeah," she said reluctantly, pulling it out of her tool pouch. "How about you start on the cable traces while I check the connections?"

The job ended up being trickier than Travis had expected. The trouble was a malfunction in one of the multiplexer nodes, triggered when the relatively long-duration network diagnostic packets interfered with the shorter-duration data pulses from Gravitics and Communications. The result was an intermittent corruption of Donnelly's missile telemetry data stream, occasionally causing the stream to vanish completely.

It only took Travis and Marx five minutes to fix, but nearly an hour to figure out. Maybe one reason, Travis reflected as they replaced the faulty node, that Craddock had blown off the job in the first place.

"Excellent," Donnelly said as Travis and Marx closed and sealed the junction box. "And now I believe you were both off-duty. Dismissed, and go get some rest. You've earned it." With a curt nod to each of them, she swung herself with practiced ease down the passageway.

"What did she mean before about writing her up?" Marx asked. "I didn't think we *could* write up officers."

"We can complain to the bosun about mistreatment," Travis told her. "It's not technically a write-up, but that's probably what she meant."

"Oh." Marx cocked her head. "Are you going to?"

Travis looked at the box. Technically, he knew, Donnelly had overstepped her bounds by grabbing him and Marx directly instead of putting the request through their respective chiefs.

On the other hand, Travis had seen plenty of cases where turf wars, personality conflicts, and simple inertia had snafued up the system. And it wasn't like the job hadn't been necessary, or that Donnelly had dragged them out of their racks. "I don't know," he told Marx. "You?"

Marx sniffed and shook her head. "Too much datawork. And afterwards you've made yourself a new enemy. As long as our chiefs don't get wind of it, I say we let it drop."

"I suppose," Travis said reluctantly. Donnelly's actions seriously offended his sense of how things should be done, but Marx's argument made sense. And questionable methods or not, Donnelly *had* gotten an important job done. "So. I guess I'll see you around?"

"It's a small ship," Marx said. "We'll have to do this again sometime."

Ten minutes later, as he fell asleep in his rack, Travis found himself rather hoping that they did.

☆   ☆   ☆

"It showed up midway through the watch," Creutz said as Ouvrard studied the readout. "Dinks says it's a mistuning in the ring, with an associated misalignment. She's not really sure whether the mistuning is driving the misalignment or vice versa, but she's pretty sure it doesn't much matter. Either way, it's trouble."

"No argument there," Ouvrard said, scrolling the readout back to the top and checking the summary graph. As if *Phobos* didn't have enough troubles. "So is the ring at risk?"

"The ring itself, no," Creutz said. "But it's definitely putting strain on the hull."

Ouvrard scowled to herself. So much for the geniuses who'd claimed that a ship this size could run on a single impeller ring without unpleasant consequences. "How much strain? Are we in danger of losing some hull plates?"

"Dinks hasn't the foggiest," Creutz said. "She's trying to run some simulations, but the data's pretty limited and there's nothing in the archives that really applies. Still, so far things are pretty tame."

And there should be plenty of warning if something *did* start to go belly-up. Ouvrard assumed.

"Nothing we can do about it out here, I suppose."

"Not really," Creutz said. "It's part and parcel with the whole screwed-up design of the damn ship. Fixing it would take a trip back to Manticore and probably another month in dock."

"And we'd probably end up with *Phobos* being taken away from us," Ouvrard murmured.

"Probably."

For a moment neither of them spoke. Then, Creutz stirred. "Speaking for myself, Ma'am, I say damn the torpedoes and full speed ahead."

"You mean continue with our mission?"

"Ah...yes, Ma'am. That was a historical reference—"

"Yes, I know," Ouvrard said, feeling a mischievous smile playing around her lips despite the seriousness of the situation. "Really, Armand, you need to develop a sense of either irony or the absurd."

"I'll keep that in mind, Ma'am," Creutz said with a lopsided smile of his own. "Though if MPARS wanted me to have a sense of irony they should have issued it to us."

"Better," Ouvrard said approvingly. "Well, keep Dinks on it. And have her start looking for a fix."

"I thought we agreed there wasn't anything she could do," Creutz said, frowning.

"That's what the book says," Ouvrard confirmed. "But Lieutenant Stroud comes from a long and distinguished school of book-be-damned tinkerers. If there's a rabbit anywhere in that hat, I'm betting she can pull it out."

Creutz frowned a little harder. "A rabbit in a *hat*?"

"Historical reference," Ouvrard told him, unstrapping from the engineering station. "I'm heading to the impeller room. If any of the nodes blow up, do let me know."

"Yes, Ma'am," Creutz promised. "I'll be sure to hand-wave it to you as you fly past."

"Nice," Ouvrard said approvingly. "You've definitely got potential."

"Thank you, Ma'am," Creutz said. "Perhaps someday I'll master the skill well enough to run for Parliament."

"Please," Ouvrard protested. "I just ate."

☆   ☆   ☆

Hanford had hoped *Rafe's Scavenger*'s fusion plant would stumble along for at least a few more hours before they had to shut it down.

It didn't last nearly that long.

And they never had a chance to shut it down.

The failure was about as spectacular as it was possible to have and still live through it. One minute everything was humming along more or less smoothly; the next, it was like someone had drop-kicked them in the direction of the Andromeda Galaxy. The ship was still shuddering when the scream of the depressurization alarm erupted, rattling the bulkheads and hatches. Wincing with the sound and the throbbing pain where he'd been thrown against the passageway bulkhead, Hanford fumbled for a handhold and changed direction toward the bridge.

The siren had gone silent, but the red warning lights were still flashing when he arrived. Shankweiler was already there, strapped into the copilot station, her hands dancing frantically across the controls. The pilot's station was empty; glancing around, Hanford spotted Gratz, who was supposed to be on duty, floating limply against the wall. "What've we got?" Hanford demanded as he slid into the pilot's station and strapped himself in.

Or rather, tried to do so. Only one of the three straps was still intact, the others torn loose from their anchors. Apparently, Gratz was away from his post because he'd been thrown there by the ship's violent motion.

"What do you *think*?" Shankweiler snarled back. "The reactor went critical and the automatics ejected it." She jabbed a finger at the mass of red on the monitors. "Only they didn't eject it fast enough. It was way closer to the hull than it was supposed to be when it blew."

Hanford swore feelingly. "Damage?"

"Well, there's good news and bad news," Shankweiler said tightly. "Bad news: the reactor room and six adjacent compartments are completely gone. The backblast through the open section fried a few more compartments—still trying to sort out how much to which ones, but life support is definitely one of them. The spare O2 cylinders are probably gone, too. Pretty much everything on the starboard side of the hull is toast, including the shuttle. Still trying to figure out who's still with us, but it looks like at least half the crew may not have made it."

"God Almighty," Hanford breathed. "What the hell is the *good* news?"

Shankweiler hissed out a breath. "Half of us *might* still be alive. We've got the air in here, and probably a little more in some of the other intact parts of the ship. And we've got our survival suits."

"And that's it?"

"That's it."

Hanford felt his hands curl into fists. A dead ship in the middle of nowhere, and only their survival suits standing between them and death. "I guess," he said, striving to keep his voice calm, "it's time to send out that mayday."

"Already done."

CHAPTER TWELVE

THERE HAD BEEN A TIME in Manticore's history, Lieutenant Commander Allegra Metzger knew, when a battlecruiser's tactical officer was not only highly regarded, but considered essential to the performance of her ship. Even more importantly, at least to some in the Navy, the TO slot had been *the* stepping-stone to the coveted rank of captain and the prestige of command.

But those days were long gone. True, on paper the TO had a considerable range of noncombat duties, most of them involving the sensors, tracking, and whatever else was happening beyond the ship's hull. And on the smaller ships—the corvettes and destroyers that patrolled the space around Manticore, Sphinx, Gryphon, and the main asteroid mining areas—those duties were still important.

But not on the battlecruisers. Not when the three that weren't in mothballs still spent most of their time in Manticore orbit trying to keep undermanned stations and underequipped systems in some semblance of readiness. Here, the tactical positions tended to be awarded to Parliamentary sons and daughters, or else to solid but unimaginative officers at the end of their careers.

As for the whole stepping-stone thing, the stagnant ship numbers had effectively put such hopes and dreams to rest. The men and women who already held command posts were for the most part not willing to graciously give them up, and while such assignments weren't officially their decision, enough of them had friends in high enough places to postpone the inevitable.

Metzger had had such dreams once, back when she'd first entered the Academy as a starry-eyed cadet. She'd envisioned herself in command, and had worked her butt off with that goal glowing like an approaching sunrise in front of her.

But slowly she'd come to realize that academic prowess and sheer competence alone weren't enough, not even with the Navy's supposed commitment to meritocracy. The rich, powerful, and noble always found a way to get to the front of a steadily shrinking line. The best of the best still floated to the surface, but they had to go through a lot more interference along the way.

Some of Metzger's classmates and, later, her fellow junior officers had become embittered over that reality. But Metzger herself had long since learned to take it in stride. She enjoyed the challenges and cat-and-mouse aspects of military tactics, there were enough drills and practices to keep her from becoming stale or overly bored, and she got to be on *Vanguard*'s bridge where the action was.

When there *was* any action, of course, which was admittedly rare. The gravitic vane accident had been the most excitement they'd had in months, and even that had been over almost before it began.

Still, with *Vanguard* actually on the move now, even if it was just a quick hyperspace hop over to Manticore-B to join Gryphon Fleet, there was always the chance that something interesting might happen.

She did, however, hope that any such interesting incident wouldn't involve any actual gunnery work. Especially given the results of their recent exercises.

The officers and chiefs responsible for *Vanguard*'s missiles, lasers, and autocannon had done their best. But the antiquated, patched, and repatched state of the ship's equipment had simply proved too much for them. The captain's grading on the various tests had ranged from good to adequate to poor.

Metzger scowled down at her soup. Or at least that was what the captain's report would say. But that wasn't exactly how it had happened. Most of the officers had done competently enough, as had most of the chiefs. But some of the officers, and way too many of the crew, hadn't. Not even close.

But the captain of a Navy ship had to also be a politician. Especially these days. *Mars*'s fate was a wake-up call, a warning that the Chancellor of the Exchequer and his friends were ascendant, and that when it came to resources and manpower, MPARS held a strong advantage over the RMN. Some of the less-than-stellar officers involved in the gunnery tests were well-connected, and Davison couldn't afford to nail their hides to the bulkhead. At least not officially.

She was wondering yet again how the captain would walk that fine line when the emergency-maneuver klaxon suddenly sounded in the wardroom.

By the time the spin section slowed to a halt two minutes later she'd finished her soup and was on her way up the lift to Axial Two and *Vanguard*'s bridge.

She arrived to find Captain Davison strapped into his station. The XO, Commander Bertinelli, was floating beside him, talking rapidly in a low voice. "Reporting for duty, Sir," Metzger announced, giving the status boards a quick look as she headed for her station behind the helm. *Vanguard*, she knew, had been accelerating toward the Unicorn One space station, which was still half the system away. That course was changing now as *Vanguard*'s bow pitched around against the background stars, bringing the ship maybe a hundred seventy degrees from her original course.

Metzger studied her displays as she strapped in. As far as she could see there was nothing out there but floating rocks. "Do we have a situation, Sir?"

"That's what we're trying to figure out, TO," Davison said gruffly. "XO, has Gravitics been able to squeeze anything more out of that flicker?"

"Nothing so far, Sir," Bertinelli said. "TO, get the captain a fine-sweep on the forward octants, will you?"

"Forward octant sweep, aye," Metzger acknowledged, keying for the sweep. On some ships, she knew, the bridge crew had served together long enough that they conversed with each other by name instead of by position. But Captain Davison was old-school, and still insisted all bridge personnel be addressed according to standard practice. His friends and apologists suggested the formality was modeled on the Peerage's own habit of referring to themselves and each other by estate titles instead of family names. The captain's detractors and *Vanguard*'s more cynical crew members held to the theory that Davison was so close to retirement he didn't think his officers' names worth making the effort to memorize. "May I ask what exactly I'm looking for?"

"Good question," Davison growled. "Gravitics lost a wedge out there—a mining ship named *Rafe's Scavenger*, about twelve light-minutes astern. No idea yet whether they lost the whole ship, lost the wedge, or just shut it down for some fool reason."

"Understood, Sir," Metzger said. Standard procedure in such cases was for the Navy ship who'd spotted the event to start setting up for a rescue mission while awaiting the slower light-speed data that would take a few minutes to catch up with the instantaneous gravitic pulses. If there was a reactor flare or some other indication of catastrophe—

And right on cue, a tiny flare flickered just off-center of Metzger's fine-sweep. "Flare," she snapped. "Bearing—"

"I see it," Davison interrupted. "Reactor failure?"

"Sure as hell looked like it," Bertinelli said. "TO, what does CIC say?"

"CIC confirms reactor failure," Metzger said, peering at the sensor data and analysis now scrolling across her displays. "No way to tell at this range whether it ejected in time or took the ship with it."

"If it took the ship, it didn't take all of it," the communications officer reported. "Getting an emergency beacon . . . and also a radio call." He clicked a switch.

"—gain I say mayday," a woman's tense voice blared from the bridge speakers. "Mining ship *Rafe's Scavenger*, twenty-five crew, unknown number of casualties. We've lost our reactor, wedge, and life support. Urgently request assistance from any ship within range. Repeating: Mayday; again I say mayday. Mining ship—"

Davison gestured, and Com switched off the speakers. "Astro, can we get to her?" he asked.

"A moment, Sir," the astrogator said, his fingers tapping out options. "Yes, Sir, we *can* make a rendezvous. But it'll be tricky. We're mostly on vector now, but we've got a lot of speed built up in the wrong direction. Recommend we increase our deceleration to one point seven two klicks per second squared and start to angle onto the proper zero-zero intercept."

The bridge was suddenly very quiet. One point seven kilometers per second squared was just about eighty-five percent for *Vanguard*'s impellers, and the highest a warship could go without starting to risk compensator failure and instant death for everyone aboard. Normally, warships didn't push their equipment that hard except in actual combat, especially not after such a lengthy period of idleness, and RMN standing orders specifically urged caution in all such questionable situations. Added to that was the current wardroom hypothesis that Captain Davison's chief ambition in life was to keep *Vanguard* in good working order until he could retire in equally good order.

But facing off against that risk and standing order was the equally firm standing order that Navy ships were to render immediate aid to civilian craft in danger. Peering discreetly over her shoulder, Metzger watched the captain out of the corner of her eye, wondering how he was going to reconcile those two directives.

It was apparently an easier decision than she'd thought.

"Helm, lay in Astro's intercept course and execute," Davison ordered. "Time to intercept?"

"Nine point five hours," Astro said.

"Going to be tight, Sir," the sailing master spoke up. "Civilian suits are usually only good for ten hours."

"Let's hope they have enough air left on the ship to cover the rest," Davison said. "Com, put a laser on them and let them know we're coming. Get a sitrep, and find out how long their air will hold out."

Metzger turned back to her station. In retrospect, of course, the captain's decision was obvious. Retiring with the shiniest ship in the fleet was one thing. Retiring with the public knowledge that you'd been a life-saving hero was far better.

Metzger winced a little as the status monitor showed *Vanguard*'s wedge ramping up to eighty-five percent. And if it came to wrecking your ship during said rescue attempt and becoming instead a hero martyr?

She wasn't sure where that one stood on Davison's list. She hoped it wasn't very high.

☆   ☆   ☆

"We have a course?" Ouvrard asked.

"Coming up now," Creutz said, peering over *Phobos*'s astrogator's shoulder. "At current acceleration it looks like we'll reach them in about nine point seven hours."

"Good," Ouvrard said, doing a quick mental calculation. Civilian survival suits typically had enough air for ten hours, plus *Rafe's Scavenger*'s had whatever was left in the undamaged parts of the ship. Nine point seven hours ought to do just fine. "Lay it in, and let's get cracking."

"Aye, aye, Captain."

And as the stars on the screen moved a little bit sideways as the ship yawed onto its new course, Ouvrard permitted herself a little smile. Suddenly, all the problems with this damn ugly-duckling ship no longer mattered. All that mattered was that there was someone in trouble out there, and that *their* ship—HMS *Phobos*—was in position to rescue them.

That felt good. That felt *damn* good.

"Course laid in and wedge at eighty percent," Creutz reported. "We're on our way, Ma'am."

"Steady as she goes, Mr. Creutz," Ouvrard said softly. "Let's go be heroes."

☆   ☆   ☆

"Did you get the whole message out?" Hanford asked.

"I think so," Shankweiler said, pulling the headphones away from her ears. "But the backup batteries are draining pretty fast. I'm not sure if the bit about both of them coming this way made it."

"Never mind that part," Hanford growled. "They're supposed to be warships, for—" he glanced over at Juarez, the religious one of the group "—for Pete's sake," he amended. "If they can't spot and identify each other across an asteroid field, that's their problem. Anyway, better to have too many rescuers than too few. I meant did they get the bit about us losing the whole canned O2 system in the explosion and only having ten hours' worth of air in these suits?"

"Yes, I'm sure they got that part," Shankweiler said. "I told them twice."

"I'm sure they know what they're doing," Juarez murmured.

"Yeah, one would hope," Hanford said, eyeing the man more closely. He had the same tension lines in his face as the rest of them, but there was also a strange sort of calmness behind his eyes. *Religious stuff*, Hanford thought with old reflexive habits of contempt for such things.

Still, paradoxically, he found himself rather envying the man.

"So now what?" Shankweiler asked.

"We shut down the transmitter," Hanford said, bringing his mind back to the problem at hand. "Leave the receiver and running lights on, but shut down everything else."

"Except the fans," Pickering spoke up. "With the reserves gone, circulating the air will help stretch out the available oxygen. The longer we can postpone tapping into our suit supplies, the better."

"Good idea," Hanford said. "But if the power levels drop too low, we shut the fans down, too. We need the receivers working in case *Phobos* or *Vanguard* needs to talk to us before they get here." Steeling himself, he turned to the edge of the semicircle. "Chou?"

"No change," Chou said, her medikit monitor sensor pressed against the side of Gratz's neck. "Still comatose. I think he's stable, but—" She shrugged helplessly. "I really can't tell. Sorry."

"That's okay," Hanford soothed. At least getting Gratz into his suit hadn't killed him. Some of the crew, he knew, had been worried about that happening.

Others, he suspected, had rather hoped for it. An extra suit's worth of oxygen would help the rest of them stretch out their own survival time. "Stay with him," he continued. "If he dies..." He looked around the circle, expecting to see some scandalized expressions or at least some guilty ones at the prospect. But there was nothing. Probably the others had already run the numbers on that option themselves.

Maybe more of them were hoping for it than he'd first thought. Maybe all of them were.

He focused on Juarez. No. Not all of them.

But whatever was going to happen, Hanford himself had now done everything he could think to do. Their lives were in the hands of the universe.

Or maybe in the hands of Juarez's God.

"Okay, spread out," he ordered. "Shut off everything except receivers, lights, and fans. As soon as you're done, we'll meet back here." He forced a smile. "When the Navy and MPARS arrive, we don't want them to have to go looking for anyone."

☆　　☆　　☆

"I don't believe it," Bertinelli said, peering at the tracking display. "Out in the back end of nowhere—the back end of nowhere in an *asteroid belt*, for God's sake—and there are *two* of us who just happen to be in range for a rescue?"

"It's not nearly as coincidental as you make it sound," Davison chided. "*Phobos* is here because she was specifically tasked with patrolling these less-traveled areas. We're here because the same less-traveled areas were the logical spot for gunnery exercises on our way to join up with Gryphon Fleet."

"Are we breaking off, then, Sir?" Metzger asked.

Davison frowned at her. "Breaking off, TO?"

"Breaking off the rescue," Metzger said. "*Phobos* is on track to reach *Rafe's Scavenger* in plenty of time. And as you said, that's why she's out here in the first place."

"True," Davison said. "But the miner's captain has stated he has at least one injured crewman, possibly more, and I'd bet heavily that *Vanguard*'s sickbay and medical staff are far superior to *Phobos*'s."

"Besides, *Phobos* barely has room for her own crew and supplies," Bertinelli added. "She certainly won't have the capacity for taking the miner in tow."

"We're taking them in *tow*, Sir?" Metzger asked, frowning.

"It's one of our options, yes," Davison said. "I presume you've never known an asteroid miner?"

"Ah...no, Sir, I haven't," Metzger admitted.

"Well, I have," the captain said. "Their businesses run very close to the edge, with a laser-thin margin for error. Even a badly damaged ship is worth something, and bringing *Rafe's Scavenger* back might make all the difference to her captain and crew."

"Not to mention that it would be nice to know how and why their fusion plant failed," Bertinelli said. "The evaluators can hardly do a proper investigation if we leave the ship drifting."

"Understood, Sir," Metzger said. It all sounded so neat and reasonable and aboveboard.

So why did she have the nagging feeling that there was something going on beneath the surface that the captain and XO weren't saying?

She returned her attention to her station, feeling annoyed with herself. One of the qualities that made for a good tactical officer was a natural suspicion of an enemy's plans and actions. Sometimes it was hard to turn off that distrust when among friends.

Still, it wouldn't hurt to keep her eyes and ears open.

☆　　☆　　☆

Phobos was two hours into her acceleration when a message came through from the MPARS Gryphon Command.

It wasn't exactly the kind of message Ouvrard had been expecting.

"You've got to be kidding," she said flatly.

"I wish I was, Ma'am," Creutz said acidly. "But they sent it twice, and it came through the same way both times. There's no garble or other mistake."

"No, I'm sure there isn't," Ouvrard growled, peering at the message again.

> To HMS *Phobos*
>
> From MPARS HQ, Gryphon
>
> HMS *Vanguard* has been identified in your sector. Vector indicates she is moving to rescue mining ship *Rafe's Scavenger*. It would be in the best interest of the service if *Phobos* was to effect the rescue. Strongly urge you to act accordingly.

Appended to the brief note was a dump of Gryphon's latest data on *Vanguard*'s position and vector, along with her estimated position and time for a zero-zero intercept with the stricken miner.

"So they're turning it into a race," she said. "They're turning a rescue mission into a damn pissing contest between MPARS and the Navy."

"That would appear to be the case, Ma'am," Creutz confirmed. "And if the numbers they sent us are accurate, we're currently in second place."

Ouvrard chewed at her lip. "Do we have *Vanguard* on sensors yet?"

"We've got her wedge," Creutz said. "But they're still out of com range."

And even if Ouvrard *could* talk to them, what would she say? That her MPARS bosses had ordered her to beat them to *Rafe's Scavenger*, and would they please let her win? What if *Vanguard*'s captain decided that for the good of *his* service *he* had to win?

Ouvrard glowered at the plot. The bitter irony of this whole thing was that under slightly different circumstances the whole conundrum would have been moot. *Rafe's Scavenger* was currently outside Manticore-B's hyper limit, as was *Phobos* herself. If *Vanguard* had also been on that side of the limit, she could have made a microjump and been there within minutes of receiving the miners' distress call. Alternatively, if it had been *Phobos*'s sister ship *Deimos* out here on patrol, the situation would again have been easily resolved. *Deimos*, which had been built from the after half of the bisected *Mars,* had inherited the battlecruiser's hyperdrive, the idea being that once both sloops were in service

Deimos could hang around outside the hyper limit and render quick aid throughout that area, while *Phobos* could stay inside the limit and handle any trouble there.

But *Deimos* wasn't here, and *Vanguard* wasn't there, and wishes weren't horses.

"Fine," she said. "I presume you've run the numbers. What'll it take for us to get there first?"

A muscle in Creutz's cheek twitched. "We'll need to run the wedge at eighty-nine percent for the next two hours. At that point we make turnover, and can crank it back down to eighty-three."

Ouvrard felt her stomach tighten. Eighty-nine percent. Four points outside the standard eighty-to-eighty-five percent that was considered safe operating range for inertial compensators.

Four very crucial, very risky points. Especially with *Phobos*'s single mistuned impeller ring continuing to stress the hull. At this point pushing past eighty percent would be dangerous enough, let alone going all the way to eighty-nine.

But she had no choice. The message from Gryphon wasn't officially an order, but she'd been in the service long enough to know how to read between the lines. If she didn't do everything in her power to win this damn stupid race MPARS Command would praise her on her brave effort, possibly add a commendation into her file, and then quietly take her ship away from her. For the good of the service, of course.

She snorted. MPARS Command be damned. The point wasn't showing up the Navy, or even obeying oblique instructions. The point was that there was a wrecked miner and a group of desperate people out there. The *Rafe's Scavenger* survivors might have enough air to wait for *Vanguard*, but there was at least one injured crewman aboard, maybe more than one, and there was no guarantee how long those injured might live.

And really, at its core, taking risks to save others was what MPARS was all about. It was what *Phobos* was all about.

It was what Ouvrard was all about.

She looked around, vaguely surprised to see that everyone else on the bridge was looking back at her. She hadn't realized her musings had taken so much time. "Tyler, set course for *Rafe's Scavenger*," she ordered the helmsman. "Acceleration—" she braced herself "—one point two seven klicks per second squared."

"Aye, aye, Ma'am," the helmsman said. His eyes flicked to Creutz, and then he turned back to his board. "Course for *Rafe's Scavenger*, acceleration at eighty-nine percent."

"And may God have mercy on their souls," Creutz murmured.

"Yes," Ouvrard murmured back. "And on ours."

☆　　☆　　☆

"Listen up!" Craddock bellowed, his voice cutting through the excited babble in the machine shop. "Yeah, I know you're all off-duty—deal with it. Fresh assignments: Bowen and Atherton—"

"Is it true we're on a rescue mission, Chief?" someone called.

"—you're on the secondary analyzer. We've supposedly got the parts to get it functional again—find 'em, and get the thing up and running ASAP. Yarrow and Long: that flutter in the Number Two gravitics display in CIC has spread to two of the others. The flutters are synched, which means there's some root cause. Find it and fix it. Benson—"

"Come on, Chief, give," another voice called. "Are we just mooning around, or are we really *doing* something for a change?"

"Yeah, we're doing something, Kilgore," Craddock shot back. "We're doing our jobs, or we're getting our butts handed to us. Got that?"

"Yeah, Chief, sure," Kilgore persisted. "But are we *doing* something?"

"Oh, for—" Craddock rolled his eyes. "*Yes*, we're doing something. *Yes*, we're on a rescue mission. *Yes*, some sand-sifter mining ship's blown her reactor and the crew's stinking up their survival suits. Anyone else?" He glanced around, and his glare fell on Travis. "Long, you waiting for a parchment invitation? You and Yarrow get your butts up to CIC. Now: Kilgore—"

"Pretty cool, huh?" Yarrow commented as she and Travis shot down the passageway. "Not that someone's in trouble, but cool that we get to do something."

"Yeah," Travis said, his heart thudding with anticipation. *This* was what he'd joined the Navy for: the chance to give aid and protection to the Star Kingdom's citizens.

He just hoped *Vanguard* was up to the task. Because worse even than not trying was to build up false hopes and then fail.

"You coming?" Yarrow called over her shoulder as she deftly negotiated a corner.

Travis set his teeth. False hopes and failure... but all of that was Captain Davison's department. All Travis had to do was fix a balky monitor.

That, at least, didn't come with any false hopes attached. "Just make sure you don't run somebody down," he called back to Yarrow. "I'm right behind you."

☆   ☆   ☆

Phobos was midway into turnover, and Ouvrard was rechecking the figures for their upcoming deceleration profile, when the ship ripped herself apart.

It came without warning: a violent rapid-fire series of jolts and twists, punctuated by screams and shouts from the intercom, the whole thing overlaid by the frantic bellow of the emergency klaxons.

The alarm volume had dropped to background intensity by the time Ouvrard managed to untangle herself from the line of overhead monitors she'd been thrown into.

"Report," she called, the word coming out more as a croak than as a true command.

There was no reply. Blinking to clear her vision, Ouvrard looked around.

The bridge was a disaster zone. Two of the crew were floating limply around the cramped space, bouncing off consoles and monitors as the ship continued to lurch. The rest of the personnel were moving slowly. Clearly conscious, just as clearly dazed.

Well, the hell with *that*. "*Report!*" she snarled, putting some teeth into the order this time.

"Fusion plant scrammed," a voice came from midway down the bridge. It was so distorted by pain that it took Ouvrard a few seconds to recognize it as Creutz's. "Emergency power and life support are on line. Wedge down. Intercom... reactor room not showing. Sensors..."

"Shuttles?" Ouvrard asked, getting a grip on one of the handholds and pulling herself toward her station. Something blurred into her eye, and she swiped the back of her hand across it, noting the swath of bright red on her sleeve as she brought the hand away.

"They're not showing either," Creutz said. "Could be just the sensors are down. The—oh, my God," he interrupted himself, his voice suddenly horrified.

"What is it?" Ouvrard demanded, pulling herself down into the nearest station and jabbing for a status report.

"The reactor pylon," Creutz said mechanically. "It snapped. It just *snapped*."

"That's impossible," Ouvrard countered, the words complete reflex as she pulled up the proper sensor schematics. The pylon connecting the reactor section to the forward part of the sloop was a solid twenty meters in diameter, containing an axial access passageway as well as a pair of heavily shielded, two-meter-diameter plasma conduits. It couldn't just break. It simply *couldn't*.

Only it had.

Ouvrard stared at the display in disbelief, her injuries and even those of her crew momentarily forgotten. The pylon had broken just forward of its midpoint, leaving the two sections of the ship connected only by the slender dorsal bracing line. The pylon and hull forward of the break had been burned black by the explosive release of the plasma jets from their containment conduits. On one of the camera views, she could see a section of the hull still bubbling as it radiated the extra heat into the vacuum. The aft section of the ship was flopping slowly back and forth, the movement threatening to break the final connection and send it drifting away.

Ouvrard had known the hull harmonic from the unbalanced impeller ring was bad. She'd had no idea that it could be *this* bad.

She took a deep breath, wincing as the lung expansion sent a stab of pain through bruised or cracked ribs. What had happened had happened. Her responsibility now was to what was left of her ship.

Or rather, what was left of her crew. The ship itself, as a ship, no longer existed.

She jabbed the intercom's broadcast key. "Initiate emergency procedures," she called toward the mike. A formality, really—anyone aboard who was still alive and functional would already have figured out that part. "Damage control: triage assessment. Medical personnel: full sweep." She glanced over her shoulder. "And send someone to the bridge," she added.

She keyed off, wondering dimly if anyone was even out there to hear.

A hand groped across her shoulder to one of the handholds. "God in heaven," Creutz murmured. "What in *hell* just happened?"

"Three things," Ouvrard said. "One: we just lost MPARS's criminally stupid race to *Rafe's Scavenger*. Two: we also just proved that this ship design sucks swamp water. Three: we got an unexpected chance to practice our wrecked ship search-and-rescue techniques."

"On ourselves," Creutz said with a shallow sigh. "Aye, aye, Ma'am. I'm on it." Carefully, he eased toward his station.

"Where are you hurt?" Ouvrard called after him.

"I'm all right, Ma'am," he replied over his shoulder.

"That's not what I asked."

"I know," Creutz said. "I'm moving. Others aren't. Triage rules say they go first."

Ouvrard eased a tentative hand against her injured ribs, wincing at the flash of fresh pain. "Very good, Commander," she said, keying for a damage-assessment schematic. "Carry on."

☆   ☆   ☆

The only really good thing about working in zero-gee, Travis had long since concluded, was that it gave you the ability to turn and twist your body into whatever angle was most convenient for the task at hand.

Still, it remained a bit disconcerting to look up and see the entire CIC crew in their stations hanging above his head.

"Five-mil," Yarrow said.

Travis returned his attention to the half-open display monitor and handed her the requested wrench. Above and behind him, the CIC hatch slid open, and he felt the ripple of air as someone came into the compartment. "Relieving you, Jones," a familiar voice said.

Travis looked up again. It was Senior Chief Inzinga, taking over from the current gravitics operator. Odd, because like Travis and the rest of his tech unit, Inzinga was supposed to be off-duty right now. Maybe there was more going on with this rescue than Craddock had said, something that had induced the captain to pull in more of his first-watch people.

And given that Travis already had a casual-conversation relationship with Inzinga, this might be his chance to find out what was going on.

"We're getting these monitors fixed," Travis said as Inzinga strapped himself into the station. "Chief Craddock pulled us off-duty—"

"Yeah, yeah," Inzinga said distractedly as he punched at his keys. "Bridge; CIC," he called toward the mike. "Inzinga. I've rewound the record and am starting my pass."

Travis looked at Yarrow, saw his same puzzlement reflected in her face. Whatever was going on, they'd apparently missed it while they were concentrating on the broken monitors.

"Okay, I see it," Inzinga said, leaning a little closer to his primary display. "Their wedge crashed, all right. We're still too far away for any real detail, but it doesn't look like the fusion plant blew."

"We should know that in about thirty seconds," Captain Davison's voice came from the speaker. "Chief Grillo?"

"Yes, Sir, I'm on it," the woman at the tracking station said briskly. "Standing by."

Travis looked at the chrono. Assume Inzinga had been called shortly after the wedge event, factor in how long it took to get dressed and then get from the petty officers' area to CIC, add in thirty seconds...

"Here we go," Grillo said. "No flare...no neutrino burst," she said slowly, reading the data off her displays. "Looks like the reactor scrammed safely. From the acceleration profile, I'd say she was in turnover when the wedge went down."

"At least we don't have another *Rafe's Scavenger* on our hands," Davison said. "So what the hell happened to her?"

"Must be talking about *Phobos*," Yarrow murmured in Travis's ear.

Travis frowned. "*Phobos* is out here? Who told you that?"

"Atherton," Yarrow said. "He heard she was heading for the same wrecked mining ship we are."

Travis huffed out a breath. A Navy *and* an MPARS ship on the same rescue mission? "Must be one hell of an important miner."

"No idea," Yarrow said. "Ten-mil."

Travis handed her the wrench, his thoughts on *Phobos* and whatever was happening out there. It didn't make sense for a ship to simply drop her wedge, especially when she was on something as time-critical as a rescue mission. Mechanical problems, then?

But a com signal traveled at the same speed as the data from her scrammed reactor. If she was in trouble, a distress call ought to be reaching *Vanguard* any time now.

"One moment, Sir," Grillo said. "There's a small star cluster right behind them. Let me see if I can get anything from occultation."

Travis stiffened. He'd taken a cursory look at *Phobos*'s stats during the big hoopla that had accompanied her launch. Now, suddenly, something in that list seemed to leap out from his memory. "Oh, no," he breathed.

"What?" Yarrow asked, peering into the open display. "Looks okay to me."

"Not that," Travis said. "*Phobos*. I think she's broken up."

"Broken *up*?" Yarrow repeated, staring at him. "That's ridiculous. Tracking already said the reactor scrammed safely."

"I know," Travis said, the horrific image of a shattered ship floating in front of his eyes. "But she only has a single impeller ring. If it gets misaligned or mistuned—"

"You'll start running harmonic stress to the hull," Inzinga finished for him.

Travis looked down to see the senior chief looking quizzically up at him.

"Sorry, Senior Chief," he apologized, wincing. He hadn't realized he was talking loud enough to be overheard.

"Never mind *sorry*, Spacer Long," Inzinga said. "Where in the world did you learn about something that obscure?"

"I wrote a paper on impeller instabilities at Casey-Rosewood," Travis said, feeling his face redden at the memory of how that paper had come to be.

"Oh, my God," Grillo murmured. "Captain, if I'm reading this right, there are multiple occultations. Not a single ship, but a partial ship plus several pieces.

"Sir, I think *Phobos* has broken up."

"That's impossible," another voice came from the speaker, sounding as disbelieving as Grillo did. "She wasn't attacked— we'd have seen the flash of a warhead or the explosion from a beam weapon."

"Unless it was a hull harmonic," Davison said grimly. "Senior Chief Inzinga, am I correct in assuming that can happen with a ship *Phobos*'s size running a single impeller ring?"

"Yes, Sir, you are," Inzinga said, his forehead slightly furrowed as he looked up at Travis. "It's highly unlikely, even with a single ring, but it can happen."

"Well, it apparently has," Davison said.

Yarrow touched Travis's arm. "We're finished," she said softly.

Travis looked at the monitor. While he'd been focusing on *Phobos*'s accident, she'd finished fixing the monitor and had put the casing back in place.

And it was time for them to go.

Only Travis didn't want to. Not now. He wanted to hear what

the captain was going to do about *Phobos*. Just because the sloop had broken up didn't mean that no one was alive aboard her. On the contrary: with the reactor safely scrammed and life pods within easy reach of everyone, there was a good chance that many or even most of the crew had made it through.

But they couldn't last out there forever. A catastrophic hull harmonic could have left hidden damage: charged capacitors, unvented plasma streams, or stress cracks that could shatter at any time. The crew were sitting inside a gigantic time bomb, and sooner or later that bomb would go off.

"Come on," Yarrow said, more emphatically this time.

Travis clenched his teeth. "Right," he said. Glancing around CIC, he silently wished them all good luck.

They, and *Phobos*'s survivors, were going to need it.

CHAPTER THIRTEEN

METZGER HAD HOPED the preliminary report would turn out to be wrong. There was every chance it would, after all, especially given the extreme unlikelihood that *Phobos* had been taken down by a hull harmonic catastrophe. Senior Chief Inzinga could easily have been jumping at shadows in reading his data.

But he wasn't. The harmonic was real.

Phobos had disintegrated. Some of her crew were undoubtedly already dead, with more to follow over the next few hours. The question now was how long that list would ultimately be.

And *Vanguard* and Captain Davison had now been presented with the ultimate nightmare dilemma. Because *Rafe's Scavenger* was also out there, just as crippled as *Phobos,* also carrying the dead and the probably soon-to-be dying.

Metzger had run the numbers. If *Vanguard* continued on her present course, there was a good chance she would reach *Rafe's Scavenger* before the miners' air ran out. Alternatively, Davison could change course and probably get to *Phobos* before the hulk disintegrated further.

But whichever path the captain chose, there was virtually no chance *Vanguard* could rescue one ship and then get to the other. Not in time.

"Still no response from *Phobos,*" Com reported. "Looks like their laser and radio went out when the ship broke apart."

"Keep trying," Davison ordered, his tone studiously neutral. He was facing forward, and Metzger couldn't see his expression from her station, but she had no doubt it was as steady as his voice.

But it was all a mask, and everyone on the bridge knew it. This was the situation that every commanding officer knew he or she might one day have to make.

Rafe's Scavenger was a civilian craft, and RMN standing orders were to render all aid and assistance to such vessels. *Phobos* was an MPARS rescue ship, with many former Navy personnel aboard.

Rafe's Scavenger had eight survivors awaiting rescue. *Phobos's* tally was unknown, but it was probably in the dozens.

Metzger had no idea which way Davison would go. She had no idea which way she herself would go if the decision was hers.

Somewhere in the back of her mind, the starry-eyed cadet who'd once dreamed of command was being very quiet.

☆   ☆   ☆

The monitor had been fixed, Craddock had decided that more people on the secondary collection system would just get in each other's way, and Travis and Yarrow had been returned to off-duty status.

"You all right?" Yarrow asked as they sat across from each other in the mess hall.

"Hmm?" With an effort, Travis brought his eyes back from his contemplation of nothing in particular.

"I asked if you were all right," Yarrow said, lifting her coffee cup carefully. The spin section had been started up again, but at half its usual speed, and in the lower gravity it was easy to let liquids get away from you.

"Not really." Travis tried a smile. "I didn't think I was letting it show."

"Next time you don't want something to show, pay more attention to your coffee," Yarrow advised. "You've been ignoring it, and you hate cold coffee."

Travis looked down at his cup. She was right, on both counts.

"Actually, come to think about it," she continued, "there's probably a regulation against taking food and not eating it. You should look into that. It would be a travesty to waste food."

"I keep thinking about *Phobos*," Travis said, not even caring that, once again, he was being ridiculed simply for following the rules. "There has to be something we can do."

"I assume the captain's working on the problem," Yarrow pointed out. "Not to mention everyone on Unicorn One and Gryphon Base. Unless you've got a magic wand stashed away somewhere,

I think you and I are pretty much out of it." She cocked her head. "You never said anything about having written a paper on impeller instabilities. Was that part of your class work?"

"No, it was a special project," Travis said, feeling the bitter irony of the situation. If Lieutenant Cyrus hadn't trumped up those charges and kicked him out of impeller school, he might have been one of the people who'd helped design and tune *Phobos*'s ring. He might have been able to keep this from happening.

Instead, he was sitting here helplessly, with agonized frustration and cold coffee.

And then, an odd thought tweaked at the back of his mind. *Lieutenant Cyrus...*

"What is it?" Yarrow asked.

"An idea," Travis said. He stood up—too fast—and started to float off the deck. He caught the underside of his chair with his toe and pulled himself back down. "I need to run some numbers. Lounge terminal's closest, right?"

"Should be," Yarrow confirmed, standing up more carefully. "You going to drink that coffee? Or should we say to hell with regs and throw it away?"

Travis hesitated, then picked up the cup and downed the contents in a single, long swallow. It tasted terrible. Grabbing Yarrow's empty cup, he set both mugs on the nearest disposal podium and pushed off his chair. "Let's go."

☆   ☆   ☆

Hanford stared at his helmet chrono, watching in strange and morbid fascination as the numbers clicked over to yet another minute. A lot of the minutes were past. A whole lot more of them still lay ahead.

And the ultimate end was still shrouded in blackness. The same blackness that shrouded his dead ship.

He scowled, forcing his eyes to shift their focus to his faceplate and the scene beyond. He'd never been the moody, introspective type. Here and now, with their lives hanging by a spider thread, was no time to start.

Or maybe it was. Certainly the rest of *Rafe's Scavenger*'s remaining crew seemed to have gone that direction. They were floating in various spots and at various angles around the bridge, some doing a slow spin, others mostly stationary. The rotating ones' faces were periodically visible, and Hanford noted that all of them seemed calm or at least resigned. That was good: slower breathing would stretch out their air supplies. The two who were facing away from him were more of a question mark, but their lack of restless twitching implied that they, too, were trying to conserve their oxygen. Gratz was still unconscious, and Chou was still watching over him, her monitor plugged into his suit's data jack.

Juarez, annoyingly, had found enough peace within him to actually take a nap.

For a long minute Hanford gazed at the man's calm, sleeping face. Then, with nothing better to do, he returned his attention to his chrono.

Another minute had passed. With a sigh, he settled back into his vigil.

☆   ☆   ☆

"Okay, here's what's we've got," Creutz said, making a final notation on his tablet and offering it to Ouvrard.

"Thank you," she said, taking it. Creutz was still moving slowly and carefully, she noted, as was perfectly natural for a man with a broken arm and some cracked ribs. But the medics had done their job well, and Creutz seemed more or less functional again.

Certainly as functional as Ouvrard herself was feeling. Her own cracked ribs were thankfully not hurting anymore, but the painkillers she'd been given were making her just a bit light-headed. Blinking away the slightly sparkling fog, she ran her eyes down Creutz's list.

It was as bad as she'd expected. Possibly a bit worse. One of the shuttles had taken a full blast of plasma in its flank and control thrusters when the conduits snapped, and wasn't going anywhere anytime soon. The other was flyable, but the wrenching of the pylon where it had been attached had put some cracks in its body and two of its three fuel tanks.

As for *Phobos* herself, she was in the process of dying.

Half the forward compartments were either breached or cut off from the central core. The impeller room, only one bulkhead forward of the bridge and the rest of the core section, was nevertheless completely inaccessible, and all attempts to communicate with possible survivors in there had gone unanswered. There was no communication at all with the aft part of the ship, the section containing the fusion plant and associated engineering compartments behind the broken pylon. There might still be survivors, but there was no way to tell until a search party could physically get back there and look.

At least they weren't going to have the oxygen countdown the survivors on *Rafe's Scavenger* were currently in the middle of. *Phobos*'s life support was twitchy but still mostly functional, at least here in the core, and the backup power cells had also escaped serious damage. The emergency oxygen supplies were also untapped, and there seemed to be enough EVA suits and lifepods for everyone who'd survived the initial explosive breakup.

Which meant that if Creutz could get the survivors gathered together in the core, they should be able to ride this out until *Vanguard* finished picking up the surviving miners and get her tail out here.

Assuming, of course, that *Vanguard* had figured out something was wrong. With Robert Davison in command, that wasn't necessarily a smart bet to make.

"Orders, Ma'am?"

"Let's start by collecting everyone we can from this side of the pylon," Ouvrard said, handing back the tablet. "I know some of the compartments are cut off—do whatever you can to get to them and get their occupants out."

"And those we can't get to?"

"Have the search teams make notes on what we'll need to get into those areas," Ouvrard said. "Cutting torches, pry bars, whatever. We'll try to get to them on the second sweep. What's the situation aft of the pylon?"

"Still too dangerous for EV teams," Creutz said. "But the coxswains say they should be able to get the Number Two shuttle flying."

"Good," Ouvrard said. "We need to get any survivors back up here before that section breaks completely free and drifts off. Do we have enough able-bodied to form another SAR team to go with them?"

"I think so," Creutz said, making another note on his tablet. "I should at least be able to put together a small one."

"Good," Ouvrard said. "I don't want *Vanguard* to have to go on a snipe hunt when she arrives."

"*If* she arrives," Creutz muttered. "At their range, they may not even know anything's happened."

"Which is why the next priority after collecting the survivors will be to get the com working again," Ouvrard said. "Or if we can't, to find some other way to signal for help. Sequential bursts from the autocannon, maybe, or similar bursts with any plasma that might not have vented."

She frowned as an odd thought drifted through the fog. Unvented plasma... "Do we know if the impeller capacitors vented?"

"Uh—" Creutz peered at his tablet. "I don't think we've got anything on that—all the data lines forward of the bridge are down. They're supposed to vent in an emergency, though."

"Yeah, and a single-ring ship isn't supposed to fall apart," Ouvrard said. Still, he was probably right.

Meanwhile, there were plenty of more immediate crises to deal with. Along with the whole trapped-and-missing-crewmen issue, there were half a dozen fires that had erupted in various places aboard the ship. At least three of those were class-D metal fires, where there was enough attached oxidizer that even venting to vacuum wouldn't put them out. So far all the fires were small, but they needed to be dealt with before they got any bigger. The emergency life-support system was currently humming away just fine, but it needed to be checked for hidden problems lest it suddenly *stop* working. *Phobos*'s death throes had given her wreckage a slow spin, and they needed to make sure that rotation wasn't going to combine with the rest of the damage to pop seams that the internal sensor system claimed were in no danger. For that matter, if and when they had the time, it would probably be a good idea to do a complete system diagnostic to make sure the internal sensors were actually reading such things correctly.

And they absolutely needed to let *Vanguard* know what was going on.

"As soon as the SAR teams have made their first sweep, pull everyone who's handy with power tools and get them looking for a safe place to cut through that bulkhead," she told Creutz. "The autocannon are probably still our best bet for getting some kind of signal out, and I want Senior Chief Dierken and Gunner's Mate Funk working on that as soon as we can get them in there."

She smiled tightly. "The two of them have had a free ride so far. They might as well start earning their pay."

☆   ☆   ☆

It took Travis twenty frustrating minutes to discover he couldn't get to the tactical programs he needed. Either they weren't accessible on the lounge computer or, more likely, weren't available on a lowly spacer third class's password.

Somewhere during that time, he noted peripherally, Yarrow gave up and wandered away. With his full attention on his search, Travis couldn't remember afterward whether or not she'd said good-bye.

But there was too much at stake for him to just admit defeat. If he couldn't get to the program he needed, maybe Chief Craddock could. Closing down the terminal, he headed out of the lounge and up the lift. Unless the techs had already gotten the secondary analysis system up and running, Craddock should be in the gravitics monitor room, presiding over the operation.

He'd exited the lift and was flying down the passageway when Lieutenant Lisa Donnelly emerged from a compartment directly into his line of motion. Her eyes widened as she saw Travis barreling toward her—

"Look out!" Travis croaked. He grabbed for a handhold, missed, grabbed for another one, got it, and with a wrench that felt like it was dislocating his shoulder he braked to a stop.

The whole incident had taken less than three seconds. Even so, Donnelly had enough time to switch from stunned surprise to full Angry Officer mode. "What the hell was *that*, Long?" she demanded, glaring at him.

"I'm sorry, Ma'am," Travis said hurriedly, trying to ease past her.

"Ship blowing up from the stern forward?" she growled, moving to block his escape path. "Someone actually on fire?"

"No, Ma'am," Travis said between clenched teeth, his mental countdown ticking away the seconds. "I'm sorry—I need to get to Chief Craddock right away."

"So *right away* that you need to run people down?" Donnelly countered. "What's the problem?"

Travis squeezed his handhold. He'd hoped he could run the numbers before he actually mentioned this to anyone. But it was clear that Donnelly wasn't going to let him go without getting *something.* "I think I may have a way to save both of the ships out there," he told her. "Both crews, I mean. But I need—"

"Whoa, whoa," she interrupted, her eyes narrowing. "What do you know about the situation?"

"I was fixing the monitors in CIC when *Phobos*'s wedge went down," he explained. "If it was a hull harmonic—sorry, Ma'am. The point is that we need to get to her before there's more damage."

"We also need to get to the miners before their air runs out."

"Yes, Ma'am, I know."

"And you have an idea of how we can do both?"

Travis swallowed. In the back of his mind, Commander Bertinelli's words rang with hollow mocking: *Your job isn't to think, Spacer Long. If modifications are called for, someone with more experience and authority than you will inform you of that fact.* "Yes, Ma'am, I do," he said. "But I need to run a tactical simulation to see if it'll work, and I can't get access to those programs. I'm hoping Chief Craddock can."

"Probably not," Donnelly said, the anger in her eyes replaced with...something else. "But *I* can. Come on, let's find a terminal."

☆ ☆ ☆

"Relieving you, Commander."

Metzger turned, frowning. Lieutenant Elmajian, the assistant tactical officer, was floating behind her. "What?"

"ATO's taking back her watch, TO," Bertinelli said from the captain's side.

Metzger felt a flicker of surprise. She'd almost forgotten she'd arrived mid-watch. "Yes, Sir," she said. "Permission to stay until the situation is resolved?"

"It's resolved, TO," Captain Davison said quietly. "As far as it can be."

"Get something to eat and then hit your rack," Bertinelli added. "That's an order."

Metzger sighed. But he was right. She'd already been late getting to sleep when the crisis hit the fan, and she could feel fatigue tugging at her eyelids. Maybe Elmajian, with fresher eyes and a fresher brain, could spot something she'd missed. "Yes, Sir."

A minute later she was heading aft down the passageway, wondering if she was more tired than she was hungry or vice versa. More tired, she decided.

But if she went to sleep now, she'd just wake up in a couple of hours with a growling stomach. No, better to grab a snack first.

Wondering distantly whether *Phobos*'s crew had had a chance for a final meal, she headed for the wardroom.

☆ ☆ ☆

For a long minute Lieutenant Donnelly just stared at him. Travis braced himself—

"You're crazy, you know," she said at last. "This can't possibly work. Not without a huge slab of luck."

"I know," Travis admitted. "But if there's even a chance—"

"No, no, I agree," Donnelly said calmly. "Luckily for you, I'm as crazy as you are." She tapped his arm and keyed the intercom. "Bridge; Missile Ops," she announced.

"Com," a crisp voice came back.

"This is Lieutenant Donnelly," Donnelly identified herself. "I need to speak with Captain Davison."

"Captain's busy," Com said.

"The XO, then."

"That's who the captain's busy with," Com told her. "And before you ask, the ATO's part of the same deep conversation. Is there some crisis with the missiles?"

"No, Sir," Donnelly said. "I have a spacer here with an idea about—"

"You have a *spacer*?" the other cut her off. "Yes, fine, thank you. Your call's been logged, Lieutenant. The captain will get back to you when he can."

There was a click, and the connection was broken.

"Ma'am, we can't wait that long," Travis said urgently. "The deadline—"

"Yes, yes, I know," Donnelly said, still gazing at the computer display. "But there's no way I can get to the captain now. Not after I've already been told to wait."

"So we're just going to give up?"

"Hardly," Donnelly said. "Remember how I got my telemetry subsystem fixed?"

"You hijacked Spacer Marx and me?"

"I cut through the clutter and went straight to the people who could do the job," Donnelly corrected.

Abruptly, she tapped his arm and launched herself toward the Missile Ops door. "Come on."

"Where are we going?" Travis asked as he hurried to catch up.

"Com said the captain was talking with the ATO," Donnelly reminded him. "That implies that the TO wasn't there. If she wasn't there, she's somewhere else. If she's somewhere else, we can find her."

"Okay," Travis said cautiously. "Where do we start?"

"The wardroom," Donnelly said. "Keep your fingers crossed that she's there and not already asleep in her cabin."

She grabbed a handhold and gave herself an extra burst of speed. "Keep up, Long," she said over her shoulder. "And let me do the talking."

☆   ☆   ☆

"Commander Metzger?" The server peered around the wardroom. "Well, she *was* here. I guess she left."

"About how long ago?" Donnelly asked.

The server shrugged.

"I don't know, Ma'am. Couple of minutes, maybe."

Travis clenched his hands into fists. A couple of minutes. Twice around the chrono. Two minutes that could mean the difference between life and death.

Or maybe not. If Donnelly's expression was anything to go by, she was a long way from giving up.

"Thank you," she said to the server. She turned back toward the wardroom door, tapping Travis's arm as she strode past him. "Come on."

"Where now, Ma'am?" Travis asked, a sudden horrible suspicion sliding in on top of his vision of dying spacers. Donnelly wasn't planning on barging in on a senior officer in her own *quarters*, was she?

"My quarters," Donnelly said over her shoulder.

Travis felt his eyes widen. Was she suggesting—? No. She couldn't possibly—

"We're going to give the TO a call, and we need a quiet place to do it from," Donnelly continued. "Move it—we've got lives to save."

CHAPTER FOURTEEN

"OKAY, THAT'S THE LAST OF THEM," Creutz said, checking off an entry on his tablet.

Ouvrard nodded, feeling a fresh flicker of guilt. The last of the survivors from *Phobos*'s aft section had been brought back aboard.

And with that list of names, they now also had the complete list of those who *hadn't* made it. Those who would never board a ship again.

Phobos had lost forty-two of her crew in the first few minutes of the catastrophe. Forty-two out of a hundred and thirty: nearly a third of her entire complement. Most of them had been in the aft section of the ship, tending and monitoring the fusion plant or else working in the machine and electronics shops.

Some of them had died quickly, in explosive decompression as their compartments were split open to space. Others had died even faster, incinerated in place as wrenched conduits spewed plasma the temperature of Manticore-A's surface into cramped compartments or down narrow passageways.

And it was Ouvrard's fault. All of it.

Because no matter how urgently MPARS Gryphon had wanted *Phobos* to be the first ship to arrive at *Rafe's Scavenger*, their carefully worded message had fallen far short of a direct order. An implied threat against her career, perhaps. But an order, no.

Ouvrard could have ignored it. She could have kept her ship within safe acceleration parameters and arrived second behind *Vanguard*. The miners would be just as alive and safe, and in the

161

grand scheme of the universe it didn't matter a tinker's damn who did the actual rescuing.

At least, that was what the Board of Inquiry would probably say. It was certainly what Ouvrard would say if *she* was one of the officers sitting on that Board.

But what was done was done. It was too late for bitter second thoughts about her decision; too early to worry about the Board she would eventually be facing. All that mattered right now was that two-thirds of her crew *were* still alive, and it was her responsibility to do everything in her power to make sure they stayed that way. There were injuries to be treated, trapped crew members still to free, the life-support systems to be monitored, and the communications equipment to be cobbled into some semblance of working order.

Speaking of which—

"Anything from Dierken about the autocannon?" she asked.

"The shuttle was able to get him and his team in through one of the forward hatches," Creutz said. "He's going to see what he can do about a signal. He also wants permission to detach Funk and a couple of the others to see if they can get into the impeller room from that direction."

Ouvrard felt her stomach tighten. The silence from the impeller room implied that there were indeed no survivors.

But miracles *did* sometimes happen. "Confirm to Dierken that Funk is to concentrate on getting to the impellers," she told Creutz. "And get me an update on the team working on it from our side."

☆   ☆   ☆

For every second that Commander Metzger's com went unanswered, Travis estimated that his blood pressure went up another ten millibars.

Because, really, what the hell was he *doing*?

He was a spacer first class, a mere gravitics tech. Metzger was a commander, the tactical officer of an RMN battlecruiser. She had multiple years of experience stacked on top of multiple years of training. If she hadn't come up with this idea herself, how good could it possibly be? What was Travis doing here, anyway?

More to the point, what was he doing *here*?

Surreptitiously, guiltily, he looked past Donnelly at the rest of the cabin. It was small, though considerably larger than his own living area, with two racks, two lockers, and the fold-down desk/swivel chair combo where Donnelly was currently seated. Somewhat to his surprise, the racks weren't as tightly made as was required in the enlisted areas. There were also a few more personal touches in here than he'd expected: an intricate lace doily tacked to the front of one of the lockers, a small metal-mesh statuette on the shelf beside one of the racks, and a few small pictures fastened to the bulkhead at the head of the other rack. Travis wasn't at the right angle to see the subject of any of the pictures, and he knew far better than to move to a better vantage point.

For that matter, he knew far better than to move at all. This was officer country; more importantly, it was female officer country. An enlisted male shouldn't be here at all—

"Metzger."

Travis jerked, the movement nearly bouncing him away from the corner of the desk where he'd planted himself. On one level, he realized suddenly, he'd hoped the TO had already gone to sleep and *wouldn't* answer. In fact, it might be better to pretend they'd gotten Metzger's com by accident and forget the whole thing.

But he wasn't the one seated beside the intercom. Donnelly was.

"Commander, this is Lieutenant Donnelly," she said briskly. "I'm sorry to bother you, but I've just been offered an idea on how we might be able to save the miners and get to *Phobos* before she breaks up completely."

"Really," Metzger said, her voice neutral. "Let's hear it."

"Actually, Ma'am, the idea came from Spacer First Class Travis Long," Donnelly said. "I think he should be the one to explain it."

Travis felt his eyes go wide. Donnelly had promised to do the talking. Now she was flipping on him?

"Very well," Metzger said. "Spacer Long?"

Donnelly gestured Travis toward the microphone.

"Go," she ordered.

Travis took a deep breath. People were going to die out there, he reminded himself firmly. If this could help save some of them, it would be worth it.

"Yes, Ma'am," Travis said. "Here it is...."

He laid it out for her as quickly and concisely as he could. The fact that he'd already run through the explanation with Donnelly made it a bit easier. The fact that he was now talking to a *much* more senior officer made it a whole lot harder.

But finally, with a minimum of stuttering, he made it to the end. Bracing himself, he waited for the TO's inevitable scorn.

To his slightly confused disbelief, the scorn didn't come.

"Interesting," Metzger said instead. Her voice sounded distracted, as if she was only paying half attention to the conversation. Maybe that was why she hadn't jumped down his throat yet. "A nice bit of outside-the-line thinking."

"Thank you, Ma'am," Travis managed.

"I've done a quick feasibility check, Ma'am," Donnelly put in, rescuing him from the need to say anything else. "The numbers and geometry look good."

"Yes, I'm doing my own right now," Metzger said.

So *that* was what was holding the rest of her attention. Travis held his breath, wondering if the TO would find some flaw that neither he nor Donnelly had spotted.

"Looks good," Metzger said. "Looks very good. Excellent work, both of you. Stand by while I com the bridge."

There was a click—"Bridge; Metzger," Metzger said. "I need to talk to the captain."

Travis frowned. *Stand by* in com conversations usually meant being put on hold or muted out of the connection while a side conversation took place. Clearly, Metzger had missed hitting the proper key.

Fortunately, it could be done at either end. He reached for the switch—

And stopped as Donnelly caught his hand.

He started to speak, changed his mind as she flashed him a quick shake of her head. He nodded, and withdrew his hand. It was Metzger's mistake, after all, not his or Donnelly's.

And actually, it *would* be gratifying to get to hear the captain's reaction to his idea.

"This is the Captain," Davison's brisk voice came. "I thought you'd been sent off-duty, TO."

"I was, Sir," Metzger said. "But I've just been handed an idea on how to rescue both *Rafe's Scavenger* and *Phobos*, and I wanted to bring it to your attention at once. If we—"

"A moment, TO," Davison interrupted. "You were *handed* an idea?"

"Yes, Sir, by one of our gravitics techs, Spacer First Class Long. If we—"

"That's Spacer *Travis* Long?"

"Yes, Sir," Metzger said, her tone going a little odd.

"I see," Davison said with a grunt. "Very well. Continue."

"Yes, Sir," Metzger said. "Of the two ships in danger, *Phobos* is the most critical. If she's indeed suffered a hull harmonic catastrophe, there could be extensive damage and substantial continued danger to any remaining crew. Furthermore, even if we assume significant casualties, there are likely more survivors there than on *Rafe's Scavenger*."

"Are you suggesting we give up on *Rafe's Scavenger* and change course for *Phobos*?" Davison asked ominously. "Leaving *Rafe's Scavenger* to die?"

"Leaving *Rafe's Scavenger*, yes, Sir," Metzger said. "But not to die. Once we're on our new course we take one of *Vanguard*'s practice missiles, clear out the warhead space, and fill it with super-compressed oxygen tanks from our shuttles. Then, at the proper time, we fire the missile at *Rafe's Scavenger*, with a cutoff timer set to kill the missile's wedge at just the right moment."

"You must be joking, TO," cut in another voice—Commander Bertinelli. "That can't possibly work."

"I believe it can, Sir," Metzger said. "I've run the numbers and sent you the relevant plot. If we get the timing and vector right, the missile will end up at a zero-zero with them. All they need to do is go outside and bring in the tanks, and they'll be able to hold out until we can collect *Phobos*'s crew and return to them."

For a long moment there was silence. Then, there was the sound of someone clearing his throat. "Ingenious," Bertinelli said. "But it won't work. The geometry and timing will be almost impossible to get right. Even if you're lucky enough to get the missile there, it's way too big for the miners to get in through their hatchways."

"They won't have to bring in the whole missile," Davison murmured, his own voice thoughtful. "Mining ships have external grapples, maneuvering packs, and EVA carts designed for moving large chunks of rock around. If the missile gets close enough, they can remove the tanks and bring them inside." He gave a little snort. "*If* it gets close enough. The XO's absolutely right on that score."

"I think we can do it, Sir," Metzger said doggedly. "We've got timers that can be adjusted to the picosecond, and our position-ing and velocity numbers are precise enough to drop it within a hundred meters of the ship. And we've got a ninety-minute window to prep the missile."

"It's ingenious, I'll give you that," Davison said. "But it's also completely impractical. The operation will continue as planned."

Travis felt his breath catch in his throat. That was it? A single glance at the plot, and the captain was going to simply reject the idea?

Metzger was apparently thinking the same thing. "Sir, I strongly urge you to reconsider," she said carefully. "Whatever's happened to *Phobos*, her crew is almost certainly in serious trouble."

"Serious trouble is what we're trained for, TO," Davison said. "*Rafe's Scavenger*, on the other hand, is in a life-or-death crisis situation. As the XO says, and your assurances notwithstanding, successfully getting a missile to a zero-zero with *Rafe's Scavenger* would be borderline impossible. Worse, your plan depends on untrained miners' ability to handle their end of the operation. We don't even know if they're still able to receive word that a package is on its way, let alone in shape to retrieve the oxygen and bring it inside."

"Sir—"

"More importantly, our standing orders put civilian assistance above aid to other Navy or MPARS ships," Davison continued. "Those orders do not allow for playing unreasonable games with civilian lives. If *Phobos*'s crew has to spend a few more hours in the cold and dark, they'll just have to manage."

"Yes, Sir." Metzger paused. "If I may, let me offer an alternate suggestion. If we change course to *Phobos* right now, as per Spacer Long's plan—"

"As per *your* plan, TO," Davison interrupted.

"Excuse me, Sir?"

"I said as per your plan, TO," the captain repeated.

"Sir, I believe I mentioned this came from Spacer Long—"

"And I'm telling you it's *your* plan," Davison said. "No one else's. Now, you were saying?"

There was a brief pause.

"If we change course to *Phobos* right now, as per the plan," Metzger said, her voice suddenly cautious, "there should be time to launch the missile, confirm it's on the correct zero-zero vector, and also get an acknowledgment from *Rafe's Scavenger* before it's too late to reset course back to them."

"And after all that we'd still arrive before their air runs out?" Bertinelli countered. "I doubt that."

"It would work, Sir," Metzger insisted stubbornly. "It would require us to run the wedge at eighty-nine percent for about thirteen minutes. But it would get us there only eight minutes later than our current projected time."

"We're pushing our limits as it is," Bertinelli reminded her. "*And* theirs. Another eight minutes could kill them all."

"Not necessarily, Sir," Metzger said, her tone respectful but firm. "That deadline assumed they'd be running most of the time on their suits, without taking full account of the air left in the ship. They should have been able to get at least an extra hour before switching to suit air."

"Speculation," Bertinelli countered. "We can't afford to take the chance. Neither can they."

Travis felt a slow anger starting to burn his throat. It was one thing to consider a plan carefully and then make an informed decision. It was something else to dismiss that plan after barely a cursory glance. Especially when that hasty decision could mean death for dozens of men and women.

That had to be said. And if Metzger couldn't or wouldn't say it, he would have to. Bracing himself, he opened his mouth—

"No," Donnelly murmured in his ear.

Travis looked at her. The lieutenant was watching him, a tightness around her eyes. "There's no point," she whispered. "He's made his decision."

"Sir, I respectfully request you reconsider," Metzger said. But Travis could hear in her voice that she, too, knew the decision had been made.

"I appreciate your suggestion, Commander," Davison said. "Now, as has already been pointed out, you're off-duty. Get some sleep."

"Yes, Sir," Metzger said.

Travis looked at Donnelly, and for a moment their eyes met. Then, lowering her gaze, Donnelly tapped the intercom cut-off switch.

"Come on," she said. "Let's get out of here."

They were out of Donnelly's quarters and the spin section and back to the zero-gee core of the ship before she spoke again. "Interesting," she murmured. "I don't think I've ever seen the captain *or* the XO show that kind of fire."

"Fine time for it," Travis muttered.

And winced, wishing too late that he could call back the words. That wasn't how a spacer was supposed to talk about superior officers. "I'm sorry, Ma'am," he apologized.

"As you should be," Donnelly said severely. "Don't ever complain or backtalk behind someone's back, Long. You have a problem, you go to them, or you go up the chain of command, or you keep your mouth shut."

"Yes, Ma'am."

"Because the next person you pull that on likely won't be as forgiving as I am." She paused. "That being said, it *was* a good idea. I wish we could have seen if it worked."

"I guess we'll never know, Ma'am," Travis said. "But they were probably right. It probably wouldn't have."

"Don't," Donnelly snapped.

Travis flinched at the sudden anger in her voice. "Ma'am?"

"Never give up on an idea just because someone doesn't like it," she said, glaring at him. "Be persuaded by facts, or don't be persuaded at all."

"Unless I'm ordered to do so?" He grimaced. Again, the words had gotten out before he'd had time to properly think about them. "Sorry, Ma'am."

"You need to learn to watch your mouth, Spacer," Donnelly warned. "Military service is a game, with players and rules. Learn to play, or learn to hurt."

"I understand, Ma'am," Travis said between clenched teeth.

"I doubt it," she said. "But you'd better start. And for the record, along with being snide, that statement was also wrong. No one can order you to give up on your ideas. All they can order you to do is not act on them. Big difference. If the idea's good, people will eventually come around."

"Though not in this case."

Her lip twitched. "No, this one's time is past," she admitted. "The point I'm trying to make is not to give up on yourself."

"Yes, Ma'am," Travis said, feeling fractionally better. "I'll try."

"You do that." She hesitated. "*Phobos* is in for more trouble, isn't she?" she asked quietly.

Travis sighed.

"I'm hardly an expert, Ma'am. But everything I've read says

hull harmonic damage goes deep. If anything dangerous is still active in there, it could go at any time."

Donnelly exhaled a tired-sounding breath. "Then I guess it's time to start praying for miracles."

"Yes, Ma'am," Travis said. "I hope they can find one."

☆   ☆   ☆

"Well, it looks like *Vanguard*'s reached *Rafe's Scavenger*," Creutz said, peering at the single sensor monitor they'd managed to get up and running.

"Good," Ouvrard said. And well within the miners' oxygen countdown. At least those survivors had made it through this ordeal alive. "Have you heard anything new from the impeller crew?"

Creutz was opening his mouth to answer when the plasma still trapped in the impeller capacitors vented violently, slicing through the remaining bulkheads and exploding with blazing death through what was left of the ship.

Ouvrard had just enough time before the bridge disintegrated around her to wonder what the Board of Inquiry would say about her failure.

☆   ☆   ☆

Three days later, after the *Rafe's Scavenger* survivors had been delivered to Unicorn One, the official list of the *Phobos* dead was finally made available.

It was only then that Travis learned to his horror that Gunner's Mate Johnny Funk and Senior Chief Dierken, the two men responsible for saving his career from Lieutenant Cyrus, had been aboard the doomed sloop.

He didn't eat for a full day afterward. He didn't sleep for two days after that.

CHAPTER FIFTEEN

"ONE HUNDRED AND THIRTY men and women," Breakwater said, his voice rising in both volume and intensity. "One hundred and *thirty!*"

Winterfall winced. The Chancellor had a flair for the dramatic, and he was certainly pulling out all the dampers today.

Unfortunately, a volume that worked in the House of Lords assembly chamber was strikingly inappropriate here in the much smaller Cabinet meeting room. Even at the far end of the ornate table, seated in what Breakwater had described as the hot-seat chair, Winterfall found the Chancellor's thundering roar to be borderline painful.

Apparently, he wasn't the only one. "Please, My Lord," Prime Minister Davis Harper, Duke Burgundy, said. His face was screwed up in distress, hardly surprising given how much closer he was to Breakwater's auditory eruption.

But even at that, there was no hint of anger or even confrontation in his voice. Burgundy, the perpetual conciliator, was as much on his normal game as Breakwater was on his. "Be gentle to an old man's ears."

"Forgive me, Your Grace," Breakwater said, notching back his volume as he inclined his head toward the other. He'd made his point, and was ready now to cut back on the histrionics. "But I make no apology for my passion. A hundred and thirty good MPARS officers and enlisted have died. I, for one, want to find out what happened."

"And *I*, for one, would appreciate it if the Chancellor would spare us his crocodile tears," Minister of Defense Dapplelake said stiffly. "If he'll recall, from the very beginning of his ridiculous *Mars* proposal First Lord Cazenestro and I told his so-called Sanity Committee—" he flashed a look down the table at Winterfall "—that the plan was insane. Well, it was, and those *hogs* have now come home to root."

"You and the Admiralty signed off on Ashkenazy's certification that *Phobos* was ready for duty," Breakwater countered.

"You barely gave us enough time to examine his test results before insisting we do so," Dapplelake shot back.

"If you hadn't finished your analysis, why did you release the ship?"

"Because you'd been badgering us for weeks to do so."

"So you're saying that a little political pressure is enough for you to ignore your jobs and put the lives of over a hundred men and women in danger?"

"That's a lie!" Dapplelake snarled, leaping to his feet. "The Defense Ministry does *not* bow to pressure. We would never have confirmed certification if we'd had any indication that there was a problem."

"Please, My Lords, please," Burgundy said, holding out conciliatory hands toward both men, his voice and expression pained. "Men and women are lost. Can't you for once put aside your political differences out of respect?"

"I beg your pardon for my tone, Your Grace," Dapplelake ground out, his eyes still on Breakwater. "But I will not sit by and have the integrity of my people impugned. From everything we were given, *Phobos* was fully fit for duty."

"Please, My Lord," Burgundy repeated, fluttering the hand still stretched toward Dapplelake. "Let us be civil here."

Slowly, Dapplelake resumed his seat. "The fact of the matter, Your Grace, is that for the final two weeks my people were barred from certain areas of the ship, and denied access to some of the test documents. If anyone knew there was a problem, it was Ashkenazy and his people." He looked at Breakwater. "And the Chancellor and *his* people."

"That's a serious charge, My Lord," First Lord of Law Deborah Scannabecchi, Duchess New Bern, spoke up. It was the first word any of the other Cabinet ministers had ventured since the

Phobos debate began, Winterfall noted. Clearly, they were used to staying out of Breakwater's and Dapplelake's mutual lines of fire. "Have you any proof of this charge?"

"I believe I do, Your Grace," Dapplelake said. "That's why I asked Baron Winterfall to come before this body to answer some questions. With the Prime Minister's permission."

"Yes, of course," Burgundy said, eyeing Winterfall apprehensively. "Baron Winterfall, if you have light to shed on this matter, please do so."

"Yes, let's see what he has to say," Dapplelake seconded, his voice dark with brooding anticipation. "And when his presentation is finished, I have a few questions of my own to ask."

Winterfall braced himself. He didn't know exactly what Dapplelake was planning to ask, but he had little doubt as to what the nature of the questions was going to be. The seemingly never-ending game of political chess between the Chancellor and Defense Minister was heating up, and Dapplelake had determined it was time to clear some of the pawns off the board.

The first of those pawns being Winterfall.

He'd suspected something like this was on the horizon a few weeks ago when Dapplelake specifically invited him to attend *Phobos*'s commissioning ceremony. He'd known it for a certainty for the past month as he began to hear murmurs from others in the Lords that the Defense Minister was increasingly mentioning Winterfall's name in connection with the doomed ship. If he could make Winterfall the face of the disaster, it would damage any influence or credibility the young baron might still have, while delivering a warning to Chillon and the others lords who'd allied themselves with Breakwater on his quest to cut back the military's share of the Star Kingdom's budget and shift those resources to his own MPARS.

But there were things Dapplelake didn't know. Or more precisely, things that Dapplelake didn't know Breakwater knew. The Chancellor had set his side of the board carefully, up to and including dangling Winterfall and the rumor of blocked documents in front of his opponent, and Dapplelake had taken the bait.

Breakwater would have been the better target, of course. But Dapplelake had probably chosen Winterfall instead after deciding that the *Phobos* incident wasn't big enough to take down the Chancellor himself.

He was probably right on that score. Little did he know that the reverse wasn't true.

"Certainly, My Lord," Winterfall said. "A question, though, first, if I may?"

Burgundy gestured. "Proceed."

"Thank you." Winterfall looked at Dapplelake. "To clarify, My Lord: you had no idea at all that anything was wrong with *Phobos*?"

"None whatsoever," Dapplelake said firmly. "As I've already said, and as you're about to confirm, the Navy and Ministry were cut out of several crucial test areas."

"Yes, My Lord," Winterfall said, a sudden uncertainty trickling across his expectations. His question should have been a subtle warning to Dapplelake that Winterfall wasn't simply going to be rubber-stamping his accusations.

Only Dapplelake wasn't showing any awareness of that. In fact, as far as Winterfall could tell from the man's expression and body language, he was totally oblivious of the fact that he was walking into a trap. Had he suddenly lost his political skills?

Or did he genuinely not know the truth?

Out of the corner of his eye, Winterfall saw Breakwater's finger twitch with a signal to continue. The blood was in the water, and the Chancellor was eager to see his rival's humiliation in front of the entire Cabinet. The fact that a junior lord like Winterfall would be handling the knife would just add that much extra twist to the situation, as well as deflecting the bulk of the inevitable political fallout away from Breakwater's own backyard.

But if Dapplelake really didn't deserve the blame . . .

Winterfall squared his shoulders. He would wield the knife that Breakwater had given him, because the knife needed to be wielded. But not here. Not in front of Dapplelake's fellow cabinet members. "Your pardon, My Lord," Winterfall said, ducking his head toward the Defense Minister and then shifting his gaze to Burgundy. "Your pardon as well, Your Grace. As Lord Dapplelake said, I have information to present. But on further consideration, I believe it would be best for me to present it to you in a more private setting."

"No!" The half-muttered word seemed to burst of its own accord from Breakwater's lips. Winterfall winced, knowing without looking exactly the kind of glare the Chancellor was now sending in his direction.

It was, Winterfall realized later, a rare mistake on Breakwater's part. Without the Chancellor's unexpected reaction Burgundy probably would have turned down Winterfall's request and insisted he continue. Now, though, the Prime Minister sent a speculative look at Breakwater, flicked his eyes back to Winterfall, then sent another, longer look at the Chancellor. "I think that can be arranged," he said. "Perhaps you'd be kind enough to wait a few minutes after the meeting."

"It's rather unfair to Baron Winterfall to presume on his time," Breakwater put in, a bubbling anger just audible beneath the words. "I, for one, would like to hear what he has to say right now." He shot a warning look at Winterfall. "Especially given that any information about the *Phobos* disaster should be shared with the entire Cabinet, not spoken in secret to only one of the interested parties."

"I never suggested Baron Winterfall's information would be spoken in secret, Lord Breakwater," Burgundy said mildly. "But you make a valid point about other interested parties." He looked back at Winterfall. "Perhaps, My Lord, you'd be available to meet with the King and Earl Dapplelake at the palace this evening? At, say, eight o'clock?"

The ghost of old reflexive fears flashed across Winterfall's mind. Back when this *Mars* thing had first started, his unexpected invitation into the King's presence had been a strange and terrifying thought.

But not anymore. Not with three extra years of Breakwater's tutelage under his belt.

Now, he simply ducked his head again in acknowledgment, his brain spinning not with panic but with the straightforward task of recasting his presentation for the newly redefined audience.

"I would be honored, Your Grace," he said. "I'll look forward to the meeting."

"As will I," Burgundy said, an odd note to his voice. "Until this evening, then. You're now excused, with the Cabinet's thanks."

Slipping his tablet into its case, Winterfall left the room. He carefully avoided looking at Breakwater on his way out.

The Chancellor would understand that this was the right thing to do. Eventually.

Hopefully before he flayed Winterfall alive and hung his hide out to dry.

☆   ☆   ☆

Despite Burgundy's casual description, Winterfall hadn't really expected the meeting's participants to consist solely of himself, the King, and the Defense Minister.

He was right about that. Burgundy himself was present, of course, and so was Breakwater. The Chancellor seemed to have calmed down somewhat since the Cabinet meeting, but Winterfall could see he wasn't so much satisfied as he was withholding final judgment. The other two participants Winterfall had thought might be invited, First Lord of the Admiralty Cazenestro and Admiral Locatelli, were conspicuous by their absence. Apparently, Dapplelake had decided he didn't need to bring in any of his support staff on this.

The one person waiting in the Palace conference room who *was* a surprise was Crown Prince Edward. Winterfall hadn't even realized that Edward's ship, *Defiant*, was near Manticore at the moment, let alone that the Crown Prince might be invited to the meeting.

Still, Winterfall had faced the King without problem or trepidation. The Crown Prince couldn't be any worse.

"Thank you for meeting with us this evening, My Lord," the King said to Winterfall, his voice and manner as gracious as always, as he took his place at the head of the conference table. "We're eager to hear this story you find too sensitive even for the privacy of the Cabinet chamber."

"Thank you, Your Majesty," Winterfall said, bowing deeply across the table. "With your permission, I'd like to start the story with HMS *Phobos*'s departure for her posting in the Unicorn Belt. Two days later, with *Phobos* still en route, the battlecruiser *Vanguard*, which had been resting in Manticore orbit for several years, was suddenly loaded with new equipment and replacement parts and ordered to prepare for a voyage. The timing, plus the fact that *Vanguard* was also ordered to Manticore-B, seemed strangely coincidental, especially in retrospect after the incident of *Rafe's Scavenger*. I therefore decided to do some checking."

He paused for a breath, wondering if Dapplelake would call him on that. In fact, Winterfall had been only peripheral in the investigation, with Breakwater and his extensive network of contacts doing most of the heavy lifting. But if the Defense Minster knew that, he apparently didn't think it worth mentioning. "A search of the Navy and MPARS records, along with a conversation with a member of *Vanguard*'s crew, showed that—"

"A moment," Dapplelake interrupted. "On whose authority did you speak with any of *Vanguard*'s crew?"

"No authority was needed, My Lord," Winterfall said. "It was a family conversation with my half-brother, Spacer First Class Travis Uriah Long."

"I don't care who he is," Dapplelake growled. "Navy officers and crew are not permitted to speak on the record without express authorization from their CO."

"Did Spacer Long reveal anything that wasn't in official Navy records?" the King asked.

Winterfall hesitated. Technically, Travis had indeed said something Breakwater hadn't found in the record. But in the sense the King meant—"No, Your Majesty," he assured the monarch. "And as I understand naval regulations, family conversations that don't violate classification standards are exempt from the usual permission requirements."

Dapplelake harrumphed, but waved a hand. "Very well. Continue."

"A search of the records revealed that the orders for *Vanguard*'s new equipment had actually begun several weeks before *Phobos* was certified and commissioned," Winterfall said. "Again, the timing raised suspicions, so we looked deeper into the lists. Buried among the rest of the equipment was a full set of repair parts for *Vanguard*'s tractor system. A system that I'm told has been inoperable for most of the past decade." He looked squarely into Dapplelake's eyes. "A system that would be necessary for her to tow a crippled ship like *Phobos*."

The room went suddenly still. "What are you implying, My Lord?" Dapplelake demanded into the silence.

"I'm suggesting, My Lord," Winterfall said, "that elements within the Navy realized ahead of *Phobos*'s commissioning that there was a dangerous flaw in its design. Those same elements permitted the sloop to head out, knowing it would fail, and arranged for *Vanguard* to be in position to retrieve the soon-to-be crippled ship and bring it back to Manticore."

"You realize what you're saying," Dapplelake said, his voice dark. "You're accusing the Royal Manticoran Navy of deliberate, cold-blooded murder."

"Not at all, My Lord," Winterfall said hastily. "I have no doubt that those involved had no expectation that anyone would die.

There is some indication, in fact, that specific concerns about *Phobos*'s impeller ring were voiced early on, but were brushed aside by MPARS and the ship's designers. I think the plan was simply to allow *Phobos* to founder and be towed back in disgrace and humiliation. The project would be abandoned, and the remaining battlecruisers left intact."

"And then *Rafe's Scavenger* came onto the scene," Burgundy murmured.

"Exactly, Your Grace," Winterfall confirmed. "The miner's critical situation prompted *Phobos*'s captain to push her ship's capabilities to the point where the fatal hull harmonic broke her apart. The rest—" he grimaced "—we all know."

Again, silence descended on the room. Winterfall stole a sideways look at Breakwater. The Chancellor still wasn't happy. But at least he seemed to realize now that Dapplelake truly hadn't been involved. For whatever that was worth to him.

The King cleared his throat. "Who?"

"Who was the person who sat back and let it happen?" Winterfall shook his head. "I don't know, Your Majesty. I'll confess that—" *we* "—I assumed Earl Dapplelake had been aware of the problem and had turned a blind eye to it. But at the meeting this afternoon I realized he had, in fact, been kept completely in the dark. That was why I asked for a more private setting in which to lay out the situation."

"We appreciate your discretion," the King said. The lines in his face, Winterfall noted, seemed to have deepened in the past few minutes. "Is there more?"

Once again, Winterfall hesitated. Should he tell them that his brother had come up with a scheme that might have saved at least some of *Phobos*'s crew?

No, he decided. *Vanguard*'s official record listed that idea as having come from the ship's tactical officer, and claiming otherwise would look like bragging, if not outright perjury. "No, Your Majesty," he said. "That's all."

Across the table, Dapplelake stirred. "In that case, and with your permission, Your Majesty, I should like to be excused. I have an investigation to initiate, and I'd like to get started as soon as possible."

"Of course," the King said. "I'll look forward to hearing the results of your inquiries."

Dapplelake smiled, a small, brittle thing. "I'm sure you will, Your Majesty," he said. "I, of course, will not."

He turned to Winterfall; and to Winterfall's surprise, the other actually inclined his head in a bow. "Thank you for not automatically thinking the worst of me," he said. "Not everyone in the Lords would have been so courteous." He flicked a significant look at Breakwater.

"You're welcome, My Lord," Winterfall said, matching the other's tone. "I'm sorry to have been the bearer of such news."

Dapplelake inclined his head again. Then he bowed to the Crown Prince, Burgundy, and the King. He looked again at Breakwater, hesitating a split second before offering the Chancellor the same courteous nod, and left the room.

"Unless there's other business, I believe we're finished," the King said. "Once again, Baron Winterfall, we thank you for bringing this to light. You and Lord Breakwater are excused. Duke Burgundy, perhaps you'd be kind enough to give me an additional minute of your time."

Breakwater and Winterfall were halfway from the palace door to their cars before the Chancellor spoke. "Nicely done," he said, his words forming little clouds in the cool nighttime air. "Not only did you cut him off at the knees, but he even thanked you for the honor of permitting him to fall on his sword."

"He wasn't involved," Winterfall reminded him. "There's no reason for him to take the blame."

Breakwater snorted.

"Reason doesn't enter into it. Never has. He's still the Defense Minister, which means all responsibility ultimately lies at his door."

"*All* responsibility, My Lord?"

"Meaning?" Breakwater countered.

"Meaning there are persistent reports that the MPARS station on Gryphon ordered *Phobos* to get to *Rafe's Scavenger* first," Winterfall said. "If so—"

"No one would ever have given Captain Ouvrard such an order," Breakwater interrupted. "At worst, someone might have offered it as a suggestion."

"Perhaps," Winterfall said. "I'm just saying that, however it happened, there seems to be more than enough blame to go around."

Breakwater was silent for a few more steps.

"You have a conciliatory spirit, Gavin," he said at last. "In a job that involves the rescue of stray dogs, that can be helpful. In politics, it isn't."

Winterfall threw the other a sideways look. Was that a deliberate swipe at his mother's business?

"I'm just trying to find the truth, My Lord," he said, making a supreme effort to brush off the jibe.

"The truth is that Dapplelake will find whoever allowed *Phobos* to fly, and then he'll resign," Breakwater said tartly. "Right now, that's all the truth that matters."

Winterfall sighed. But Breakwater was probably right. The House of Lords, it had been said, was built on privilege and pride. Dapplelake's pride would dictate that he take the blame for his subordinates' actions.

"I wonder who Burgundy and the King will choose to replace him," Breakwater continued thoughtfully. "Well, no matter. Whoever it is won't have Dapplelake's stubbornness. Especially not after a scandal of this magnitude. No, I think we're on track to finally crank back the money and personnel sink that our illustrious Royal Manticoran Navy has become."

"Yes," Winterfall murmured. Fleetingly, he wondered what effect Breakwater's proposed budget slashing might have on his brother's own career.

But he couldn't afford to think that way. As always, it came down to the greatest good for the greatest number. The Navy had seen its day, and it was time for MPARS and other parts of the Star Kingdom to start getting their fair share of the pie.

Besides, from the way Travis had talked about the frustrations of life aboard *Vanguard* there was every chance he would simply serve out his five T-year hitch and get out. Whatever Breakwater was able to push through, Travis would be long gone before he was affected by any of it.

"In fact, it might be a good idea to sit down right now and draft a few proposals," Breakwater said into his thoughts. "We'll want to have something ready when Act Two of the *Phobos* scandal hits. I trust you had no further plans this evening?"

"No, My Lord, not at all," Winterfall assured him.

"Good," Breakwater said, pulling out his uni-link. "Castle Rock's still out of town. Let's see if Chillon and Tweenriver are available."

CHAPTER SIXTEEN

WITH A TIRED-SOUNDING SIGH, Burgundy settled into his overstuffed chair in the King's Sanctum and shook his head. "Well," he said.

And stopped.

For a moment his single word hung in the air like a piece of broken insulation floating uselessly in a service accessway. Edward looked surreptitiously at his father, wondering if the King would diplomatically suggest the Prime Minister offer something a bit more useful.

But he didn't. Nor, Edward suspected, would he. From everything Edward had heard, the Prime Minister had been doing this more and more lately: stopping to think in the middle of conversations and forgetting to start again.

Not that it was a huge loss in most of those conversations. Burgundy was a mousy sort, marginally competent at managing Cabinet meetings, but a far cry from the dynamic, forceful Prime Ministers who'd cracked the whip over the Lords during the reign of Edward's grandmother. Queen Elizabeth had known what she wanted, she'd found men and women who could made sure she got it, and the Lords be damned if they got in her way.

Burgundy, in contrast, was a doormat. Edward still didn't know how he'd managed to be elected Prime Minister, but he suspected it was a matter of Burgundy being no one's first choice but everyone's second.

The truly sad part was that he *had* been more alive once. Back in his early days in the Lords he'd done his share of wheeling and dealing, and had in fact been on Elizabeth's side on several of the reforms she's steamrolled through that body.

But the energy had long since faded away. Michael's ascent to the throne, and his calmer, less confrontational style of rule, had been matched by the fading of Burgundy's own fire. Perhaps Burgundy was one of those mirrorlike men who had no independent political personality, but who could only reflect the light from their leader, mentor, or monarch.

Rather like Winterfall, in fact. Even just seeing the young baron here tonight Edward had had the distinct sense that he was an eager young lord whom Breakwater would inspire, use, and then discard.

And when it was all over, Winterfall would probably even thank Breakwater for the experience.

Burgundy was still staring off into space, with no sign that he would be following up on his original comment in the near future. The King likewise seemed to have descended into a deep rumination. If there was to be a conversation, Edward decided, he would have to take the lead. Clearing his throat, he looked at Burgundy and raised his eyebrows.

"I presume, Your Grace, that you'll be able to persuade Dapplelake to stay on?"

Burgundy twitched, as if surprised at the break in the silence. "What? Oh. Yes, of course I'll try. But I may not succeed. Dapplelake has a great deal of stubborn integrity, and you could see that he was taking this whole thing personally."

"Then he needs to rethink his priorities," Edward said bluntly. "He's been the Navy's chief bulwark in the Lords against Breakwater's plans to take our ships away and turn the Navy into a social club. You saw him tonight—he was practically salivating at the prospect of getting that impediment out of his way."

"You have no idea, Edward," the King said tiredly. "He's already submitted a new proposal to sell off our battlecruisers, either to Haven or possibly at the kind of warship sale the Havenites are holding at Secour this fall."

"He isn't suggesting we take them to the Secour sale, is he?" Burgundy asked, sounding worried. "Those are all supposed to be surplus Havenite ships. I don't think they'd appreciate us crashing their party with our merchandise."

"That won't be an issue," Edward soothed. "The BCs have spent way too much time in mothballs. We couldn't possibly get them in shape—for anything—in less than a year."

Burgundy huffed out a breath. "Thank goodness. We can't afford to have a major trading partner mad at us."

"We'll be fine," Edward said absently, his mind suddenly racing. The Secour warship sale had been announced nearly five T-years ago, with the Republic of Haven sending out an open invitation to all interested parties to attend, examine, and hopefully buy. The Republic's purpose in holding the sale appeared to be twofold: first, to clear out some unneeded but still serviceable warships; and second, to provide a reason for a general get-together of the systems in the region.

The invitation had made it clear that Haven was serious about having as large an attendance as they could get for the proposed month-long meeting. So serious, in fact, that they'd offered to send fast couriers to transport interested parties whose worlds didn't have hyper-capable ships of their own.

Naturally, Breakwater had moved swiftly to crush any interest in the meeting, arguing that the last thing the RMN needed was more obsolete ships for its trophy room. But for once his tactic had misfired. King Michael had simply ignored the ship-sale aspect of the meeting when presenting it to Parliament, focusing instead on the twin virtues of hospitality and neighborliness. In the end, not only did Parliament vote to send *Diactoros*, one of the Star Kingdom's two fast couriers, to the Secour meeting, but also authorized the RMN to offer passage to interested governments in Ueshiba and Minorca, systems too far from Haven to make the Republic's own transport offer practical. *Diactoros* and her escort, the heavy cruiser *Perseus*, had left on their grand circle tour nearly eight months ago, to the small notice of Parliament and the muted annoyance of a Chancellor distracted by the nearing climax of the *Mars* project.

Given the final debacle of that project, and the subsequent sharpening of both Breakwater's attention and his attitude, it was doubtful the Chancellor would sit idly by if the Navy asked to send a third ship to the Secour meeting.

Unless he thought it would get him something he wanted...

Burgundy and the King had settled into a slightly desultory conversation about ship sales and Manticoran security by the time Edward had the details worked out. He waited for Burgundy to finish his current point, then cleared his throat. "Your Grace; Your Majesty," he said. "If I may, I have an idea."

His father gestured. "Please."

"Let's start back at the beginning of the *Mars* project," Edward said. "Why was that initiated in the first place, especially given that what Breakwater actually wanted was system patrol craft? *Mars* was cut up because she had two reactors and two impeller rings, and we can't build either of those technologies. Every impeller and shipboard reactor in the Star Kingdom has been imported from the League, and they're damned expensive."

"Indeed they are," Burgundy agreed with a wry smile. "We really should learn how to build them ourselves."

Edward inclined his head. "Exactly."

Burgundy's smile vanished. "You're joking."

"Not at all," Edward assured him, stealing a quick glance at his father. The King was watching him closely. "The technology is complex, but well-known. There's no reason in principle we couldn't set up our own manufacturing facilities. Once we have those, we can make any ships we want—system patrol craft, miners, merchants, or more warships."

"With all due respect, Your Highness, this isn't exactly a new proposal," Burgundy pointed out. "Dapplelake has suggested it on more than one occasion. The problem isn't the technical aspects, but the time and the necessary expertise. Not to mention the start-up money."

"Which we have plenty of," Edward said. "Manticore, Limited's reserves are more than enough to cover both the R and D and the actual plant manufacture."

"Manticore, Limited's reserves are a year and a half away," the King reminded him. "The way things are going, even if we sent off for it tomorrow there's every chance the money would arrive just in time to watch the last battlecruiser being cut up for scrap."

"And we *couldn't* send off for it tomorrow," Burgundy added. "Not the kind of funds you're talking about. Not without approval from Parliament."

"Which is why we need to lay the groundwork first," Edward said. "What neither of you has said so far, but which all of us are undoubtedly thinking, is that building an impeller manufacturing plant for the handful of ships the Star Kingdom needs would be like creating an automated fifty-ton hammer to crack walnuts. Even at the prices the League charges, it's still more cost-effective to import the nodes and reactors. *But.*"

He lifted a finger in the air. "What if we were able to build ships, not just for us, but for the entire region?"

He had, he decided, seen more enthusiastic responses in a fish tank. For a moment both men just looked at him, then exchanged a look between themselves, then turned back to him. "Haven's already got the infrastructure to do that," the King pointed out. "But all right, let's think it through. Assuming we could find the necessary people and train them to this sort of thing, how do you propose to induce our neighbors to buy from us instead of Haven or the Solarians?"

"Step one: we see what's selling," Edward said. At least neither of them had dismissed the idea out of hand. "The Secour sale is the perfect opportunity. We send a team to see what Haven's offering and what the customers are looking to buy.

"Step two: once we have that, we dazzle them with what *we* can do. One of our ships, *Casey,* is supposed to be undergoing a refit, though Breakwater's interference has kept the work in an on-again, off-again limbo. I propose we not only put the refit on track again, but that we pull out all the stops and make her the most advanced light cruiser anyone in this neighborhood has ever seen.

"Step three: once *Casey* is up and running again, we send her on a tour of the region and drum up some business. Part of our pitch will be that, unlike Sol or Haven, we won't have simply a limited selection of stock ships, but can custom-design whatever the buyer wants. By the time the funds and equipment arrive from Sol for our new node and reactor facilities, we'll hopefully have enough people trained and enough orders to get the thing rolling."

"I don't know," Burgundy said doubtfully. "Even the best-case scenario will have us in a financial hole for several years. If the orders don't come in, we'll never be out of it."

"Yes, there are risks involved," Edward said, forcing patience into his voice. Did Burgundy not have even a *spark* of his old fire left? "But if we don't move forward, we fade away. If our fathers and grandfathers hadn't been willing to take risks, none of us would be here in the first place."

Burgundy's face was screwed up with uncertainty. "I don't know." He lifted a hand toward the King. "Your Majesty?"

"It *is* a risk," the King agreed. "But Edward's right. Like all organisms, we either grow or die."

"The Lords won't go for it," Burgundy warned.

"Not if we feed them the whole thing at once," the King agreed. "I presume you have a plan to cover that, Edward?"

"I do, Your Majesty," Edward said. "We propose sending another team to Secour, but we frame it as an enquiry into whether or not there's a market for used battlecruisers."

"Is Haven even sending a battlecruiser?" Burgundy asked. "I remember the heavy cruiser *Péridot* being the biggest thing on the sale list."

"Doesn't matter what they're bringing," Edward said. "We can still use it as our excuse."

"At least to Breakwater," Burgundy said. "But the rest of the Lords aren't nearly as committed to that course. What would we tell *them*?"

"You're right, the BC story should be our and Breakwater's little secret," Edward said, frowning with thought.

"We've already sent out *Diactoros* and *Perseus*," the King pointed out. "What happens if the Minorcans, say, decide to buy one of the Havenite ships?"

"Right," Edward said, nodding as he saw where his father was going. "We tell the Lords it occurred to us that we'd sent only one escort ship with *Diactoros*, and that we wanted to offer an escort to any of the passengers we ferried to Secour who wants to ride home in a new ship."

"I think we can sell that," the King said. "And of course, Haven shouldn't care that we've sent two delegations."

"Not at all," Edward agreed. "All we have to do is show up and smile."

"And *not* tell them we're hoping to cut into their future business," the King said pointedly.

Edward winced. "Yes, we'll want to make *very* sure that whoever we send doesn't mention that."

"Why do any of our people need to know at all?" Burgundy asked. "Can't they just take detailed notes on the ships being offered?"

"Because they'll do a better job if they know what they're

looking for," Edward said. "As a corollary, whatever ship we send has to be loaded with as many experts as we can squeeze aboard without Breakwater and his cronies noticing and getting suspicious."

"Who are you going to get to assemble this group?" Burgundy asked. "I presume you won't be doing that all by yourself."

"No, I'll definitely need help," Edward agreed. "First Lord Cazenestro or Admiral Locatelli are the logical choices, but their daily activities are too public. A single red flare, and Breakwater would be all over it. I need someone who's knowledgeable but farther off Parliament's radar. That's why I was thinking Commodore Kiselev."

"Who's he?" Burgundy asked.

"The current CO of Casey-Rosewood," Edward said, "which means he's pretty much invisible except at budget time. Between the two of us, we know most of the officer corps personally. And with his access to Casey-Rosewood's records—not to mention the whole range of BuPers's files—we can also look for talented POs and enlisted to round out the crew."

"And we sell this to Breakwater as testing the waters for a sale?" Burgundy wrinkled his nose. "I don't know. If he catches on to what you're doing, I'm not sure even your status will be enough to protect you."

"True," the King said. "Which is why Edward will be staying completely away from this."

Edward spun back to his father, feeling his mouth drop open. "*What?* No."

"It's not open to debate, Edward," the King said firmly. "You can get the ball rolling, but after that you're out. You're the Crown, and the Crown has to pick and choose how and where it gets involved in politics."

Edward hissed softly between his teeth. This was *his* idea, damn it. Not only that, but this was the best hope for the Navy's continued survival. He *had* to be involved.

But he knew an order when he heard one. Besides, frustrating or not, his father was right. "Understood," he said. "I have business tomorrow at Casey-Rosewood anyway. I'll speak with Kiselev then and see if he's game to handle this."

"And then you'll return to your ship."

"I will, Your Majesty," Edward promised.

"Very well." The King looked back and forth between them. "Then I believe we're finished here. Davis, you'll talk to Dapplelake first thing tomorrow?"

"Yes, Your Majesty," Burgundy promised. "I presume I can add your weight to my arguments?"

"Absolutely," the King assured him. "Make sure he knows his resignation will *not* be acceptable to the Crown."

"I'll do my best." With an effort, Burgundy worked his way out of the confines of his chair. "But as I said, he's a very stubborn man." He bowed to the King, then Edward. "Good evening, Your Majesty; Your Highness."

Edward waited until the other had left the room. "To coin a phrase, Dad, this is one royal mess," he said.

"You don't know the half of it," his father said. "Breakwater was bad enough on his own. But with Winterfall in his pocket—" He shook his head.

Edward frowned. "*Winterfall*? You're joking."

"One would think so, wouldn't one?" Michael said ruefully. "But whether Breakwater was simply lucky or whether he saw something in Winterfall that no one else did, his new protégé has suddenly blossomed into someone who needs to be watched."

Edward shook his head. "Sorry, but I don't see it. He looks to me like just another of Breakwater's—what did you call them once? Sock puppets?"

"That's the term," Michael said. "And I hope you're right. The Star Kingdom can't afford another influential politician who truly believes the universe is a safe and cozy place. You can trust Commodore Kiselev?"

"Absolutely," Edward assured him. "He was my division CO on *Bellerophon* when I was young and green, and he pretty much took me under his wing. We'd probably have been closer friends if we hadn't both been making so damn sure we didn't run afoul of the rules against fraternization. On top of which, of course, was his concern that he didn't look like he was sucking up to his future monarch."

Michael nodded. "I remember those letters you sent. I was just wondering if you might have grown apart."

"In distance, yes," Edward said. "In attitudes, no. I should have at least a preliminary answer from him before Captain Davison's knighting ceremony on Sunday."

"Good." The King made a face. "Hardly seems something we should be honoring him for, does it?"

"He *did* save eight civilians," Edward pointed out. "These days, that all it takes to be considered a hero."

"I suppose," Michael said with a sigh. "It's a shame the geometry didn't work out for his tactical officer's missile idea."

"Probably just as well he didn't try it," Edward said. "The chances were pretty slim; and even if it *had* worked, Breakwater would probably have screamed for a demotion on the grounds that he wasted an expensive missile in a noncombat situation."

Michael snorted. "I still can't believe that's an official Defense Ministry policy."

"Yet another cost-saving measure we can thank Breakwater for." Edward stood up. "And now, with your permission, I need to go. Cynthia will have the kids in bed by now, and I promised her we'd spend an actual evening together, with grown-up conversations and everything."

"Of course, and do give her my love," the King said. "I don't know if I've mentioned this lately, Edward, but I think your grandfather's stipulation that the Crown be married to a commoner has worked out extraordinarily well in your case."

"She *is* a gem, isn't she?" Edward agreed with a smile. "Give my regards to Mary."

"I will," Michael promised. "We'll see you on Sunday. And let me know how it goes with Kiselev."

CHAPTER SEVENTEEN

METZGER LOOKED UP from the tablet to the man gazing stolidly at her from across the desk. "You've got to be kidding," she said.

"Not at all," Kiselev said, his eyes boring into hers with uncomfortable intensity. "I trust you noticed the part wherein, if you agree, you'll be promoted to commander and replace Alex Thomas as *Guardian*'s XO?"

"Oh, yes, I saw that," Metzger murmured, the universe seeming to spin around her head. It was like a dream come true.

A whole cluster of dreams, actually. To finally make full commander, to be assigned as a ship's executive officer, *and* to actually head off on a voyage that would take her outside the somewhat claustrophobic confines of the Star Kingdom—any one of those by itself would have been enough to make her day. Or her week, or her whole year.

And all she had to do was in exchange was do a quiet end run around Parliament and the anti-RMN Lords like Earl Breakwater.

Come to think of it, that actually counted as another plus.

"You're sure Captain Eigen isn't going to make a stink about us stocking his ship with new people?" she asked. "Losing his XO and half his officer complement could be taken as a pretty hefty slam."

"No, no, he's already aboard with this," Kiselev assured her. "I take it you haven't actually met the man?"

"Just briefly, and all at the pleasantries level."

"Well, you'll like him," Kiselev assured her. "He's sharp and cool-headed, and as passionately dedicated to the Navy and the Star Kingdom as anyone you could find."

"And apparently doesn't mind playing his cards under the table."

"We aren't doing anything under the table," Kiselev protested mildly. "*Guardian*'s XO was slated for rotation to a dirtside command anyway, and most of the other officers who are being swapped out are on equally reasonable career tracks. Breakwater can look as close as he likes, and it'll still come up looking clean." He shrugged. "And of course Admiral Locatelli will be there to soothe any questions or concerns that anyone *does* come up with."

"Assuming he's still System CO when the dust settles," Metzger warned. "From what I hear, Dapplelake's going through the upper ranks with a torch and pitchfork."

"Locatelli will survive," Kiselev said. "Wherever the *Phobos* communication breakdown happened, it won't have been at Locatelli's end. He's too good an officer to play fast and loose with vital information."

"Until now," Metzger murmured.

"Not really," Kiselev said. "Remember, every scrap of data you collect at Secour will be duly and legally turned over to Parliament. There's nothing underhanded about this." He shrugged. "It's just that Parliament may have a—shall we say—slightly different interpretation of why that data was gathered."

"Understood." Not that Breakwater would see it that way, of course. But the ostensible purpose for this trip would play to the Chancellor's goals, and it was amazing how wishful thinking could distract even the smartest people. "When is this all slated to happen?"

"It'll be a gradual procedure," Kiselev said. "Figure three and a half months to get to Secour, with the meeting and sale starting in six, and we have a couple of months to get everyone aboard *Guardian*. Plus a little extra time to let the officers and crew work up before you head off into the universe."

The last few words came out rather wistfully, and Metzger felt a twinge of guilt. Few of the RMN's current officers or enlisted had ever been outside the Manticore system, and she could understand Kiselev's quiet regret that he wouldn't be going along. "Look at the bright side," she offered. "If this works, maybe you'll get to be the one to take *Casey* around to show everyone in a couple of years."

Kiselev gave her a lopsided smile. "Is it that obvious?"

"We all want to go," she said quietly. "I was just lucky in the draw this time."

"Hardly," Kiselev assured her. "That idea of yours—that supply missile thing?—was brilliant. I've reviewed the data, and I still think Davison should have taken the shot."

Metzger's twinge of guilt deepened. She still didn't know why Davison had insisted on crediting that idea to her instead of Spacer Long, despite her objections. But she and the entire bridge crew had heard him enter it into his log, and they all knew the quiet hell there would be to pay if any of them contradicted his version of events.

She'd heard later that the captain had written a vaguely worded commendation into Long's record. Hardly a sufficient acknowledgment for the boy's ingenuity.

But maybe she could do something right now to help the balance things out. "What about enlisted?" she asked. "You going to leave *Guardian*'s crew intact, or bring in new spacers and noncoms?"

"It'll be a mix," Kiselev said. "Again, we're looking for people with particular expertise in their areas."

"And who can keep their mouths shut?"

"Not necessarily," Kiselev said. "It'll only be the senior officers who know the real mission. Why, do you have someone you'd like to see aboard?"

"I do," Metzger said. "Spacer First Class Travis Long."

"Travis *Long*?" Kiselev echoed, frowning. Swiveling around in his chair, he started punching keys on his terminal.

"Yes," Metzger said, thinking furiously. Throwing Long's name into the hat had been an impulse. Now she needed to come with some logic to back it up. "He's quite good at his job," she said. "He's also quick on his feet in a crisis. There was an EVA accident aboard *Vanguard*, and he pitched right in with the rescue when one of the gravitics techs got blown off the hull."

"I see," Kiselev said absently as he peered at his display. "Yes, I thought I recognized that name. Did you know he originally started out training as an impeller tech?"

Metzger frowned. Normally, if a recruit washed out of a specialty, he got dumped into the bosun's mate slot, and that was that. "No, I didn't," she said. "What happened?"

"Not what you're thinking," Kiselev said, sounding oddly evasive. "Let's just say his instructors weren't happy with him."

"With *him*? Or with his work?"

"With him personally," Kiselev said. "That's really all I can say." He was silent another moment. "Interesting. I notice that Long has also had a small run-in with another of our proposed *Guardian* officers. Marine Colonel Jean Massingill, back when she was head of the boot camp section."

"So we *will* be taking some Marines?" Metzger asked. "I assumed we'd save all the rack space for your analysts."

"I wish we could," Kiselev said. "But regs say you have to have at least three Marines aboard for security." He gestured to his display. "In Massingill's case, we get a sort of double value. Her husband is a former League yard dog and one of the best ship experts we have. On top of that, the colonel herself has had some disagreements with Locatelli lately, and I get the feeling he'd like to have her out of his sight for a while."

"So sending them both will be a win for everyone."

"So it would seem," Kiselev said. "Interestingly enough, one of her first frictions with the Admiralty was a few years ago, and seems to have been in the wake of her run-in with your same Spacer Long."

"Really," Metzger murmured. Kiselev, Massingill, and Metzger herself, all senior officers with private stories tucked away concerning Spacer Travis Long. Pretty rarefied atmosphere for a lowly spacer who'd been in for such a short time.

"But that's all beside the point," Kiselev continued. "The point was that his false start into impellers means Long has some basic knowledge and training in two different fields. That's rare for an enlisted of his rate."

"Which might make him useful for our purposes," Metzger pointed out.

"Agreed," Kiselev said. "I'll see what I can do. Anyone else you'd recommend?"

"Our aft weapons officer, Lieutenant Lisa Donnelly," Metzger said. If she was going to reward Long for his idea, she might as well go all in and give Donnelly similar points for cutting through the chain of command and bringing him to her attention while there was still time to do something. "I can probably come up with a few more, depending on how many people you want to shuffle around."

"We'll see," Kiselev said, making a note on his tablet. "So: you, Long, and Donnelly. Okay, I'll get the ball rolling, and you can expect your orders within the next few weeks."

"Yes, Sir," Metzger said as they both stood and shook hands across the desk. "Thank you."

"No thanks needed," Kiselev assured her. "You've earned it."

It was only later, as Metzger headed back to Landing for Captain Davison's knighting ceremony, that she began to have second thoughts about tossing Long's and Donnelly's names into this slightly clandestine operation. True, it would give them the rare chance to do a real spaceflight. But if Breakwater got wind of the real purpose of the trip, the two young people would be right there with her and Captain Eigen in the center of the Chancellor's laser sights.

Still, for all Breakwater's legendary volume and bombast, there probably wouldn't be much he could do to any of them. The worst that could happen would be that they all might be demoted or shunted off to exile on Gryphon for a while. No, the probable rewards definitely outweighed the possible risks.

And really, certain parts of Gryphon were said to be quite nice.

☆　　☆　　☆

Captain Wolfe Guzarwan was halfway through his thick, spice-rubbed steak when a small plastic rectangle came sailing through the open door of *Fenris*'s wardroom and landed neatly between his plate and his pitcher of margaritas. "What's this?" he asked, peering down at it.

"Your invite to the ship sale," Dhotrumi said, a satisfied grin plastered across his face as he stepped into the wardroom. "A genuine Ueshiba governmental ID card, with all the trimmings."

"Genuine, huh?" Guzarwan said. Wiping his fingers on his napkin, he picked up the card and looked more closely. Sandwiched between thin sheets of translucent plastic was a neat array of embedded chips and circuitry. "I thought you said the IDs from that merchantman were too damaged to get anything from."

"*Vachali* said they were too damaged," Dhotrumi corrected snidely. "But Vachali doesn't know squat about things that don't go boom or bang."

"I wouldn't make fun of the colonel's limited range of expertise if I were you," Guzarwan warned. "So this will pass as real?"

"It'll get you in at the front of the line," Dhotrumi assured him. If the implied threat of Vachali's inflated self-importance was worrying him, he was keeping it a dark secret. "'Course, I don't know if anyone on Secour's ever even—"

"Anyone on *Marienbad*," Guzarwan corrected. "Secour is the system, Marienbad is the planet."

"Yeah, thanks, Professor," Dhotrumi said with an air of strained patience. "Let's try it again. I don't know if anyone anywhere *in* Secour has ever met someone from Ueshiba, let alone scanned one of their IDs. That includes Marienbad, random asteroids, comets, and meteors, and possibly hypothetical space monkeys living on any or all of the system's three suns. That better?"

"Wonderfully better," Guzarwan assured him, mentally shaking his head. One of these days Dhotrumi was going to go smart-ass on the wrong person, and end up picking his teeth out of the nearest bulkhead. "I'm more worried about the Havenites calling scam than the Secourians," Guzarwan said.

"Doesn't matter *who* looks at it," Dhotrumi insisted. "It'll get you in just fine. Anyway, now that I've got the coding I can make more. How many do you want?"

Guzarwan wiggled the ID slowly between his fingers. "I think this will do."

Dhotrumi's eyes narrowed. "*One* ID? I thought we were going after the cruiser *and* the battlecruiser."

"We are," Guzarwan said. "Well, maybe one more. Yes, make it one more ID. Then you can concentrate on working up a few uniforms."

"Uniforms," Dhotrumi said, his voice gone flat. "Let me guess. You've changed the plan again."

"*Our* part, yes," Guzarwan said. "Your part, no. As long as you can crack the Havenite Navy's start-up procedures, you're fine. You'll just follow Vachali and do what he tells you."

"I can hardly wait," Dhotrumi said sourly. "How many uniforms do you want?"

"Let's say twenty Republic of Haven Navy and twenty Cascan Defense Force," Guzarwan said. "Make it a mix of ranks."

Dhotrumi blinked. "Twenty *Cascan* uniforms?"

"Twenty Cascan uniforms," Guzarwan confirmed. "You've got the specs our clients sent us, right?"

"Right," Dhotrumi said uncertainly. "It's just . . . *Cascan*?"

"Because they've also assured me that the Cascans will be at Secour in force," Guzarwan continued. "Apparently, Haven already has one sale in the box."

"I hope it's not the cruiser," Dhotrumi muttered.

"On the contrary," Guzarwan corrected. "We very much hope it *is* the cruiser." He pointed a finger at Dhotrumi. "The only question is whether you think Mota and his team are up to cracking a warship. If they're not, you're going to have to do both of them."

"Mota will do fine," Dhotrumi said. "We know from the sale list that the cruiser's an *Améthyste* class, and I've got all the back doors for those. Everything else is just access and lockdown codes, and he can handle those."

"Assuming the Havenites haven't found the back doors and cleared them out," Guzarwan warned.

Dhotrumi waved a hand. "No problem—they'll have left a few ghosts behind. People never get everything. Yeah, Mota can handle the cruiser." His mouth twisted sideways. "The real question is whether Vachali can have Kichloo and his team ready to handle their half of the boom and bang stuff."

"They'll be ready," Guzarwan said. "Vachali has enough people to pick from, and they've got six more months to train and drill."

"Yeah," Dhotrumi said, not sounding convinced. "I hope that's enough."

Guzarwan eyed him. "You got a problem I should know about?"

Dhotrumi's shoulders hunched briefly. "I'm just thinking, Cap'n. Far as I know, no one's ever tried a stunt like this before. And that was when we were just gonna grab *one* ship. Now we're talking two of them."

"You're thinking about it the wrong way," Guzarwan soothed. On one level, it was ridiculous to have to soothe a pirate. But system hackers like Dhotrumi tended to be nervous types, and Guzarwan had learned over the years that this was the way to calm them down and get them back to their jobs. "Don't think about the problems. Think about what this score will do for us. With two new warships—"

"Two *used* warships."

"Two *extra* warships," Guzarwan said, feeling his patience starting to thin. Nervous *and* pedantic; and meanwhile, his steak was getting cold and his margaritas were getting warm. "You just worry about cracking the impeller and command systems. We'll do the rest."

"Yeah," Dhotrumi muttered. "I just hope the Havenites or Secourians don't have anything that can chase us. Because I already told you that we'll never get the weapons up and running in time to be of any use. I told you that, right?"

"Don't worry about pursuit," Guzarwan said. "We'll have our wedges up before any of the other ships even know there's a problem." He smiled tightly. "You ever see what a wedge does to an unprotected ship?"

Dhotrumi winced. "No."

"I'll make sure you're on the bridge for at least one of them," Guzarwan promised. "It really is a sight to see."

"And we'll do all of them? Haven's *and* Secour's?"

"And everyone else's," Guzarwan promised. "Every last one."

He gestured toward the door. "Now if you don't mind, I have food that needs to be attended to. Get started on that other ID and my forty uniforms. I want them ready before we raise the Warshawskis and head for Secour."

BOOK THREE

1533 PD

CHAPTER EIGHTEEN

LIKE NIGHT AND DAY was one of those figures of speech that Travis had grown up with, along with everybody in the Star Kingdom and probably every human being in the Diaspora. It was pervasive, quoted way too often, and aside from literal night and day he'd long since concluded that the term was hyperbole, a lazy choice of words, or both.

His life aboard *Vanguard* had certainly been a long, slow slide into night. With a few exceptions the battlecruiser's officers and petty officers had seemed placid and coasting, with their priorities more on making life run smoothly than making sure one of His Majesty's warships stayed as close to fighting trim as possible. The enlisted were even worse, with on-duty hours spent moving at half-speed—or avoiding work altogether—and off-duty ones filled with gambling, stealing or repurposing official ship's equipment, and engaging in other activities he didn't even want to think about.

And drinking. The drinking had particularly rankled. RMN rules put strict limits on the amount of alcohol available aboard, but that never seemed to stop anyone.

It had often made Travis feel like he was literally under siege on his own ship. He would be at the terminal in his section, trying to study toward his gravitics system operator rating, while drunken shouts and laughter went on outside his door. Every third day, it seemed, he would come upon a job that had been logged as completed, only to find it not only not finished but barely even begun. Reporting it to Craddock or Bowen seldom did any good, and by his third month aboard he'd learned that if he wanted those jobs completed his only practical recourse was to finish them himself.

And at least twice a day he found himself dodging, kicking, or getting slammed into by cleaning and damage-control remotes that had been rigged for jousting, racing, demolition derbies, or hide-and-seek in the service tubes and accessways. Often in tubes and accessways that should have been cleaned by those selfsame remotes, but clearly hadn't been.

Esterle's accident with the gravitic array, and the subsequent halfhearted investigation had set his teeth on edge. The *Phobos* incident, and the emotional gut-punch of losing the two men who had put themselves on the line to save him from Lieutenant Cyrus's vendetta, had all but sealed the black sense of frustration and despair that had been gradually settling in around him. It had gone so far that when his half-brother Gavin had come to him after *Vanguard*'s return to Manticore and asked about the disaster, Travis had told him that as soon as his five T-years were up he would be out.

It was a thought he'd never before even dared to put into mental words, let alone audible ones, and it was as soul-crushing an admission as anything he'd experienced aboard the ship. It was a statement of defeat, a recognition that the glowing life of Naval service he'd envisioned for himself hadn't happened.

He hadn't fitted into the world of his childhood and youth. Now, it was clear that he didn't fit into the Navy, either.

And then, two months after *Phobos*, he'd been promoted to petty officer third class and transferred to the destroyer HMS *Guardian*.

Night, and day.

Vanguard's officers had been soft and lax. *Guardian*'s officers were tough and demanding. Not in the unthinking, uncaring martinet way that Travis remembered from some of his drill instructors at Casey-Rosewood, but in the make-damn-sure-the-job-gets-done way. More than that, they operated according to the rules and regs, just the way Travis had hoped for when he first joined up. With *Guardian*'s officers, everyone always knew exactly where they stood and what was expected of them.

At the same time, running parallel with that theoretically rigid attitude was a carefully tailored flexibility that might almost have been mistaken for laxness. Failures were spotted and the guilty parties properly taken to task, but not every failure made it into the official record. Minor problems arising from ignorance or inexperience were simply corrected, with a stern lecture but no permanent consequences. Only when the lesson failed to take root did the official hammer come down on the perpetrator, with the second lecture often laced with some of the most creative invective Travis had ever heard.

But in Travis's experience, that second discipline was seldom needed. As with *Vanguard*'s enlisted, *Guardian*'s crew seemed to take their cue from the officers' standards and attitude. Captain Eigen set the bar high, and his people responded in kind.

It was a command philosophy that saved Travis's neck in more ways than one. His promotion to petty officer had put him in official command of the destroyer's gravitics techs—all two of them—and the casual rule-breaking that had been the norm on *Vanguard* would have driven him insane with a losing effort to keep order. On *Guardian*, though, the techs were competent, respectful of authority—even Travis's—and adhered to the regs well enough that their occasional lapses weren't too hard to overlook.

Especially since Travis himself made plenty of mistakes in his first weeks, most of them minor, all of them frustrating. Again, *Guardian*'s unofficial patience level came to his rescue, as both the bosun and the lieutenant in charge of the destroyer's electronics exercised the same tough patience with him that he was learning to exercise with his subordinates. Slowly, under their tutelage, he learned to strike the same delicate balance they did.

The crew wasn't composed of robots, of course, and there were still plenty of hijinks during off-duty hours. But again unlike *Vanguard*, everyone seemed to understand that there were lines they weren't to cross, and they mostly stayed behind them.

And as for his efforts toward his gravitics specialist rating...

☆　☆　☆

"There," Lieutenant Ioanna Kountouriote said, jabbing her slightly crooked forefinger at the center gravitics display. "Did you see it?"

"Yes, Ma'am," Travis managed, fighting back the sudden bout of nausea that had hammered across him as the ship crossed the Alpha wall back into N-space. He'd experienced this once before, back when *Vanguard* did her microjump between Manticore-A and Manticore-B, and at the time he'd hoped that the severity of the sickness was at least partially due to the crossing-the-wall hazing he and the other first-timers had also been going through.

But it was just as bad the second time as it had been the first. At least this time he'd known enough to adjust his meal schedule so that his stomach would be empty, which relieved him of the worry that he was about to flood CIC with yuck.

Adding to the aggravation was the fact that Kountouriote and the other officers and ratings around him seemed completely unfazed by the experience. He hoped they were just faking it.

"That was the secondary gravitic ripple coming from the energy bleed off our Warshawski sails as we translated to N-space," Kountouriote identified the twitch. "It's pretty small, especially compared to the noise the hyper footprint kicks out, and it's almost undetectable even from your own ship. But transitionals like that add to your database on how your nodes are doing. All part of the sys op's job." She waved at the display again. "Now you know what one of those is supposed to look like."

"Yes, Ma'am," Travis said, taking a slightly deeper breath as the nausea faded away. "Thank you, Ma'am."

Kountouriote grunted. "No problem. Thank the captain that he likes to see young skulls full of vacuum filled with something more useful than sports scores and card-draw odds."

"I would never bother with card odds, Ma'am," Travis assured her.

"That's why you usually lose," the petty officer two consoles down at the lidar station murmured.

Travis smiled lopsidedly. Six months ago, back on *Vanguard*, a comment like that would have dropped him into a pit of frustration and silent anger. Now, he could recognize it as plain simple truth. "Which is why I don't usually play," he said.

"Eyes on the prize, Long," Kountouriote said tersely. "Here we go. Watch what happens when the Warshawski sails reconfigure as the wedge."

Across the compartment at Travis's right the door slid open. Reflexively, he tensed as he shot a look sideways. Captain Eigen had dropped into CIC once while Travis was watching over Kountouriote's shoulder, and despite the fact that *Guardian*'s commander had given Travis permission to observe during non-action periods he couldn't shake the feeling that he was someplace where he wasn't supposed to be. Someday, Eigen was bound to realize that, too.

But it wasn't the captain. It was, instead, Commander Metzger.

"Ladies and gentlemen," Metzger greeted the group as she floated in and headed toward her station. Like Travis, she'd been promoted when she came aboard *Guardian*, from lieutenant commander to full commander, and from tactical officer to executive officer.

And as the rest of the officers and ratings in the compartment murmured their return greetings, Metzger's eyes locked onto Travis's. "Long," she added.

"Ma'am," Travis said, turning quickly back to the board as his heartbeat picked up again.

Because somewhere along the line, the newly minted XO seemed to have taken an unusual interest in the newly minted gravitics technician third class, Travis Long.

Travis had certainly not expected any such attention when he discovered they'd both been transferred to *Guardian*. But in retrospect, he realized that it was almost inevitable. Outside of *Vanguard*'s bridge crew, he was the only one who knew that the missile delivery plan during the *Phobos* crisis had been his idea, not Metzger's. It only made sense for her to keep an eye on him to make sure that secret didn't spread elsewhere and possibly embarrass the people involved.

It sounded paranoid, he knew, and probably was. But there was no getting around the fact that the only other nonbridge person besides Travis who knew about the lie was Lieutenant Donnelly...who was *also* now aboard *Guardian*. Throw in Colonel Massingill, the Casey-Rosewood commander who'd had him on the carpet over Chomps's stolen cookies, and it was starting to look like everyone he'd ever had a major run-in with had been put aboard this one particular ship. Maybe even with the goal of keeping an eye on him?

He rolled his eyes, feeling a surge of disgust. Ridiculous. No, this was just the normal shake-up that periodically took place in every ship's company, probably with the added push of officers cashing in favors to get to fly a real honest-to-Pete interstellar trip. The fact that Metzger, Donnelly, and Massingill were all here was surely pure coincidence.

Still, when Travis was a child his uncle had warned him never to trust in coincidence. It had seemed like good advice then, and it was probably good advice now.

Something on the display caught his eye, eleven or twelve light-seconds inward from them. "Is that another wedge, Ma'am?" he asked, pointing to it as he forced his mind away from shadowy conspiracy theories and back to the task at hand.

"Sure is," Kountouriote said, tapping the intercom key. "Bridge; CIC. New contact bearing zero one seven by zero one three; distance one-point-seven million klicks. Passing to plot now. From the wedge strength, looks like a merchant." She clicked off her mike. "Probably Solarian design," she added to Travis. "At a guess, *Llama II* class."

"Acknowledged," Captain Eigen's calm voice came from the CIC speaker. Another one, Travis suspected, who either didn't feel translation sickness or hid it well. "Patty, get a com laser on them. Find out if they're buying or selling. Then—" His voice cut off as he closed his mike.

"Buying or selling?" Travis murmured.

"Here for the ship sale, or just a random merchant," Kountouriote murmured back. "Though given it's Secour, the odds of the latter are probably pretty slim."

"Oh," Travis said, frowning at the display. He'd barely been able to tell that it was an impeller wedge, let alone the design, origin, and class of the ship riding between the stress bands. "You really got all that just from her wedge, Ma'am?"

"It's an art *and* a science," Kountouriote said in a lofty voice. "It comes from experience."

"Or it comes from learning how to snow the new kids on the street," Metzger put in dryly. "Her vector suggests she's in from Casca or Zuckerman, which means either the Solarian or the Havenite merchant circuit, and both of those use Llamas."

"Oh," Travis said, his face warming.

"Like the lieutenant said, there's an art to filling in the gaps," the lidar operator spoke up. "But if you don't fill them in right, the snow blows back in your own face." He tapped his display for emphasis. "Y'see, that's not a *Llama*. It's a *Packrat III.*"

"A *Packrat?*" Kountouriote echoed, leaning closer to her displays. "What the hell's a *Packrat* doing out—?"

"Greetings, *Guardian*," a cheerful voice boomed from the CIC speaker. Another difference between *Vanguard* and *Guardian*,

Travis noted approvingly: unlike Captain Davison's more traditional approach to bridge/CIC communication protocols, Captain
Eigen's SOP was to automatically pipe all outside signals straight
to the Tactical crew.

Which really only made sense. The men and women in CIC
would be the first to analyze and interpret any situation that
arose, and the captain wanted them in the loop right from the
start. "This is the merchantman *Wanderer*, Captain Oberon Jalla
at your service. Am I reading this ID right? You're Manticoran?"

"Yes, we are," the captain's reply came over the speakers. "Are
you here for the Havenite sale?"

The conversation flagged as the question started its twelve-
second round trip. "What's the problem with a *Packrat* freighter,
Ma'am?" Travis asked quietly.

"They're just not very common out here, that's all," Kountouriote said. "They mostly do the outer Solarian League routes."

"Could be someone's trying to expand their business into this
region," Metzger suggested.

"Countess Acton won't be happy with *that* news," someone
else said.

"The countess has been talking for years about building more
freighters to add to the one she's already got," Kountouriote
explained to Travis. "More League competition is likely to put
those plans on the back shelf."

Travis nodded. Acton and Samuel Tilliotson were the rival owners of Manticore's two single-ship freight companies, both of them
running short-haul routes with the Star Kingdom's neighbors. His
mother had looked into investing in one of the firms when Travis
was a teenager, but had decided that with Havenite and Solarian
freighters handling the bulk of the traffic in the area it was unlikely
a local group could get enough foothold to turn a serious profit.

"Good lord, no," Jalla's answer came. "The Concordia Shipping
Company of Third Brunswick is hardly in the market for new
ships, especially warships without a scrap of real shipping space.
But we *do* have some passengers aboard from Ueshiba who may
be looking to buy."

"Really," Eigen said. "*Official* government passengers?"

Travis frowned as the time-delay once again temporarily interrupted the conversation. Odd—Ueshiba was several degrees off
the vector Kountouriote had marked as *Wanderer*'s entry angle.

Had they taken a detour? He looked over at the plot, trying to gauge vectors and angles...

"Waste of time," Kountouriote murmured.

"Excuse me, Ma'am?" Travis asked, frowning.

"I can see those wheels turning in there," Kountouriote said, pointing a finger at his head and turning it around. "You're trying to figure out whether or not they really *did* come from Ueshiba. Like I said, waste of time. For starters, the grav waves out here aren't nearly as well mapped out as we'd like, and if their captain managed to catch one he could have gone way off direct vector. He also might have stopped off somewhere after Ueshiba. Zuckerman, Casca, maybe even Ramon." She winced. "Though there's not much at Ramon to draw outworld visitors."

A shiver ran up Travis's back. A hundred years ago, Ramon had been systematically ravaged and looted by the Free Brotherhood, who had spent several years sucking the planet dry before moving on to Zuckerman and fresh victims. The Ramonian economy still hadn't completely recovered from that devastation.

The politicians in Parliament who were so eager to dismantle the Navy might have forgotten about Ramon and the threat of groups like the Brotherhood. It was for damn sure the Ramonians never would.

"They're working to get their society and infrastructure back together," Metzger said. "But you're right—there's not much trade to be had there. Still, it was more or less on *Wanderer*'s route. Maybe they decided to swing by and take a look. Ham, pull me up the specs on *Packrats*."

"Far as I know, they're as official as you can get," Jalla's voice came over the speaker. This communications time-delay stuff, Travis decided, was a pain in the butt even when you were used to it. "Why do you ask?"

"Because Manticore sent a courier a few months ago to pick up the official Ueshiba delegates," Eigen said. "Did they not arrive?"

"Here's what we've got on the *Packrat*, Ma'am," the rating at Tracking One murmured, his words accompanied by a set of simultaneous flickers as he sent the schematic to all the other stations. "Six hundred fifty meters long, about a million tons, one-gee toroidal spin section, six transfer shuttles. A little on the small side, but otherwise pretty straightforward freighter design."

"Crew size?"

"Twenty to twenty-five, Ma'am," the rating said. "There's also room for probably fifty or sixty passengers."

"I don't know anything about any courier ship," Jalla came back. "Hang on—let me patch you into the head of the delegation."

There was a short pause. "I thought *Diactoros* had an escort," Travis said.

"They did," Kountouriote said. "HMS *Perseus*. It would take something pretty nasty to take her out."

"Impossible," Tracking said sourly. "According to Parliament, there's nothing out here but rainbows and fluffy bunnies."

"Captain Eigen, this is Moss Guzarwan, plenipotentiary and chief delegate of the Ueshiban Government," an authoritative voice came over the speaker. "How may I help you?"

"I was inquiring as to why you're aboard a freighter instead of the Manticoran fast-courier ship *Diactoros*," Eigen said. "She was sent to bring you here, along with representatives from some of our other neighbors."

Another time-delay silence descended on the compartment. Apparently, everyone in CIC had run out of other things to talk about.

"I know nothing about any courier," Guzarwan said. "Wait a moment. You said a *fast-courier*? Well, of course. This is a *Packrat* merchantman, Captain. Obviously, I and my party left Ueshiba long before your courier arrived."

"Why didn't you wait for it?" Eigen said. "No offense to Captain Jalla, but I'm sure *Diactoros*'s accommodations are more comfortable than his."

"That's for sure," the Tracking One rating put in. "*Packrats* are about as bare-bones as you can get."

"To be perfectly blunt, Captain, some members of our government weren't convinced you would actually send the courier as you'd promised. Though I wasn't one of them, I assure you. Since we didn't want to miss the meeting, when we learned Captain Jalla was bringing *Wanderer* to the Secour system anyway, we decided to add a second string to our bow by sending a back-up delegation. As, I assume from your presence, Manticore itself did?"

"It's a bit more complicated than that," Eigen said. "I hope Captain Jalla finds enough business here to justify a voyage of this length."

"Oh, we're paying him well for his services," Guzarwan said dryly after the usual pause. "On top of that, he's hoping he can buy a pair of P-409-R processing cores for his impeller ring without having to go all the way to Haven or else paying the ridiculous mark-up that the local merchants charge."

"P-409s are an expensive item," Eigen commented. "What kind of problem are you having?"

"Long, you know anything about P-409-Rs?" Metzger asked into the silence. "I understand you've had some training in impeller tech."

"I'm not sure we actually use the 9-Rs, Ma'am" Travis said, trying to remember those early classes at Casey-Rosewood. Impeller nodes were insanely complicated things, but like everything else in the universe they were built from a limited list of components. P-409s were an important part of that list: processing cores that could be linked together to create the massive computer power necessary for managing plasma on an atom-to-atom basis in the impeller nodes. Processing cores were fast, densely packed, incredibly powerful, and—as Eigen had already mentioned—incredibly *not* cheap. "*Casey* may use them, but I think the 9-B is the most modern type we have onboard."

"Havenite ships must use them," Kountouriote pointed out. "Or maybe they've got their own knock-off version. Not much point otherwise for Jalla to think he can score some here."

"We're having Klarian instability problems with two of our nodes," Jalla's voice came back on. "Nothing serious yet, but my engineer says it could get that way if we don't replace the cores. I figured the Havenites would have brought a modern warship or two to ride herd on the sale, and was hoping they'd have enough spares that they could afford to sell one or two of them. I don't suppose *you* have any you'd be willing to part with?"

"Sorry," Eigen said. "I've checked with Logistics, and we don't have any of that particular type aboard. Would a P-409-B work for you?"

"That's a point," Metzger commented. "About the warships, I mean. I doubt the ships the Havenites are selling are modern enough to need top-of-the-line components. Though I suppose they may have undergone upgrades at some point."

"Makes me wonder how Jalla came to need something that advanced," Kountouriote added. "*Wanderer* doesn't read out as anything nearly that new."

"There's that," Metzger agreed. "Maybe we'll get a chance to ask him."

"I don't think so, but thanks for the offer," Jalla said. "I have to go now—captain stuff to do, you know. Safe flight to you."

"And to you," Eigen said. "We'll see you in orbit."

There was a brief tone, the signal that *Guardian*'s transmission had ceased. "And that's that," Metzger commented. "Interesting that Ueshiba was anxious enough that they sent two separate delegations. I wouldn't have bet they had enough spare cash for *any* kind of serious system defense."

"It's about time they had *something*," Kountouriote said. "They'll be sitting ducks out there if anything like the Brotherhood ever comes around."

"So will everyone else," Metzger said. "Including possibly us. Long, is there a problem?"

Travis twitched. "Excuse me, Ma'am?"

"You're frowning at that plot like there's something wrong with it," Metzger said. "Is there?"

Travis hesitated. There was indeed something that felt wrong about this whole thing. Wrong, or at least not quite right.

But he had nothing solid, or even anything nebulous that he could point at. And until he did...

"No, Ma'am." Travis stole a sideways look at her, to find her watching him closely. "Nothing."

"I see," Metzger said, in a tone that said she didn't quite believe him. "If that changes, be sure to let me know."

"Yes, Ma'am," Travis murmured. "I will."

☆   ☆   ☆

With a muttered curse, Jalla keyed off the com. "Well, *damn* it all," he said, turning to face Guzarwan. "That's a hell of a development. What now?"

Guzarwan shrugged, trying to look casual about it, though he was anything but. *Damn* the Manticorans, anyway. He'd heard reports that they were sending a courier around to their neighbors, Ueshiba included. But all his calculations had indicated that they still had four to eight more days before the real Ueshiba delegation showed up and popped his balloon. Four days would have been all the time he needed to grab the Havenite ships and get out.

Only now Manticore had thrown a wrench in the works by sending a second ship ahead of its own delegation. And not only another ship, but a damn *destroyer*.

Did they know something they shouldn't? No—that was impossible.

So why the hell were they here?

"Chief?" Jalla prompted. "What now?"

"We stay with the plan," Guzarwan growled. "Or would you rather give up and go home?"

"No, but—" Jalla waved in *Guardian*'s general direction.

"So we weren't expecting to have another armed ship here," Guzarwan said. "So we'll just have to be a little more on top of our game, that's all."

"You mean more improvisation?" Jalla asked pointedly. "What the hell's a Klarian instability, anyway?"

"Nothing you have to worry about," Guzarwan said. "It's a minor little glitch that almost no one's ever seen, and wouldn't care about if they did. And I know how to fake one—all it takes is a little twitch every once in a while. I needed a reason—besides us—for you to have brought *Wanderer* to Secour."

"You'd already given a reason," Jalla countered. "You told them you'd paid us, remember?"

"There are other freighters doing the local circuit," Guzarwan reminded him. "Probably two or three of them during the time we supposedly hired you. One of those would have been a more plausible ship to hitch a ride on, especially since they were already heading this way and you presumably weren't. The more reasons you can give someone, the more likely they'll find one they can hang their hat on."

"I don't like it," Jalla declared, shaking his head. "And you should *never* have mentioned a specific part. Especially something as advanced as a 9-R. Hell, our impellers use 8-Ds, not even the same class. Eigen's bound to wonder why we want something like that."

"Fine—let him wonder," Guzarwan said with a shrug. "Wondering's good for the soul."

"Not if he wonders in the wrong direction," Jalla warned. "Where did you even hear about—? Oh, no. You didn't."

"I didn't what?"

"You got it from the spec sheets we pulled from that military transport we hit off Boniface, didn't you?" Jalla demanded. "Damn it, Guzarwan—if they know 9-Rs are used in Solarian missiles, they're *definitely* going to be wondering the wrong direction."

"Would you kindly relax?" Guzarwan growled, starting to get annoyed. What was Jalla so wired up about this for, anyway? "The Solarians aren't exactly in the habit of giving out their missile specs to every backworld navy in the galaxy. The farthest Eigen's going to go with this is to wonder if we got an impeller upgrade, and how we could afford something like that."

"And if he asks?"

"If he asks—which he won't—I'll reluctantly confess I'm trolling for a cheap 9-R so I can resell it back home."

"You already said *we* need it."

"So I lied."

Jalla's nose crinkled.

"I don't like it," he declared. "If Eigen decides to get suspicious, we're going to be in deep. *Really* deep. Dhotrumi's already said his team probably can't crack the weapons codes in the time we've got. Even if he can, do we even have anyone who knows how to fire a Havenite missile or laser?"

"We could figure it out," Guzarwan said, tapping his teeth thoughtfully with the tip of the antique Fairbairn-Sykes knife he'd taken off the body of one of his first victims so many years ago. "But all we really need is to make sure the Manticorans get neutralized and stay that way."

"You got a way to neutralize a Manticoran destroyer?"

"'Course I do," Guzarwan said with grim satisfaction. "The way to deal with a big dog is with a bigger dog."

"Meaning?"

"Meaning we just have to tread water until we're close enough to the planet for a decent signal."

"And then?" Jalla prompted.

"And then," Guzarwan said, "it'll be time for the Havenites to hear from some seriously concerned citizens."

CHAPTER NINETEEN

FIFTEEN AND A HALF HOURS LATER, *Guardian* arrived at Marienbad.

The place was comfortably crowded, probably as packed as the planet's orbital space had been since the original colony ships arrived. Along with *Guardian* there were two Havenite warships: a battlecruiser and a heavy cruiser, plus sections of what looked like a non-hyper-capable corvette that was in the midst of an orbital assembly. Floating near the half-finished ship was the heavy freighter that had presumably brought in the pieces from Haven.

The two larger warships were equally intriguing. The cruiser's spin section, instead of the usual toroidal or cylindrical shape, was built more like a dumbbell, with a pair of wedge-shaped pieces turning around the amidships part of the main hull. Metzger had heard of such designs—the theory was that the dumbbell could be locked in place vertically during combat, working in conjunction with the pinched-side shape of the compensator field to squeeze out a few more gees of acceleration—but had never seen one in person. Hopefully, that was one of the ships for sale and she would be allowed aboard for a closer look.

The battlecruiser was even more interesting. Instead of a spin section, the amidships habitation area was compact and built close-in to the rest of the hull. Metzger had heard Haven was experimenting with a new grav-plate system for their hab sections. Apparently, that research had borne some fruit.

Elsewhere in the orbital lanes was a pair of fast courier ships, both of them broadcasting Havenite transponder codes. The original invitation had offered courtesy transport for the more hardscrabble systems in the region, and it looked like some of them had taken Haven up on the offer, just as some of Manticore's neighbors had taken the Star Kingdom up on theirs.

Of course, how a system that couldn't afford a multimonth trip to Secour could afford to buy even a surplus warship was another question entirely.

Crowded, of course, was a relative term when dealing with the vast amount of space contained in even a set of mid-distant orbital lanes. In this case especially, with all of the orbiting ships except the battlecruiser having already struck their wedges, a casual observer would barely have noticed anything at all was there.

Struck wedges, and nodes that had already gone cold. Apparently, *Guardian* was running fashionably late to the party. As was *Wanderer*, whose lower acceleration had now put her about four hours behind them.

"Captain, we're being hailed," Alfonse Joyce announced from the com station. "Commodore Jason Flanders of RHNS *Saintonge*."

"Thank you," Eigen said, keying his com. "Commodore Flanders, this is Captain Eigen of His Majesty's Ship *Guardian*. Greetings, and our thanks to you and the Republic for hosting this get-together."

The com display lit up to reveal a brown-haired man dressed in the green-and-gray Havenite uniform, a set of commodore's insignia glittering on his shoulderboards, the ensemble completed by a full and meticulously groomed beard. "Captain Eigen," the other said gravely. He wasn't smiling, Metzger noted, and there were tension lines at the corners of his eyes. "On behalf of the Republic of Haven, and RHNS *Saintonge*, I'd like to welcome you to Secour. I'm glad to see you're still getting good service from your *Protector*-class destroyers."

"They're getting a bit creaky, but otherwise are fine vessels," Eigen said. "I should inform you that another pair of ships, the fast courier *Diactoros* and her escort, are still on the way. I apologize for their delay—I see you have the meeting already underway. Hopefully, they'll arrive sometime in the next few days."

"Not a problem," Flanders said with a dismissing wave of his hand. "We expected representatives would be coming and going over the entire month, and have planned our discussions and demonstrations accordingly. *Diactoros* and her assembled delegates will be welcome and brought up to speed whenever they arrive."

"I'm glad to hear that," Eigen said. "I can't help noticing you seem preoccupied, Commodore. Is there some other problem?"

"Yes and no," Flanders said, his voice going a little sour. "I suppose it depends on how accommodating and neighborly we're all feeling today. I've received a communication from one of the delegates expressing concern at the presence of a non-Havenite warship here."

"You're joking."

"Yes, I know," Flanders said, a hint of a smile tugging at his lips. "I suppose you could take it as a compliment that he evidently thinks a Manticoran destroyer could hold her own against a Havenite battlecruiser. But as I say, he's concerned about it."

"What did you tell him?"

"Nothing, yet," Flanders said. "My first impulse was to suggest he sounded ridiculous and that if he had a problem he was welcome to go home. But that wouldn't exactly have been neighborly."

"Not to mention accommodating," Eigen agreed. "So what shall we do about it?"

"The head of our delegation, Ambassador Boulanger, has suggested we put you in an orbit one-eighty around from the complainer," Flanders said. "That way, he wouldn't have to look at you, or whatever it is about you that bothers him."

"I don't think I've ever had my own angry nemesis before," Eigen commented dryly. "Not sure whether to be proud or ashamed."

"I wouldn't bother with either if I were you," Flanders said, matching his tone. "I don't think he's as much angry as he is sniveling."

"That *does* take some of the drama out of it," Eigen agreed. "So we're to be sent around back to the children's table?"

"As I say, that's the ambassador's suggestion," Flanders said. "But I'm not happy with it, on several levels. I was hoping you might have a clever alternative."

"I'm sure we can come up with something," Eigen said. "May I ask who this person is?"

Flanders shook his head. "Sorry, but he asked me to withhold his name and world, lest Manticore retaliate for his legitimate concerns, unquote. Whatever paranoid lens he's viewing you through, it apparently stretches far enough to cover the whole Star Kingdom."

"Sounds like a pretty odd duck to be sent to a multisystem meeting," Eigen said. "But all right. He's worried that we'll make trouble? Fine. Let's try this. We settle into orbit close in to you—a thousand klicks, say—running ahead of you with our beam to your axis. Then we strike our wedge. First hint that we're trying to make trouble, you fire up your laser and fry us."

Someone behind Metzger muttered something under their breath, and Metzger felt her own stomach tighten. That was a *terrible* position for a warship to be in. Riding that close to a battlecruiser with a lowered wedge was risky enough. But to compound the tactical disadvantage by deliberately lining up with the other ship's axial laser was as bad as it could possibly get. Surely the offer was simply Eigen attempting to be sarcastic.

Flanders clearly thought so, too. "You're not serious."

"Why not?" Eigen countered. "What better way to show that we trust you? Alternatively, if he wants assurance that you're the alpha dog on this particular street corner, this should ease his fears on that score, too."

"Yes, but—" Flanders strangled off the sentence. "No, I can't agree. The whole thing is insane. Furthermore, the Republic of Haven is not in the habit of letting minor worlds dictate its policy. *Especially* policy toward its friends and allies."

"Accommodating and neighborly, remember?" Eigen reminded him. "We're the big boys who can afford to humor the new kid in town."

"Captain—"

"More to the point," Eigen continued, "that's the orbital attitude I was planning to take anyway. Except for the part about being directly in your sights, of course. I noticed that your ships are lined up more or less the same direction. I thought it might be prudent to have at least one set of missiles lined up transverse, just in case something unexpected shows up."

There was a brief pause.

"Interesting," Flanders said. "Are you expecting something unexpected, Captain?"

"Not at all," Eigen assured him. "But one of the lessons of history is that trouble seldom announces itself. And if some trouble *did* show up, its best move would be to come up over the horizon on our flanks."

"Have you any reason to suspect any such in-system trouble?"

"Again, not really," Eigen said. "But if there were someone out there who, say, didn't like this kind of a regional conference, his best move might be to commandeer some armament from the surface and try to catch us napping."

Flanders smiled faintly. "I see you're a worst-case-scenario type of person."

"Probably," Eigen agreed. "But we don't see much actual combat in our neighborhood. Mental exercises and borderline paranoia help pass the time."

Flanders's smile broadened. "Indeed," he said. "Very well, then. If we're going to play to the gallery, we might as well go all the way. In the spirit of cooperation with the Star Kingdom's trust, and to make sure someone doesn't hit the wrong button and accidentally slice you in half, we'll strike our wedge and shut down our forward reactor."

Metzger felt her eyes go wide. Was Flanders really offering to shut down half his ship's power just to placate someone's bizarre delusions about the Star Kingdom?

"That's hardly necessary, Captain," Eigen said. From his tone, he was as stunned as Metzger was at Flanders's suggestion. "Your weapons safeguards are more than sufficient—"

"Especially since we were planning to shut it down for maintenance anyway," Flanders continued with a touch of sly smile on top of his perfectly innocent tone. "The dorsal radiator system needs some work, and we need it cool enough in there for our remotes to function. We might as well score some points with one of our neighbors while we're at it."

Eigen chuckled.

"Well played, Commodore," he said, inclining his head. "I think we're in for an interesting visit."

"It could happen," Flanders agreed. "And now to more pleasant business. I'd like to invite you to a dinner we're hosting tonight aboard the heavy cruiser *Péridot* at twenty-hundred local, Marien-bad Central Meridian time. I trust you'll be able to attend?"

Metzger glanced at the clock that had been set to the local time's twenty-three-hour day. It was just after fifteen hundred, which gave them nearly five hours. "I'd be honored," Eigen said. "May I ask the purpose of this meeting?"

Flanders cocked an eyebrow.

"Do all meetings have to have a purpose?"

"Not at all," Eigen said. "But when diplomats are involved, that's usually the case."

"And so it is here," Flanders confirmed. "I'd prefer the topic be kept confidential for the moment. But I can assure you it's of as much interest to the Star Kingdom as it is to the Republic."

"Interesting," Eigen said. "We'll be there."

"Thank you," Flanders said. "One other thing. The ambassador has requested that this be a small gathering, with no more than two members from each represented system, and one of them an official government delegate if possible."

"Which we can't provide," Eigen reminded him.

"Understood," Flanders said. "Not a problem—Ambassador Boulanger can brief your delegate and the others you're transporting whenever they arrive. I mostly wanted to alert you that you and your guest may be hemmed in by stuffy government types."

"Thanks for the warning," Eigen said with a wry smile. "But we've faced our own politicians and survived."

"Glad to hear it," Flanders said. "Until twenty-hundred, then. *Saintonge* clear."

Flanders's image vanished. Eigen keyed off the com from his end and nodded toward the back of the helmsman's head. "Take us in, Vitoria. Be careful not to ruffle any feathers along the way."

"I'll do my best, Sir," she promised dryly.

Eigen swivelled around. "Comments?" he invited.

"Asking us to play lap dog to the Havenites is an odd request," Metzger said. "I'm wondering if we can get Flanders to tell us who forced the issue."

"We'll look for an opportunity to ask him," Eigen said. "TO? You look intrigued by something."

"I was thinking about that Havenite heavy cruiser out there," Calkin said. "It seems to me that's way too much warship for someone who's looking to simply defend his system. For that, he'd do better to buy some corvettes or a pair of destroyers."

Metzger pursed her lips. Calkin had a point. Heavy cruisers, like battlecruisers, were designed mainly for force projection outside a system's home territory, with significantly less use as system defenders. The only reason the RMN had so many of the larger hulls was because the fleet had been thrown together in a hurry when the colony had expected to face the Free Brotherhood's own massive fleet.

"And yet the Havenites brought one," she pointed out. "That could mean they already have a buyer."

"My thoughts exactly," Eigen said. "Another good reason to attend the dinner tonight. Maybe we can find out who that buyer is." He looked at Metzger and raised his eyebrows. "Since we don't have an official government delegate, Commander, I guess it'll be you and me."

"I'd be honored, Sir," Metzger said. Earlier, she'd hoped the cruiser was for sale so she could get a look inside. Sometimes, on rare occasions, wishes were granted ahead of anticipated schedule. "Is this considered a perk of rank, or an obligation?"

"I don't know yet," Eigen said. "Let's see what kind of table the Havenites are setting."

☆　　☆　　☆

"Petty officer in Laser One!" Ensign Joji Yanagi's smooth baritone called out over the hum of the computers and ventilation fans.

Lieutenant Lisa Donnelly rolled her eyes. Yanagi had begun this nonsense a month ago, about the time serious boredom had started to settle in around *Guardian*'s crew. It was allegedly a loving homage to the classic announcement given when a senior officer entered the bridge, but Donnelly had no illusions as to what the bosun's or tactical officer's response would be if one of them ever caught him at it.

She'd toyed with the idea of giving him a small slapdown in hopes of preempting a more serious verbal flaying farther down the line. But his antics helped defuse the boredom-driven tension in *Guardian*'s Weapons Department, and there really weren't any regs against sarcasm unless it edged into insubordination or was fired directly into a superior's face. Besides, it was no worse than some of the stunts Donnelly herself had pulled back at the Academy.

Still, it was nice when she could occasionally give him a figurative elbow in the ribs. "Yanagi, you thickhead, this isn't just a petty officer," she admonished, pulling herself into his view from behind one of the techs working on the half-disassembled missile tracking module strapped to the central work bench. "This is Gravitics Tech Third Travis Long."

"Really," Yanagi said, bending backwards at the waist as if to get a better look at the young man floating stiffly in the open hatchway. "Sorry, Ma'am."

"As well you should be," Donnelly said as she floated toward them. "Before we came aboard *Guardian*, Long and I served together on *Vanguard*."

She had the satisfaction of seeing the subtle change in Yanagi's face as he finally made the connection. "Oh," he said, the faint sarcasm in his voice morphing into equally faint but genuine respect. "Honored to meet you, Long."

"And you, Sir," Long said, eyeing the other cautiously.

"Will you take over for me, Mr. Yanagi?" Donnelly continued, nodding back over her shoulder at the gutted tracking module. "Long and I have some business."

For the briefest fraction of a second she could see in Yanagi's eyes the question of what kind of business a weapons officer and a gravitics petty officer could possibly have together. But whatever his conclusions or suspicions, he was smart enough not to voice them.

"Yes, Ma'am," he said. Nodding at Long, he kicked off the bulkhead and flew past Donnelly, threading his way deftly between a pair of diagnostic consoles.

"Ignore him," she advised the still tense-looking Long as she came to a halt beside him. "His heart's in the right place, even if you can't say the same about his brains. What can I do for you?"

Long's eyes were still on the spot where Yanagi had disappeared. "What did you tell him, Ma'am?" he asked, his voice tight. "Commander Bertinelli instructed me—"

"Relax," Donnelly said quickly. She'd received the same heavy-handed warning from *Vanguard*'s XO about contradicting Captain Davison's official record of the *Phobos* incident. "I've just told them about your courage and quick-thinking in jumping off the hull to help rescue Esterle after the gravitics array fried her suit."

"Oh." Long's eyes started to come back, then narrowed again as the plural apparently made it through to his brain. "You told *them*?"

"I use it as a cautionary tale," she said. "Rules and regs are there for a reason, but sometimes you have to bend them a little."

Once again, his eyes changed, and she belatedly remembered his rather rigid view on such matters. "So what brings you here?" she asked, trying to change the subject before she found another pile of awkwardness to step into.

It took Long another half second to regather his thoughts. "P-409-R control modules, Ma'am," he said. "That freighter we talked to on the way in—*Wanderer*—said they needed a 9-R for some node problems."

"Do we even have any 9-Rs aboard?" Donnelly asked, frowning as she ran a mental inventory.

"There aren't any in the ship's stores listing," Long said. "The highest version I could find were 9-Bs."

"Then they're out of luck," Donnelly said with a shrug. "Unless the Havenites have some. So where do I come in?"

Long's face screwed up. "Here's my problem, Ma'am. The instability *Wanderer* said they were having—" He hesitated. "I'm probably wrong, but—"

"None of that," Donnelly said sternly, her thoughts flicking back to Captain Davison's brusque dismissal of Long's missile idea. "Remember what I said about ideas? Spit it out—I've got work to do."

"Yes, Ma'am." Long braced himself. "The problem is that I just don't see the instability *Wanderer*'s captain was talking about. There's the correct sort of flicker, but the timing isn't right. Or at least, I don't think it is. A Klarian instability is supposed to be random but cyclical, hitting only when the bad node is at rein peak. I did an analysis of the flickers, and they just don't seem to be hitting at the right times."

"Let me get this straight," Donnelly said. "It's random, but still has a pattern?"

"Right," Long said. "I know that sounds weird, but that's the way Klarians work. Only this one doesn't. It's almost like someone just hits a switch marked *flicker* whenever he feels like it." His lip twitched. "Of course, the captain *did* say two of the nodes were affected. That could be screwing up my analysis."

"Let's assume it's not," Donnelly suggested. With one of *Guardian*'s tracking modules lying guts-out on the table, the last thing she had time for was a detailed lecture on impeller node operation. "What's your theory?"

"It's not a theory, exactly," Long hedged. "It just occurred to me . . . would someone use 9-Rs in weapons systems?"

A chill ran up Donnelly's back. "Oh, *that's* a pleasant thought," she muttered. "You thinking we might have a Q-ship on our hands?"

"It wouldn't have to be a full Q-ship," Long said hastily. "I mean, that would be an act of war, wouldn't it?"

"Not unless they fired on someone," Donnelly said, her brain kicking in on boosters. RMN missiles didn't use 9-Rs, but more advanced League or Havenite missiles might use something that advanced. Unfortunately, she was hardly up-to-date on other star nations' weaponry.

But with a little luck, maybe she could rectify that shortcoming.

"Come on," she said, kicking off toward the monitor station. "Commander Calkin has a wish-list of missiles he'd like Parliament to buy the Navy someday. Let's find out just how detailed his specs are."

☆   ☆   ☆

The Havenites' table turned out to be excellent.

Or maybe it was only very good. Metzger didn't have much experience in elegant dining to compare it to.

But it was really, *really* good. The appetizers were some kind of crisped vegetable, with a sweet yet tangy citrus-based dipping sauce she couldn't quite identify. The soup was thick and steamy, with generous chunks of vegetable and mini-dumplings, plus its own interesting set of spices. The main course consisted of leaf-wrapped rolls containing layers of meat, vegetables, and rice, laid across a bed of tomato pasta.

Tucked away to one side, looking a bit out of place beside the more elegant dishes, was a platter of chicken wings cooked in BBQ sauce. Metzger puzzled over that one for a while until she overheard one of the stewards comment to another guest that it was one of Commodore Flanders's favorite foods.

Still, the rest of the spread was obviously not standard ship's fare, but had been laid on specially by the Havenites for their distinguished and hopefully cash-laden guests. The underlying message was clear: Haven was the big shining beacon on the hill in this part of the galaxy, and they knew how to treat their friends.

And judging by the smiling faces and empty plates around the U-shaped table, the message had been duly noted. By the time they reached the coffee and small but delicious honey-flavored dessert cakes, Metzger guessed half the guests were probably ready to renounce their home systems and defect.

Certainly such a move would be a giant step up for most of them. Micah and Zuckerman, for example, were both relatively small systems with modest economies and no more than half a dozen small system defense craft between them. Ramon had also sent a delegation, undoubtedly here courtesy of Haven's courier-ship offer, and Metzger could see in their faces the low-level strain that was probably characteristic of everyone living on that ravaged world.

Or maybe the strain Metzger thought she saw was merely a product of her own imagination, generated by the memory of that earlier CIC conversation and with Ramon's history fresh in her mind. Still, if the strain was only her own projection, the grim determination in the Ramonians' faces definitely *wasn't* her imagination. Their world was climbing back from the abyss, and the delegates were clearly determined to make the kind of connections and alliances with their neighbors that would hopefully assure that such a catastrophe never happened again. Which, when it came right down to it, was pretty much the situation for all of them.

All except Manticore, Haven itself, and possibly Casca. The Cascans had a genuine if somewhat rudimentary navy, she knew, with at least one hyper-capable ship and a few smaller system defense craft. The Cascan delegates to the dinner had dressed the part, as well, both of them resplendent in full military uniforms. The older of the two, seated prominently at Commodore Flanders's left, wore captain's insignia.

If and when Breakwater succeeded in destroying the Royal Manticore Navy, a small corner of Metzger's mind mused, the uniforms and glitter would probably be the last to go.

Fortunately, even ingrained cynicism could fight only an uphill battle against good food, and as the evening progressed Metzger found herself relaxing and enjoying both the meal and the company. Still, she couldn't help remembering one of her father's favorite quotes: *the tastiest bait hides the biggest hook*. Most of the time, in Metzger's experience, the adage wasn't true.

Sometimes, though, it was.

"Thank you all for coming here this evening," Commodore Flanders said as the stewards worked their way around the outside of the table, removing the dessert plates and refilling the coffee cups. "I know you're all anxious to return to your ships so as to be ready for tomorrow's set of ship tours, so I'll keep this short. But some of you have asked why the Republic of Haven has decided to sell off some of our surplus warships at what we all agree are ridiculously low prices."

"And those who haven't asked are certainly wondering about it," the short, balding man seated at his right added quietly.

"Indeed," Flanders said, inclining his head to the man. "That's Ambassador Boulanger's diplomatic way of reminding me that

I'm not the featured speaker here. Allow me to yield the floor to Captain Gordon Henderson of the Cascan Defense Force."

He sat down and the uniformed man to his left rose to his feet. "Thank you, Commodore," he said gravely. "As Commodore Flanders suggests, and Ambassador Boulanger confirms, our time here at Secour is limited. Allow me therefore to come right to the point.

"Ladies and gentlemen, I believe this region of space has developed a pirate problem."

A small murmur rippled around the table. Metzger looked sideways at Eigen, noting the emotionless set to his face. Either he was quick on the uptake, or Henderson's news wasn't exactly unexpected.

"Let me assure you this isn't some random thought the Cascan government pulled out of a hat," Henderson continued when the buzz had died down. "Ten years ago, one of the freighters on a circuit between Micah, Zuckerman, Ramon, Manticore, and ourselves disappeared. At the time we assumed she'd been lost due to navigational error or equipment failure. But there were just enough questions to raise our suspicions, so we began to keep closer watch on all such traffic. We also began comparing notes with freighter captains and the occasional courier who came by, as well as sifting carefully through the regional data brought by all such ships.

"Our diligence was rewarded. During the next three years, we noted the disappearance of two more freighters, under equally mysterious circumstances."

"What makes you think they were victims of anything more than simple accidents?" a thin man with dark skin asked. Metzger hadn't caught his name earlier, but she was pretty sure he was one of the group from Suchien.

"I agree," Kanth Padua, the chief Yaltan delegate, said. "Less than one ship per year seems rather thin pickings for a serious pirate gang."

"It's not quite as thin as you might think," Henderson said. "The more important point is that those are only the ones we know about. If a League company, say, was starting a new run into this region and the pirates snatched the first freighter before it even arrived, we'd never hear about it."

"Indeed, it could be that their primary interest up to this point has been systems closer to Sol," Ambassador Boulanger said. "They certainly have more commercial traffic ripe for the picking. It's possible that what the Cascans have tumbled onto is someone's first tentative efforts to expand their operation into our region."

"I'm not sure we have enough shipping to make that worthwhile," the Ueshiba delegate, Guzarwan, pointed out. "But on the other hand, any loss hits us harder than it would a League member system."

"Excuse me?" Jalla asked, lifting his hand slightly. "A question, if I may?"

Metzger looked across the table at Eigen, caught the captain's eye, and lifted her eyebrows in silent question. Eigen gave her a small shrug in return, and an equally small shake of his head.

Metzger nodded and returned her attention to Jalla. All the other delegates, as far as she'd been able to discern, had brought a fellow diplomat or at least a fellow countryman along as their dinner companion. Guzarwan, in contrast, had left the other Ueshibans in *Wanderer* and instead brought the freighter's captain.

It seemed a strange choice, maybe even an insulting one. But whatever Guzarwan's rationale for his decision, apparently Eigen didn't know what it was, either.

"Certainly, Captain," Flanders invited, without any hint of offense or question that Metzger could hear. Maybe the commodore already knew why Jalla was aboard.

Or maybe he was just better at taking such cultural quirks in stride. Given Haven's prominence and position among its neighbors, it was likely their senior naval officers received more diplomatic training than those in the RMN.

"Let's assume you're right," Jalla said. "How do you propose we proceed?"

"The Cascan government has come up with a set of three tiered responses," Henderson told him. "Ideally, all the systems in the area will be willing and able to adopt all three, but we understand there are political and economic realities. At any rate, here they are, in increasing order of cost and difficulty.

"First: we gather data. What I mean by that is that we not only make sure to analyze the downloads from each ship that visits our systems, but that we speak directly to the ships' personnel about any problems they might have had and ask for their routine computer status dumps to track down and quantify those problems. If there are pirates poking around someone's hyper limit, there may be clues buried in routine data that will help us nail down which systems have been targeted. Conversely, if we're wrong and the disappearances *are* indeed accidents, that same data may help us pinpoint rogue grav waves or other anomalies that future ships can then avoid."

"A suggestion?" Jalla spoke up. "If this analysis can be done quickly enough, you may be able to send a copy with the same freighter on the next leg of its trip. That way, the systems farther down the line would have both the raw data *and* a preliminary analysis to build on."

"Excellent idea," Henderson said, nodding.

"You're talking about a *lot* of data and analysis," Ramon's chief delegate, Petrov Nahnawa, said doubtfully. "I'm pretty sure we don't have the manpower to spare. I doubt some of the rest of you do, either."

"We're not asking you to overstrain your resources," Henderson assured him. "Especially you on Ramon—God knows the length of the road still ahead of you. If you can't do much, just send the raw data and the next system down the line can do more of the crunch work. But anything you *can* do will be helpful."

"I wasn't trying to drop bricks on you, either," Jalla seconded. "I was just thinking like a ship's captain. Naturally, we have a vested interest in everyone doing whatever they can to keep the spacelanes safe."

"As do we all," Henderson said. "Which leads us to the second response. My government suggests that we look into the creation of emergency data pods. We're envisioning these as missile-sized devices which, in the event of a ship's imminent destruction or capture, can be loaded with all relevant data and sent inward toward the inhabited parts of a system."

"Seems a bit like overkill," Hrdlicka, Secour's host-system representative, said. "Freighters are already equipped with radios and com lasers. If a beleaguered ship can't get a signal out with one of those, I'm not sure a data pod will tip the balance."

"It never hurts to have another string to one's bow," Henderson said. "Especially since an experienced pirate will know to look for lasers and radio transmitters and destroy them. They may not be looking for a data pod."

"And what we have in mind here would be a relatively 'stealthy' system," Flanders added. "The Cascans are thinking in terms of something very small, with minimal radar or lidar signature, that uses old fashioned reaction thrusters, so there won't be any impeller signature to be picked up at all."

"Exactly," Henderson said. "There's a good chance even a pirate close enough to target a freighter's communications array wouldn't see something that size when it separated from their target, especially if it was simply dropped and programmed to light off its thrusters several hours after it was deployed. Obviously something moving that slowly will take a *long* time to get to its destination in-system anyway—too long to do the launching ship any good, to be honest—so there wouldn't be much point in activating it the instant it hits space. But when it *does* reach the local system authorities, at least it'll confirm a piracy problem for them before the next ship comes along."

"Still, we're talking about a *lot* of refitting here," one of the Micahan delegates pointed out. "You can't just strap something like that to the forward cargo module with a pull string threaded through the hatch to set it off. You'll need a whole infrastructure to hold, service, and launch it."

"And all that infrastructure will take up cargo space," Jalla put in. "Not much, granted, but still. I don't know about everyone else, but my business runs pretty close to the wire."

"Well, a pirate attack would certainly solve that problem, wouldn't it?" Henderson countered, a bit tartly. "Along with every other problem you might have."

"Captain," Boulanger warned.

Henderson grimaced. "My apologies," he said, inclining his head to Jalla. "I didn't mean to sound callous."

"My apologies in turn, Captain," Jalla said. "You're right, of course. If the choice is between death and a thinner profit margin, obviously we'll all just have to tighten our belts."

"Question," Padua said, lifting a finger. "Obviously, you've put a lot of thought into this. It's also obvious that Haven already knows at least the bare bones. Can we assume, then, that Ambassador Boulanger and Commodore Flanders are here in part because Haven is taking an official interest in sponsoring this anti-piracy effort?"

Henderson looked down at Boulanger. "Would you care to field that one, Ambassador?"

"Certainly," Boulanger said, getting to his feet. "The Republic of Haven and the Cascan government have indeed been in touch over the past several years on this issue, and the RHN has begun preliminary work on their data pod idea." He gestured to Henderson. "Which leads in nicely to point three on Captain Henderson's agenda."

"Yes," Henderson said, his voice going darker. "Point three is that we, the endangered systems, are going to have to arm ourselves."

This time, Metzger noted, there was no shocked conversational ripple. Clearly, everyone had already figured out where the conversation was ultimately headed.

Most of them had also done the math. "Not a chance," Nahnawa said firmly. "Not a ship like this."

"You wouldn't start with a cruiser or destroyer," Flanders said. "A frigate or even a couple of corvettes would give you enough firepower to chase off most would-be attackers."

"Especially if we can get the shipping companies to settle into a fixed schedule or circuit," Henderson added. "They're more or less doing that now, of course, but they could certainly tighten things up a bit. If you know when a ship is likely to be coming in, and from what direction, you can send a corvette out to the hyper limit to meet it."

"Assuming you *have* a corvette," Nahnawa muttered.

"You escort it in, then escort it out again once the cargo's been switched for the next batch," Henderson continued, ignoring the interruption. "Neat and straightforward. If the pirates are lurking at that position, you'll be in perfect position to take them out."

"And if wishes were gold, we'd all be rich," Nahnawa persisted. "Be reasonable, Captain. We haven't nearly the resources to buy, maintain, and crew a ship like that."

"I'm afraid we can't help much with the crew or maintenance," Flanders said, "aside from reminding you how much the loss of a single merchant's cargo would mean for your economies." He sent Henderson a significant look. "You may want to ask Captain Henderson later for the details of Casca's losses in that regard. As to the initial outlay, though, if you'll look at the price listings we gave you, you'll see that we're selling these ships at barely above scrap metal prices. Even the corvettes, which we'll have to break apart, crate and ship, and reassemble, are being offered under cost."

"That's very generous of you," Padua said, his eyes narrowed slightly. "May I ask why the Republic of Haven is suddenly so eager to help a group of minor worlds acquire warships?"

"The obvious reason is neighborliness," Boulanger said. "We may be a couple of hundred light-years from some of you, but with the League over twice as far away this local group of systems is really all that we have. Your ability to defend yourselves makes for a quieter, more peaceful region, and stability is good for everyone."

"Especially for those who actually own most of the shipping companies that are at risk?" Guzarwan asked pointedly.

"Of course that's part of it," Boulanger agreed without embarrassment. "But politics, security, and economics aren't zero-sum games. The safer you are, the more you can focus on developing new products for the rest of us to buy, as well as raise your own standards of living enough to buy more from us. The fact that Haven happens to have the biggest slice of the local economic pie right now doesn't mean much when the pie is continually getting bigger."

"There's one other factor to consider," Eigen said quietly. "Hyperdrive technology and capabilities are being improved every day. It may not be long before ships will be able to access bands above Beta and Gamma, maybe even far above them. When that happens, we'll all be much closer neighbors than we are now. The more we cement our friendships while we're still distant, the better chance we'll remain friends and allies when we're only weeks apart."

"An interesting choice of words, Captain Eigen," Guzarwan said, his voice dark and suspicious as he eyed Eigen closely. "*Ally* implies a military situation. Is there something about all this you're not telling us?"

"*Ally* also means partner or associate," Flanders pointed out. "I'm sure that's all Captain Eigen meant."

"Or not," Henderson said calmly. "Because in a sense he's right. The tiered response I just outlined is based on mutual defense. But defense alone doesn't win a war. At some point, the battle must be taken back to the enemy. Which is why..." He looked expectantly at Flanders. "Commodore?" he prompted.

Flanders inclined his head to the other. "Which is why," he said, "as of thirteen hundred today, the Republic of Haven Naval Ship *Péridot* has officially become the Cascan Defense Force Ship—" He raised his eyebrows in silent question.

"*Péridot* will do for now," Henderson said. "If my government chooses to rename her, we'll do that later at her commissioning ceremony."

Flanders nodded. "CDS *Péridot*, it is, then. May she serve you well in your hunt."

"Thank you." Henderson turned back to face the rest of the table, and it seemed to Metzger that he was standing just a little taller now in the Alpha Spin Section's artificial gravity. "Because as I said, we aren't going to just sit around and react to this threat," he continued grimly. "If there's a pirate gang working the region, they have to have a base. We, and CDS *Péridot*, intend to find that base." He held out his hands, palms upward. "We hope we can count on your support in this endeavor. Financial and military support from those who can afford it; moral and logistical support from those who can't."

Metzger looked at Eigen. "A call to alliance," she murmured.

He shook his head minutely. "A call to war," he murmured back.

Metzger looked away again. A call to war . . . and there was no doubt that Henderson and the Cascans fully intended that the Star Kingdom be part of their pirate hunt. Possibly the biggest part.

And as all the various implications of that tumbled together through her mind, she realized that her father had indeed been right.

But at least the bait had been *very* tasty.

CHAPTER TWENTY

THE CASCANS' BIG ANNOUNCEMENT pretty much ended the meeting. Henderson said a few more stirring words, and wasted a minute or two with vague talk about joint strategies and rosy plans for the region's future. But none of it meant anything without the approval of the various Parliaments, Senates, Diets, and Regents, all of which were far away, and none of which had sent anyone even remotely authorized to make any such sweeping deals. Everyone in the compartment knew it, which meant there wasn't much point in continuing the conversation. Especially since all the food was gone.

Which was probably just as well. There were a dozen questions Guzarwan wanted to ask, none of which he dared speak aloud.

Starting with who the hell this other group was who'd decided to intrude on his territory.

Guzarwan's clients on Canaan had assured him that he was the only pirate gang in town. Apparently, his clients didn't know jack. Not only was someone else here, but they'd obviously been at it for several years.

Though in retrospect that revelation went a long way toward explaining why Haven had organized this ship sale in the first place. Guzarwan had puzzled long and hard about that. It had seemed such bizarre serendipity when Canaan first approached him and proposed this scheme.

Or maybe there was no luck to it at all. It was just barely possible that Canaan had engineered the piracy problem in a deliberate attempt to prod Haven into setting up this very sale.

233

Guzarwan snorted under his breath. No, that one wasn't even barely possible. Not Canaan. Whether they'd known about the other pirates or not, the ship sale had surely been Haven's idea.

Which was just as well. No collusion or manipulation by Canaan meant no trail for anyone to backtrack in the aftermath of the operation. And no trail to Canaan meant no trail to Guzarwan.

Still, he had to give a nod to the Cascan bean-sifters. Pirate operations that careful and leisurely should have continued for years before being noticed. Casca had been right on top of things, even if it had taken them a few years to recognize what exactly was happening.

And at the end of the day, all that mattered was that Henderson and Flanders thought they were ahead of the game. Guzarwan simply had to make sure the Cascans didn't fold their hands and leave before the *real* game got going.

He waited patiently while the well-wishers and pedantic chatterers finished congratulating the new interstellar power, studying Henderson carefully until the last visitors—the two black-uniformed Manticorans, as it happened—said their good-byes and headed to the lift. Then, gesturing Jalla to follow, he headed across the compartment to his unsuspecting prey.

Henderson and Flanders were talking quietly together amidst the muted clinking as the stewards removed the last of the dishes. Both men turned as Guzarwan stepped up to them. "Ambassador Guzarwan," Flanders greeted him with a nod.

"Commodore Flanders," Guzarwan said, returning the nod. "Captain Henderson," he added, nodding in turn to Henderson. "Congratulations on your new acquisition, by the way. I presume you'll be commanding her on her return to Casca?"

"Yes, though that won't be for another week or two," Henderson said. "My crew knows the basics, but we're not yet up on the specifics of handling a ship this size."

"I'm sure your people will pick it up quickly," Guzarwan said. "That was also a very enlightening discussion. Especially given that your analysis closely parallels some of the meditations at the highest levels of the Ueshiban government."

Henderson glanced at Jalla. Apparently, Ueshiban phraseology was something else he wasn't up on. "What do you mean?"

"Your mysterious pirates," Guzarwan explained. "Some of the

delegates here tonight were skeptical. I'm sure you saw that as clearly as I did."

"The evidence perhaps isn't as clear-cut as one might hope," Flanders said diplomatically. "But sooner or later, I think, they'll come around."

"Perhaps sooner," Guzarwan said. Glancing at the bustling stewards moving around them, he lowered his voice. "It may be that we have additional data directly supporting Captain Henderson and his conclusion."

"Really?" Henderson asked, frowning. "What sort of data?"

"I'd rather not say more until I've had a chance to review our records," Guzarwan said. "They're mostly a set of anomalies in—no," he interrupted himself firmly. "Balance and preparedness in all things. I cannot and must not speculate until I'm certain."

"Which will be...?" Henderson prompted.

He could almost taste it, Guzarwan saw: proof that he hadn't just been swinging wildly into the air and making a fool of himself. Sometimes, it was almost too easy. "My analyst and I should have had sufficient time to study and meditate on the data by tomorrow," he assured *Péridot*'s new commander. "In fact, I wonder if you'd be willing to host another such get-together here tomorrow evening?"

"Well—" Henderson looked uncertainly at Flanders. "That may not be convenient. As I said, for the next few days we'll be in the process of transferring command, and there will be a lot of extra people moving around the ship."

"Yet you still plan on showing the other delegates around," Guzarwan reminded him. "I heard you confirm tours for tomorrow with both the Manticorans and Yaltans."

"That's not quite the same as a formal dinner," Henderson said.

"It doesn't have to be as elaborate as tonight's assembly," Guzarwan said. "And if cost is the issue, the Ueshiban delegation will be happy to underwrite the meal."

Henderson stiffened, just enough to show Guzarwan that he'd hit the mark. "The Cascan government just bought a heavy cruiser," he said tartly. "I think we can afford to host another meal for the delegates. Do you want everyone who was here tonight to be here tomorrow, as well?"

"Not necessarily," Guzarwan said. "In fact, not at all. The only ones I really need to speak to right now are the Manticorans and Yaltans. And the two of you, of course." He paused, as if pondering the problem. He could propose the obvious solution if neither of the other two came up with it, but it would be better if the suggestion came from one of them.

Fortunately, Flanders was able to add two and two. "If Mr. Padua and Captain Eigen are here anyway for the tour, we could just invite them here to Alpha Spin afterward for an informal meeting," he suggested. "I'll make sure I'm here, and that way you'll have all of us."

"And without risking a public slight of any of the other delegates," Henderson added. "That works for me. Does it work for you, Mr. Guzarwan?"

"It does indeed," Guzarwan said. "Excellent. I'll bring my analyst in for the tour as well, and we'll be set. Hopefully, by then I'll have news worth sharing."

"We'll look forward to hearing it," Flanders said, a touch of grimness in his voice. "One question. Does this have any bearing on your concerns about the presence of a Manticoran warship?"

"Again, Commodore, I'd rather not go into details at this point," Guzarwan said evasively. "Let's just say that there *may* be a connection." He smiled tightly. "I promise that by tomorrow I'll have something definitive."

"I hope so," Flanders said. "The Star Kingdom has been a good friend over the years. I'd hate to see that relationship damaged. Especially for no reason."

"If there's damage to be had, I assure you, it *will* be for good reason," Guzarwan promised.

"Very well," Flanders said, still looking troubled. "Until tomorrow oh-nine-hundred, then."

"Yes," Guzarwan confirmed softly. "I wouldn't miss it for the world."

☆   ☆   ☆

Ever since the end of the meeting, Metzger had been looking for a way to ask Eigen the question that had been nagging at her since practically the beginning.

Not that she hadn't had plenty of time for her ponderings. Indeed, for a while it had looked like her captain was planning to skip the trip back to *Guardian* entirely and simply rack aboard *Péridot*. He spoke to each of the delegates, some of them for several minutes, before they broke off the conversations and headed back to their own shuttles. By the time Eigen finally gestured her to the Alpha Spin lift, she concluded that there really wasn't any diplomatic phrasing possible for her question.

And so, as their shuttle headed across space toward *Guardian*'s distant running lights, she simply, point-blank, asked it.

"So how long have we known about the pirates, Sir?"

"I didn't actually *know* anything, XO," Eigen said. "But I've heard rumors. Well, actually, even *rumor* is too strong a word. Let's just say there've been some vague indications that something might be happening out there. They come mainly from between-line readings of Havenite communications, plus the whole ship-sale and regional-meeting thing in the first place. All filtered through minds that like to connect dots whether there are any actual connections there or not."

"Looks like they got this one right, though."

"Possibly," Eigen said. "For what it's worth, I'm not even sure how much the Havenites knew before tonight. Though now that I think about it, Flanders's reaction when I first proposed that *Guardian* take up a crosswise orbital attitude might indicate that he also had his suspicions. Still, best guess is that this whole thing has been driven by Casca right from the beginning."

"And even *they* don't seem to know a whole lot," Metzger murmured. "I wonder if Jalla knows something."

"Could be," Eigen said. "Merchant captains do hear things. Might explain why he talked Guzarwan into bringing him to the meeting tonight."

"To see what we knew?"

"And hopefully to add in anything he had that we didn't," Eigen said. "What concerns me most is that if the Cascans' information and deductions are right we may have a bigger problem on our hands than just some random pirate gang."

Metzger eyed him. "Meaning...?"

"Meaning that Kanth Padua was right," Eigen said. "Three scores in three years may keep a gang going, but it's hardly enough to make them rich. They may be taking more ships than Casca realizes." His lip twitched. "Or they may have themselves a sponsor."

"You mean as in a mercenary group?"

"Professional mercenaries typically don't bother with small-time freighter attacks," Eigen said. "I'm thinking more along the lines of a rogue state employing privateers."

"Oh, that's a lovely thought," Metzger said, wincing. "Testing the waters for an attack, you think?"

"I have no idea," Eigen said. "They could be hoping for conquest, planning to settle some old score, or be running some manifest-destiny craziness. Worse, it could be the remnants or successors to the Free Brotherhood or some similar group."

"Hence, *Péridot* and Casca's plans for a neighborhood tour," Metzger said. "I wonder if they'll want the RMN to tag along."

"Oh, I'm sure they will," Eigen said sourly. "Luckily, that's not our problem. That'll be for Lord Angevin to field when he and *Diactoros* get here."

"I hope the King at least warned him this might be coming before they left."

"If not, Angevin's a diplomat," Eigen said. "They're supposed to be trained to land on their feet."

"I hope so," Metzger said. "Have you decided who you're going to take back to *Péridot* for the full tour tomorrow?"

"Probably just you," Eigen said. "You heard Henderson—they're going to be up to their shoulderboards tomorrow with Cascans learning the ropes and Havenites trying to teach them. If Kanth Padua hadn't wanted a tour too I doubt he'd have let us come aboard at all." He eyed her curiously. "Why, were you hoping to curl up in your cabin with a good book?"

"I was actually thinking that Massingill might be a better choice," Metzger said. "Not Colonel Massingill—her husband, the Solarian ship design whiz."

"Gill Massingill," Eigen said, making a face. "I have to tell you, XO, I'm really not thrilled at having a civilian aboard my ship, even if he *is* former Navy. Not sure how the Havenites will take it, either."

"There are civilian diplomats all over the place," Metzger reminded him.

"Different pot of scampi," Eigen said. "The lines of command and authority there are odd but well-defined. In Massingill's case, he's technically under my authority, but as a civilian things aren't so clear."

"Mm," Metzger said noncommittally. To her mind, the situation wasn't nearly so fuzzy. Massingill was aboard a Navy ship, she and Eigen could give him orders, and he would follow them.

"They should have just reinstated him as a PO and been done

with it," Eigen continued. "Too late to worry about that now, I suppose."

"I doubt he'd have accepted, considering some of the feelings he left behind when he took early retirement," Metzger said. "My point is that he's likely to see a lot more on this first pass through *Péridot* than I will."

"I suppose that makes sense," Eigen said. "Fine—I'll take him tomorrow. We'll see about talking Henderson into a more leisurely tour later, after the Havenites have finished their training and gone back to *Saintonge*."

"He may try to bargain a tour against Manticoran help with their pirate hunt," Metzger warned.

Eigen snorted. "I'm sure he will. And I'd bet my pension that Breakwater's going to be absolutely *thrilled* about this one."

"Yes," Metzger said. "Still, that might be one way to get the BCs out of mothballs."

"That it would," Eigen agreed. "Silver linings, XO. Silver linings."

"Yes, Sir," Metzger murmured. Assuming, of course, that the battlecruisers could be made ready for flight quickly enough. And that crews could be found for them. And that whoever might be sponsoring the pirates didn't turn out to be more than a match for the inexperienced fighting force the RMN had become.

Silver linings, maybe. But it was a good idea to remember that the saying also assumed there would be a cloud.

And that sometimes that cloud turned out to be hellishly big.

☆　　☆　　☆

"Sorry," Donnelly apologized as she finally floated back over to where Travis had spent the last hour in a hopefully unobtrusive vigil. "The reassembly was trickier than any of us expected. A bit of metal grit had gotten into one of the components and was shorting out a pair of pins."

"Not a problem, Ma'am," Travis assured her. It wasn't like he had any claim on her time, after all.

Besides, he was finding it surprisingly restful to float all alone in a corner of Laser One, with no studies silently clamoring for his attention and none of the other off-duty petty officers wanting him to do something for or with them. It was almost like actual solitude.

Except that, unlike solitude, here he had the bonus of being able to watch Lieutenant Donnelly at work.

She wasn't beautiful, not in the way holo-stars were beautiful. But paradoxically, her lack of physical perfection actually made her more attractive. It freed Travis's mind to focus on her graceful movements in the zero-gee, and the melodic ring that somehow permeated her voice even when she was giving orders or discussing the care and feeding of laser tracking feedback moderators. Her intelligence and attention to detail came through, too, as she improvised solutions and short-cuts that her techs had missed.

And wrapped around all of it was her dedication to her job, her ship, and the entire Royal Manticoran Navy. Every free moment she could spare from her work with the module was spent at her terminal as she tried to track down the answer to Travis's question. To see if *Guardian* might indeed be facing a disguised warship.

"Anyway, I hope you weren't too bored," Donnelly continued, half-turning to settle into the corner beside him and holding up her tablet where they could both see it. "Okay; good news and bad news. The bad news is that I'm guessing there are two, possibly three, *very* nasty missiles that use the 9-R control module. The good news is they're so advanced that the League has them on a Class-AA restriction. That means that they're not only forbidden to be sold or shipped anywhere outside the League's own battlecruisers, but there are actually little men with tablets who periodically go around the League counting the things and making sure none of them has walked off." She considered. "It could be little women. The files don't specify."

"And none of them is missing?"

"Not as of my last data, which is admittedly over a year old," Donnelly said. "But if they're that paranoid about the things, I think it's likely they're all still accounted for." She twitched a mischievous smile. "If you're still concerned, you can always give *Saintonge* a call. I'd guess Commodore Flanders is back from *Péridot* by now, and it's possible the RHN has some actual specs to work from."

"I think I'll save that conversation for another day, Ma'am," Travis said, daring to joke a little. "If I may ask, though: if you don't have the missile specs, how do you know they have 9-Rs?"

"Pure, unadulterated guesswork," Donnelly said. "The Navy bought a few of the previous model for the *Casey* refit, and extrapolating upward from those gets us to 9-Rs. Again, it's just a guess, but it *does* follow the League's usual upgrade pattern."

"I see," Travis said, trying to think. "So you're saying it's as likely that they got an impeller upgrade as that they've got missiles hidden away somewhere?"

"More likely, actually," Donnelly said. "At least missiles that use 9-Rs."

Travis sighed. "Understood, Ma'am. Thank you for your time."

"No problem," she assured him. "Nice to see that brain of yours is still chugging away."

Travis looked sideways at her. Was she mocking him?

But if she was, she hadn't stayed to see the reaction. Her attention was on her tablet, switching it back to an exploded view of the still partially unassembled module. "Anyway, back to work," she added. "See you later." Kicking off the wall behind them, she headed back to the table.

No, Travis told himself firmly as he swam his way down the passageway toward the spin section and his quarters. Back at Casey-Rosewood, he'd had a small stirring of feelings for his classmate Elaine Dunharrow. He'd subsequently been transferred to gravitics, and had never again been closer to her than twenty meters. Aboard *Vanguard* he'd risked his life for Bonnie Esterle. She'd left without even a hug, and he'd never seen her again. Shortly after that, Donnelly herself had grabbed Travis and thrown him together with communications tech Suzanne Marx for that junction box problem. Marx had sounded mildly interested in getting together again someday, but that had never happened. Whatever it was that made up the package that was Travis Uriah Long, women clearly didn't find it attractive.

And on top of that, Lisa Donnelly was an officer, and Travis was enlisted, and RMN rules forbade fraternization between ranks. Strictly speaking, he couldn't even be Donnelly's friend, let alone anything more. No, it would be best if he just forgot the whole thing and focused his attention on his job.

His job, and why something still felt wrong about *Wanderer* and her purported need for exotic control modules.

CHAPTER TWENTY-ONE

"THIS IS THE NUMBER TWO-FOUR escape pod cluster," Flanders said, pointing to the set of glow-yellow rings painted around the pods' access hatches. "Vac suit storage there and there; emergency bubble suit lockers there. You'll notice that they flank both sides of the forward lift pylon. That way, if spacers are coming up from Alpha Spin, either via the lift or the ladder that runs alongside the lift shaft, they'll be able to spread out to the suits and pods without crowding."

"Question?"

Gill Massingill gave himself a little twist around his handhold and turned toward the speaker. It was the Ueshiban representative, Guzarwan, floating beside a red-rimmed opening that marked one of *Péridot*'s emergency pressure hatches. "Yes?" Flanders asked.

"You say *if* they're coming up from Alpha Spin," Guzarwan said. "Where else would they go if they didn't go here?"

"There are other escape pods and suit lockers on Spin Five," Flanders said. "That's the outer part of the spin section."

"Alpha and Beta both," Henderson added.

"Right," Flanders said, nodding. "Those would be the primary escape route for spacers who were in there at the time."

"Though there probably wouldn't be many," Henderson said. "The only time the ship would be in that kind of danger would be in battle, and the spin sections would be locked into their vertical positions and the crew already distributed to battle stations."

"Ah," Guzarwan said. "Another question, if I may." He gestured over his shoulder at the pressure hatch opening and the hatch itself just visible inside its bulkhead pocket. "This is a pressure hatch, correct, designed to close in case of depressurization? Yet all the suits and escape pods are on *that* side." He pointed to the pod hatches beside Flanders and Henderson. "What happens to crew members who are forward of here if the section loses pressure and the hatch closes?"

"They'll have access to one of the pods farther forward," Henderson said. "This cluster is mostly backup for anyone in Alpha Spin or moving between forward missiles and the hyper generator section."

"There were more pod clusters forward?" Guzarwan asked, frowning. "I don't remember seeing anything like this along the way."

Gill looked over at Captain Eigen, resisting the impulse to roll his eyes. Guzarwan was obviously a complete prat when it came to ships—the earlier escape pod and suit locker markings had been about as blatant as it was possible for such things to be. Yet somehow the Ueshiban had managed to miss them. If he was really this ignorant, he should have brought *Wanderer*'s captain with him on the tour to answer some of these basic questions instead of wasting everyone else's time.

Because the man he *had* brought, his hatchet-faced, pot-bellied assistant Kichloo, certainly wasn't offering any running footnotes. Kichloo had hardly said a word the whole trip, in fact, but the way he looked wide-eyed at everything around him tagged him as the same level of amateur as Guzarwan. Right now, in fact, he was floating behind his boss, his hands and face pressed against the pressure hatch opening as if he was hoping the royal coronet would be in there.

Though come to think of it, comparing Kichloo's face to a hatchet was being rather unfair to hatchets. Maybe an ancient stone hatchet. Kichloo's expression was about as warm and mobile as a granite cliff face, but without the cliff face's natural charm.

It was just as well he was an advisor and not a regular politician, Gill decided. Winning any kind of popular election with a face and cold-fish demeanor like that would be a pretty steep uphill run.

"The pods and suit lockers were more spread out elsewhere on the ship," Flanders said, with a tactful calmness Gill had trouble achieving even on his best days. "They're clustered here because, as I said, this area serves the spin sections."

"Oh," Guzarwan said, sounding a bit deflated, as if he'd hoped he'd caught the commodore in a mistake. "I see," he added, looking around the passageway as if seeing it for the first time.

At the other end of the group, hovering together behind Flanders and *Péridot*'s new Cascan captain, Henderson, Gill spotted the Yaltan and Ramonian representatives exchanging looks of strained patience. Even they knew more about the ship than Guzarwan did. In a perfect world, he decided, Guzarwan would simply die of embarrassment right here and now.

"Commodore Flanders, how has this type of split spin section worked for you?" Captain Eigen spoke up, probably trying to move the conversation away from Guzarwan and his ignorance.

"Not as well as we'd hoped," Flanders said, clearly relieved at the change of subject. "Being able to lock the spin section vertically inside the compensator field translates into a few extra gees' acceleration in n-space. But of course, once you lock it down you in essence no longer *have* a spin section, which means zero-gee throughout the ship. Not especially desirable for anything long term. And of course, the shape means you have less useable space to begin with than you have in a standard toroidal section."

"That's more or less what I thought," Eigen said. "I'd heard that some of the League navies were playing with this design for a while, but I never heard what the outcome was."

"Oh, it went on for a while," Flanders told him. "Various shipyards built everything from destroyers all the way up to battlecruisers." He waved a hand around them. "Obviously, that's where we got our inspiration for the *Améthyste*-class cruisers."

Gill smiled cynically. Inspiration, hell—from what he'd seen so far, a lot of *Péridot* was a straight, unashamed rip-copy of Solarian designs, right down to the layout of the ductwork and the service accessways.

Still, given that Haven was selling the ship at a substantial loss, it sounded like they'd already written off the dumbbell spin section as a dead-end design. Under the circumstances, he doubted anyone in the League would squawk about copyright infringement. At least the downsides of the arrangement were now abundantly clear.

The grav-plated habitation and command modules on the Havenites' battlecruiser, on the other hand, were an entirely different kettle of fish. That approach had some interesting possibilities, and it would be highly interesting to see what other innovations they'd come up with since moving on from straight League designs. Hopefully, Captain Eigen could cadge an invitation over there later so he could have a closer look.

But whether he could or not, *Guardian*'s secret mission was already a success. From what Gill had seen of *Péridot* and the other Havenite ships, he was sure Manticore could compete with the Republic in the ship-building business.

Assuming, of course, that King Michael could get the Exchequer to loosen up the necessary funds for fusion plant and impeller manufacturing facilities.

Gill hoped so. He *really* hoped so. It would be so gratifying to work with brand-new ships again, instead of the RMN's collection of mechanical fossils.

"Make a hole!" someone shouted from one of the hatchways leading inward. A pair of men in Cascan uniforms and a woman wearing Havenite ensign's insignia floated through the hatchway. The woman caught sight of Flanders and winced. "Excuse me, Sir," she amended in a more subdued voice.

Flanders waved silent acceptance of the apology and pressed close to the side of the passageway as she led the two Cascans aft. "We *did* warn you all it was going to be a zoo here today," Henderson said dryly.

"That's all right," Eigen said for all of them. "Please; lead on."

Henderson gestured to Flanders. "Commodore?"

Flanders nodded and pushed off his handhold, sending himself floating aft after the three spacers. "Down past the lifts to the spin section modules we have another escape-pod cluster," he said over his shoulder. "Aft of that is the hyper generator and its associated workshops."

The group followed. Settling in behind Eigen, Gill continued studying the design and equipment as they went, making mental notes of every detail.

And idly dreaming of the shipyard he would someday be in charge of.

☆   ☆   ☆

"The shuttle from *Saintonge* has docked with *Péridot*," *Wanderer*'s chief engineer called through the open bridge door. "Jalla? You get that?"

"I got it," Jalla called back, his own voice uncomfortably loud as it echoed from the clamp enclosure he had his face pressed against. Somewhere back there something was jammed.

There it was. "Six centimeters farther back," he ordered the man at the other end of the long crate. The other nodded and inserted the probe gingerly into the nearest gap.

And with a click loud enough for Jalla to hear all the way at his end the clamp popped free. "That's it," Jalla said, pushing back from the enclosure with relief. *Wanderer* had just the one missile, and Guzarwan was pretty sure they would have to use it sometime tonight. It would be highly embarrassing, not to say probably fatal, if they couldn't even get it out of its packing crate. "What are you all floating around for?" he growled at the other crewmen hovering around the cargo bay. "Get this thing out of its crate and into the launcher." He craned his neck. "The launcher *is* ready, right?" he called.

"Mostly, Chief," a distant voice called back.

"What the hell is *mostly*?" Jalla snarled. "Get it ready, or I'll *mostly* kick your butt into next month. *Move* it."

He turned back to the crewmen scrambling over the crate. One single missile, paid for in blood, jealously hoarded for nearly six years against any temptation to spend it.

Tonight that self-denial would end. Tonight, they would get to spend that missile.

And in return, they would be leaving the system with warships. Warships loaded with all the missiles anyone could ever want.

There was a loud thud as one of the men's wrenches slipped off a bolt and bounced off the deck. "Watch it," Jalla snapped. "You break it, I break you. Now, *move* it."

☆　　☆　　☆

The disguised false-front compartments in the aft section of *Wanderer*'s shuttle were cramped and hot, with only a little ventilation and no light at all.

Vachali hardly noticed. He was a professional, and he did whatever was necessary. Besides, he'd been in far worse settings throughout his violent life, facing far nastier enemies, and with far less reward beckoning from the other end of the tunnel.

The wait was almost over. He was convinced of that. True, it had been over five hours since he and the others had closed themselves in their hidey-holes, just before the shuttle docked with *Péridot* and their great leader and pompous chatterjay Guzarwan headed in for the grand tour. And true, Vachali had been expecting to get the signal for the past hour. But it was surely almost time.

And then, there it was: a small vibration on his wrist, silent and invisible.

Time to go.

The first step was to make sure that no one was loitering nearby in the shuttle's cargo area. Vachali accomplished that with a slender fiber-op cable through an innocent-looking scratch in the door's corner. It was barely possible that one of *Péridot*'s crewmen had wandered in, given that Guzarwan had deliberately left the shuttle's hatch open to the docking port to show that he had nothing to hide. Unlikely, but still possible. And part of Vachali's job was to ward off even unlikely events that could get him and his team killed.

The area was clear. With *Péridot*'s transfer of ownership to the Cascans still going on, everyone aboard clearly had better things to do than poke around someone else's shuttle.

They would be regretting that lack of curiosity before the night was out.

The hidden door was designed to open silently, and it did its job perfectly. Vachali floated out, making sure his concealed handgun was close at hand, and made his way to within view of the open hatch. From the passageways and compartments on the other side came the muted murmur of voices and machinery, but no one appeared to be nearby. Getting a grip on one of the handholds, he keyed his viber with the activation signal.

The rest of his team had apparently been as bored and impatient for action as he had. Ninety seconds later, all fifty were gathered behind him, just out of view from the hatchway.

"Shora?" Vachali murmured, not because he needed to confirm the other's readiness but because it was traditional to touch base with the second-team commander before going into action.

"Team ready," Shora confirmed.

Vachali nodded, his eyes flicking across the stolid faces and coiled-spring-ready bodies. They were certainly a colorful lot. Eleven were in vac suits, with bright-orange stripes to make them more visible in marginal lighting. Twenty wore Republic of Haven naval uniforms. The other nineteen, plus Vachali himself, were dressed in Cascan Defense Force outfits. The EVA team members had their hip pouches in place; the uniformed men had their bulkier kit cases floating at their sides. "EVA teams: go," he ordered.

Silently, the vac-suited men split into two groups and headed for the shuttle's two side airlocks. "Com team, with me," he continued. "The rest in twos: thirty seconds apart or as conditions warrant. Labroo, you have my case."

A moment later Vachali, Shora, Mota, and two of the others were swimming their way down the passageway toward the cozy little interior nest that housed *Péridot*'s bridge, CIC, and—most important of all at the moment—the ship's communications center.

If all went by the plan, *Péridot* would soon be theirs. If all *didn't* go by the plan ... well, the ship would still be theirs. It would just cost a lot more blood.

☆   ☆   ☆

The tour had been fascinating, but by the time the group gathered in the lifts heading down into *Péridot*'s Alpha Spin section Gill was ready to call it a night. His eyes were tired, his throat was scratchy with the slightly lower humidity the Havenites maintained on their ships, and his head was crammed to overflowing with all the mental notes he'd taken over the past few hours.

On top of that, his muscles were on the edge of a general all-over ache. People who'd never experienced zero-gee, he knew, usually had a mental picture of floating around like wingless angels in effortless bliss, when in fact it was at least as strenuous as travel through a normal gravity field. *None of the weight, all of the inertia*, as one of his instructors used to say. Gill was definitely looking forward to giving his upper body a break while his legs did all the transport work for a change.

Earlier that afternoon, he'd hoped they could take one of the two narrow ladderways down to the wardroom, on the theory that you could learn a lot about a ship's designer by how he put together his ladders. Now, he was more than content to take the lift.

From what Captain Eigen had said on the shuttle that morning, Gill had expected the gathering in *Péridot*'s wardroom to be a much smaller affair than Commander Metzger's description of the previous night's dinner. He was therefore somewhat surprised to find the wardroom, if not packed to the bulkheads, nevertheless comfortably crowded. Something over half of them were officers, in a mixed group of Havenite and Cascan uniforms, while the other half were apparently the civilian delegates and their assistants.

The size of the crowd had evidently taken Eigen by surprise, too. "Captain Henderson?" he murmured as their group filed out of the lift.

"I'm afraid this is my doing," Guzarwan spoke up before Henderson could reply. "It occurred to me that my earlier suggestion of limiting tonight's gathering wasn't very polite, not to mention highly undiplomatic. So I passed around a more general invitation this morning to the other delegates and arranged to have your steward fly some extra provisions up from the surface. All at Ueshiba's expense, of course."

"I already told you there was no need for that," Henderson growled.

"Yes, you did," Guzarwan agreed. "But I beg you to indulge my government just this once. After all, if we're going to be allies—" he inclined his head at Eigen "—it would best if we were also friends." He gestured across the room, toward a short, balding man having an animated discussion with a few other men. "I *did* of course clear it with Ambassador Boulanger, who I assumed would inform both of you."

"Well, he didn't," Flanders said stiffly. "More importantly, as *Péridot* is now under Cascan command, the ambassador has no authority whatsoever aboard her. He had no business authorizing *anything*, let alone a gathering like this."

Guzarwan winced. "Yes, I see," he said. "My apologies to you, Sir." He turned to Henderson. "And especially to you, Captain Henderson. I was under the impression that, given all the RHN personnel aboard, that the transition was still ongoing."

"No, Commodore Flanders is correct," Henderson said, his voice marginally less annoyed. It was, Gill reflected, hard to stay mad at a person who was so abjectly apologetic for his lapse of judgment. "We'll let it pass this time. But in the future, bear in mind that it's the captain who has final authority aboard his or her ship. Civilian diplomats and even the captain's own superiors are required to clear all operations and orders."

"I understand, Sir," Guzarwan said, ducking his head. "My apologies."

"Now that we've got that settled, can we get to the main reason we're all here?" Eigen asked. "You said you would have information for us."

"And my research has indeed borne fruit," Guzarwan confirmed. "Unfortunately, there's still one piece that has yet to fall into place. Captain Jalla is crunching the data aboard *Wanderer*, though, and we should have the entire story within a very few minutes."

"Why is *Jalla* doing the research?" Eigen asked, gesturing toward the silent Kichloo. "I thought Mr. Kichloo was your analyst. If there's still work to be done, why is he here instead of back aboard *Wanderer* doing it?"

"Because I wanted him at my side when I present our findings," Guzarwan said, some stressed patience creeping into his voice. "Besides, the remaining work is all computerized data-crunching, which Captain Jalla can oversee as well as Mr. Kichloo. It will be only a few minutes more, I assure you."

Flanders and Henderson looked at each other. "I suppose we can keep everyone entertained a little longer," Henderson said, his eyes flicking over to the buffet the stewards had laid out. "But this had better be worth it."

"Trust me," Guzarwan promised. "It will."

☆　　☆　　☆

The trick to not looking like you were traveling in a bunch, Vachali had long ago learned, was simply to not travel in a bunch.

There were risks to that approach, of course. In this case, if one of them was spotted and challenged by a genuine Havenite or Cascan, there would be no backup right at hand to help cajole, bluff, or shoot their way out of the situation. But with two ships' worth of Havenites to draw on, plus an unknown number of Cascans being groomed for ship's operations, the odds were that a few freshly unfamiliar faces wouldn't even be noticed.

Still, to be on the safe side, he made sure he and Mota traveled the axial passageways together. Mota was one of the best hackers in the business, but the kid was pathetically inept at cajoling, bluffing, *or* shooting.

But as expected, neither of them rated even a second glance from anyone else in the passageways. Just as importantly, from the casual pace of the other crewmen and the equally casual tone of their conversations, it appeared that the watch was starting to wind down. Guzarwan had figured that would be the situation, but it wasn't something Vachali had been willing to take on faith.

There was no guard outside the communications room when he and Mota arrived. Shora, who'd led this particular intrusion, was already in place, floating outside the hatch and pretending to study his tablet. He waited until Vachali and Mota were ten seconds away, then popped open the hatch and floated inside.

He was talking to the Cascan-uniformed man and woman in

the compartment when Vachali arrived, closing the hatch behind him. "—down your system and route everything through the bridge while we're running the tests," Shora was saying to the clearly puzzled ratings. "The ensign will explain further—ah; here he is now." He swivelled on his handhold toward Vachali, his free hand slipping momentarily beneath his tunic, then swivelled back again to face the two Cascans.

Neither of them even had time to gasp before he shot them.

Vachali looked over his shoulder, to see Mota's anxious face peering in through the hatch viewport. He gestured the other in, and Mota popped the hatch. "Clear?" he asked, his nose wrinkling with the faint smell of ozone.

"Clear," Vachali assured him. He didn't much care for the afterscent of shock rounds, either—the acrid smell of an honest lead-loaded 10-millimeter always seemed more manly, as well as more honest. But using darts that could deliver a lethal current surge from an air-propelled weapon was a hell of a lot quieter than even a silenced handgun. Quieter, really, than anything except a knife. And for the moment, silence was the name of the game. "How long?" he asked.

"Not very," Mota assured him as he maneuvered into an angled position above the two dead Cascans and got busy with the com board. "Everyone in place?"

There was a chorus of acknowledgments from the rest of his team, scattered around the other control areas of the ship.

"Okay," Mota said. "Here we go."

He leaned in close to the keyboard, punching away like a berserk woodpecker. As he worked, Shora swivelled the chairs around, putting the corpses' backs to the hatch so that even the small amount of blood staining their tunics wouldn't be visible to anyone who glanced casually through the viewport. Vachali, for his part, stayed close to the hatch, his back blocking the view, while the scene was being set.

For all his inexperience with guns and glib, Mota was definitely good at computers. Barely forty-five seconds later, he tapped a final key and nodded. "Bridge, CIC, and Alpha Spin are locked out of the intercom system," he reported. "You're good to go."

Vachali nodded. "Shora?"

Shora had already pulled the headset off one of the Cascans and put it on. He nodded to Mota, and the tech tapped a key.

"Attention, all personnel," Shora said in a clipped, military tone and a pretty fair Havenite accent. "All RHN personnel returning to *Saintonge* are to report immediately to the RHN shuttle at Docking Port Three. I say again, immediately. All other non-essential RHN and CDF personnel are to report to Beta Spin for a special assembly with Commodore Flanders and Captain Henderson. Repeating—"

He ran through the message again, then signaled Mota to key off. "Okay," he said. "Let's see if it works."

Two minutes ticked slowly by. Shora and Mota repositioned themselves to face the dead Cascans, feigning an animated conversation with the bodies, again for the benefit of any passersby. With the scene playing out, Vachali could now move out of the way of the viewport and into guard position out of sight beside the hatch. If the ploy didn't work, the three of them and the other two loitering nearby would have to move immediately on the bridge and CIC. At that point, Guzarwan's neat little hijacking would morph into a ship-wide running battle, with a toss-up as to whether they and the other teams scattered around the ship near the armory, engineering, and impeller rooms would be able to win the day.

And then, the viber on Vachali's wrist came to life, and he breathed a quiet sigh of relief. "They're on the move," he reported.

"The Cascans seem pretty excited, too," Shora confirmed, his voice sounding distracted as he concentrated on the spotter message coming through on his own viber.

"Probably heard about all the extra food Guzarwan had brought up and figure they're in for a treat," Vachali said. Guzarwan had called it, all right, straight down the line. "Order Team Two to meet me at the Havenite shuttle and Team One to start moving to their Plan A positions. Mota, you have the uni-link relay system frozen?"

"Completely," Mota assured him.

"Good," Vachali said, pulling his uni-link out of his belt. "Open it up for mine—I need to let the chief know he's on."

Mota nodded and busied himself with the board again. "You're in."

"Teams are on the move," Shora added, keying an acknowledgment signal into his viber. "They should be ready when you are. How long do you want Mota and me to hang here after they finish hacking the rest of the security system?"

"Until the chief or Kichloo say otherwise," Vachali said. "And stay on your toes. I'll probably need you before this is over."

CHAPTER TWENTY-TWO

"MOVEMENT," VACHALI'S VOICE CAME TERSELY over Guzarwan's uni-link. "Prime."

"Understood," Guzarwan said solemnly, carefully suppressing the grim smile that wanted to come out. Phase One was complete, and from Vachali's report it sounded like the plan was exactly on track.

Now, with the Havenites and Cascans heading like obedient sheep to the pens where their herders had sent them, it was time for Phase Two.

"You have news?" Flanders asked as Guzarwan put away the uni-link.

"Yes," Guzarwan said, putting some darkness into his voice. "And I'm afraid it's worse than I expected." He turned, caught Boulanger's eye from halfway across the Alpha Spin wardroom, and beckoned him over.

"Well?" Flanders prompted.

"I'll be happy to share the full story with you in a few minutes," Guzarwan said as Boulanger joined them. "But first, I need to have a private word with Captain Eigen and Ambassador Boulanger."

"What sort of word?" Boulanger asked.

"No," Flanders said flatly before Guzarwan could answer. "Not without me."

"Or me," Henderson seconded.

"I'm sorry, gentlemen," Guzarwan said, just as firmly. "It turns out that there's a larger civilian component to this than I'd

255

realized. I have to give Ambassador Boulanger an opportunity to respond privately to the allegations I'm about to present to you and the rest of the company."

Flanders looked at Boulanger. The other shrugged helplessly.

"I have no idea what this is about," he said.

Flanders eyed him another second, then turned back to Guzarwan.

"And Captain Eigen?" he asked, making the question a challenge.

"He's the highest Manticoran official present," Guzarwan said. "I know he's not a civilian, but it's the best I can do. All I can say right now is that he and Mr. Boulanger need to hear this together, and in private."

"I have no objection," Boulanger said. "In fact, I'll admit to being intrigued."

"I have a great number of objections," Flanders growled. "Captain Eigen?"

"I don't like it, either," Eigen said. "But I'm willing to go along."

"Captain Henderson?" Flanders asked, turning finally to the Cascan. "This vessel is under your command. You have the final say."

"I agree that it's ridiculous, not to mention insulting," Henderson said reluctantly. "But unless we want to whip up some truth serum or a torture wheel it doesn't look like we'll ever find out this big bad secret unless we play along." He fixed Guzarwan with a glare that was probably designed to shrivel junior officers. "Five minutes," he added sternly. "No more."

"Five minutes should be sufficient," Guzarwan promised.

Henderson still looked like he was sucking on a sour grape, but he nodded. "All right. There's a storage compartment at the aft end of the wardroom. You can talk there."

"If it's all the same with you, Captain, I'd prefer to use the conference room near your office on the next level inward," Guzarwan said diffidently. "The one we saw on the tour earlier. It's more private, and there are larger displays I can link my tablet into."

"Fine," Henderson growled. "Just get on with it."

"Thank you." Guzarwan gestured to Boulanger and Eigen. "Gentlemen?"

He led the way to the lift, wondering if any of the others had noticed that Kichloo had drifted away at the same time he'd called Boulanger over to join the conversation.

They probably hadn't. Kichloo was very good at drifting, after all. And military people, despite their fancy uniforms and warships, really weren't all that observant.

"Can you at least give us a hint?" Boulanger asked as the lift started up.

"All in good time, Ambassador," Guzarwan said. "All in good time."

The lift car came to a halt, and the doors slid open. Eigen took a step toward the opening—

And abruptly reversed direction as Kichloo rolled like a silent ocean wave into the car, the muzzle of his gun pressed into Eigen's stomach. "Softly, now—very softly," Guzarwan warned, his own gun pressed against Boulanger's side. "No shouting, yelling, or screaming. Not even so much as a preliminary deep breath. I assure you we can kill you much faster than you can summon help."

Eigen recovered first. "Who are you?" he asked, his voice tense but under good control.

"The new masters of this ship," Guzarwan told him. "Depending on your actions over the next few minutes, the transfer of ownership can go through peacefully or with serious loss of blood."

Boulanger let out a long, shuddering breath. "Captain, you can't let them—"

"Quiet," Eigen said.

He hadn't so much as raised his voice, but Boulanger broke off his protest and sputtered into silence.

"Very good," Guzarwan said approvingly. "Here's how it's going to work. You and Ambassador Boulanger will accompany us to the bridge and persuade the duty officer to hand over the lock codes for the impellers, helm, and navigation. Once we have the codes and my men have started bringing up the wedge, you'll give the abandon-ship warning and order the crew to the escape pods. We take off, you get picked up by *Saintonge* or *Guardian* or one of the other ships, and the incident will be over. Granted, you'll end up with some egg on your faces, but at least you and the rest of the men and women aboard will still be breathing. I think that's a fair exchange."

It was, Guzarwan reflected, probably the most ridiculous and naïve plan imaginable, and he was pretty sure Eigen knew that. But the Manticoran's expression never even cracked. "I suppose it's the best we're going to get," he said. "A bit problematic taking us half a ship's length at gunpoint, though."

"I think we can stay close enough together that no one will notice," Guzarwan assured him.

This time, Eigen was unable to completely suppress the flicker of hope from his face. Traveling casually together in close order, with the captor's gun necessarily pressed closely against the prisoner's side, added up to the best odds for turnover that a prisoner was likely to get.

"I suppose we don't have a choice, do we?" he said, his voice studiously neutral.

"No, you don't," Guzarwan agreed. "Let's get to it, then, shall we?"

Eigen's eyes took on a cold glint. "Yes," he said softly. "Let's."

☆　☆　☆

The men of Team Two, as per Plan A's instructions, had gathered themselves casually along the passageways. They drifted away from their positions as Vachali passed, forming a loose group behind him. Labroo, Vachali's second in command, was anchoring the far end of the line, and passed Vachali's overnight case to him as he joined the assembly.

By the time he reached the Havenite shuttle, he had a solid mass of other Cascan Defense Force uniforms behind him.

The two Havenite crewmen manning the docking collar were talking with a lieutenant, who Vachali guessed was the shuttle's commander, when the group arrived. "Ensign," the lieutenant greeted Vachali, frowning as Vachali waved the group to a halt. "You going to a party?"

"I guess that's up to *Saintonge*, Sir," Vachali said. "We just got orders from Captain Henderson that we're supposed to hitch a ride over there with you." He hefted his equipment case. "We were told to bring our overnight kits with us, too."

The lieutenant and crewmen exchanged puzzled glances. "I wasn't informed," the lieutenant said, frowning. "You have a chip?"

"I got the impression it was a last-minute decision," Vachali told him. "The captain said he'd have someone call and confirm it."

"No one's called yet," the lieutenant said, frowning. Pushing off his handhold, he glided to the intercom in the bulkhead near the collar and caught another handhold there. "Let me see if the bridge knows anything about it." He keyed the intercom. "Bridge; Bay Three; Lieutenant Riley," he said. "I have a CDF group who say they're supposed to ride over to *Saintonge* with us. Has anyone cut or logged orders to that effect?"

"Lieutenant, this is CDF Commander Kaplan," Shora's voice came from the speaker, with a Cascan accent that was even better than his Havenite one. "Yes, we know all about it. Captain Henderson and Commodore Flanders have both authorized the transfer, but there's a glitch in the software and we're having trouble getting a chip coded. Let them aboard and go ahead and take off—we should have the problem fixed in a few minutes, and will transmit the official orders to you en route."

"Yes, Sir," Riley said. He still didn't look happy, but Vachali guessed that such snafus had been common as the Cascans removed Havenite programs and protocols from the various computers and installed their own. "Bear in mind that I can't dock with *Saintonge* with unauthorized passengers aboard."

"They'll be authorized before you get there," Shora promised. "I'll call Commander Charnay right now and fill him in on the situation, then transmit a copy of the orders to both of you once we have them on chip. Good enough?"

"As long as Commander Charnay's happy, I'm happy," Riley said with a touch of cautious humor. "Thank you, Sir."

"No problem, and sorry about the glitch," Shora said. "Safe flight."

Riley keyed off the intercom and jerked his head toward the hatch. "Don't just float there, Ensign—you heard the man. Get your people aboard, and let's burn some hydrogen."

☆   ☆   ☆

The first risk point came exactly where Guzarwan had expected: as he and the others emerged from the lift into Axial Three and his prisoners discovered the whole area was deserted. "Hold on," Eigen said, his head twisting back and forth as he looked both ways down the long passageway. "Where is everyone?"

"Somewhere else, of course," Guzarwan said calmly, floating a couple of meters farther back. If Eigen was concerned or suspicious enough he might choose to make his last stand right here, and Guzarwan had no intention of having his gun within grabbing range.

Fortunately, in zero-gee the concept of a sudden leaping lunge didn't exist. With only his fingertips on one of the handholds maintaining his position, Eigen would have to either grab the handhold, pull in and then push out, or else rotate ninety degrees and shove off with his feet, and either move would be telegraphed in plenty of time for Guzarwan to decide how nasty his countermove would be.

Eigen knew all that, too. He was still staring at Guzarwan with blood in his eyes, but he was making no move to come at him.

Time to ratchet it down a little. "Relax, Captain," Guzarwan said in his most soothing voice. "The crewmen on duty are, obviously, at their duty stations. The rest are across in Beta Spin."

"What are they doing there?" Boulanger asked, looking back and forth as if he was still expecting the missing crewmen to jump out and say boo.

"I invited them to a party," Guzarwan said, tapping his viber. Where the hell was their backup?

Apparently waiting for a parchment invitation. Five meters down the passageway, Wazir and Zradchob popped into view from one of the spin section maintenance compartments. "We're here, Sir," Wazir said briskly.

"Thank God," Boulanger bit out. "Quick—sound an alarm. The ship's being..." He trailed off, his brain belatedly catching up with the curious fact that neither their captors or rescuers were reacting in the slightest to each other.

Eigen had already figured it out, of course. "Don't bother," he told the ambassador bitterly. "I think you'll find they're together."

"Of course," Guzarwan confirmed, beckoning to the newcomers. "Escort the captain and ambassador to the bridge," he ordered. "Shora will need them there." He cocked an eyebrow at Eigen. "You'll be good, Captain, won't you?"

"Of course," Eigen said softly as Wazir nudged his arms behind his back and fastened a slender plastic cable-tie around his wrists. "Just as good as I have to be."

"I'm sure you will," Guzarwan said, an unexpected shiver running up his back. Even trapped like a caged animal, there was something in the Manticoran's voice that momentarily chilled his blood. "Take them."

A minute later, they were gone. "I thought Shora said we already had the bridge," Kichloo said as he opened his shirt and pulled out the wide wraparound belt that had doubled as a fake pot-belly.

"I wanted them to think they're still useful," Guzarwan explained as he punched the lift call button. "Especially Eigen. He's still hoping he can alert the bridge crew in time to sound the alarm."

Kichloo grunted. "I heard the Manticoran Navy was all useless fancy-pants dukes and duchesses."

"So did I," Guzarwan said. "Maybe Eigen's a throwback."

The two lift cars arrived. Guzarwan locked them in place, wedging the outer doors open just to make sure they weren't going anywhere. By the time he'd finished, Kichloo had half of the miniature shaped charges out of their pockets and floating in a loose cluster in front of him. "One per?" he asked.

"Make it two," Guzarwan decided. "Unless there were some pressure hatches you missed?"

"No, I got 'em all," the other said. "Want me to go do Beta?"

Guzarwan nodded. "Go."

It took ninety seconds for Guzarwan to affix two of the charges to each of the hatches that opened on the emergency ladders, fastening them to the viewports where they would cause the most destruction if the people trapped in Alpha Spin were foolish enough to try to open them. Two more charges went onto the floors of each of the two lift cars.

When he was finished, he picked a spot where he could cover both of the pylons and drew his gun. It was possible that Flanders or Henderson had noticed that the five minutes they'd given him were up, had investigated the conference room and found it empty, and sent someone up one of the ladders to see what had happened to the lift cars. Guzarwan didn't want to start any premature commotions, but he wanted someone sounding an alarm even less.

No one had shown up by the time Kichloo reappeared in the non-spinning part of Axial Two, giving Guzarwan a thumbs-up as Guzarwan's section rotated past him. Guzarwan pushed off the rotating part and brought himself to a floating stop beside the other man. "Any trouble?" he asked.

Kichloo shook his head. "I checked with the EVA team—everything's ready—and confirmed all our people are clear of this section."

"Good," Guzarwan said. "Let's do it."

Ten meters forward down the passageway was the first of the ungimmicked pressure hatches. Guzarwan and Kichloo positioned themselves on the forward side of the door, and Guzarwan nodded. "Do it."

Kichloo nodded back and tapped the activation code on his viber.

And from seemingly all around them came a multiple dull thud as the exterior hatches in *Péridot*'s amidships area were blasted open.

The raucous hooting of the decompression alarms and the sudden wind at Guzarwan's back had barely begun when the pressure hatch in front of him and Shora slammed across their view, cutting off the airflow as the automatics kicked in to isolate the hull breach.

But for once, the safeties weren't going to do their job. Peering through the hatch's viewport, Guzarwan could see the other red-rimmed openings still wide open, their protective hatches frozen uselessly in place in their wall pockets by the nano-enhanced glue that Kichloo had surreptitiously injected into each opening during the tour.

There was a lot of air in even a partial section of a ship the size of *Péridot*, and it would take more than a handful of seconds to drain all of it out into space. But it was already too late for anyone aboard to take any action to stop it. Most of the officers and crew were in the two spin sections, which had become separate islands of air, sealed off from the rest of the ship by the very pressure hatches designed to protect them.

There were micro airlocks in each of the spin section pylons, of course, that could normally be used to let vac-suited crewmen into the vacuum to find the damage and make repairs. But with the charges Guzarwan and Shora had now rigged to the hatch viewports, that option was no longer available. Any attempt to open the hatch would blow the charges, killing the person in the airlock and rendering it useless.

In fact, given that they'd put two charges on each hatch, it was entirely possible that the blast would also rupture or deform the inner hatch. Unless the captives had been cautious enough to set up a secondary barrier further inside, that would depressurize a good portion of the spin section and kill everyone who was unlucky enough to be in that area.

"Send an acknowledgment to the EVA teams," Guzarwan instructed Shora. With one last look through the viewport, he pushed off the pressure hatch and headed forward. "And order the engineering teams to move in."

He pulled out his uni-link and keyed it on. "Mota?"

"Here, Chief," the hacker's voice came.

"Link to the shuttle laser and tell Jalla to start bringing up his wedge," Guzarwan ordered. "Then lock down the com board and get busy cracking the bridge lock codes." He looked at his chrono. "*Wanderer*'s wedge will be up in forty minutes. Make sure we're right behind her."

☆ ☆ ☆

Gravitics Specialist First Class Jan Vyland, Travis had found, wasn't nearly as outgoing or helpful as Lieutenant Kountouriote. In fact, he thought of her as something of a cold fish, an opinion that was shared by at least a sizeable percentage of the petty officer contingent.

But if she wasn't interested in actually helping Travis learn the ropes of gravitics readings, she nevertheless didn't mind him hanging around during her watch and watching over her shoulder. As far as Travis was concerned, that was good enough.

Though at the moment there wasn't anything much for him to watch. All of the ships in orbit were floating peacefully along in the simple elegance of Newtonian mechanics. Elsewhere in the system, a grand total of two wedges were on the plot, belonging to a pair of mining ships maneuvering through the rings of one of the system's three gas giants.

Most of *Guardian*'s crew probably saw them as what they were: simple asteroid miners. For Travis, though, such ships were a ghostly reminder of the ill-fated *Rafe's Scavenger* and the even more ill-fated *Phobos*. Those memories, combined with the general quiet and inactivity of the watch, had stretched a gloomy haze across his mind.

He was practicing running the wedges' strength and position in a back-of-the-brain calculation when the door across CIC slid open. He turned, wondering if the Officer of the Watch had decided to make a snap inspection.

It wasn't the Watch Officer. It was, in fact, probably the last person Travis had expected.

"*There* you are," Lieutenant Donnelly said, floating in the hatchway. "I've been looking for you."

"Yes, Ma'am, I was here," Travis said, feeling his heart rate pick up. She'd been looking for *him*? "Captain Eigen gave me permission to observe when I'm off—"

"Yes, yes, fine," Donnelly interrupted. "Those P-409-R control modules you asked me about. What do you know about Clarino surge dampers?"

Frantically, Travis searched his memory. Was this a trick question? Some kind of test?

If it was, he'd just failed it. "I don't think I've ever heard of them," he admitted. "Are they important?"

"Maybe," Donnelly said. "That weapons thing you were worried about was still nagging at me, so I did a little more digging. It turns out that the node Klarian instability they talked about *does* affect the 9-R modules. *But* it's even harder on surge dampers, and they're at least as expensive and tricky to get hold of as 9-Rs. So why didn't Jalla ask about replacing those, too?"

"Uh..." Travis frowned. "Maybe he didn't want to bother us with details?"

"He had no problem going on about the 9-Rs," Donnelly pointed out. "Which he trotted out as one of the reasons he was willing to haul wedge all the way here from Ueshiba. Add in the fact that his instability wasn't behaving like a Klarian *and* that he's got a Ueshiban delegation aboard that *Diactoros* was supposed to be bringing...?"

Again, Travis heart rate ratcheted upward. Only this time it didn't have anything to do with Donnelly's presence. "So where does that get us?"

"I don't know," Donnelly said. "But I thought it might be worth checking whether or not Jalla ever asked *Saintonge* about selling him any 9-Rs."

"Kind of sloppy not to, if it was part of a cover story," Travis pointed out.

"Very sloppy," Donnelly agreed. "But even smart people get sloppy sometimes." She gestured at the hatch. "I think Patty Boysenko's on com duty on the bridge. Let's see if she'll give *Saintonge* a call for us."

CHAPTER TWENTY-THREE

BACK IN THE SOLARIAN LEAGUE, where Gill Massingill had cut his teeth, one of a yard dog's most important jobs was to keep track of times, distances, and locations. So when Captain Henderson allotted Guzarwan five minutes for his private meeting with Captain Eigen and Ambassador Boulanger, Gill had naturally noted the time and started a private countdown.

They'd been gone nine of those five minutes, and Gill was wondering if he ought to point that out to Henderson, when the scream of a depressurization alarm burst across the buzz of Alpha Spin conversation.

Gill's first instinct was to look up at the small strips of crepe cloth hanging from the ceiling. They were waving gently in the airflow from the ventilation system and the wardroom's human factors, but there was no universal movement that would indicate the direction of a leak. Wherever the depressurization was coming from, it wasn't in Alpha Spin.

Or at least, it wasn't in Alpha Spin Five. One of the two spin decks further inward?

That was clearly what the Havenites thought. Gill looked away from the indicator strips to see that several of them were already heading up the ladders built into the lift pylons. A couple of the Cascan Defense people were right behind them.

Gill had a different priority. Moving crossways against the flow of uniforms heading toward the lifts and around the clumps of nonmilitary planetary delegates standing in frozen bewilderment, he headed for the nearest of the bulkhead-mounted vac suit lockers.

Only to discover that the locker wouldn't open. The latch moved and gave the usual disengaging click, but the door stayed firmly shut.

"Trouble?"

Gill looked over his shoulder. Commodore Flanders was coming up behind him, aiming for the locker next to Gill's. "It's jammed," Gill told him, turning back to the locker and frowning at the mechanism. It looked like there was something in the gap just above the latch.

Flanders reached the other locker and tried it. Like Gill's, the latch worked fine but the door itself stayed closed. "What the *hell*?" Flanders demanded, yanking at the latch one more time and then moving to the next locker. It, too, was jammed closed.

Gill crouched down and peered into the gap. Sure enough, something was stuck in there. On impulse, he leaned close and sniffed.

One sniff was all he needed. "*Damn* it," he snarled, shouting to be audible over the alarm. "Commodore Flanders—"

The last word came out in a bellow that rang in his ears as the decompression alarm abruptly cut off. Gill looked up hopefully, but the emergency lights were still flashing red. The crisis hadn't ended; someone had merely shut off the cacophony.

"What is it?" Flanders asked.

"It's glued shut," Gill told him, pointing to the locker door. "Standard Number Three nano-based formula, probably injected with a hypo." He looked around at the other lockers lining the walls. "Ten to one they're all like this."

For a long moment Flanders just stood there staring at him. Then, abruptly, he yanked out his uni-link. "Everyone on the spin ladders—stop what you're doing," he shouted into it. "Stay away from the hatches. Don't touch them. Repeat, don't touch the hatches!" He listened another second, then swore and jammed the device back into his belt. "Someone get up there!" he shouted, jabbing a finger at a pair of junior officers near the ladders. "You two—*go*! Tell them not to touch the hatches."

The officers were already on their way, bounding up the ladders three rungs at a time in the deck's two-thirds gee.

"What is it?" Gill asked.

"We've been sabotaged," Flanders bit out, "and whoever it is has also shut down the intraship relay system. If they've rigged the hatchways—"

He broke off as the officers who'd just headed up the ladder reappeared, sliding down again.

"What the—?" Flanders began.

And stopped as the rest of the people who'd disappeared up the pylon earlier also reappeared, returning at a more subdued pace than they'd left.

"Daurignac?" Flanders called, beckoning to a woman bringing up the rear of the forward group. "Report."

"There's something on the viewport, Sir," the woman said, her face tight as she strode over to him. "Two somethings. I couldn't tell what they were, but I didn't like the looks of them. I ordered everything left alone until you could take a look."

"They're explosives," the Cascan captain, Henderson, said as he crossed the wardroom toward them. He was breathing heavily, and Gill belatedly noticed he was coming from the direction of the other ladder. *That* was different—in Gill's experience, ship captains normally didn't rush headlong into potential danger, at least not until someone more junior or expendable did a first-pass assessment.

"Guzarwan," Flanders said darkly, making the name a curse. "Him and his people. It has to be."

Gill's contemplation of Henderson's heroics vanished in a sudden flash of horrified understanding. His own captain had been with Guzarwan. If Guzarwan was a saboteur—"We have to get out of here," he said, ignoring the fact that he was interrupting Henderson's description of the mystery objects. "If they've depressurized the ship, we may be the only ones left. We have to get out and see what they've done with Captain Eigen."

"Good idea," Flanders growled. "How do you propose we do that without suits?"

"We don't have *suits*?" Henderson demanded.

"Sealed in the lockers," Flanders told him. "We can check the escape pods, but I'm guessing they've got those locked down, too."

Henderson swore. "So now what?"

"Maybe they don't know everything," Gill said, frowning in concentration. He'd worked on plenty of similar ships back in the League, with a lot of different yard dogs. And if a dumbbell-shaped spin section was a new one on him, basic human nature wasn't. "Come on—I've got an idea."

He set off at a fast jog through the now silent crowd to the forward ladder and started up. Flanders and Henderson were right behind him.

Half a minute later, they arrived at Alpha Spin Four, the innermost deck, one level above the living/work space of the section and dedicated to equipment and storage. From here, there was nothing but uninterrupted lift pylon stretching between them and the booby-trapped hatch at the main hull. "You know how to disarm a bomb?" Henderson asked.

"Nope," Gill said, looking around. "But we may not have to. Not yet, anyway." A few meters from the ladder, beside the forward-edge bulkhead, was a service airlock. Beside it was an equipment locker that, according to its label, contained tool kits, oxygen bottles, and safety line. Mentally crossing his fingers, Gill pulled open the door.

"What the *hell*?" Flanders muttered.

"Yep," Gill agreed, gazing at the two vac suits stuffed more or less neatly together at the side of the locker. "Strictly against regulations to have suits in here. *Anyone's* regulations, probably. But EVA crews get tired of having to tromp over to a locker and fill out a sign-chart every time they need to make a quick run outside. So a lot of them finagle a suit or two off the stores listing and stash them where they can just throw them on whenever they need to."

Henderson had crouched down and was pulling the suits out and onto the deck. "Looks like medium and a large," he said. "You suppose there are any more in the other pylon?"

"You can check," Gill said. "But I doubt it. Getting two suits off-record is hard enough without trying for three or four. Besides, the reactor side of a spin section is where more of the nasty stuff is located and where you need to be more careful. You don't mind the datawork and safety checks so much when you're going into a yellow or red zone. There are more green zones here on the forward side—that's where people think they can play things more casual."

"So we've got suits and an EVA hatch," Flanders said, straightening up. "I don't suppose we have any demolition experts in Alpha Spin who could go in and disarm the hatch bombs?"

"*I* certainly don't have any," Henderson said. "Besides, what's the point? Even if we could get the hatches open, there's vac on the other side. From what I could see of the status lights through the viewport, it could be the whole amidships section."

"With the rest of the ship probably in Guzarwan's hands by now," Flanders said bitterly. "We're sitting ducks, Gordon. Sitting, *crippled* ducks. We've got to get word to *Saintonge* about what's happened."

"They've locked down intraship communications," Henderson reminded him. "That probably means all external com systems are locked, too. Even if we could get to a console we couldn't get a signal out."

"We could use one of the radar arrays," Gill suggested. "They won't have shut them down, and you can tie a suit's com into one without too much trouble."

Flanders and Henderson exchanged looks. "I thought Eigen said you were a former impeller tech," Flanders said.

"I have experience with a lot of different systems," Gill said evasively. Now was not the time to explain that he'd been sent here to scope out Haven's ships in hopes that someday Manticore could come in and undercut their prices. "The aft radar would be best—if *Péridot* is holding its same attitude we should be able to contact both *Guardian* and *Saintonge* from there."

"How do we get there?" Henderson asked. "Over the hull and in through one of the aft hatches?"

"There are sensors on *Péridot*'s external hatches," Flanders warned. "If Guzarwan is monitoring them he'll know where we come in."

"I presume the sensors can be bypassed," Henderson said.

"No need," Gill said. "They either bypassed or blew at least one of the hatches in order to depressurize the amidships. We find that hatch, go in, use one of the minilocks to get into a pressurized part of the service accessways—either the starboard one by the hyper monitor or the portside one by the pump room; either will get us past the reactor and the impeller room—and head aft."

He ran out of air and explanation and stopped, suddenly aware that both men were staring at him. "You sound like you've got more than just a *little* experience with these ships," Flanders said, his eyes narrowed. "Where'd you learn all this, anyway?"

Gill sighed. Admiral Locatelli had sworn all of them to a black-rimmed oath of silence, and had made it very clear what would happen to anyone who blabbed. But if they were going to get out of this, he needed these men to trust him. "I used to be a yard dog in the League," he conceded. "*Péridot* looks to be based on the League's *Antares*-class cruisers, and I did a fair amount of work on those."

"Interesting," Flanders murmured, his eyes narrowing a bit. "I wondered why Manticore had sent a nondiplomatic civilian. So you just came here to look things over?"

"Doesn't matter why he's here," Henderson cut in impatiently. "What matters is that he knows how to get to the aft endcap without being caught. That just leaves the question of who goes with him."

"I don't need anyone else," Gill assured him. "I can handle things just fine."

"Two always have a better chance than one," Henderson said firmly. "We've got two suits; that means we send two people. I'm the captain, which makes it my responsibility. Help me on with this, will you?"

"This isn't necessary, Sir," Gill said urgently. The last thing he needed while trying to get past saboteurs or terrorists was to have a newbie along for the ride. "Accessways aren't exactly the safest part of the ship, you know. There are tight spots, edges that can snag a suit, and sometimes power junctions are left open. One brush with the wrong wire, and you'll fry."

"We'll all fry anyway if this doesn't work," Henderson countered. "Now, help me into the damn suit."

Flanders hissed out a sigh. "No," he said reluctantly. "I worked in aft engineering aboard *Péridot* when I was an ensign. I know that section of the ship, including some of the accessways. I'll go with him."

"My ship, my responsibility," Henderson repeated harshly.

"The best person for the job," Flanders countered.

For a couple of seconds the two men stared at each other. Then, Henderson inclined his head. "You're right," he said with clear reluctance. "What do you want me to do?"

"Go back down and check out the escape pods," Flanders said as he unfastened his tunic. "I'm guessing Guzarwan found a way to lock them down, too, but maybe you can get around his blocks and get one of them working. Do I assume their radios are locked down until they're ejected?"

"Yes," Henderson said. "I see where you're going—if we can get one loose, we can call *Saintonge* from there and give the alarm."

"Right," Flanders said, picking up the suit and starting to put it on. "Meanwhile, Massingill and I will try his aft-radar idea. With luck, one of us will get through."

"Agreed," Henderson said. He held out his hand. "Good luck, Commodore."

Flanders gripped the other's hand briefly. "And to you, Captain." He gestured to Gill. "Shake a leg, Massingill. We have a ship to save."

☆   ☆   ☆

Com Specialist Second Class Patty Boysenko was ready and willing to give *Saintonge* a call.

Lieutenant Grace Burns, Officer of the Watch and daughter of Baron White Springs, was neither.

"No," she said, her voice carrying all the weight and pomposity of someone new to her position and determined to make the most of it. "Regulations don't permit random or unauthorized communications with non-RMN vessels. *Especially* communications with no official military purpose."

"This *has* a military purpose, Lieutenant," Donnelly insisted. "If Jalla didn't actually inquire about the components he told us he needed—"

"Then what?" Burns interrupted. "Seriously. What? He forgot, or changed his mind, or is planning to do it later. Are you suggesting *Guardian* be brought to Readiness One over a simple housekeeping issue?"

"We're trying to find out what Jalla and Guzarwan are up to," Donnelly said between clenched teeth.

"What makes you think they're up to anything?" Burns held up a maddeningly placating hand. "Never mind. You think you have a case? Fine. Go persuade someone who can authorize the call to do so, and I'll be happy to have Boysenko make it."

"*You* can authorize the call," Donnelly bit out, trying hard to keep a grip on her rapidly disintegrating temper. Burns was in charge of the aft tracking equipment, and the two women had had a pair of small run-ins over equipment usage on the long voyage from Manticore. Burns's side of the argument had been overruled both times, and this was obviously her payback.

Burns shook her head. "Not according to regulations."

Donnelly looked at Long, wondering briefly if he appreciated the irony of Burns's professed rule-stickler attitude. From the intensely focused expression on his face, he probably hadn't even noticed it.

"Fine," she said, turning back to Burns. "We'll be back. Ma'am."

"What now?" Long asked when the bridge hatch was once again closed behind them.

"We call Commander Metzger," Donnelly said grimly, pulling out her uni-link.

"Wait a second," Long said, suddenly looking uncomfortable. "Do we—? I mean, are you sure about this, Ma'am?"

"Aren't you?"

Long's face screwed up with uncertainty.

"I don't know," he admitted.

"Well, I am," Donnelly said. "You may have a knack for outside-the-line thinking, but I have a knack for hunches. Trust me on this one."

She keyed her uni-link, not waiting to see whether he decided to trust her, and not really caring either way. "Lieutenant Donnelly for Commander Metzger," she instructed the computerized switchboard. "Tell her it's urgent."

☆   ☆   ☆

The Havenite shuttle from *Péridot* was nearly to *Saintonge* when the promised passenger authorization for Vachali and the others finally came through.

"About time," Lieutenant Riley growled, peering at the display. "I don't know. This thing looks a little rough."

"Yeah, sorry about that, Sir," Guzarwan's voice came over the cockpit speaker. "We're having some transmission problems. Everything's coming out muddy. *Saintonge*, did you get the copy we sent you?"

"Negative, *Péridot*," a new voice came on. "We got something from you, but it's all scrambled."

"Okay, we'll try it again," Guzarwan said. "Shuttle, are you having any com problems of your own? We're reading some static coming off your systems."

"Not seeing anything," Riley said, leaning closer to his repeater displays. "Crevillan?"

"Nothing I can see, Sir," the coxswain at the helm reported.

"Would you try a reboot anyway?" Guzarwan asked. "Anything you can do to boost reception would help when we try to send this again."

"*Saintonge*?" the lieutenant asked.

"We're not reading any problems here, either," *Saintonge* said doubtfully. "But I suppose it can't hurt. Go ahead."

"Acknowledged," Riley said. "Rebooting com system now." He gestured to the copilot. "Go ahead, Prevost."

"Aye, Sir," the copilot said briskly. She keyed her board. "Rebooting now."

And with the shuttle's connection to *Saintonge* momentarily broken, Vachali shot all three of them in the back.

He took a few seconds to confirm they were dead, then popped the cockpit hatch and looked into the shuttle's passenger section.

Fifteen of his twenty men had their fake uniform tunics off and were busily getting into the shuttle's vac suits. The other five were also out of their Cascan uniforms and were switching over to Havenite ones.

The rest of the passengers, the group of real Havenites who'd been returning from *Péridot*, were bobbing slowly in their crash harnesses. Dead.

Again, Vachali gave himself a moment to make sure everything was as it should be. Then, he jerked a thumb toward the cockpit behind him. "Dhotrumi? Move it."

"Right." Dhotrumi said. He caught the top of one of the seats and sent himself flying through the hatch into the cockpit, doing up the neck of his new tunic as he went. Vachali followed, heading to the pilot's station while Dhotrumi stopped above the dead copilot and busied himself with the com board. By the time he finished, Vachali had both bodies out of their seats and had swapped out his own Cascan tunic for a Havenite one. "Ready?" he asked Dhotrumi as the two of them strapped into the command stations.

"Ready." Dhotrumi keyed a switch to bring the com back up.

As utterly unclear as Dhotrumi could make it.

"What the *hell*?" *Saintonge*'s Com officer protested, his voice coming through scratchy, distorted, and barely audible. "What did you do, Shuttle, pour liquid metal in the works?"

"I don't know," Vachali said, trying to match the late Lieutenant Riley's voice. But not trying very hard. Dhotrumi's sabotage had rendered any hope of vocal recognition impossible. "If it helps, the good news is that *Péridot*'s orders came through this time. Did your copy make it?"

"If you count digital mud pies, sure, this is great," Com said sarcastically. "I *swear* you guys are going back to remedial com tech class as soon as we head for home."

"Hey, we did everything by the book," Vachali protested. "I don't know what happened. Maybe our glitch somehow matched up with *Péridot*'s glitch and that's why we could get the transmission and you couldn't."

Even through the distortion, Com's contemptuous snort came through loud and clear. "*Sure* it did. Yeah, never mind the trip home—we're starting those classes as soon as you're back aboard. Just make sure you have those orders ready to show Security when you dock."

"Yeah, about that," Vachali said, snapping his fingers softly and raising his eyebrows in question when Dhotrumi looked over. The other nodded and gave a thumbs-up. "Computer's also showing a glitch in the docking system," Vachali continued. "This may take a little longer than usual."

"You got to be kidding me," Com growled. "What did you do, bring in a class of Secourian third-graders and have a water fight?"

"Hey, we'll get it fixed," Vachali promised. "Prevost is back there looking into it now. I'm sure it'll just take a few minutes."

"I swear, Riley, I'm going to send all three of you back to boot camp," Com bit out. "Fine. Send me the telemetry, will you? Maybe we can figure it out from this end."

"Will do," Vachali said. Not that the telemetry would come through any clearer than the voice communication, of course. Dhotrumi had seen to that. "Sending now. Want me to stay open?"

"Thanks, but you're hurting my ears," came the sour reply. "While you're shut down, you can run some diagnostics or maybe reboot again."

"We'll do that," Vachali said. "Shuttle out."

He keyed off and half turned toward the open hatch. "EVA teams?"

"Ready," Labroo called.

"Stand by the hatches," Vachali said. "Two minutes."

He turned back to the helm controls. *Péridot* had been easy. Guzarwan and Kichloo had had the advantage of being invited aboard before the attack, and the fact that the cruiser had been on Haven's for-sale list meant that Mota could research the computer systems ahead of time and look for back doors and wall cracks he could exploit.

Saintonge was an entirely different pan of penne. He and Labroo probably knew as much about Havenite battlecruisers as anyone outside the RHN, but they were a long way from knowing all the critical little details that would make or break this operation. Vachali's men would be going in essentially cold, and even with only a skeleton crew aboard to oppose them they were seriously outnumbered. Add in the fact that Dhotrumi would be starting largely from scratch on *Saintonge*'s computer systems, and they were definitely facing an uphill climb.

But that was okay. In fact, it was better than okay. Uphill climbs were Vachali's specialty. Impossible odds, impossible challenges—that was what separated the lions from the sheep.

Vachali was a lion. He'd proved that time and time again. He would prove it again tonight.

Saintonge was coming up fast. "One minute," he called over his shoulder. "Repeat: One minute."

CHAPTER TWENTY-FOUR

LIEUTENANT BURNS SWIVELLED AROUND in her station as Travis and Donnelly floated back onto the bridge. Her face, Travis noted, started to shift into a condescending expression as she saw who it was.

Until, that is, she saw who was right behind them.

"I understand Lieutenant Donnelly wants to make a call to *Saintonge*," Metzger said without preamble. "You have a problem with that, Lieutenant?"

"Uh..." Burns's throat worked as she flashed a dagger-edged look at Donnelly. "I—it's not regulation—"

"I asked if you had a problem with that."

Burns's eyes flicked to Donnelly and back to Metzger. "No, Ma'am."

"Good." Metzger gestured to the young woman at the Com station. "Patty, put through the call."

"Yes, Ma'am." Boysenko turned back to her board and keyed a switch. "*Saintonge*, this is Com Spec Boysenko aboard HMS *Guardian*," she said. "Commander Metzger would like to speak with your Officer of the Watch."

"*Guardian*, acknowledged," a crisp voice came back. "Hold for the First Officer, Commander Charnay."

Travis stole a sideways look at Donnelly. Her eyes, he saw, were on Burns, a small but grimly satisfied smile tweaking her lips. Some undercurrent was going on there, he gathered, but he had no idea what it was.

The com display lit up with the face and shoulders of a dark-haired man with a lined face and a small, neatly trimmed mustache. "Commander Metzger, this is Commander Charnay," he identified himself. "How may I help you?"

"I have a small but possibly important question, Commander," Metzger said. "On our way into Secour, *Wanderer*'s captain said he was having trouble with two P-409-R control modules and was hoping to buy replacements from you. Can you tell me whether or not he ever made such a request?"

"I doubt we'd have sold him one even if he'd asked," Charnay said, his gaze dropping to something off-camera. If he was annoyed at being asked to do what was essentially yeoman's work, he didn't show it. Maybe the fact that *Guardian*'s XO thought the matter worth asking about personally had suggested to him that he treat it similarly. "No, I'm not seeing anything about P-409-Rs in the log. It's possible he's planning to ask later."

"Possibly," Metzger agreed. "If I may impose a bit further, Sir, could you also check on Clarino surge dampers?"

"Nothing on those, either, Commander," Charnay said, eying her thoughtfully. "May I ask what this is about? *And* why a senior officer is involved?" He lifted a hand suddenly. "Excuse me."

For a moment, he looked off-camera, and Travis could hear voice murmuring unintelligibly.

"I'm sorry, Commander Metzger, but I have to go," Charnay said. "We've got an incoming shuttle that's having problems with its docking system, and I need to give this my attention."

"Understood, Commander," Metzger said. "Thank you for your time."

The screen blanked. "Well, Lieutenant?" Metzger asked, turning to Donnelly. "What now?"

"I don't know, Ma'am," Donnelly admitted, flicking a glance at Burns. Travis followed her eyes, and found the same self-satisfied smile on Burns's face as he'd seen earlier on Donnelly's. Definitely something going on there. "If *Wanderer* was lying about their problem..." Her lips compressed briefly. "But even if they were, I... I'm sorry, Ma'am. I don't really know where to go with it."

"I don't think lying is an officially actionable offense," Burns murmured.

Metzger's eyes remained on Donnelly. "Then I suggest you do

some additional research or thinking and see if you can come up with something."

Donnelly nodded, a small wince flicking across her face. "Yes, Ma'am."

Metzger turned to Burns. "As you were, Watch Officer," she said. With a final look at Donnelly, she turned and headed for the hatch.

"You two are also invited to leave," Burns said quietly, eyeing Donnelly and Travis. She swivelled around, turning her back to them—

"Bridge; CIC," a voice came from the speaker. "Lieutenant, I was just running a visual on *Saintonge*. Something strange seems to be going on over there. There are a bunch of EVAs moving along the hull."

"It's nothing, Carlyle," Burns said. "They're having trouble docking a shuttle, that's all."

"Bring it up," Metzger called from the hatch.

Burns swivelled around again, her eyes flashing, and for a fraction of a second Travis thought she was actually going to tell the XO that *she* was Officer of the Watch, not Metzger, and that if there were any orders that needed to be given Burns would be the one to give them.

Which would of course be not only insubordinate but pedantic and pointless, given that the XO could assume the watch anytime she felt like it. More to the point, Burns was a lieutenant and Metzger was her XO and they would both be living on the same ship until they got back to Manticore.

But Travis hadn't imagined that flash of Burns's eyes.

"You heard the XO," the lieutenant growled.

"Yes, Ma'am." The man at the TO position keyed a switch, and the image of *Saintonge* appeared.

There wasn't really much to see, Travis realized, especially given that the battlecruiser was still end-on to *Guardian*'s flank, the positioning Commodore Flanders and Captain Eigen had agreed on earlier. *Saintonge*'s bow endcap was foremost, her bristling armament of autocannon, counter-missiles, and internal X-ray laser almost casually pointed in *Guardian*'s direction. Behind the endcap the tip of one of the battlecruiser's missile launchers was visible, peeking coyly out at the universe. Further aft, the dorsal and ventral radiator fins from her forward fusion plant jutted out high over the hull, while behind them the matching set of radiators from the aft plant were also visible. The image included some infrared, and it was readily apparent that only the aft reactor was running and hot.

Conspicuous by its absence was the usual wide toroidal spin section, or even *Péridot*'s dumbbell-shaped equivalent. Those in the know had told Travis that *Saintonge* had a different kind of habitation section, something that utilized grav plates instead of centrifugal effects to create its artificial gravity. Travis had no idea how energy-efficient such a design was, but it certainly made for a sleeker shape.

"Where are they?" Metzger called.

"They *were* there, Ma'am," Carlyle said, sounding midway between embarrassed and confused. "They've either gone in or are behind the bow endcap where I can't see them. I'm sorry, Ma'am."

"That's all right, Ensign," Metzger assured him. "How many did you see?"

"At least eight or ten," Carlyle said. "What I got is all recorded, if you want to take a look."

"Maybe later," Metzger said. "For now, just keep an eye on things over there. If the Havenites are doing some major hull work, it might be nice to know what kind. Anyone else have anything on *Saintonge*?"

One by one, in rapid succession, the lidar, radar, and tracking stations called in negatives. Not surprising, really, given that all of *Guardian*'s active sensors were currently shut down. Emissions from devices capable of probing thousands of kilometers into deep space were far too powerful to use this close to other ships, especially with small-craft traffic in the area.

"Nothing on *Saintonge* from Gravitics, Ma'am," a final voice said hesitantly, and this one Travis recognized as Specialist Vyland. "But I think I'm getting something from *Wanderer*."

"What, specifically?"

"It's hard to tell, Ma'am," Vyland said. "She's beneath the planetary horizon, so all I'm getting is a refraction pattern. But it looks to me like she's bringing up her nodes."

Travis and Donnelly exchanged looks. *Wanderer*, the ship with the supposed Klarian problem, was starting her wedge?

"Really," Metzger said, thoughtfully. "Patty, had *Wanderer* given any indication that she was planning on going anywhere?"

"She didn't send out any general calls, Ma'am," Boysenko said. "Do you want me to signal her and ask her intentions?"

Metzger looked at the helm display, still showing *Saintonge*. "Not yet," she said slowly. "Guzarwan was supposedly doing the *Péridot* tour today. Let's give Captain Eigen a call and see if Guzarwan mentioned anything to him about what he and his ship were up to."

☆   ☆   ☆

"Okay," the young and exceedingly frustrated voice came over the cockpit speaker. "You got the patch loaded? I got no idea *why* you'd need it, but—hell with it. Let's try it again."

"Acknowledged," Vachali said, smiling tightly to himself. The vibers had only a limited range, especially with a battlecruiser's worth of metal running interference. But the range was good enough. One by one the reports had now come in as the EVA teams reached their assigned hatches, used their cutters, pressure-dupes, and induction jumpers to bypass the sensors and locks, and slipped inside the ship.

And at last it was time for the lion to strike.

He made sure to make the docking a little rough, just to add a final touch of realism to the operation. The indicators went green, and he shut down first the thrusters and then the rest of the board. Unstrapping, he left the cockpit and joined Labroo, Dhotrumi, and the other two waiting by the hatch. "Stay behind us until we're clear," he murmured to Dhotrumi, giving the other a small shove toward the rear of the group. He didn't expect the Havenites to bring much security to one of their own incoming shuttles, but there was no point in taking chances. The last thing they could afford was to have their chief hacker catch a stray bullet. "And everyone remember we're still outside the gravity zone. Aim and fire accordingly."

The hatch swung open, revealing three men and a woman, all in tech coveralls. None of them Marines; none of them, as far as Vachali could tell, even armed. Sloppy. "About time," the nearest tech growled as he floated forward. His eyes barely even acknowledged the shuttle's passengers before shifting to the docking mechanism. "What the hell—?"

The rest of his question or complaint was lost to eternity as Vachali and the others shot all four of them.

Labroo was through the hatch and into the connecting passageway before the bodies finished their slow bounce off the bulkheads. He looked both ways and gave the all-clear hand signal.

"Quietly, now," Vachali warned as the team collected their kit cases and floated out through the hatch. The longer they could keep *Saintonge*'s crew fat, sassy, and oblivious to what was happening to their ship, the better. "Very, very quietly."

☆ ☆ ☆

Gill's plan had been simple. He and Flanders would exit the Alpha Spin service airlock, use the thruster packs from the locker to jet up to the main hull, find one of the hatches the saboteurs had gimmicked, and get inside.

After that, of course, considering that the ship was full of an unknown number of enemies, things would probably get more complicated. But at least the opening move was easy.

Or it was until he discovered that one of the thruster packs was completely dry and the other had no more than five seconds of burn time left.

"Great," he growled as he and Flanders hung from the handholds outside the lock. There was less than half a gee at this level of Alpha Spin, but it still made for more weight than he was used to dealing with in a vac suit. "Now what?"

"We climb the pylon, of course," Flanders said calmly, hooking his safety line onto the ring beside the lock. "Come on—to the top of the section."

He bent his knees and jumped, catching the seam ridge at the edge of the Spin Five roof and pulling himself up.

"Great," Gill muttered again. He had no idea where the Havenite was going with this plan, but without anything better to offer he had no option but to follow.

A minute later they were standing at the base of the forward pylon, on the antispinward side, where facing the pylon meant they were also facing the direction of the rotation. Gill gazed up toward the main hull fifty meters above them, trying to ignore the dizzying movement of the starry background as it circled around them at Alpha Spin's rotation rate of three RPM. The pylon was like a giant white sequoia, a solid five meters in diameter, without a single handhold in sight.

And really, why would there be? There were handholds all over a ship's main deck areas so that EVA crews could get around, but there was no gear and no attachments on the pylons that were likely to need maintenance outside of a full dock-based overhaul. Anything in the habitation part of the spin section that needed work would be handled with the rotation stopped, based at airlocks like the one he and Flanders had just used. The pylon area was essentially a no man's land, where no one had any reasonable likelihood of spending time or thruster fuel.

"You said we're *climbing* it?" he asked.

"Correct," Flanders said. Digging into his belt pouch, he came up with a multidriver and extended the longest of its blades. "You should have one of these," he said, holding it out for Gill's inspection as he flipped his safety line up over his shoulder to run down his back. "You'll want the longest blade," he added, transferring the multidriver into his right palm like he was gripping a Roman short sword.

Gill found his multidriver and set the blade to match Flanders's. Wondering what exactly the commodore had in mind.

Because on the face of it, this stunt wouldn't work. Gill had already noted the lack of handholds, which meant the only way up was to jump. The plus side of that was that once they left the Alpha Spin surface where they were standing, they would be free of the pseudogravity caused by the spin section's centrifugal motion. At that point, they would be in a Newtonian vector, heading off at an angle to Alpha Spin until they ran into something solid.

Which would happen very quickly, of course. The fact that their section of the pylon had a higher absolute speed than the more inward sections meant that jumping straight up would bounce them right back into the pylon as they caught up with it again, probably no more than a meter or two closer to the main part of the ship than they were already.

The problem was that they wouldn't stay there. They would bounce into the pylon and then bounce right off again, and without any connection with the spin section they would again be in free-fall.

In theory, as long as they maintained some of their original upward momentum they would continue to bounce, kangaroo-style, until they reached the main part of the ship. In practice, though, they would lose some of that momentum to friction each time they hit the pylon.

And if they lost enough of it they would be in serious trouble. Their last bounce would send them drifting away from any further contact with Alpha Spin, and their next likely contact with *Péridot* would be when the Beta Spin pylon spun around a third of a minute later to slam into them.

The impact all by itself would be pretty devastating. Worse was the fact that it would likely send them angling away from the ship without any hope of getting back. Even the five seconds' worth of fuel left in Flanders's thruster pack wouldn't make the difference.

And at *that* point, the next object they were likely to intersect would be Marienbad itself.

He was opening his mouth to point all of that out to Flanders when the commodore bent his knees and jumped.

As Gill had predicted, he got only a meter up before his vector caught up with the pylon and slammed him into it chest-first. As he hit, he swung the multidriver in a wide sideways arc, windmilling it over his head toward the edge of the white metal above him.

Abruptly, the swinging arm stopped, stretched out above him. Flanders also stopped, hanging from the pylon as if he was pinned there.

Which, Gill belatedly realized, he was. Flanders's swinging arm had neatly threaded the blade of his multidriver into a small, unobtrusive safety-line anchor ring in the pylon's surface.

Gill huffed out a grunt of mixed admiration at Flanders's cleverness and annoyance at himself for not thinking it all the way through. No, the pylons weren't equipped with handholds...but of *course* they had their share of safety-line anchor rings. In the dim starlight, without the more obvious markings of handholds to look for, he'd completely missed the relatively minor bumps in the surface.

But now that he knew what to look for, he could see several lines of them extending up the pylon toward the main hull. This might work, after all.

"Whew," Flanders grunted, turning his head awkwardly to look at the hull below him. "Wasn't sure I still had it. Some of my crazier shipmates liked to hotdog up the pylons like this back when I was serving aboard her."

"I thought you said you were an officer," Gill reminded him, studying the layout of the rings. The next one up was a good three meters above Flanders's head, and this time they wouldn't have the advantage of a solid surface to jump from.

"There was a school of thought at the time that said officers should be able to do anything enlisted could, only better," Flanders explained. "I'm thinking you can climb up my line, stand on my shoulders, and jump to the next ring."

"Right," Gill said. On the other hand, if he took a couple of steps farther back from the pylon, and gave it a good, strong jump...

Only one way to find out. Backing up three steps, he faced the pylon and jumped.

He nearly didn't make it. The speed differential was higher than he'd gauged, and he slammed into the pylon only a half meter or so above Flanders. A quick swipe with his multidriver got him connected to the next ring up, and a moment later he was once again hanging "down" in Alpha Spin's pseudogravity.

"Or you could climb up *my* safety line," he suggested, flipping it back over his shoulder.

"Show-off," Flanders grunted, and Gill winced a little as the commodore's weight came onto the safety line. "I remember a new PO who tried that same leapfrog stunt on his first try up the pylon. Misjudged the speeds and caught the guy below him with the toe of his boot."

"I assume he did better his next time around," Gill said, setting his teeth as the strain of their combined weight threatened to break his grip on the multidriver.

"No, because there wasn't one," Flanders said. "That was the first *and* last time anyone let him play. Steady, now."

The commodore crawled across Gill's back and pulled himself up until he reached the business end of Gill's anchored multidriver blade. Planting his boots on Gill's shoulders, he jumped.

A moment later he was hanging from the next ring up, and it was Gill's turn.

Climbing a safety line in partial gravity was about as tricky and awkward as he'd expected. But he made it in reasonably good time, and without kneeing Flanders in the kidneys more than once. He pulled himself up onto the Havenite's shoulders, visually located his target safety-line ring—

And jerked violently as something flashed past from his right. Reflexively, he bent his knees, dropping into as low a stance as he could manage.

"Watch it!" Flanders snapped.

"I see him," Gill bit back. On the main hull, anchored to the upslope of one of the cruiser's sets of missile tubes, was a vac-suited figure holding what looked like a shoulder-carried missile launcher. He was lining it up for another shot when the spin section's rotation carried him out of sight around the curve of the hull.

"Go!" Flanders snapped.

Gill was already in motion, straightening his knees in a convulsive spasm that sent him flying up along the pylon's surface. Whatever sabotage Guzarwan had done to Alpha Spin's suit lockers and escape pods, he apparently hadn't trusted it enough to skip the common-sense tactic of layering in a backup. In this case, he'd put someone in position to shoot down anyone or anything that got out.

Two seconds ago, Gill had been worried that his jump might not get him high enough to reach his target ring. But adrenaline was a wonderful thing. His outstretched hand made it to the ring with ten centimeters to spare, and with a quick jab of the multidriver he was anchored. "Suck it in," he warned Flanders, pressing himself as close to the pylon as he could.

"Like that helps in a vac suit," Flanders gritted out. "Watch it—there's another one aft on the bunkerage tanks."

Gill turned his head to look. Sure enough, another launcher-equipped figure was rolling into view on the hull bulge that held *Péridot*'s fuel and other supplies. He winced, trying to press even closer to the pylon.

But the figure rolled out of sight again without even attempting to fire. "Well, *now* they're just being nasty," he muttered.

"No, I don't think so," Flanders said thoughtfully. "I gather you never saw any actual combat back in the League?"

"That was my wife's area of expertise," Gill said, his thoughts flicking briefly to Jean, going calmly about her life on *Guardian*, as oblivious as the rest of the crew as to what was happening aboard *Péridot*. If Guzarwan had plans for the RMN ship as well...

"Those are tactical field rocket launchers," Flanders told him. "Fire small heat-seeking or optical-guided missiles. Guzarwan must have put the gunners out here in case we got one of the escape pods working."

"Yeah, I figured out that part," Gill growled. "I'm guessing they can splat us just as permanently as they can a whole pod."

"*If* they can hit us," Flanders said. "Given a ship's general background glow, heat-seeking should only work against us if we use thrusters, which we aren't. Given that their first shot missed us, I'm also guessing they didn't fine-tune their optics enough for fire-and-forget on suit-sized targets. About all that's left is to bull's-eye us manually, and we're one hell of a small *and* moving target."

"And they only have a limited number of shots," Gill said, his brain finally unfreezing enough to see where Flanders was headed. "Which means they have to decide whether we're worth spending a missile on."

"Plus every one they spend on us leaves them one less they can use against the pods if Henderson gets one or more of them free."

Gill nodded. "So we go on?"

"We go on," Flanders agreed firmly. "One's on the dorsal hull, the other's ventral, so they've pretty much got the whole rotation covered. But right as we move into or out of view will be their hardest shots. We'll try to time our major activity for those periods."

Gill grimaced. Though with one rotation of Alpha Spin happening every twenty seconds, those windows of opportunity were going to be pretty damn small.

But it was all they had. "Got it," he agreed. "You've got the next move. Pick your time, and let's do it."

☆   ☆   ☆

"I'm sorry, *Guardian*," the voice from *Péridot* came over the bridge speaker. "I'm afraid I'm still unable to raise Captain Eigen."

"That seems very odd, Petty Officer Wazir," Metzger said. Her voice was calm enough, but Travis could see that her face was starting to darken with suspicion, anger, or both. "In that case, let me speak with Captain Henderson. Or Commodore Flanders, if he's still aboard."

"I'll try," Wazir said. "Hold, please."

There was a short tone marking the loss of *Péridot*'s signal. "Patty, have you ever heard of a ship losing the whole intraship uni-link relay system but still maintaining external communications?" Metzger asked.

"No, Ma'am," Boysenko said firmly. "Actually, I've been trying to figure out how something like that would even be possible. There are half a dozen ways to get messages around inside a ship, and it doesn't sound like *Péridot* has any of them up and running."

The com toned again as *Péridot*'s signal came back. "I'm sorry, Commander Metzger, but both Captain Henderson and Commodore Flanders are unavailable," Wazir reported. "I've left messages for both of them to call you when they can."

"Thank you," Metzger growled. "You've been very helpful."

"You're welcome, Commander," Wazir said. "I'm sure Captain Henderson will return your call soon." Once again, a tone from the com signaled a disconnect.

"Doesn't much understand sarcasm, does he?" Donnelly murmured in Travis's ear, her lips close enough for her breath to tickle.

Travis shrugged. It was indeed possible Wazir was particularly dense. On the other hand, having been at the receiving end of officer sarcasm, he was hard-pressed to know what else Wazir *could* do but accept Metzger's comment at face value.

"What now, Ma'am?" Burns asked.

Metzger was silent another moment.

"Carlyle, you said you had footage of the EVA activity at *Saintonge*?"

"Yes, Ma'am," Carlyle's voice came from CIC.

"Cue it up and send it here," Metzger instructed. "Patty, call Colonel Massingill and have her report to the bridge."

Travis felt his muscles tighten reflexively as memories of his Casey-Rosewood confrontation with Massingill flashed back at him. An instant later he relaxed again as his brain caught up with him. Whatever Metzger wanted with Massingill, it couldn't possibly have anything to do with him.

Still, whatever welcome he'd started out with here, he'd probably outstayed it. From the stiff expression on Burns's face, possibly even more so. "With your permission, Ma'am?" he asked. He got a grip on the tech station's handhold beside him, readying himself to beat a hasty retreat as soon as he had permission to do so.

Burns opened her mouth. Metzger got there first. "As you were, Long," the XO said. Abruptly, she turned and looked at him, as if only now remembering he was still there. "How are your gravitics specialist studies going?"

Travis blinked at the complete non sequitur. "Ma'am?"

"How are you at reading gravitics profiles?" Metzger said impatiently. "Come on, come on."

"I'm...all right, Ma'am," Travis managed. "I've reached Level—"

"Good enough," Metzger interrupted him. "Get yourself over to CIC. Jan, is *Wanderer*'s wedge still coming up?"

"Yes, Ma'am," Vyland's voice came.

"Patty's about to wake up Lieutenant Kountouriote and send her to CIC," Metzger said. "I want the two of you to dig into the gravitics and wring out everything you can about that ship. I'm sending Long over, too, because he's here and three sets of eyes are better than two."

"Understood, Ma'am," Vyland said. Whatever her thoughts might be about Travis being attached to the *real* gravitics specialists, they didn't make it through into her voice.

"Commander Calkin will be arriving to coordinate the rest of the sensor analysis," Metzger continued. "If there's anything odd or nonstandard about *Wanderer*—anything at all—I want to know about it."

Metzger gestured to Travis. "Go."

"Aye, aye, Ma'am," Travis said. Grabbing the handhold, he sent himself flying toward the hatch.

"And after you roust Massingill, Kountouriote, and the TO," Metzger added behind him, "I want to give *Saintonge* another call. Whatever's going on in *Péridot*, they need to know about it."

CHAPTER TWENTY-FIVE

THE BATTLE FOR *SAINTONGE*'S BRIDGE had been bloody. Bloodier than it should have been.

For starters, there shouldn't have been two Marines on guard outside the hatch. All the pre-operation intel had said there might be a single guard on duty, more likely none at all. Either one of the EVA teams had screwed up their infiltration and some hatch alarm had gone off, or something about the *Péridot* operation had leaked out and alerted *Saintonge*'s commanders that something was going on.

Vachali scowled as he gazed at the three twisted bodies lying on the deck in the bridge's unpleasant-feeling half gee, leaking blood and generally being in the way. The Havenite deaths he didn't care about. After all, they were all slated for the great beyond anyway.

The problem was that in the course of the capture two of his men had also been shot. One was still functional, though the pain-killers were likely to mess with his aim and possibly his judgment. The other, though, was out of today's fight. Depending on when they were able to get *Saintonge* out of the system and focus on some medical care, he might well be joining the Havenites on their journey into eternal blackness.

Still, as with everything, there was a bright side. His men's primary weapons were silent, but when the Marines opened up with their much noisier return fire the whole forward end of the ship had come alive. With Dhotrumi's control of the com room preventing any official information or warnings from getting out of the bridge, CIC, or anywhere else, the curious and confused men and women converging on the battle area had been easy targets for the EVA teams already in place. Between their rapid-fire carbines, gas canisters, and hunter drones, they'd destroyed most of the resistance in those first few minutes. The rest of the crew had been sent scurrying away to cower in out-of-the-way compartments, where they were pinned down and could be rooted out at Vachali's leisure.

And now that Vachali had the bridge, he had the ship.

Or at least, he would soon. The critical question was *how* soon. "Well?" he demanded.

"I've got good news and bad news," Dhotrumi said, glancing disdainfully at a smear of blood on his sleeve that he'd picked up from the edge of the console. "The good news is that I've got chunks of all the main passageways except Axial One thinking they've got major fires and have therefore opened vent pipes to vacuum. No one's getting through any of those until they break out the suits and build a few micro airlocks, by which time we'll have those areas locked down. Labroo says that Impeller Two is still being contested, but we should have it soon, and we've already got control of Impeller One, Reactor Two, and Main Engineering, including the hyper generator. Reactor One was shut down when we got here—we're not going to get it up to power anytime soon, but we don't need it. We've got the preliminary cracking system up and running; as soon as it's finished, we can get started. Regardless, I should have the codes for startup in a few minutes."

Vachali nodded. Except for the Aft Impeller glitch, they were still pretty much on schedule. "So what's the *bad* news?"

"Well, I've still got a little ringing in my ear from that gunfire," Dhotrumi said blandly. "It'll probably pass, though."

"It'll pass like a boot in the rear, smartmouth," Vachali growled. "Get back to work."

"Aye, aye, Sir." With a grin, Dhotrumi turned back to his board.

Vachali looked around at the bodies. As soon as Gad finished securing Forward Impeller, he decided, he'd have him send one of his men back here and find a locker or storage room to get the corpses out of the way. Until then, he would just have to work around them. Walking past Dhotrumi and one of the bodies, he slipped into the helm station and started studying the controls. In about an hour, if things went according to plan, he'd be taking this thing out of orbit.

"Boss?" Munchi's voice came over the speaker from the com room. "We've got a call from the Manticorans. You want me to tell them the intercom system is out?"

Vachali hesitated. That was indeed the cover story that Guzarwan had instructed them to use if any of the other orbiting ships happened to call. It was safe, efficient, and discouraged the caller from trying back.

But he'd just received a report via the shuttle's laser com system that *Guardian* had tried calling *Péridot* for their captain a few minutes ago and that Wazir had spun that same cover story for them. The idea was to allay any suspicions, not enflame them, and having two Havenite ships reporting the exact same problem was likely to stack things in the wrong direction.

"No, I'll talk to them," he said. Backing up from the helm to the Watch Officer's station, giving his Havenite tunic a quick check for stray bloodstains, he settled into the padded seat and strapped in. "Go ahead, Munchi," he ordered.

The com display lit up to show a middle-aged woman wearing a Manticoran commander's tunic. She looked a little tired, but beneath the heavy lids her eyes were alert enough.

"This is Lieutenant Vachali, *Saintonge* Watch Officer," Vachali identified himself. "What can I do for you, *Guardian*?"

"Commander Metzger," the woman identified herself in turn. "I wonder if I might speak to Commander Charnay."

"The commander is occupied elsewhere," Vachali said, resisting the awful temptation to point her at the body lying at the rear of the bridge near the plotting station. Now was clearly not the time, but Metzger's reaction would undoubtedly have been priceless. "Perhaps I can help you?"

"There's some kind of problem with our communications with *Péridot*," Metzger said. "I can't get them to link a call to our captain, and they seem unable to get a message through to your commodore, either. I wondered if you'd heard from him."

"Not that I know of," Vachali said, lowering his eyes to the board in front of him. He couldn't pull up the ship's log until Dhotrumi unlocked the bridge computer system, but of course Metzger had no idea he was looking at a blank display. "According to the log, we haven't had any contact with him since he left for *Péridot*."

"Is that unusual?"

"Not really," Vachali said. "Commodore Flanders isn't the type who feels it necessary to check on his officers every ten minutes. I know he was going to be assisting Captain Henderson in showing some of the visitors around *Péridot* today. They probably just got caught up in the activities and lost track of time."

"That doesn't explain the glitch in *Péridot*'s intercom and internal relay systems," Metzger pointed out. "Especially since I thought Havenite intercom systems had triple backups."

"Sometimes multiple systems go out together," Vachali pointed out. "I've seen a single relay box take out an entire sector of a ship's power systems. Also remember that they're switching *Péridot*'s systems over to Cascan programs and protocols. That's bound to wrinkle things up a bit."

"Perhaps," Metzger said. "Thank you for your time, Lieutenant. I'll just have to keep calling until they get things sorted out."

"That's probably best," Vachali agreed, stifling a grin at the thought of Wazir and Guzarwan suffering patiently through repeated Manticoran nagging. "I'm sorry I couldn't help you further. Would you like me to log a note for Commander Charnay to call you when he gets a chance?"

"That would be very helpful," Metzger said, nodding. "Thank you."

"My pleasure, Ma'am," Vachali said. "*Saintonge* out."

He keyed off the com, feeling pleased with himself. More pleased than he should be, really, considering that all he'd done was pull the wool over a woman's eyes. He swivelled around—

To find Dhotrumi swivelled toward him, his eyes wide. "What?" Vachali growled.

"What the hell was *that*?" Dhotrumi demanded. "Havenite ships don't have triple com backups, you idiot."

Vachali's warm glow vanished. "Oh, hell," he growled, running the conversation rapidly back through his mind. The damn woman had set him a damn *trap*. And he'd walked right into it.

Or maybe he hadn't. "She said it, but I never agreed with her," he pointed out.

"You didn't deny it, either," Dhotrumi pointed out.

"Maybe I was just being polite," Vachali said. "Either way, it leaves her with uncertainty, and uncertainty slows people down."

"Maybe," Dhotrumi said. "But I wouldn't count on it slowing her down too much."

"Then you'd better get this thing cracked so we can get the wedge up and get the hell out of here, hadn't you?" Vachali said.

"Yeah. Right." Dhotrumi gave Vachali a final glare, then turned back to his board.

Vachali shifted his eyes to the man working at the aft end of the bridge, his back to the other two, clearly trying to look inconspicuous. Stepping over to Dhotrumi, he leaned down and put his lips right behind the other's ear. "By the way," he murmured, "the next time you call me an idiot in public, I'll wreck your face."

Dhotrumi didn't miss a beat. "The next time you screw up that badly in public," he countered in the same low voice, "the chief will wreck *your* face."

Vachali grimaced. Guzarwan probably would, too. "Just do your job," he growled.

Turning, he headed back to the helm, glaring at the bridge displays. The previous owners had set them to give the three-sixty display a corresponding three-sixty view of the space around them. Not especially useful, but impressively panoramic.

And dead center in the display in front of the helm and watch officer stations was the Manticoran destroyer.

It looked so harmless, Vachali thought sourly to himself, floating all alone in space. So harmless, and so vulnerable, with its wedge down and its portside flank lined up with *Saintonge*'s forward weapons cluster.

But it was neither harmless nor helpless. It was a warship, crewed by trained Naval personnel, and with a full arsenal of weapons.

And he and Guzarwan had damn well better not forget that.

Swearing under his breath, he maneuvered into the helm station. "Tell Labroo to get Aft Impeller under our control," he snarled toward the intercom. "And someone call Gad. Tell him I want these damn bodies off my bridge."

☆　　☆　　☆

"Huh," Boysenko murmured in a bemused sort of way. "I didn't know Havenite ships had triple intercoms."

"That's because they don't," Metzger said, glaring at the blank display, as if she could see through the afterimage back to *Saintonge* and Lieutenant Vachali. "I made that up."

She turned around, noting in passing that Burns was still strapped, stiff and straight, into the Watch Officer station. Probably still annoyed that the XO had effectively usurped her command.

Right now, Metzger couldn't be bothered with hurt feelings. "Colonel?" she invited.

Massingill was hovering at the missile station, peering at a display that was currently showing Carlyle's loop recording of *Saintonge*'s EVA activity. Unfortunately, as Metzger had already noted, there wasn't much to see. Carlyle had apparently come in right at the tail end of whatever was going on, and *Guardian*'s electro-optical sensors hadn't been pointed the right direction before that.

"I don't know, Ma'am," Massingill said slowly. "That many people, that spread out... unless they're doing some bizarre check of the entire hull, I can't see anything it could be except an incursion."

Metzger looked at the looping video, chewing at the inside of her cheek. Unfortunately, she *could* think of any number of things it could have been, all of them completely innocuous. It could have been routine maintenance, with several different systems tagged to take advantage of the battlecruiser's down time. It could have been a training exercise for EVA teams—the RMN didn't do routine exercises of that sort, but the RMN was chronically strapped for cash and the Republic of Haven Navy wasn't.

Or it could indeed have been a routine check of the entire hull. With only a handful of seconds to go on, and no idea how long the spacers had actually been out there, it was hard to draw any definitive conclusions.

But there was also *Péridot*, another RHN ship, supposedly having bizarre problems with its internal communications coincident with Captain Eigen being aboard. There was Metzger's little triple-intercom comment, which *Saintonge*'s watch officer seemed to have missed, though perhaps he was simply too polite to correct a foreign officer. There was even Long's and Donnelly's weird P-409-R question that still hadn't been answered.

And all of it added up to... what?

Metzger hated uncertainty. That was one of the best things about serving with the Navy: the fact that a hundred years of fine-tuning had created a list of regulations, procedures, and protocols that covered nearly any situation an officer could possibly find herself in. Regulations that should have banished uncertainty to the paving stones of hell.

Yet here she was, up to her neck in it.

Was there some kind of threat out there, as Massingill seemed to think and Metzger's own gut was reluctantly seconding? Or was it just a bizarre series of coincidences that added up to exactly nothing?

And if there was a threat, what exactly was she supposed to do about it?

Abruptly, she realized that the twisting in her gut wasn't just agreement with Massingill that this wasn't adding up. The twisting was fear. Deep, genuine fear.

The Star Kingdom of Manticore had never experienced a war. The closest it had ever come to one was the brief tangle with the Free Brotherhood, and that had been a hundred years ago.

Metzger and the rest of the Navy had been trained to fight. But neither she nor any of *Guardian*'s officers, from Captain Eigen on down, had ever actually done so. Nor had they ever really expected to.

What was she supposed to do? Was she supposed to decide that the threat was real and sound Readiness One?

But what if it wasn't? Captain Eigen had promised Commodore Flanders that *Guardian* would hold station relative to *Saintonge*. If she violated that agreement without cause, would there be diplomatic consequences down the line?

Worse, would there be military ones? *Saintonge*'s forward laser was pointing directly at *Guardian*'s flank, and the fact that Flanders had promised to disengage it wasn't particularly comforting.

The consequences might not stop with Manticoran-Havenite relations, either. It was someone else's concerns that had pushed Eigen and Flanders into the positioning agreement in the first place. If Metzger unilaterally violated that agreement, would that delegate lodge a formal protest with Landing over her actions? She had no idea what the possible political and trade ramifications might be; what she *did* know was that Defense Minister Dapplelake had given *Guardian*'s senior officers specific orders to be as diplomatic and cooperative as was humanly possible.

She looked back at Burns...and as she did so it dawned on her that the stiffness in the young lieutenant's face wasn't from Metzger's supposed insult at taking over her watch. It was, instead, fear. The same fear and uncertainty Metzger herself was feeling.

And Burns was looking to her executive officer to come up with a response to those fears.

Metzger felt her back straighten a little. Uncertainty and the fear of petty consequences were for cowards. She was an officer of the Royal Manticoran Navy; and by God and by her King, she would do whatever she had to.

"Colonel, I want you to assemble a response team," she said to Massingill. "I realize you and the other two are the only actual Marines we have aboard, but I'd guess we have our fair share of people who've tested well with small arms and hand-to-hand combat. Find them, collect them, and get them ready."

She could see in Massingill's face the obvious objection: that skill on a firing range or salle did not exactly translate into combat readiness and skill. But she was a Marine, and Marines followed orders. "Aye, aye, Ma'am," she said. Pulling herself fully into the missile console station, she called up the personnel files and got to work.

Metzger turned to Burns. "Lieutenant Burns, as you've probably already deduced, I'm relieving you," she said formally. "But stay here—I may need you."

"Yes, Ma'am," Burns said, and to Metzger's ear the younger woman's voice sounded marginally calmer. "Should we—I mean, do you want to raise *Guardian*'s readiness level?"

Metzger looked at the view of *Saintonge* floating in the center of the main display, some of her momentary resolve evaporating back into caution. *Not too far*, she warned herself. *Don't push it too far.*

And not just out of consideration for the outside world, but also for her own crew. She didn't want to stress them out, or look too jumpy. Not until and unless she had a few more facts under her belt.

"Signal Readiness Two," she told Burns. "Then get over to the plotting console and start running a full diagnostic on ship's weapons and targeting systems. Let's see just how ready *Guardian*'s prepared to be."

☆   ☆   ☆

Guzarwan was studying his tablet, reviewing the course he'd composed, when a little crowing yelp came from the tech station. "Got it!" Mota announced, looking at Guzarwan in triumph. "We're in. You got helm, reactor, impellers, and all the peripherals that go with them."

About time. "Send out the codes," Guzarwan ordered, jabbing the intercom. "Impellers; bridge," he called. "Mota's feeding you the access codes—plug them in, and get the startup sequence going."

He got an acknowledgement from both impeller compartments and rekeyed for Shora. "We're starting the impellers," he said. "Pull your men inside and make sure the hatches are sealed."

"What about the two Havenites out there?" Shora asked. "You want us to take them out?"

For a moment Guzarwan was tempted. Part of the startup procedure was to bring the spin section to a halt, and as the dumbbells slowed the rapid rotation that had so far defeated his men's attempts to pick off the two would-be escapees would cease to be a problem.

But even small radar-guided missiles were expensive, and at this late date spending one to take out a couple of troublemakers wasn't worth the effort. If he could keep them trapped outside, that was all he needed. "Don't bother," Guzarwan him. "Just make sure your men seal the hatches once they're in."

"Got it."

Guzarwan turned back to the helm, smiling tightly as the displays started coming up in response to Mota's cracked access codes. Setting his tablet floating in front of him where he could easily read his calculations, he began feeding in the numbers.

☆   ☆   ☆

Gill's first warning was the slight change in his inner ear as he started yet another climb over Flanders's back. "Commodore?" he called.

"I feel it," Flanders confirmed, his voice grim. "They're getting ready to lock down the spin section."

Gill felt a chill run through him. The only reason for this kind of dumbbell-shaped spin section in the first place was that locking it vertically made for more efficient compensator field when traveling through n-space. And the only reason Guzarwan might care about n-space efficiency—"He's starting up the impellers?"

"Sounds like it," Flanders said tightly. "Which means that he somehow got the lock codes...and I know none of my people would have given them up. Not willingly."

Another shiver ran up Gill's back. "Let's hope he's just got a really good hacker team," he said, trying to put out of his mind the nastier ways Guzarwan might have gotten the codes. "Either way, we've got to get inside."

"No argument here," Flanders said. "It looks like our playmates agree."

Gill looked at the main hull. Sure enough, the two sentries had disappeared, presumably back inside. "You realize they're still going to be waiting for us," he warned.

"I'm sure they are," Flanders agreed. "Just keep going. And no talking from here on—they're probably monitoring our channel."

Their progress inward to the slower-moving sections of the spin section, combined now with the section's decreasing speed, made their leap-frog jumps both easier and longer. Three double-jumps after Alpha Spin began its slow-down, they reached the hub.

Gill had been making a mental list of all the hatches he could remember in this part of an *Antares*-class ship and wondering which one Flanders was heading for. The answer, as it turned out, was none of them. Instead, Flanders slipped into an open gap at the edge of the hub, led the way on a zigzag course through the still-operating mechanism, and finally slipped into a service accessway equipped with single-person-sized airlock.

Ninety seconds later, they were both again inside the ship.

Gill keyed off his suit radio, gestured for Flanders to do the same, and touched his helmet to the other's. "Let me guess," he said. "Officers should be able to do everything the enlisted can?"

"And we had some pretty crazy enlisted when I was aboard," Flanders said, an edge of dark humor in his voice. "Okay. You said the starboard accessway?"

"I *did* say that, yes," Gill said, wincing. "But that was when *Péridot* was locked down and we had plenty of time. Now, we don't. What's it going to take, about forty minutes to bring up the wedge?"

"Probably down to thirty-five now," Flanders confirmed. "So if the accessways are out, that means the regular passageways. If we eliminate the ones with access to the reactor and Aft Impeller—they'll surely be guarding those—that leaves us . . . not a lot of options."

"Maybe we can split the difference," Gill suggested. "We'll use this accessway to get past the amidships section of Two that they depressurized, then drop back into one of the Three passageways for a bit, then back up here into one of the Four accessways until we pass the reactor, then back to Three until we get close to Aft Impeller, then back to Four the rest of the way to the aft radar."

"Not sure how much time that'll save us," Flanders said doubtfully. "Especially when you add in the risk of getting seen and shot. But you're right, it's probably the best we're going to get.

Okay; we're in Four-Three right now. We'll keep going until we're past amidships, then drop in to Three and hope our luck holds."

"Sounds good," Gill said. "I don't suppose there's any kind of armory or weapons locker back here?"

"Yes, but I don't have the lock code. And I doubt we have the time to break into it."

"Too bad," Gill said. "A couple of guns would have felt good about now. Well, never mind. Let's get out of this vacuum chamber and back to civilization."

☆　☆　☆

"She's definitely got an above-average wedge signature, Ma'am," Lieutenant Kountouriote called toward the gravitics station mike. "But it's nowhere near military class, either."

"You can see it best right when she was settling into orbit," Vyland added, tracing the image on her display with her stylus. "You see that little vector tweak at the end? It's brief, but it shows more power and compensator juice than a freighter of her type ought to have."

"Anything new on the weapons debate?" Metzger's voice came over the speaker.

"Nothing yet," Commander Calkin said from the CIC command station behind Travis. "Unfortunately, *Wanderer*'s still below planetary horizon, so we can't get anything fresh on her. But the records we have on her way in don't show anything out of the ordinary."

"What about *Saintonge*?" Metzger asked. "Anything new there?"

"Nothing obvious, Ma'am," Calkin said, and Travis felt the movement of air behind him as the TO swivelled around to look at some of CIC's other overhead displays. "Still running just the aft reactor, with no indication of weapons activation—"

"Whoa!" Travis snapped, jabbing a finger toward one of the gravitics displays. "What was *that*?"

"Where?" Kountouriote demanded.

"It looked like *Péridot*, Ma'am," Travis said, tensing as he belatedly realized he'd just interrupted a senior officer. "I think she's activating her nodes."

"Ioanna?" Metzger asked.

"Just a second, Ma'am," Kountouriote said, running the recording back to the proper spot. "He's right. *Péridot* is bringing up her nodes."

Calkin hissed softly between his teeth. "Ma'am, this is starting to get more than a little worrisome. I think it's time we brought up our own nodes."

"I agree," Metzger said grimly. "Problem is, we promised Commodore Flanders we wouldn't."

"Flanders isn't there for us to talk to," Calkin reminded her. "And we haven't been able to reach him, his XO, *or* Captain Eigen."

"No, we haven't," Metzger conceded. "But... Patty, give *Péridot* another try. See if you can bypass the com systems somehow and get to Flanders. Maybe link through one of the shuttles."

Calkin muttered something under his breath, and unstrapped from his station. "Kountouriote, take over," he said. Launching himself at the hatch, he opened it and left the compartment.

"Where's he going?" Travis muttered to no one in particular.

"Probably the bridge," Kountouriote said. "Looks like he wants to have a word with the XO without all of us listening in."

Travis nodded. He could certainly understand Calkin's point. With strange things happening with *Péridot* and *Saintonge*, it only made sense for *Guardian* to bring up her wedge. For that matter, it probably made sense to go directly to Condition One, full battle readiness. Tactical Officers like Commander Calkin were supposed to think that way.

But Travis could also see Metzger's point. So far all they had was a freighter and an RHN ship bringing up their wedges, which was hardly even vaguely aggressive, let alone combat-level threatening. The fact that neither of the two Havenite ships was talking to *Guardian* was irrelevant—they didn't have to answer to the Star Kingdom for anything they did.

Going to Readiness One probably wouldn't be visible from the outside world, though pouring power into the laser might be detectable at the relatively close ranges of the other orbiting ships. The problem was that, given *Guardian*'s current positioning, bringing up the wedge and sidewalls would be immediately visible to at least *Saintonge*, and probably *Péridot* as well. Travis wasn't sure whether or not that would be considered an aggressive move, especially the sidewall part, but he could see the XO not wanting to risk it. Relations between Haven and Manticore were cordial, and Metzger clearly didn't want to put any dents in that friendship.

On the other hand...

"Maybe there's a way to split the difference, Ma'am," he said. "The agreement was for *Guardian* to hold station and keep our wedge down, right?"

"That's my understanding," Kountouriote confirmed, looking up at him. "So?"

Travis hesitated. Once again, he was offering unsolicited advice to a superior officer. He'd gotten along well enough with Kountouriote, and she'd been good about teaching him the ins and outs of gravitics, but this might be pushing the line.

"Spit it out, Long."

Travis braced himself. "Maybe we could leave the wedge down and just ease out of position, Ma'am," he said. "If we drop a few kilometers inward, we'll not only get out of *Saintonge*'s direct laser line, but we'll also start moving away from her. Which will also take us closer to *Péridot*," he added as that added bonus only now occurred to him. "I know she's a lot farther away than *Saintonge*, Ma'am, but any distance we're able to close can only help our sensor analysis of what's going on over there."

"And if *Saintonge* points out that we're drifting off-station?" Kountouriote asked.

"We act surprised, Ma'am, and tell them a green helmsman keyed in the wrong program," Travis said. "In fact, warning us about our movement might get their XO to come out of wherever he's hiding."

"Or at least should get us *some* senior officer to talk to," Kountouriote said, nodding thoughtfully. She hesitated another moment, then keyed the intercom. "Bridge; CIC. Commander, we have a suggestion."

Travis listened tensely as Kountouriote described the plan, half wishing he could see Metzger's face, half relieved he couldn't.

It was something of a shock, then, when she agreed. "Helm, starboard thrusters. Slow burn; ease us inward at point one klick a minute. Be ready to reverse. Long?"

"Yes, Ma'am?"

"Report to the bridge," Metzger ordered. "If *Saintonge* squawks, I want a properly green helmsmen to parade in front of him."

Travis felt his eyes widen. Between his specialty badge and his rank insignia, there was no way he could pull off such a charade.

"Excuse me, Ma'am—"

"I know, it's ridiculous," Metzger continued. "But these are the same people who didn't seem to know how Havenite intercoms worked. Let's see if they also don't know about *Manticoran* rank and insignia."

"Yes, Ma'am," Travis said. "I'm on my way."

And as he headed around the curve of the ship toward the bridge, he wondered distantly if he would go down in history as a footnote, or as the prime offender in a major interstellar incident.

CHAPTER TWENTY-SIX

VACHALI HAD BEEN WRONG about all resistance aboard *Saintonge* being subdued. It turned out there was a handful of Marines still capable of making trouble.

"We got three of them before they pulled back," Labroo's grim voice came from the intercom. "Don't know for sure if any of them are dead, but we probably got at least one. All they've got are frangible rounds, though, and the micro-airlock barriers we set up are working just fine."

"Keep an eye on them, and watch for other exits from the hab module," Vachali ordered. "I'd rather not try to depressurize the whole module yet—that kind of thing brings out desperation, and I want to wait until we've reached the rendezvous and have a full complement aboard before we have to face down any Light Brigade charges."

"Don't worry, we'll hold them," Labroo promised. "Trev's pulled one of the reconnaissance drones and got it in the accessways. If he can find the route into Marine country, we can send in another one with a gas canister."

Vachali grunted. "Just make damn sure no one gets out."

"Yeah, don't worry. They won't."

Vachali clicked off. "Boss?" Munchi spoke up behind him. "Not sure, but I think *Guardian*'s on the move."

"On the move where?" Vachali demanded, searching the bridge's screens for the tactical display Munchi said he would be bringing up.

"Mostly down and starboard," Munchi said. "Really doesn't make much sense."

Vachali found the tactical. Munchi was right: the Manticoran destroyer was sinking slowly toward the planet far below, the laws of orbital mechanics mandating that it pick up a bit of extra speed as it did so. "They trying to get away from us?" he asked.

"If they are, they're doing a pretty stinking job of it," Munchi said. "Thrusters are slow, but even Manticoran thrusters can't be *that* pathetic."

Vachali chewed at his lip. Back when *Guardian* first arrived, Commodore Flanders had assured Guzarwan that he would make sure the Manticorans behaved themselves. *Guardian*'s movement, however small, was technically in violation of that promise, and as unofficial captain of the battlecruiser it was Vachali's job to slap the Manticorans down for it.

Only he couldn't. A high-level agreement like that required a senior officer to deliver the warning that *Guardian* get its tail back into position, and Vachali's uniform was only that of a lowly lieutenant. In theory he could throw Dhotrumi or even Labroo into a higher-ranking uniform; in actual practice, all such uniforms were either locked away in the hab section with the majority of the ship's surviving crew or else wrapped around inconveniently bloodstained bodies.

"Boss?" Munchi prompted.

Vachali bared his teeth in a snarl. "Ignore it," he said.

Munchi pursed his lips. "Okay. Whatever you say."

He wasn't convinced, Vachali knew. But he didn't care.

Because the cold, hard fact was that whatever *Guardian* was up to, whether its drifting movement was accidental or deliberate provocation, it didn't matter. Even if the Manticorans knew for a fact what was going on—and they didn't—there was still nothing they could do. No RMN ship would take it upon themselves to fire on a Havenite warship, certainly not one holding this many hostages, absolutely not without first trying to negotiate those hostages' release. Vachali could easily stall them until *Wanderer* had her wedge up, her missile prepped, and *Guardian* in her sights.

So let the Manticorans stew. Right now, Vachali had more important things on his mind.

Like getting *Saintonge*'s damn codes cracked and getting his new ship the hell out of here.

He turned his attention back to Dhotrumi's station, scowling at the program data flowing across the display. And it had better be soon.

☆   ☆   ☆

Getting to the aft endcap turned out to be considerably easier than Gill had expected. Not only did he and Flanders encounter no resistance, barriers, or booby traps, but they didn't see a single one of the hijackers along the way.

That was the good news. The bad news was that they didn't see a single member of *Péridot*'s crew, either.

Where were they? The depressurized amidships section that had trapped Gill and the others in Alpha Spin would serve equally well to pin down the personnel in Beta Spin. But surely no more than half to two-thirds of the crew would have been in there when Guzarwan blew the amidships hatches. Were the rest of them, the ones who'd been on-duty, locked up somewhere out of the way?

Or were they all dead?

He didn't like that answer. If Guzarwan was willing to kill everyone in the bridge and impeller rooms, he was probably also willing to kill everyone still in the spin sections.

And if he was willing to do *that*, he was undoubtedly willing to kill everyone aboard *Guardian*, too.

Including Jean.

A hard knot formed in Gill's throat. Colonel Jean Massingill was a Marine, and a good one. She'd been through hell and back in the little brush fires that periodically erupted around the Solarian League's borders, collecting more medals and scars than she'd ever really wanted, and had been ready to retire to a desk job when the Star Kingdom's representatives came calling.

Those desk jobs had been a mixed bag. The Casey-Rosewood stint, for one, had been slathered with more politics than she'd liked. But at least the jobs had been safe. If Jean hadn't always appreciated that, Gill certainly had.

Now she was in danger again. Serious, deadly danger.

And she didn't even know it was there. She and *Guardian* could get shot out of the sky before she had so much as a hint that anything was going down.

But she would now. Gill couldn't protect her, not from here. But he could at least warn her.

"Status?" Flanders murmured.

"Done," Gill said, finishing his last connection and surveying his handiwork. Tying *Péridot*'s com system into her aft radar wasn't pretty, but it would work. Theoretically. "You want to talk to them, or should I?"

"You're Manticoran," Flanders said. "They're more likely to listen to you."

Gill nodded.

"Here goes." He keyed the radar. "*Guardian*, this is Alvis Massingill. Repeat: this is Alvis Massingill, calling RMN *Guardian*."

He keyed to repeat and switched to receiving. The speaker remained silent. "How long?" Flanders murmured.

"Hard to tell," Gill said. "Figure one to three minutes for the rating in CIC to notice that the radar they're being painted with is modulated, then another two to three to convince the Watch Officer that he or she isn't crazy. Tying in voice to their radar shouldn't be too hard—Com and Helm are next to each other, and the helm has its own link to the radar—"

"Massingill, this is *Guardian*," a voice boomed from the speaker.

Hastily, Gill dialed back the volume. *Guardian* was more alert than he'd expected. "Commander Metzger," the voice continued at a quieter level. "Report your status."

"*Péridot* has come under attack, and appears to have been taken," Gill said. "The hijackers appear to have gained enough control to start bringing up her wedge."

There was a brief moment of silence. Then, in the background, he heard a sound that sent a ripple of both fear and hope through him: the klaxon of Readiness One.

Guardian was preparing for battle.

But it was a brittle hope, and it might already be too late. By his estimation, *Péridot* was already ten to fifteen minutes into its node warm-up procedure, and *Guardian*'s impellers would take the same forty minutes as *Péridot*'s to reach full wedge. A ten-minute head start would theoretically be all the hijackers needed to take their newly functional ship out of orbit and slash her wedge across *Guardian*'s half-formed stress bands, destroying the destroyer's nodes and leaving her helpless.

A second pass with that same functional wedge would rip *Guardian* into a nightmare of twisted scrap metal.

The klaxon's background blare dropped to a distant whisper. "Who, and how many?" Metzger asked.

"I don't know how many," Gill said. "But we think Guzarwan is part of it."

"*We?*"

"Commodore Flanders is with me," Gill said. "We were able to escape from Alpha Spin after Guzarwan's people sealed us in."

"You brought Commodore Flanders out instead of Captain Eigen?" a male voice cut in. Commander Calkin, Gill tentatively identified it.

"Commodore Flanders once served on *Péridot* and knows the ship," Gill said, part of his brain wondering why the hell he had to justify his actions to anyone. "Not to mention that he's *Saintonge*'s commander. I don't know what Guzarwan is planning, but I think you'll need all the help you can get."

"I'm sure we will," Metzger said grimly. "But that help won't be coming from *Saintonge*. We think she's been taken, too."

"*What?*" Flanders demanded, crowding Gill out of the way as he pressed closer to the speaker. "How?"

"Presumably, the same way *Péridot* was," Metzger said. "We know a shuttle arrived from *Péridot*, and we observed what looked like the last few seconds of an EVA incursion. Since then, all calls get stopped at Com, with the man there claiming the XO and other senior officers are unavailable."

"It's the same scam we're also getting with *Péridot*," Calkin added. "Have you seen Captain Eigen? We haven't been able to contact him."

"Captain Eigen and Ambassador Boulanger disappeared with Guzarwan shortly before the attack that locked down the spin sections," Gill said grimly. "We haven't heard anything from or about them since."

He'd expected at least one angry curse to be audible through the speaker. The utter black silence that followed his statement was in some ways even more chilling.

"I see," Metzger said. "What are your current resources?"

"Thin," Gill admitted. "We haven't seen any other officers or ratings, and without a secure com system we can't easily hunt for any. We have the resources of *Péridot* herself, but only to the point where the hijackers have control."

"Which we assume precludes the reactor, impellers, bridge and CIC," Flanders added.

"We also have no weapons, or any way to get any," Gill finished.

"Understood," Metzger said. "Recommendations?"

"I don't know," Gill said reluctantly. "I was hoping that you had some ideas."

"I have one," Flanders said. "Commander Metzger, I presume *Guardian* has a laser and is carrying a full complement of missiles?"

"Yes, to both," Metzger said cautiously. "What are you proposing?"

"You know what I'm proposing, Commander," Flanders said, his voice stiff. "As captain of RHNS *Saintonge* and commander of Havenite forces in-system, I'm directing you to destroy *Péridot* and *Saintonge* before their hijackers can fully activate their wedges and escape the system."

Again, Gill expected an audible gasp or curse. Again, there was only silence. Maybe Metzger and Calkin had already known Flanders was going to say that.

Maybe Gill had known it, too.

"You know we can't do that, Commodore," Metzger said. "Firing on a Havenite ship would be an act of war."

"These aren't Havenite ships anymore, Commander," Flanders said bitterly. "They're pirate vessels, and as such are not entitled to share space with civilized nations."

"That may be. But—"

"No *buts* about it, Commander," Flanders cut her off. "Now, you'll need to log both my order and my personal command code to confirm my authorization when the—when this is all over."

Gill felt his stomach tighten. When this was all over, and Metzger and the entire Star Kingdom were hauled before a Havenite court on the charge of starting a war.

"The code is as follows," Flanders continued, and rattled off a complex series of numbers and digits. "Do you need that repeated?"

"No, Sir," Metzger said, her voice stiff and formal.

"Good," Flanders said. "I know this is going to be hard, Commander Metzger. But if you can't frame it as what's best for the galaxy, frame it as what's best for your people. Because if you don't destroy them, I guarantee the first ship they'll go after will be yours."

"I'm thinking about my people, yes," Metzger countered. "I'm also thinking about yours. You have, what, around a thousand men and women on those two ships?"

"Nine hundred eighty, plus your captain and several planetary diplomats," Flanders said. "None of that matters. Whatever action you do or don't take, none of them is going to survive the day. If any of our people are still alive, it's only because Guzarwan hasn't had time yet to kill them."

"What if we send a boarding party?" a new voice cut in.

Gill stiffened. It was Jean. *His* Jean.

What was she doing on *Guardian*'s bridge?

"Do you have armored assault shuttles?" Flanders asked.

"Negative."

"Then your boarding party will be dead before it even gets close," Flanders said bluntly. "You're way the hell over there, we're way the hell over here, and there's no place to hide along the way. Guzarwan will have plenty of time to prepare, and if he can't kill them with *Péridot*'s wedge, he'll kill them with shoulder-launched missiles. These people are well-equipped, and they came prepared. I have no intention of adding two functional RHN warships to their arsenal."

There was a moment of silence. Gill tried to conjure up his wife's face against the soft glow of the radar status board. Tried to imagine the rigidly controlled expression she was even now hiding behind.

Because Flanders was right. They *had* to make sure Guzarwan and his killers didn't leave Secour with his prizes.

And at the moment, Gill couldn't see any way to do that except at the cost of all of their lives.

"I assume there's no way for you to get to the impellers and shut them down," Metzger said. "More time means more options."

Gill smiled, his eyes unexpectedly misting up. *More time means more options.* The same phrase, the same exact words, that Jean trotted out whenever Gill was frustrated by some insurmountable problem. She must have said it aloud just now, and Metzger had picked up on it.

But in this case, there was no way to buy more time. Not with the hijackers in control of all the critical sections of the ship.

There was only one thing left they could try.

"There may be a way, Commander," he spoke up. "We know that most of the officers and visitors are trapped in Alpha Spin, and we can probably assume that Guzarwan has at least some of the enlisted in Beta Spin. Assuming the sections are now locked vertically—are they, by the way?"

"Yes."

"Then what we've got is a flank that's wide open," Gill continued. "A single, close-in shot could theoretically cut through both the fore and aft impeller rings without opening and depressurizing either of the spin sections."

"He's right," Flanders said, an odd note to his voice. "A single properly aimed laser shot or a close pass with a missile's roof or floor, and you could cut through *Péridot*'s flank without killing anyone but the hijackers."

"Along with any of the crew still in the main hull," Calkin put in.

"I doubt there's anyone left," Flanders said.

"What about the reactor?" Metzger asked. "Won't a shot like that risk taking down the bottle?"

Gill looked at Flanders... and in the Havenite's eyes he saw they had indeed both come to the same inescapable conclusion.

Péridot was doomed. One way or another, *Guardian* had to take it out.

But Metzger was clearly reluctant to open fire on them. So he and Flanders would offer just enough hope to persuade her to take the shot.

The fact that there *was* no such hope was irrelevant.

"We'll be all right," Flanders assured her, with a sincerity that even Gill found convincing. "Even if you nick the edge, it should just blow the plasma out that side of the hull and leave the rest of the ship intact."

"All right." Metzger still didn't sound happy, but Gill could visualize her face settling into what he'd always referred to in officers as *command mode*. She'd made her decision, and now she was committed to carrying it out. "We'll hit *Péridot*'s portside flank. Is there anywhere you two can go where you'll be safe?"

"I know some places," Flanders said. "We'll be all right. Good luck, and good shooting to you." He took a deep breath. "*Péridot* out." He keyed off. "Shall we just leave the setup as is?" he added to Gill.

"Might as well," Gill said, his heart aching. Ever since Jean had left active Marine duty, he'd always assumed he would have a chance to say good-bye to her before their final parting.

And indeed, he'd just had that opportunity. He was here, she was on *Guardian*'s bridge, and he could have said his farewells.

Only he couldn't. The words he would have said, and the way

he would have said them, would have tipped Metzger off that the tale Flanders had spun was nothing but feathered air. The XO might have had second thoughts, and with enough second thoughts the missiles would stay in *Guardian*'s tubes and Guzarwan would get away clean. "There isn't really a chance, is there?" he asked, just to be sure.

"Realistically?" Flanders shook his head. "No. It would take a miracle to cut through the impellers and not breach the bottle, too. When that happens—" He spread his hands wide.

"That's what I figured. So what now?"

Flanders rubbed at his chin. "You said I have five seconds' worth of fuel in my thruster pack?"

"About that, yes," Gill said, frowning. "Why? You want to make a campfire we can sit around?"

"I was thinking something more constructive. If we can get into the reactor room without being shot, there may be enough fuel for me to start a fire."

"Ah," Gill said, a hint of unexpected hope flickering through the ashes. "And when the suppression system comes on, the hijackers will have to evacuate or suffocate?"

"Exactly," Flanders said. "I'm hoping you know a quick way to scram a fusion reactor."

"I know at least three of them," Gill said, the flicker of hope warming to a solid ember.

Because if the reactor was already cooling down from a scram when the bottle was breached, there was at least a chance the blast would only take out the hull nearest the breach, as Flanders had described, and not the entire ship. Granted, it wouldn't be nearly as intact as the commodore had implied, but parts should at least still be habitable. "I'm guessing we're talking the accessways?"

"We are indeed," Flanders said. "Follow me."

☆   ☆   ☆

"Very well, Commander Metzger," General Chu said, his eyes boring out of the com display like twin lasers. "I don't know the format for Havenite command codes, so I can't confirm that Commodore Flanders's authorization is legally valid. For that matter, given the unorthodox transmission and associated voiceprint degradation, I can't even confirm that that *is* the commodore."

"There are other aspects of the communication that convince me the transmission is valid, Sir," Metzger said.

"Regardless, it's clear we don't have time to debate the issue," Chu said. "I do agree with you that alerting the pirates that we're on to them would be counterproductive. The Secourian Defense Force will therefore hold off any overt action or communication for the time being. But understand this: we will *not* allow enemy ships to threaten our world, our people, or our commerce. You're authorized to take whatever action you deem proper to neutralize these ships. If you're unable to achieve that goal before their impellers are fully active, we'll take our own action against them."

"Understood, General," Metzger said, her voice steady. "Thank you for allowing me time to rescue our captain and the other personnel trapped aboard."

Chu's lip twitched.

"Don't misunderstand me, Commander Metzger," he said, a shade less stiffly. "Their lives are valuable to us, as well. But our priority must be with our own people."

"As it should be," Metzger said. "Again, thank you. We'll keep you informed."

"Do that, Commander," Chu said. "And good luck."

The transmission ended, and it seemed to Travis that the lines in Metzger's face grew a little deeper. "TO?" she asked.

"The laser would be the best for the kind of surgical strike we're talking about," Calkin said doubtfully. "But with us mostly broadside to *Péridot*, there's no way to turn into firing position fast enough for them not to have time to counter. They'd see the movement, and all they have to do is roll and pitch to put their wedge between us and them."

Metzger pursed her lips. "Ioanna, what's their wedge looking like?" she called.

"Still less than halfway up," Kountouriote's voice came from the speaker. "But the TO's right. Even a partial wedge will diffuse a laser somewhat, maybe enough to render it useless."

"And even if the shot got through, that much of a shift in *Péridot*'s attitude would mean we'd need two shots to take out both impeller rings," Calkin added. "Getting one through would be dicey enough. Two would be seriously pushing it."

"But at least their reactor would be clear of our shots," Metzger pointed out. "Though that's not much help if we take out the central plasma lines. So a missile is our best bet?"

"Probably," Calkin said reluctantly. "We'll still need to rotate into alignment with *Péridot*, but we've got a ten- to twenty-degree slack in our initial launch vector, so we don't have to be *quite* lined up with her before we fire. If they're not paying close attention we may be able to ease into position without them noticing."

"And if they do, they still might buy our green helmsman excuse," Metzger said reluctantly.

"If they bother to ask," Calkin warned. "They might just open fire instead."

"We'll just have to hope the Havenites locked down their weapons systems better than they did their impellers," Metzger said. "Assuming we get that far, who do you recommend to set up the shot?"

"I'd give it to Lieutenant Donnelly," Calkin said. "She's consistently shown excellent or outstanding in simulations."

"Fine," Metzger said. "Get her started, but I'll want the two of us to look over her course and programming before we commit. And have her use a practice missile—we're going to do enough damage without risking a warhead going off along the way."

"Aye, aye, Ma'am." Calkin glanced at Travis, as if wondering why he was still on the bridge when the crew were supposed to be at their assigned Readiness One stations. But he turned back to his board without asking. Keying the intercom, he began talking softly into the mike.

Asked or otherwise, it was a good question. And it was one Travis didn't have an answer for. He'd started to leave when Metzger signaled Condition One, but halfway to the hatch the XO had waved him back. She'd finished her conversation with Flanders and Massingill, then moved immediately to the question of how to destroy *Péridot*'s nodes without killing the ship and everyone aboard.

Meanwhile, Travis remained floating in a corner of the bridge, wedged between two overhead displays and trying not to block either, trying to stay inconspicuous as he awaited orders.

And watching the bridge personnel age right before his eyes.

Metzger and Calkin were bad enough, with the lines and shadows in their faces deepening and darkening. But Colonel Massingill was worse. Her face had gone steadily more rigid as Flanders's description of *Péridot*'s situation drained away more and more hope. Now, with the decision made, the stiffness in her expression had dissolved, leaving behind it the face of someone gazing at death.

Which she was. Travis knew enough about the positioning of impeller nodes to know it would be almost impossible to successfully cut through both rings with a single shot without also slicing away enough of the reactor's peripheral containment equipment to precipitate a catastrophe. If the blast was contained enough, or the reactor was ejected soon enough, the two spin sections and their occupants might survive. But the rest of the hull would be shattered.

Massingill surely knew that. And if she and Travis knew it, Metzger and Calkin must know it, too. So why were they going through with the charade?

A bitter taste tingled at the back of his tongue. Because they had no choice. Guzarwan had to be stopped, and this was the only way to do it without straightforwardly blasting *Péridot* to atoms. Even if the chances were slim, they were better than no chance at all.

The RMN oath included a willingness to die for the Star Kingdom. It had never occurred to Travis that such an oath might also include a willingness to kill your own for the same cause.

Back on *Vanguard*, he'd disagreed with Captain Davison's decision not to trade a slim chance of rescuing *Phobos* for the near-certainty of rescuing *Rafe's Scavenger*. Disagreed with it violently. Now, looking back, he could better see the situation the captain had been in, and the heart-wrenching decision he'd had to make.

It was the same decision Metzger had just made. And it carried the same cost.

Part of that cost would be the life of Colonel Massingill's husband.

"Colonel?"

As if someone had thrown a switch, the deadness vanished from Massingill's face as her heart and soul shifted back from being a wife to being a Marine. "Yes, Commander?"

"What's the status on your assault team?"

"The bosun and I have collected nine likely names, and Sergeants Holderlin and Pohjola are gathering them outside Shuttle Two for a quick assessment and briefing." Massingill's eyes flicked to Boysenko. "We just need to get Boysenko down there to join them."

Metzger turned her head, her eyes widening momentarily with surprise. "*Patty?*"

"I did competitive shooting in high school, Ma'am," Boysenko said, a slight quaver in her voice. "I've kept up with it."

"I see," Metzger said, back on balance. "Very well. Report to Shuttle Two. Colonel, let me know when you're ready to move."

"Aye, aye, Ma'am."

Massingill flicked a glance across the bridge at Travis...and as she did, a memory flashed to his mind. Massingill, her face looking so much younger than it did now, gazing up at him from her desk as Gunner's Mate First Class Jonny Funk—the late and still heart-wrenchingly missed Jonny Funk—described for her the boots' theft of cookies from the Casey-Rosewood mess hall.

At the time, Travis had thought it was the worst thing that had ever happened in his whole life. Now, it seemed unbelievably banal.

The glance ended, and Massingill and Boysenko headed together for the hatch. A moment later, they were gone.

"You think this is a good idea?" Calkin asked quietly. "Flanders warned that Guzarwan's men have hand-held missiles. Not much point in sending a shuttle full of people to *Saintonge* if it's just going to get swatted out of the sky."

"*Saintonge* is a lot closer than *Péridot*," Metzger pointed out. "Whoever's over there won't have nearly as much time to react. I think there's a fair chance they can get to her, especially if the hijackers are still working on taking over the ship. Anyway, we have to try."

There was a brief pause. Possibly, Travis decided, his best chance to get out of here. He cleared his throat—

"You know how to work a com board, Long?" Metzger asked, looking over at him. "No, of course you don't. Doesn't matter—there isn't anyone out there for us to talk to anyway." She pointed to Boysenko's vacated station. "Strap in."

Travis felt his eyes goggling. "Yes, Ma'am," he said, fighting the confusion. What in the *world*? Maneuvering himself into position, he fumbled the straps into place. "Uh...Ma'am...?"

"I don't know, either," she said absently, drifting toward him as her eyes shifted methodically between the various displays. Looking for information. Looking, maybe, for hope. "All I know is that you're not really needed at Three-Ten Damage Control," she continued, "and that you've demonstrated a talent for outside-the-lines ideas. Right now, that's what we need."

Travis swallowed hard. "Ma'am, I don't know—"

"No—don't *know*," Metzger interrupted. "Don't think. Just let your brain spin and see what it comes up with." A ghost of a pained smile flicked across her face. "And if you don't get anything, we're no worse off."

Travis felt his stomach tighten. No, Metzger and *Péridot* might not be worse off. But *he* would be.

Because thirty seconds ago, he'd been an observer to the unfolding drama. Now, suddenly, he'd become one of the participants.

And if he didn't come up with something, he would forever feel responsible for what was about to happen.

Which meant that he'd damn well better come up with something. And he'd better do it fast.

Keying the computer to bring up everything the RMN had on Havenite *Améthyste*-class cruisers in general and *Péridot* in particular, he began to read.

CHAPTER TWENTY-SEVEN

"GOT IT!" DHOTRUMI SAID TRIUMPHANTLY. "WE have got control. Hooray for me."

"Yeah, and about time," Vachali growled, keying the intercom. "Impellers, you're a go. Get us up and running."

He got acknowledgments and keyed off. "About *time*?" Dhotrumi echoed. "You're joking, right? Show me *one* hacker this side of the League who can get into a military computer that fast."

"When we find him, I'll be glad to introduce you," Vachali countered. Actually, he was pretty damn impressed that Dhotrumi and his team had cut through the barriers as quickly as they had. That was why Guzarwan had hired the kid in the first place, of course, but even so it had been a remarkable performance.

Not that he would ever tell Dhotrumi that. He was puff-headed enough as it was, and Vachali had long ago learned that complimenting people only made them lazy.

"So what do we do for the next forty minutes?" Dhotrumi asked.

"Well, *I'm* going to run our new ship," Vachali said. "How about you seeing if you can keep your streak going by cracking the weapons systems?"

Dhotrumi shook his head. "It's not a matter of cracking the codes," he said. "Impeller and helm systems are designed for idiot grunts to start up if they have to. Weapon-work requires a lot of people and a lot of specialized training, and that's not this team's particular skill set. Once we're back at base we can tackle that. But not here."

"Whatever," Vachali growled. Guzarwan had warned him in advance that that would be the case. But it never hurt to try again, especially with Dhotrumi in the flush of self-congratulatory victory. "In that case, how about figuring out what that weird vibrating radar thing was a minute ago?"

Dhotrumi snorted.

"It was probably Munchi hallucinating. Ships use pulsed radar all the time. No one uses the kind of thing he described." He waved a hand. "If you're worried, call Guzarwan and ask. It supposedly came from *his* ship."

Vachali looked at the main display. He would love to call Guzarwan, if only to let him know that *Saintonge* was up and running.

Unfortunately, the only secure way to do that was via communication laser...and whether by accident or design, *Guardian*'s slow drift had dropped it squarely between *Saintonge* and *Péridot*.

He scowled, running his eyes along *Guardian*'s lines. The destroyer was still lying crosswise to *Saintonge*, its portside flank wide open to anything the battlecruiser wanted to throw at it. Vachali didn't have anything he *could* throw, of course, but *Guardian* didn't know that.

The question was, how much *did* the Manticorans know?

It was a critical question. Were they still lying there fat and sassy, taking *Péridot*'s and *Saintonge*'s communication-problem lies at face value? Or had they seen through the ruse and were they even now gearing up for battle?

"Is *Guardian* bringing up its wedge?" he asked suddenly.

"No idea," Dhotrumi said, peering briefly at the display and then going back to his monitors. "A good gravitics man could probably tell you. Too bad we don't have anything like that here."

"Can they tell that we're bringing up ours?"

"The exact same complete lack of an idea," Dhotrumi said sarcastically. "How many types of genius do you expect me to be, anyway?"

"Whichever types don't have a smart mouth," Vachali growled. "Fine. Just get back to work."

"Whatever you say."

Vachali glared at *Guardian* another moment, then turned away. No matter what they knew, he told himself firmly, they couldn't possibly know enough. "And have Munchi keep an eye on them," he added. "If they start turning toward us—or turning *any* direction—I want to know about it."

☆   ☆   ☆

Finally, the missile was ready.

Jalla took a final look across the hold at the mechanism, poised by the open hatch like an arched snake, then maneuvered his way back through the airlock that led into *Wanderer*'s bridge. The lock cycled, and he floated through the inner hatch, popping his helmet as he did so. "Buju, get a laser on *Péridot*," he ordered his second officer as he started stripping off his vac suit. "Tell the chief we're ready."

"You can tell him yourself," Guzarwan's voice boomed from the bridge speaker. "Good job."

Jalla threw a glare at the back of Buju's head. So the other had anticipated the order and already set up a link to *Péridot*. Never mind that Jalla had expressly forbidden him to break communication silence until he got a specific order to do so.

Guzarwan liked a certain amount of initiative among his team. Jalla didn't, and Buju was going to hear about it when this was all over.

"Yeah, missile prepped and ready," Jalla growled toward the com station. "Impellers are coming up nicely. We should be ready to move in twenty minutes."

"Good," Guzarwan said. "Bearing in mind that you *won't* move until I tell you to."

"Got it." The chief liked a little underling initiative, but there were limits. "Anything from Vachali?"

"He's got control," Guzarwan said, his voice souring. "I don't know if they've got the wedge started yet. It seems *Guardian* has managed to lose station right into the middle of the laser path between us."

Jalla felt a tingle run up his back. "*Guardian*'s out of position? I thought Flanders promised they'd stay put. Under threat of whatever he told you he'd threatened."

"Flanders isn't in charge anymore, is he?" Guzarwan growled. "Don't worry about *Guardian*—with their wedge down, they probably can't turn fast enough that you won't be able to get up over the horizon and target them."

"*Probably?*"

"And they haven't got a clue as to what's going down anyway," Guzarwan added. "Just relax, okay?"

David Weber & Timothy Zahn

"Yeah, easy for *you* to say."

"What easy?" Guzarwan shot back. "*I'm* in sight of them. *You're* not."

"Maybe we should remedy that," Jalla said. "Why don't I fire up the thrusters and take them out right now? I figure I can be in targeting position in—"

"Whoa, whoa," Guzarwan interrupted. "You fire now and Marienbad will scramble every ground-based defense they've got."

"So?" Jalla countered. "What have they got that can bother us?"

"Until our wedges are up? Who the hell knows? Not to mention that we're going to need enough time after we take out *Guardian* to kill everything else up here. I don't want anyone even suspecting there's a problem until it's too late to get their wedges up. So calm it down."

"I'll calm it down," Jalla said reluctantly. "But you keep an eye on *Guardian*, okay? Keep a *good* eye."

"I am," Guzarwan promised. "Don't worry. The only thing *Guardian* can do is destroy us, and the Manticorans would never do that to an RHN ship. Not unless they wanted to start a war that there's no way in the universe they could win. Not against Haven."

Jalla exhaled noisily. "If you say so."

"I say so," Guzarwan said. "Just sit tight, okay? And relax— you'll get to fire your missile. I promise."

☆   ☆   ☆

"Bridge; CIC," Kountouriote's voice came from the bridge speaker. "Commander, gravitics just picked up a twitch from *Saintonge*. Looks like they're bringing up their impellers."

Metzger suppressed a grimace. So Guzarwan's people had cracked *Saintonge*'s codes, too. She'd hoped fervently that *Péridot* had been a fluke. "Acknowledged," she said, tapping the intercom key. "Shuttle Two; bridge. *Saintonge*'s got their nodes started. What's your status?"

"We're nearly there, Ma'am," Massingill's voice came back, sounding even grimmer than it had when she'd been on the bridge. Though that could have been Metzger's imagination. "A few more minutes, and we'll be ready to suit up and load the shuttle."

"Understood." Briefly, Metzger considered reminding Massingill that she not only had to get to *Saintonge*, but she also had to retake it before the forty-minute clock ran down. If she didn't, *Guardian* would be forced to destroy the other ship whether Massingill and her team were still aboard or not.

But she kept her silence. Massingill surely already knew that. "Bridge out," she said instead, and keyed off.

In fact, the sobering thought struck her, maybe Massingill was counting on it. By the time her shuttle headed out she would likely know whether Flanders's gamble had worked, or whether her husband was dead.

And if he was . . .

Metzger felt her throat tighten. She'd known many long-married couples separated by death where the surviving partner had lost the will to live. If Massingill chose not to outlive her husband, she could hardly find a better way to go out than in a single, massive, Wagnerian charge against impossible odds.

And whether or not she committed suicide by combat could well hinge on whether Metzger could find a way to stop *Péridot* while still keeping Alvis Massingill alive.

Metzger focused on the back of Travis Long's head. He was leafing through the data on *Améthyste*-class cruisers, scrolling pages at probably one every ten seconds. The kid was a fast reader, or at least a good skimmer. Probably one reason why he was doing so well in the informal Gravitics Specialist classes Kountouriote was running him through.

Metzger looked away, wondering distantly why she'd kept him here on the bridge. It had been an impulse decision, one that violated standard protocol but otherwise seemed harmless. It still seemed harmless; but she could tell from the sideways looks Calkin and the rest of the bridge crew occasionally threw at Long that they were all wondering about it.

Metzger didn't really have an answer for them. Granted, Long's Unicorn Belt idea about using a missile to carry oxygen to *Rafe's Scavenger* had been inspired. But his more recent suggestion to let *Guardian* drift off-station as a way of testing *Saintonge's* vigilance hadn't been anything out of the ordinary, and his concerns about Guzarwan's control circuit gambit hadn't gone anywhere at all. When you added it up, there really wasn't all that much to make Travis Long stand out from the pack of other clever but inexperienced young petty officers.

"Ma'am?"

Metzger turned to Calkin, putting Long out of her mind. "What is it, Drew?"

"An idea, maybe," Calkin said. "Instead of using the missile's wedge to try to cut through both impeller rings, what if we ignore the aft ring and go for an angled cut that'll take out just the forward ring and the forward endcap?"

"Sounds pretty drastic," Metzger pointed out. "Won't cutting that deep with the edge of a stress band do bad things to the rest of the ship?"

"A lot of it, but not all," Calkin said. "If we make the cut as far forward as we can, the edge effects should take out the impellers and neutralize the bridge, but leave everything from amidships aft mostly habitable. Certainly the reactor should make it through all right, and hopefully all or most of the spin section."

Metzger chewed at the inside of her cheek. *Péridot* only needed one impeller ring to raise the wedge and escape. But with that much damage, the surviving pirates might decide it was no longer worth the effort to steal. At which point they would do...what? Give up and simply abandon ship?

Or would they pay Metzger back by abandoning ship only after slaughtering everyone else aboard?

Maybe it didn't matter. Maybe none if it mattered. The more she looked at the problem, the more it looked inevitable that the day would end with a wrecked Havenite ship and a dead Havenite crew.

But there was nothing to gain by giving up. "Run some simulations," she told Calkin. "See what shakes out."

"Right." Calkin turned back to his board. Metzger glanced at Long—

And paused for a longer look. There was something about Long's back and shoulders, a stiffness that hadn't been there a minute ago.

And the tech manual on his display was flipping pages now at less than two seconds each.

Long wasn't looking for inspiration anymore. He'd found it. Now he was looking for...what?

Metzger didn't know. But somehow—unexpectedly, unreasonably, even ridiculously—a small hint of fresh hope was taking root in the back of her mind.

Long had an idea. Maybe a useless one. But at this point, Metzger would take anything she could get.

In the meantime, there was still a Plan A that needed her attention. "Weapons; bridge," she called into the intercom. "Lieutenant Donnelly: report."

☆   ☆   ☆

The accessways directly port and starboard of *Péridot*'s dorsal radiator complex were more tightly packed with equipment and conduits than the route Gill and Flanders had taken earlier to the aft endcap.

It was also damn hot. On the other side of the bulkhead, Gill knew, were the massive and heavily shielded pipes that carried the reactor's waste heat to the huge radiator fins jutting outward from the hull. This particular accessway contained part of a step-down coolant grid, designed to protect nearby parts of the ship from the much hotter central heat-sink, plus a set of strategically placed hatchways in case a remote had to be sent into the main radiator system itself.

The radiator area was theoretically hot enough to kill anyone not wearing the proper gear who got within a hundred meters of it. Not that anyone could actually do that. Even here in the step-down area, the pipes were hot enough to cook on.

The plus side was that this wasn't a place where any of Guzarwan's hijackers would want to spend their time. Probably why Flanders had chosen this route in the first place.

And now they were here.

"You figured out where you're going to start that fire?" Gill murmured as Flanders finished unfastening one of the reactor control room's ceiling sections.

"Slight change of plans," Flanders murmured back. "I think instead I'm going to try sending the thruster pack into the moderator system coolant lines. If the impact bursts enough of the pipes, the coolant should blast out hard enough to simulate smoke to the detectors. Since there's no actual fire, even if whoever's in there gets to an extinguisher, there won't be anything he can do to convince the detectors the fire's out. The stage-two response should then kick in and flood the compartment, and they'll have the choice of getting out or suffocating. The moderator coolant is lower-temp than the rest of the system, so we should be okay in there." He eyed Gill. "What about you? You picked out which scram method you want to use?"

"We'll go with the two easiest," Gill said. "Let me give you the run-downs, and you can choose which you want to go for after they clear out—"

"That's okay," Flanders interrupted. "That'll be your part of the job. You just do it, all right?"

"Sure," Gill said, feeling his eyes narrowing. "But wouldn't it be better if we both knew what to do?"

"I won't be down there with you," Flanders said. "Not in any shape to work, anyway. I'll get them out; you'll scram the reactor. Got it?"

"Yes, Sir." Now, belatedly, Gill realized why Flanders was still wearing the thruster pack instead of having it off and ready to go.

It *was* ready to go. Because Flanders was going to be wearing it in.

In hindsight, of course, it was obvious. Gill should have seen it coming before they even left the endcap. Even with a target as big as a cooling grid, simply aiming the thruster and turning it loose was more likely than not to end in a clean miss. With Flanders wearing it, controlling it the whole way, it was virtually guaranteed that it would land where it was supposed to.

It was also virtually guaranteed that Flanders would die in the effort. If enemy gunfire didn't get him, the shattered pipes would.

Should Gill say something? Should he argue the point, or volunteer to go in Flanders's place?

He probably should. But he knew he wouldn't. Flanders had made up his mind, and *Péridot* was one of his nation's ships. It was his job.

More to the point, Gill didn't have anything better to offer.

Flanders pulled out the last connector and gestured toward Gill's helmet. "Remember: no talking."

Ten seconds later, they were ready.

Through Flanders's faceplate, Gill saw the other give him a brief farewell smile. Then, turning to the ceiling, the Havenite eased the section open a crack and peered through into the reactor room. Gill got a grip on a nearby support strut, ready to pull himself forward the minute Flanders made his move.

Only Flanders didn't move. He just floated there, his faceplate pressed against the crack. Then, slowly, he eased the section back into place, floated away, and gestured Gill to take a look. Frowning harder, Gill took the other's place and eased open the section.

There were four men in the reactor room, or at least four within his angle of view. Three were strapped in at various consoles, while the fourth floated near them in guard position, his head turning methodically toward each of the hatches leading into the room, a carbine ready in his hands.

All four of them were wearing vac suits.

Gill looked at the scene for another couple of seconds. Then, carefully setting the section back in place, he floated over to Flanders. The other had already unfastened his helmet, and Gill followed suit. "Well," Gill murmured. "So much for *that* approach. Any other ideas?"

"No, just the same one," Flanders said grimly. "Only now, instead of blasting into the grid, I run down the guard. If I can get that carbine away from him, I can shoot him and the others. If I make it, and if I still have ammo left, I'll try to shoot the grid. Once we spark a stage two and the automatics lock out everyone else, we're back to you getting in and scramming the reactor."

"That's insane," Gill told him. "That guard's a good ten meters away, and he and all the rest of them are also wearing sidearms. You don't have a chance."

"You got a better idea?"

"Yeah, I do," Gill said. "You charge the guard; I charge the guys at the console. That creates double the chaos, double the targets, and double the chances that one of us will get a gun while we're in good enough condition to use it. And don't give me that look," he added. "You know it's the only way that makes sense."

Flanders huffed out a breath. "Maybe," he conceded. "But it's not right. You're a Manticoran; this is a Havenite ship. This shouldn't be your fight."

"Tell that to Guzarwan," Gill said sourly. "Anyway, it became my fight the minute they marched the captain away as a hostage. Not to mention locking me into that damn ridiculous dumbbell spin section of yours."

Flanders flashed an unexpected smile. "Now, *that* one we definitely agree on," he said with a hint of humor. "Always thought those things looked ridiculous, not to mention cramped. You have a preference as to which console you go for?"

"Main control board," Gill said. "There are two men there, which gives me a choice of two guns to go for instead of just one. Plus, if everyone down there knows what they're doing, they'll be a little leery of shooting toward the main controller. Certainly more leery than shooting toward the monitor station."

"And if they *don't* know what they're doing, a few ill-considered rounds could end up scramming the reactor for us," Flanders agreed. "We'll need to find better entry points. You saw how I unfastened the ceiling section?"

Gill nodded. "I think my best shot will be something over there." He pointed to a space between a return coolant pipe and an air-exchange driver. "It's right over main control, and there's a solid bar above it that I can use to kick off of."

"Good," Flanders said. "I'll see what I can find above the guard. Work quiet, work fast, and signal me when you're ready."

☆   ☆   ☆

The missile was programmed and ready, and Commanders Metzger and Calkin were doing their final check on the numbers, when Travis finally found the answer he'd hoped was there. "Commander Metzger?" he called. "I think I may have something."

Metzger was at his side in an instant. Faster than Travis had expected, in fact, robbing him of the ten seconds he'd counted on to let him double-check his conclusions. "Go," she ordered, leaning over his left shoulder.

Travis braced himself. He would just have to trust that he was right. "The molycircs in the nodes," he said, pointing to the *Péridot* schematic he'd pulled up. "The ones that handle the synchronization of the Casimir cells. Specifically, the ones *here* and *here*, at the core of the clusters closest to the hull."

"Yes, we see them," Calkin said. The tactical officer had come up on Travis's right shoulder, sandwiching Travis uncomfortably close between the two officers. "So?"

"You said it yourself, Sir, earlier," Travis told him. "Edge effects. The gravitational strength drops off rapidly from the edge of an impeller stress band, but the effect *does* extend a few dozen meters out before it becomes negligible. And molycircs are highly susceptible to transitory stresses."

"What exactly are you suggesting?" Metzger asked, though her tone made it pretty clear that she already knew.

"We don't have to actually hit *Péridot* to kill its wedge, Ma'am," Travis said. "If we can run the edge of the missile's stress band within twenty or thirty meters of the hull, that's all it'll take. It'll wreck the focus, kill the stabilization, foul up all the other nodes as they try to synch up into stand-by, and that'll be it for that ring."

"And if we run the missile parallel to the hull, we'll take out both rings in the same pass," Metzger murmured. "And there goes the wedge."

"Yes, Ma'am," Travis confirmed. "And they're not going to get the nodes retuned, either. Not anytime soon."

"What about the reactor?" Calkin asked. "It has molycircs, too."

"Yes, Sir, but all of them are deeper in toward the center of the hull," Travis said, pulling up a different page. "The gravity transient shouldn't get close enough to affect them."

"Besides, even if it does, it'll just shut everything down in a controlled scram," Metzger said, reaching over Travis's shoulder to the intercom. "Exactly what it'll do to the nodes, in fact. Weapons; bridge. Donnelly?"

"Donnelly, aye," Donnelly's voice came back instantly.

"Get back to your board," Metzger ordered. "I need a fast reprogramming."

☆ ☆ ☆

"Missile away!" Mota's voice boomed from the bridge speaker. "From *Guardian*—damn it all, they're *firing!*"

Guzarwan snapped his head around to the tactical display, feeling his tongue freeze to the roof of his mouth. No—it was impossible. The Manticorans, firing on a Havenite ship? That was an act of *war*.

But the missile was there. It was *there*, damn it—a blur on the tactical as its thirty-five-hundred-gee acceleration ate up the thousands of kilometers separating the two ships. Guzarwan had one final glimpse of the missile as it bore down on *Péridot's* stern—

And then, nothing.

Guzarwan stared at the tactical, a sense of utter disbelief swirling through his mind. According to the track, the missile had shot out from *Guardian*, angled the last few degrees to line up on *Péridot*, and continued straight on toward its target.

And after all of that effort, the Manticorans had missed.

They'd *missed*.

It was impossible. But it was true. The track plainly showed the missile running parallel to the portside flank, a good ten kilometers out, then heading off toward the eternity of the universe.

They'd *missed*.

No one out here was supposed to have much experience with real warfare, Guzarwan knew. Even Haven, who'd tackled pirates and the occasional lunatic interstellar nomad group, was barely above amateur status. But this was just ridiculous. Even if the missile itself didn't zero in, *Guardian* should at least have been able to get it close enough to its target for its stress bands to do some damage. But they hadn't even managed that.

Could *Péridot* have some automatic ECM running that had confused or disabled the missile? Mota hadn't been able to tap into any of the weapons or active defenses, but it was possible the Havenites routinely left some of their passive defense systems running on general principles. Guzarwan hadn't spotted any evidence of such a setup on the status monitors, but it was the only thing that even halfway made any sense.

And if that was indeed the case, then he and Vachali were even more home free than he'd thought. If none of the Manticoran missiles could touch them, *Péridot* and *Saintonge* could not only bring up their wedges at their leisure, but they could also cut their mowing-machine swath through the other orbiting ships with impunity. *Guardian* would be the first, of course, lest one of his new ships accidently stray within laser range—

"Chief!" Thal's frantic voice came from the speaker. "The wedge has collapsed!"

Guzarwan's heart skipped a beat.

"What the hell are you talking about?" he demanded.

"It's collapsed," Thal repeated. "The whole system—both impeller rings—they've shut down. We're trying to restart, but—God, the diagnostics have gone crazy."

And in a horrible, suffocating instant, Guzarwan understood.

The Manticoran missile hadn't missed at all. It had done exactly what it was intended to do.

Somehow, that close pass had scrambled the impeller rings. Scrambled them badly enough to shut down, and to take the half-formed wedge with them.

And now, far from being immune to *Guardian*'s weapons, *Péridot* stood utterly open and defenseless against them.

Thal was still blabbering about tuning and synchronization and molycircs, his voice joined now by a chorus of frantic reports coming from other parts of the ship. But Guzarwan wasn't listening. There was a way out of this, he knew. There was *always* a way out. He wasn't going to give up, not now. Not after the Manticorans had so clearly demonstrated their reluctance to destroy Havenite property and lives. Not when he had two ships' worth of hostages to bargain with.

Certainly not with the ultimate hole card, *Wanderer* and its missile, still unsuspected up his sleeve.

"Everyone shut up," he called toward the mike. "Shut *up*."

The cacophony trailed away. "All right," he said into the tense silence. "Everyone shut up and listen. Here's what we're going to do..."

CHAPTER TWENTY-EIGHT

GILL HAD JUST FINISHED unfastening his section of ceiling when *something* seemed to zoom by.

An instant later, he realized how absurd that sounded. He was floating in zero-gee, in the middle of a tangle of pipes and conduits that pretty well precluded the possibility of *anything* moving quickly, let alone moving so fast that he hadn't seen it.

But yet the sense remained.

Frowning, he looked around. Nothing seemed to have changed. He leaned out from the air-exchange box that was blocking his view of Flanders.

To find that the other was looking around, too. In the gloom of the accessway Gill couldn't make out Flanders's expression through his faceplate, but he had the sense from the other's posture that he was feeling the same confusion.

The commodore spotted Gill looking at him, and for a moment they gazed across the cramped space at each other. Then, motioning Gill to stay put, Flanders worked his way through the equipment to his side. He touched his helmet to Gill's—

"I just had the strangest feeling," the Havenite's faint voice came. "Like a mini-groundquake. I know that's ridiculous, but..." He lifted a hand helplessly.

"Not really," Gill assured him. "Only to me it felt like something shot past."

"Weird," Flanders said. "After forty years in the Navy, I thought I knew every twitch or grunt a ship could make. But that was a new one. What the hell are they *doing* down there?"

Gill looked at the status display at the inside edge of his faceplate, freshly aware of the red glow that marked the silenced com. But if the reactor crew was in vac suits, and couldn't easily use the hard-wired intercoms... "Let's find out," he suggested, pointing to the com control.

Flanders nodded and reached for his own control. Twisting his face so that he wouldn't even be breathing toward his mike, Gill turned on his com and ran slowly through the frequency presets. He reached the fifth one—

"—to Shuttle Port One," Guzarwan's harsh voice came. "Stay in good retreat formation—remember there are still at least two Havenites running around loose, plus probably a few more gone to ground elsewhere."

"Never mind the Havenites," someone bit out. "What about the damn Manticorans? If they decide to blow us out of the sky—"

"If they wanted to blow us out of the sky, they'd have done that instead of just wrecking our impellers," Guzarwan bit out. "Stop yapping and get your butts to the shuttle."

Flanders tapped Gill's arm and tapped his com switch. Gill nodded and shut his off, as well, then touched his helmet to Flanders's. "Any ideas?" he asked.

"About what *Guardian* did just now? Or about what we should do next?"

"Either or," Gill said. "I'd go with the second question, because frankly I haven't a clue as to how they scrambled *Péridot*'s nodes without gutting us like a fish. But somehow, they managed it."

"With the happy result that the rats are pulling out," Flanders said with grim satisfaction. "And once they're gone, the ship is ours. You know how to assemble an emergency micro airlock, right?"

"I've knocked together a few in my day," Gill confirmed. "But I don't know the first thing about disarming bombs."

"You won't need to," Flanders said. "We use the airlocks to reseal the outer hull hatches they blew, then repressurize the amidships section."

"But the hatches to the spin sections are still booby-trapped. How do we clear them?"

"Again, we don't have to," Flanders said. "Once the area is repressurized the bombs are welcome to blow through the view-ports. Hell, they can disintegrate the entire hatch if they want. As long as everyone inside is out of the blast range, I don't care."

"So we just stand off and throw bricks at them or something until they go off?"

"Something like that." Flanders's face settled into hard lines. "And once we've got *Péridot* back . . . well, we'll see what our options are."

Gill felt something hard settle into his stomach. There was a simmering death in Flanders's eyes that Gill hadn't seen there before. It was just as well, he thought soberly, that that death wasn't aimed at him and his people. "Sounds good," he said. "Let's do it."

☆   ☆   ☆

It worked. To Travis's mild surprise and infinite relief, the plan actually *worked*.

Kountouriote's gravitics sensors confirmed *Péridot*'s wedge had collapsed. Carlyle's infrared sensors further confirmed a dip in the cruiser's heat that suggested the reactor's systems had taken a mild hit as well before the automatics restabilized the power levels.

And as the quiet and cautious triumph rippled across *Guardian*'s bridge, Travis felt a warm glow of satisfaction filling him.

The glow lasted exactly forty-five seconds before the com board he was still strapped to went crazy.

The first furious and frantic calls came from the Havenite courier ships in distant orbit, their watch officers demanding to know who the hell was throwing missiles and who the hell they were throwing those missiles at. Travis was still fumbling with the unfamiliar controls when Marienbad's ground command chimed in, a surprisingly calm General Chu acknowledging the event, though pointedly asking if this was what Manticorans considered keeping an ally informed.

Fortunately, before Travis could even begin to figure out what to say or do, someone he hadn't even seen enter the bridge nudged his hands aside and keyed everything over to the Tactical station, where Calkin had settled in and was starting in on the explanations.

Travis wished him luck with that one.

A minute later the newcomer had helped Travis out of his straps and taken his place at Com. "Over here, Long," Metzger said, beckoning.

Travis pushed himself to her side. "Yes, Ma'am?"

"Well done, Petty Officer," she said, peering at her displays. "Now for *Saintonge*. Any thoughts?"

Travis frowned. "I thought you were sending Colonel Massingill to deal with them."

"Sent, past tense," Metzger corrected. "Massingill's shuttle left about a minute ago."

"Oh," Travis said, frowning at the tactical. He hadn't even noticed that one go by.

The shuttle was there, all right, arrowing toward *Saintonge*'s bow endcap. So far, the battlecruiser wasn't showing any response.

"I'm mostly wondering if you've got any other thoughts on taking out impeller rings," Metzger continued. "We're not exactly in position to try the same trick again."

"No, Ma'am," Travis agreed. Missiles had a certain level of maneuverability, but it was only a few degrees at the most.

And of course, turning *Guardian*'s bow to *Péridot* had left her stern pointed toward *Saintonge*. Battlecruisers like *Vanguard* had aft lasers back there to use against enemy ships. Elderly destroyers like *Guardian* didn't have so much as an autocannon.

And they certainly couldn't get away with the same slow yaw rotation that had gotten *Guardian* lined up for the shot on *Péridot*. Not now. *Saintonge* would be watching them like a giant hawk. "I'm afraid I don't have any other ideas, Ma'am," he admitted. "I don't know the standard tactical responses in this situation."

Metzger snorted. "The standard tactical response in this situation is to not *get* in this situation," she said. "If you're already there, you roll wedge or else use your laser or missiles to beat the crap out of the enemy before he does it to you. Here and now, we're not in a position to do either."

"Except as a last resort."

"Except as a last resort," Metzger said grimly. "And if we don't, General Chu will. He will, and he should."

"I understand," Travis murmured. "I'm sorry, Ma'am."

"Never mind *sorry*," Metzger countered. "My point is that unless the *Saintonge* hijackers have been sloppy at their job, Massingill is unlikely to find any useable allies over there. If the rest of the Havenites are dead or contained, she won't be able to do more than buy us a little time. It's up to us to find a more permanent solution."

"A solution that doesn't involve destroying the ship," Travis said. "Understood, Ma'am."

"Commander, we're getting a signal from one of *Péridot*'s

shuttles," Com spoke up. "Correction: it's one of the ones *Saintonge* sent over there earlier today. Audio only, on laser carrier."

"Wants to keep this private, I see," Metzger muttered. She hunched her shoulders briefly and keyed her board. "*Péridot* shuttle, this is Commander Metzger, Executive Officer of HMS *Guardian*. I assume that's you, Guzarwan?"

"It is indeed, Commander," a familiar voice answered. "Congratulations on your splendid maneuver a few minutes ago. My technical people still don't know exactly what you did, but it was most effective."

"We're glad you liked it," Metzger said. "We'll be using it on *Saintonge* next. You might want to warn your people there."

"Already done so," Guzarwan said. "But I'd recommend not trying it a second time. Not unless you want to risk a war with Haven."

Metzger's eyes flicked to Travis. "On the contrary, I think Haven would thank us for keeping their warships out of enemy hands."

"They might," Guzarwan said. "*If* you had any proof that *Saintonge* was, in fact, in such hands at the time of your attack. I doubt you could muster anything that would satisfy them. Certainly not the more aggressive faction of the RHN. I presume you're familiar with the truism that an unused military either fades away or finds a reason to go to war?"

Metzger's lips compressed briefly. She *did* have such proof, Travis knew. More than that, she had Commodore Flanders's explicit order to destroy both *Saintonge* and *Péridot* if necessary.

But that was apparently something she wasn't yet prepared to share with the enemy.

"What do you want, Guzarwan?" she asked instead.

"I called to explain the new reality." The banter was gone from Guzarwan's voice now, with only coldness remaining. "Thanks to you, *Péridot* is no longer of any use to us. My men and I have therefore boarded a shuttle and will soon be joining our friends aboard *Saintonge*."

"Traveling along our line of fire?" Metzger asked pointedly. "What makes you think you'll reach your destination?"

"For starters, my men have control of *Saintonge*," Guzarwan said. "Along with the ship herself, we have a great many Havenite hostages whom we weren't planning to kill but whom we also don't especially need alive. I doubt you'd enjoy watching us execute them one by one in full video view of the other ships and the entire population of Marienbad."

"They're military men and women," Metzger said, her voice steady. "They're prepared to die for their nation."

"Of course they are," Guzarwan said. "But Ambassador Boulanger may not be so sanguine about giving *his* life for the Republic. Are you, Ambassador?"

"Don't flatter yourself, Guzarwan," a new voice said calmly. "A diplomatic post carries the same risks as a military one."

"Perhaps," Guzarwan said. "Still, I doubt Commander Metzger would want *Guardian* to be the instrument of your death. And she *certainly* wouldn't wish to be the instrument of her own captain's death."

Someone behind Travis snarled a quiet curse. Metzger's expression didn't even twitch. "You really think I'd hesitate over one life in the midst of a battle?"

"I'm sure you wouldn't," Guzarwan agreed. "But that's not really the situation, is it? Your ship's not in any danger, I have your captain and a Havenite ambassador, and you really can't justify killing them when there are other, less violent options for stopping me."

"Really?" Metzger asked. "What options are those?"

"I haven't the faintest idea," Guzarwan said. "But I know you won't give up looking for them until we raise *Saintonge*'s wedge and head for the hyper limit. Perhaps not even then."

"You're absolutely correct on that point," Metzger said. "So let me offer you a deal. If you surrender your hostages and abandon *Saintonge*, I'll give you safe passage to your own ship and allow you to leave unhindered."

"Please, Commander," Guzarwan chided. "We've put in far too much effort to simply walk away. Especially when we still have the upper hand."

"You're sure about that?"

"You aren't?" Guzarwan countered. "Fine—here's my counteroffer. Since you've already cost us one warship, give us the other and we'll call it a draw. As a good-faith gesture, we'll leave Captain Eigen and Ambassador Boulanger aboard this shuttle when we disembark. As soon as they can cycle the flight systems back around, they'll be free to leave and join you aboard *Guardian*."

"Very generous of you," Metzger said. "And the rest of *Saintonge*'s crew?"

"They'll be put into escape pods and sent out as soon as we're ready to leave orbit."

"And you'd let them go? Just like that?"

"Just like that," Guzarwan assured her. "Of course, some of those pods will be on tight intersect courses with the atmosphere, so you'll have to make a choice between rescuing them or chasing us. But I'm sure you'll make the right decision."

"Guzarwan—"

"I have to go now, Commander," Guzarwan cut her off. "I'll speak to you again once we're aboard *Saintonge*. Oh, and I presume I don't have to tell you that trying to tractor us in to *Guardian* will be the same as opening fire on us. Ambassador Boulanger and Captain Eigen will be the first to be executed, with the crews of the two Havenite ships next in line. I'm sure you'd enjoy the temporary promotion to captain, but I doubt such an incident would do much for your long-term career advancement. Until later, Commander."

There was a click, and Travis looked at the board to see that the shuttle's carrier laser had winked off. "Here they come, Ma'am," Carlyle's voice came from the speaker. "Shuttle leaving *Péridot* and bearing our direction. Moving at full speed."

"I see them," Metzger said. "Drew, did you get everyone out there calmed down?"

"More or less," the TO said. "No one's happy, but none of the other ships is in any position to do more than just yell right now."

"What about Chu?"

"He says that if we plan to fire any more missiles we're to damn well inform him of that fact beforehand. Aside from that, I get the impression he's rather impressed by our ingenuity." Calkin flicked the backs of his fingertips across Travis's shoulder. "I told him ingenuity was just SOP for the RMN. Anything from Colonel Massingill?"

"They're nearly there," Metzger said, leaning closer to her displays. "What's happening to *Saintonge*?"

"I don't know," Calkin said, frowning. "Carlyle?"

"She's... *jittering*, Sir," Carlyle said, sounding confused. "Running her thrusters... it seems like almost at random."

"It is," Metzger said sourly. "They've spotted Massingill's shuttle and are trying to keep it from docking."

"Massingill will figure something out." Calkin waved at the

display. "Meanwhile, Guzarwan and his hostages are ten minutes out from *Saintonge*. We need to decide what we're going to do with them."

☆   ☆   ☆

"Okay, we're doing it," Vachali's grouchy voice came over the shuttle speaker. "But bouncing everyone around like this is going to play hell with our containment."

"Why, are you getting bounced around more than the Havenites?" Guzarwan scoffed. "*They're* the ones trying to move. *You're* in fixed positions."

"Fixed like we're riding a hurricane," Vachali countered. "I thought these grav plates were supposed to dampen out jitters like this."

"I guess they don't. Or else you just don't know how to sweet-talk them."

"Yeah, right," Vachali growled. "Come on, Chief, this is ridiculous. I say let 'em aboard and have at it. Bouncing around like this won't stop them forever."

"I'm not interested in stopping them," Guzarwan said, getting a hard grip on his temper. Vachali was a good fighter, but a lousy strategist. "Not right away, anyhow. We want Metzger dithering around until the last minute, hoping she can find a way to pull this out of the fire. If we let the shuttle dock and play Capture the Hill, it'll be over way too fast. Better to let them pop in through a bunch of different hatchways—probably the same ones you froze the sensors on—and go out in their own private blazes of glory. Not knowing what's happening will slow Metzger down, make her think she's still got a chance. Right now, that's what we want."

"If you say so," Vachali grumbled. "I'd still rather have 'em all in a bunch."

"It won't matter," Guzarwan said patiently, stifling the urge to roll his eyes. "This is the Manticoran Navy, remember? They're not going to have more than three or four Marines aboard. Probably not even that many. You've got fixed positions, and you'll be dealing with a few professionals plus a few more amateurs. Trust me—it'll be a duck shoot."

"Yeah. I suppose."

"More to the point, if they dock, their shuttle will be attached to the hull," Guzarwan went on. "If, instead, they have to go in through the hatches, they'll probably have the pilot hang around, just drifting...and with your thrusters already moving you around, he won't even notice when you maneuver him into range of one of your com lasers and fry their transmitters."

"Ah," Vachali said, understanding finally coming. "And since their suit coms will be relayed through the shuttle...?"

"The whole team will be cut off," Guzarwan confirmed. "Metzger won't have any way of knowing what's going on, or whether the team's even alive or dead. Like I said, it's all about uncertainty and buying time."

"I'd rather just blow the shuttle now and be done with it," Vachali grumped. "But you want to play it cute, fine. You're the boss."

"That's right, I am," Guzarwan said, putting an edge on his voice. "Get back to work. I'll let you know when we're ready to dock."

"You sure you don't want to go EVA, too?" Vachali asked sarcastically.

"I'll let you know when we're ready to dock," Guzarwan repeated. "Out." With a sharp flick of his finger, he cut off the com.

"He's right, you know," Eigen said from behind him. "It won't work. None of it will."

Guzarwan swivelled in his station to look at his two hostages, strapped into two of the fold-down jumpseats on the cockpit aft bulkhead. "You don't think so?"

"I know so." Eigen nodded past Guzarwan. "I can see the gravitics readouts from here. *Guardian*'s going to have her wedge up before *Saintonge*."

"Probably," Guzarwan agreed calmly. "And?"

"So she'll be fully maneuverable before *Saintonge* will be," Eigen said. "Even if you've got enough wedge up to partially protect you, you'll never be able to roll before she can line up along your bow and open fire."

"You assume she'll risk war with Haven over a measly little battlecruiser that the RHN probably won't even miss," Guzarwan pointed out. "But, really, the argument's moot. No matter how fast or maneuverable *Guardian* is, she'll still have to turn around if she's going to bring her bow weapons to bear." He waved a hand toward the distant planetary horizon behind them. "Sadly for *Guardian*, halfway through her turn Jalla will bring *Wanderer* up over the horizon and put his missile through her unprotected flank."

Boulanger's eyes went wide. Eigen didn't even flinch.

"You assume Commander Metzger will be so focused on *Saintonge* that she won't be keeping an eye on everyone else in the system."

"No, actually, I assume there's no way she'll guess *Wanderer* has a military-grade missile aboard," Guzarwan countered. "But it'll be interesting to watch. Don't you think so?"

"If you're still alive to see it."

"There's that," Guzarwan agreed. "Still, in light of this new information, perhaps you'd be interested in making some kind of deal that would ensure *Guardian*'s survival."

"What kind of deal?"

"I don't know," Guzarwan said frankly. "Some way to disable her weapons would be best. As I've already said, we're not interested in causing any more deaths here. Since we aren't going to be able to activate *Saintonge*'s weapons, disabling *Guardian*'s would put us on an even keel. At that point, once our wedge is up we can all retire from the field and go our separate ways."

Eigen snorted.

"Even if I was willing, how exactly do you think I could disable *Guardian*'s weapons from here?"

"I haven't the faintest idea," Guzarwan said. "It would probably involve contacting someone aboard and making the deal. Figuring that part out is your job." He made a show of consulting his chrono. "But I'd advise you think quickly, because in approximately twenty minutes this offer will go away."

"As will *Guardian*?"

Guzarwan smiled. "Yes. As will *Guardian*."

CHAPTER TWENTY-NINE

"THERE IT GOES AGAIN," Marine Sergeant Pohjola commented, nodding out the shuttle viewport as *Saintonge*'s starboard thrusters flared, sending the massive battlecruiser drifting to their right. "Sort of like a slow-motion pinball. Docking with something bouncing around like that would be a real trick."

Massingill nodded. She'd figured that was what *Saintonge*'s hijackers were up to when Pohjola first spotted the battlecruiser's random thruster blasts.

Just as well she'd never planned on docking the shuttle in the first place. "I hope they're enjoying themselves," she said. "Just make sure you keep us some distance. Holderlin, you ready?"

"We're ready, Ma'am," Sergeant Holderlin said calmly from inside the aft-starboard airlock. His three teammates were lined up behind him, Holderlin's own rock-steadiness in sharp contrast to their restless fidgeting.

Massingill didn't blame them. RMN basic training had included a couple of units of close-quarters self-defense, but no one who went through those classes ever seriously expected to use any of it. Now, not only were they going to be fighting, but they were going to be fighting in a foreign environment, against an unknown enemy, and for a nation and people that weren't even their own.

Personally, Massingill didn't mind fighting for the Havenites. Right now, she didn't care who she was fighting for or, really, whether she was fighting for anyone or any cause at all. All she cared about was that she was getting to take the battle to the people who'd killed her husband.

A suffocating bitterness rose into her throat, burning with anger and grief. Alvis had been safe enough when he spoke to Metzger. He'd certainly been alive. But that safety must have somehow deserted him after that. Either the hijackers had found them, or he and Flanders had gone off to do something crazily heroic in an effort to save Flanders's precious ship.

Thanks to *Guardian*, Flanders's ship had been saved. But Alvis had never called back.

And he should have. He should have called to tell *Guardian* that the attack had been successful and that the hijackers were preparing to abandon ship. He should have called to warn Metzger that Guzarwan had hostages, including Captain Eigen.

But he hadn't called. Not then, not now. And he should have.

If he was still alive.

Of course he hadn't gone to ground like Flanders had said they would. He'd probably tried to do something stupid. Scram the fusion plant, maybe, to keep *Péridot* from blowing when the missile wedge sliced through the hull. Or maybe he and Flanders had gone to try to rescue the hostages. She could easily see Alvis trying one or the other hair-brained scheme.

Only it hadn't worked. And he was dead.

"Five seconds," Pohjola called.

Massingill took a deep breath and did a last check of her team. All three of them looked as nervous as Holderlin's group. "You ready?" she asked them.

"Yes, Ma'am," Boysenko said. The other two—Riglan and O'Keefe—merely nodded wordlessly.

Combat butterflies, one of Massingill's DIs had called them. They'd be fine once they hit deck and the shooting started.

Probably.

"Go!" Pohjola called.

In a single smooth motion Holderlin popped the outer hatch and flung himself out into space, the Alpine-style safety lines pulling the others in rapid order out behind him. "Five seconds," Pohjola called again.

Massingill nodded, getting a grip on her thruster control with one hand and taking hold of the outer hatch release with the other. With only three four-man teams available, they'd decided Holderlin's group would penetrate *Saintonge* near the forward fusion plant radiator, with the goal of attacking either the bridge or CIC, while Pohjola's team would breach somewhere in the vicinity of the hab module, where they could choose between harassing whoever was guarding the trapped Havenites or else tackling the fusion reactor room. Given the situation, standard procedure would normally have dictated that Massingill's team find a point of entry near one of the impeller rooms, with the goal of damaging or otherwise shutting down the ring.

Massingill had come up with something slightly more creative. Whether it was brilliantly creative or stupidly creative remained to be seen.

"Go!"

Massingill keyed the hatch and pulled on the hand bar, hurling herself out into the vast nothingness outside. She felt the three slight tugs on the Alpine line as the other three fell out behind her in sequence, then keyed her thruster. The tension on the line increased sharply, the shuttle's stern flashed by, and the line tension decreased as her team kicked in their own thrusters. Checking to make sure all three were still attached, Massingill shifted her eyes toward the massive battlecruiser beneath them.

As always, Pohjola's timing had been perfect. She and the others were angling straight toward *Saintonge*'s hab section, with its fancy grav plates that Alvis had been hoping to get a look at. Far more interesting to Massingill at the moment was the narrow zero-gee sheath running around the outer edge of the hab section that allowed for personnel and equipment transfer without such traffic having to go through the ship's living quarters. Part of that sheath was given over to the docking ring for the battlecruiser's four shuttles.

One of the docking ports was currently empty. One of them was occupied by the shuttle the first group of hijackers had brought over from *Péridot*.

And as *Saintonge*'s crew hadn't expected an incursion from its own spacecraft, so too the hijackers probably weren't expecting a counterattack from theirs.

Alone, Massingill could have made the touchdown and reached the docked shuttle in two minutes. Dragging three amateurs along behind her, it was closer to four.

"What happens if we can't get it open?" Riglan asked nervously as Massingill worked at the cockpit drop-lock, a small emergency escape route that she'd never heard of anyone actually using. "I mean—"

He broke off as Massingill popped the outer hatch. "I'll go first," she said as she maneuvered herself into the cramped space. "When it cycles again, it'll be Riglan, O'Keefe, and Boysenko."

The disadvantage of drop-locks, Massingill had been taught, was that they offered no freedom of movement whatsoever if you came under fire. Their advantage was that the small volume translated to a quick cycling time. Another three minutes, and the team was at the shuttle's docking collar, peering cautiously into the deserted bay and passageway beyond.

Massingill gave a scan with her suit's audio sensors, just to make sure, then gestured to the others to pop their helmets. "Looks clear," she murmured, feeling a twinge of guilt as they opened their heads to the outside air. Her own Marine vac suit included a full sensor package, and was designed to be kept zipped during an incursion.

Unfortunately, the others' standard-issue ship suits weren't so well equipped, and the risk of blundering into an enemy because you couldn't hear him was higher than the risk of taking gas, debris, or a grazing shot. Hence, it was buckets-off from here on.

Not that their helmets would be much good against a full-on shot anyway, she knew. Or their suits, either, for that matter. "Sling your helmets—make sure your headsets are muted but receiving—and let's go."

They headed down the passageway, swimming quickly and mostly quietly through the zero-gee. Guzarwan's shuttle, Massingill knew, would be docking soon, and someone from the first group of hijackers would be there to meet it.

Whatever Guzarwan had planned for his reception committee, it was about to get a little bigger. And a whole lot livelier.

☆   ☆   ☆

"It's risky," Metzger said reluctantly. "But I think you're right. We really don't have any other choice."

"Well, if we're going to do it, we need to start now," Calkin said. "We're not going to beat Guzarwan's shuttle there as it is."

Floating behind them, Travis felt his throat tighten. He'd hoped they might be able to use the same trick on *Saintonge* that they had on *Péridot*. But the mathematics of geometry—*Guardian* was still orbiting below *Saintonge* and stern-first to her—plus the physics of inertia—it would take nearly six minutes on thrusters for *Guardian* to rotate the necessary one-eighty degrees to bring her weapons to bear, plus however more minutes it would take to gain altitude to match her orbit to *Saintonge*'s current level—had combined to made that tactic unusable. There simply was no way to get into a position where they could send a missile wedge along the *Saintonge*'s axis to take out her nodes.

And with nothing cleaner to go with, Metzger and Calkin had fallen back on their original plan for *Péridot*: to instead send a missile at *Saintonge* at an upward angle where it would slice across its bow endcap, tear through its forward impeller ring, bridge, and CIC, and hopefully disrupt things enough to keep her from bringing up her wedge.

And, as an inevitable consequence, kill every Havenite unlucky enough to be trapped in that third of the ship.

But the timer was rapidly counting down, and Metzger had to do *something*. Sixteen minutes from now, if Kountouriote's calculations were correct, *Saintonge* would have her full wedge and be ready to make a run for the hyper limit and freedom. The fact that *Guardian* would have her own wedge up three minutes before that sounded like it should be a tactical advantage, but really wasn't. Not unless *Guardian* wanted to destroy the battle-cruiser, which Metzger had already made clear that she didn't.

So instead of a kill, *Guardian* would try for a decapitation.

"Still, if we're fast enough, Captain Eigen shouldn't be all the way to the bridge before we're ready to fire," Metzger continued. "Especially if Massingill's able to pin them down in their shuttle. Any idea what the penetration of autocannon shells on a stationary target would be?"

"Not sure anyone's ever run those numbers," Calkin said. "I wouldn't count on them doing any good, though. Explosives designed to take out a missile coming in at five thousand klicks per second probably won't do much against an armored endcap or impeller ring." He waved a hand. "But we can try it first if you'd like."

"Probably not worth it." Metzger hit her intercom key. "Missile Ops; bridge. Status?"

"Nearly ready, Ma'am," Donnelly's voice came back. "We were having trouble charging the capacitors, but we're back on track. Two minutes, max, and we'll be ready."

"Let me know when you are." Metzger broke the connection and looked at Travis. "Long?"

Travis winced, his eyes flicking guiltily away from her to the tactical display. What was he supposed to say?

Because he had nothing. The XO was clearly still hoping he could come up with something clever. But he had nothing.

The physics were as clear as they were unyielding. The minute *Guardian* kicked in full thrusters and started her yaw rotation, *Saintonge* would undoubtedly start an upward pitch of her own in hopes of rotating her ventral stress band and putting it between her and potential attack. Even an incomplete wedge would diffuse the fury of *Guardian's* laser, and it would certainly destroy the wedge of an incoming missile.

If *Saintonge* won the leisurely pas de deux, the hijackers would escape. If *Guardian* won, she would get her shot, and do her best to destroy as little of the Havenite battlecruiser as she could manage.

Either way, they were all looking down the throat of disaster.

"Long?" Metzger repeated.

"I'm sorry, Ma'am," Travis said. "I—nothing's coming to me."

"Don't worry about it," Calkin said with a grunt. "You're already one for two in the idea department today. That's not a bad average for anyone. Ma'am, I need you to look over these numbers."

Travis frowned, Calkin's voice vanishing into the background of his perception as a sudden thought flicked across his mind. *We're having trouble charging the capacitors*, Donnelly had said...

"Commander, Guzarwan's shuttle has reached *Saintonge*," Carlyle's voice came from CIC. "Docking now."

"Thank you," Metzger said. "Missile Ops; bridge. Lieutenant?"

"Prep countdown starting now, Commander," Donnelly reported. "We'll be ready to launch by the time *Guardian's* in position."

"Acknowledged. Helm—"

"Commander?" Travis cut in. "I'm sorry, Ma'am—"

"Spit it out, Long," Calkin snapped.

Travis braced himself. "I was wondering what happens if you wreck one of a reactor's radiator vanes."

"There's a small spike in the plant heat output, and then it settles down," Calkin said impatiently. "That's why each reactor has *two* radiators, so that one can take up the slack if the other's damaged in battle."

"Wait a minute, not so fast," Metzger said, her eyes narrowed in thought. "If I remember right, the temp spike gets smoothed and rerouted because the engineers in the reactor room make that happen. I doubt the hijackers have a full slate of trained personnel back there."

"No, no, you're right," Calkin said, his scorn fading into sudden interest. "The reactor was already going—they didn't need to put anyone with any brains back there. If the RHN has the same automatic backup scram system we do—" Abruptly, he shook his head. "Doesn't matter. *Saintonge's* running its aft reactor, and there's no way we can hit either of its radiators from our position. Not without slicing off the aft third of the ship and probably blowing the reactor along with it. If we're going to do that, we might as well put a missile down its throat and be done with it."

"We don't need a missile," Metzger said suddenly. "We've got one. We've got *Massingill's shuttle.*"

"Hell on wheels," Calkin murmured, his hands abruptly skating across his board. "Can we even get it going fast enough to do the kind of damage we need?"

"You run the numbers—I'll get Massingill," Metzger said, gesturing to the man at Com. "Simons, get me Colonel Massingill."

"Too late, Ma'am," he said tightly. "Massingill and her crew are already engaged."

☆   ☆   ☆

It was about as perfect a setup as Massingill could ever have hoped for. Two hard-faced hijackers were waiting for the shuttle from *Péridot*, their carbines slung over their shoulders, their full attention on the task of docking the incoming vessel.

And *Saintonge's* new commander had even shut down the ship's random twitchings while the shuttle docked and hadn't yet started them up again. Peering down the barrel of her carbine as the passengers filed out, Massingill waited for the critical moment when the hostages came into sight. A quick two- or three-shot to take out the primary guards, then a hail of covering fire, and Captain Eigen should have the few seconds necessary to get himself and Ambassador Boulanger to cover. Then an ordered retreat to the fallback spot Massingill had picked to make her rearguard stand while the others got the hostages back into the shuttle, and her part in this drama would be almost finished.

As usual with military plans, it didn't work out that way.

Ten passengers had emerged, some heading for the bridge, the others hovering outside the shuttle as they apparently waited for further orders or traveling companions, when two oblivious hijackers came bouncing around the curve of the outer ring behind Massingill's group and careened smack into the center of their formation.

There was no option. Cursing under her breath, Massingill let go of her carbine with her right hand, leaving it pointed at the docking bay, then snap-drew her sidearm and shot both of the newcomers. "Fire!" she barked at her team.

And with that, as the old phrase so succinctly put it, all hell broke loose.

The four Manticorans opened fire, sending a barrage of 10mm rounds into the group by the docking collar. The hijackers were also in motion, some trying frantically to retreat to the cover of the shuttle, others realizing they were too far out of position for any chance of escape and coolly drawing their sidearms or trying to bring their own carbines to bear. Massingill let her team handle the distraction fire, concentrating her own efforts on sniping out the most competent-looking of the enemy. Vaguely, she heard a voice shouting from her headset, but the gunfire was too loud for her to make out any of the words, and she was too busy to pay attention anyway.

She'd killed five of the enemy, and the rest of the Manticoran fire had taken out two more, by the time the rest made it back into the shuttle. A few random shots came from around the edge of the collar, but another couple of rounds from Massingill and the rearguard pulled back.

And an echoing silence descended on the passageway.

Massingill took a quick moment to check her team. They seemed uninjured, though all three looked a little traumatized and more than a little tense. No surprise there.

Unfortunately, there was no surprise left anywhere else, either. Guzarwan was under cover, the hostages were still in his hands, and the whole ship had been alerted to the threat. Even if Holderlin and Pohjola were successful in pinning down their share of the hijackers, that still left an unknown number of reinforcements available for Guzarwan to send up Massingill's kilt.

"Massingill! Massingill?"

Massingill worked her jaw, trying to clear away some of the ringing in her ears. The voice was coming from her headset. Probably a follow-up to whatever *Guardian* had been trying to tell her earlier. "Massingill," she replied into her mike.

"New orders," the voice said. "Urgent. Take your shuttle—"
And then, abruptly, all was again silence.

"Say again?" Massingill called, glancing down at the radio. Her equipment seemed to be functioning all right. "Say again, *Guardian?*"

But there was nothing. She started to key to a new frequency—

"Colonel Massingill?" a distant voice called. From inside the shuttle, Massingill's numbed ears tentatively concluded. "This is Guzarwan, Colonel. I want to offer you a deal."

Massingill felt her lip twist. At this point, a conversation was probably either stalling or an attempt to zero her in from the direction of her voice. "Fall back," she murmured to the others. "Riglan first—"

"I won't bother trying to bargain for your captain's life, Colonel," Guzarwan continued. "I know how you military people are, all stiff and noble and self-sacrificing. So let's try this instead.

"Tell me, Colonel: what would you trade for your husband Alvis's life?"

☆ ☆ ☆

It had taken five minutes of careful maneuvering, but *Saintonge* and the target were finally in the proper positions. "Go," Vachali ordered.

On the status board, one of the com lights lit up . . . and with a mere two seconds' worth of fire from *Saintonge*'s mid-starboard com laser, the Manticoran shuttle's own communications capabilities were neatly and permanently fried.

And with the attackers' link to *Guardian* gone, it was time to do something about that ruckus back in the docking bay. "Labroo, get your people to Docking Three," he ordered into the intercom. "Kichloo's managed to lead the chief into an ambush. Go get them out of it."

"On our way," Labroo said briskly. "What's status?"

"Seven casualties, we think," Vachali said. "The chief and the others are pinned down but safe. And watch your flanks—two other teams came aboard, and one of them may be waiting to hit you along the way."

"Let 'em try. I'll call when they're clear."

"Boss!" Dhotrumi cut in. "*Guardian*'s on the move—yaw rotation to port. You get that, Munchi?"

"I got it," Munchi confirmed from the helm. "Boss?"

"Go ahead," Vachali said, feeling his lips curl back in a vicious grin. So the Manticorans were making their final bid to stop *Saintonge* from leaving the system. Too bad for them. "We want a—what was it again?"

"An upward pitch," Munchi told him.

"Right," Vachali said. "Whatever we do to get our bottom wedge—"

"It's called the floor."

"Whatever the hell it is, get it between us and *Guardian*," Vachali said impatiently. Smartmouths, every single one of them.

"Yeah, got it," Munchi said. "What about the shaking? You want that back on?"

"Don't bother," Vachali said. The random ship movements would drain power from the thrusters, and *Saintonge* needed all the power it could get to keep its lumbering battlecruiser's defensive pitch movement ahead of the smaller and nimbler destroyer's turn.

Besides, the shaking hadn't stopped the Manticorans from boarding. It probably wouldn't do any better at spoiling their aim in the running gunfight back there.

But that was all right. The Manticorans' time had run out, and even their nuisance factor was about to be erased. "And call Jalla," he added. "Tell him to get his butt over the horizon.

"Tell him it's time to use his missile."

☆   ☆   ☆

"Simons?" Metzger demanded, her throat tightening as she stared at the monitor. Suddenly, without even a sputter, the carrier signal from Massingill's team had vanished. "Simons, talk to me."

"It's the shuttle, Ma'am," Simons said, peering at his displays. "It's stopped relaying our signals. They must have fried its systems somehow."

"Did Massingill get the message?" Metzger asked, switching her gaze to the tactical. *Saintonge* was on the move, pitching her bow upward, hoping to raise her floor high enough to put it between her and *Guardian*. "Come on, look alive. Did she get the message or not?"

"Ma'am...no, Ma'am, I don't think so," Simons admitted. "The first time through there was a lot of gunfire, and the second time was cut off." Simons gave her a hooded look. "I'm sorry, Commander."

"Never mind *sorry*, Com," Metzger bit out, her mind racing. "Tell me how we can reestablish contact."

"I—" Simons lifted a hand helplessly. "Another shuttle could do it, Ma'am. But—"

Metzger jabbed at her intercom. "Docking One; bridge. Get that shuttle into space—emergency launch."

"Aye, aye, Ma'am," a voice came back. "It'll be clear in five minutes."

"You've got two," Metzger said tersely and keyed off the intercom.

"They can't do it, Ma'am," Calkin said, almost gently. "Not in time. Unless Massingill somehow got more of the message than we thought, we're going to have to go with either the laser or a missile."

"I know." Metzger tapped the intercom. "Missile Ops; bridge. Confirm readiness." She took a deep breath and looked back at Calkin. "Stand by to fire."

CHAPTER THIRTY

IT WAS A TRICK, Massingill's suddenly numbed mind knew. A stupid, meaningless trick designed to pin her and her team in place until Guzarwan's reinforcements could arrive.

But somehow that didn't matter. If there was even a chance that Alvis was still alive...

"Colonel?" Riglan asked tentatively.

"Get to the fallback," Massingill told him. "All of you. Wait for me there." She threw a sideways look at Riglan's pinched face. "You hear me? Fallback position, damn it."

"You still there, Colonel?" Guzarwan called.

"I'm here, Guzarwan," Massingill called back, shifting her attention to the passageway beyond the docking collar, then to the collar itself. So far, no signs of reinforcements from outside or a sortie from inside. The counterattack was probably forming up somewhere behind her. "Talk fast. Is Alvis there with you?"

"Here? No, he's safely locked down with the rest of the officers and dignitaries in *Péridot*'s Alpha Spin section. But he won't be safe much longer. Have you ever heard the phrase *dog in the manger*? It refers to selfish individuals who, if they can't have something they want—"

"I know what it means," Massingill cut him off. "Get to the point."

"The point is that before we abandoned *Péridot* we left the survivors a little going-away present," Guzarwan said, his voice suddenly ice-cold. "A small but powerful bomb in the fusion bottle regulator. If it goes off, the reactor goes with it. And for a few moments our little trinary system will have a fourth sun."

Massingill felt a curse bubbling in her throat. "What's the deal?"

"You let one of my men out to reseal the hatch and let me fly this shuttle back to *Wanderer*," Guzarwan said. "I then tell you where the bomb is and how to disarm it. A simple trade, really—I get away; you get your husband back. Oh, and you also get *Saintonge*, assuming you can take it back from Colonel Vachali and his team. I make no promises on that one."

Massingill squeezed the barrel of her carbine. It sounded good. Very good.

Too good. "How's the bomb triggered? Radio signal?"

"It's on a timer," Guzarwan said. "But don't worry—you'll have plenty of time to get to *Péridot* and disarm it. Assuming you leave within the next few minutes, of course."

"Don't believe him, Ma'am," a nervous voice whispered.

Massingill looked up in surprise. In open defiance of her direct order, Riglan and the others hadn't so much as budged from their positions.

Or rather, two of them hadn't. Riglan and O'Keefe were still there, but Boysenko was nowhere to be seen. "I ordered you the hell out of here," she bit out. "Now, *go*."

"Don't believe him, Ma'am," Riglan repeated, sounding more nervous than ever. He was also making no move to leave. "He's trying to stall."

"I know what he's trying to do," Massingill said, her heart feeling like it was tearing itself apart. A convenient bomb, on a convenient timer, and he was even throwing in *Saintonge*. No, the deal was way too good to be true.

Especially since she already knew that Alvis was dead.

Which just left Captain Eigen and *Saintonge* still in the equation.

And with that, Massingill knew what she had to do. "Counter-offer," she called. "You bring Captain Eigen and the ambassador to the hatch so I can see they're still alive. Then I'll come seal the docking hatch myself and you can go."

"You know I can't give up my hostages," Guzarwan said. "If I did there'd be nothing to prevent *Guardian* from shooting me out of the sky."

"I'm not asking you to give them up," Massingill said. "You can keep them until you're aboard *Wanderer*. I just want to confirm they're safe and unhurt."

There was a pause. "Stand ready," Massingill murmured to

Riglan. "You and the others—well, you and O'Keefe. Where's Boysenko?"

"She left a little while ago," Riglan said reluctantly. "It was— well, the shooting was mostly done."

Mostly, but not quite? Massingill grimaced. But it was unfortunately all too common. Some people could handle live combat. Others couldn't. "Doesn't matter," she told Riglan. "When the shooting stops, wait a moment and see if the captain comes out. If he doesn't, then get to the fallback and wait for orders from Holderlin or Pohjola."

Riglan's eyes went wide. "*Ma'am*?"

"You heard me." Massingill turned back toward the shuttle, the cold lump that combat always brought to her stomach dissolving away. It was almost finished, and there were no longer any life-altering decisions to be made. If Guzarwan agreed to her terms, she would head to the shuttle and step into the hatchway as if preparing to close the collar.

But instead, she would open fire on the hijackers, emptying her carbine in three-round bursts, killing as many of them as she could before their return fire ended the burden of decision-making forever.

It was Eigen's only chance. It was also the way a Marine should go out. She flicked her selector to burst mode and filled her lungs. "Guzarwan? Do we have a deal?"

And then, to her utter amazement a new voice crackled in her ear. "Massingill, this is *Guardian*," Commander Metzger said. "I have urgent new orders for you."

☆   ☆   ☆

"Understood, Commander," Massingill's voice came from the bridge speaker. "Pulling back now. I'll be in space in two minutes."

"Good," Metzger said. Her voice seemed calmer, Travis thought, but the tension in her face more than made up for it. "We're prepping another shuttle now to come get you after you eject."

"That won't be necessary, Ma'am," Massingill said. "Can you send Pohjola or Holderlin to pick up the rest of my team?"

"Already done," Metzger said, frowning. "What do you mean, it won't be necessary?"

"One other thing," Massingill said. "Guzarwan said there was a bomb—"

Without warning, her voice cut off. "Simons?" Metzger demanded.

"It's *Saintonge*'s wedge, Ma'am," Simons said. "It's rotated high enough to cut us off."

"It's all right," Calkin said. "She got the orders. It's just a question now of whether she can wreck the radiator in time."

"That's not the only question," Metzger said grimly. "She said something about a bomb. Did she mean a bomb aboard the shuttle? Is that what she meant about not needing to send another one?"

Calkin hissed between his teeth. "Well, if the bomb holds off to the right second, it'll make even more of a mess of the radiator. If it doesn't..."

Metzger nodded heavily. "If it doesn't, we still have the missile."

☆   ☆   ☆

Kichloo eased his head around the hatch, and Guzarwan braced himself to watch the lieutenant's head get blown off.

But it didn't. Instead, he took a long look around and then gave a thumbs-up. "They're gone."

"Massingill too?" Guzarwan asked.

"Her, too," Kichloo confirmed, sounding puzzled. "I wonder what spooked them."

"Maybe Manticorans are naturally nervous," Guzarwan said. But he would have sworn from the tone in Massingill's voice that she was about to make a grand, self-sacrificing stand of some sort.

Maybe she'd gotten new orders from the other teams. That could be good, or very, very bad.

Either way, it was time to get the hell out of here.

"Get them out," he ordered Kichloo, gesturing toward the closed cockpit hatch.

Kichloo nodded and shoved off the bulkhead to the hatch. He opened it and floated inside, and a moment later Eigen and Boulanger floated out into the main shuttle. "They behave themselves in there?" he asked as Kichloo emerged behind them.

"Yeah, but not from lack of trying," Kichloo said darkly. "Eigen was trying to run up the thrusters."

"Good trick, with your hands tied behind your back," Guzarwan commented, eyeing the Manticoran.

"It would have worked if you hadn't shut the board to standby," Eigen said, peering out the hatch as Kichloo caught his upper arm and steered him toward the opening. "Or if my people had kept you busy longer. Though I see they made a pretty good showing as it is."

"They did," Guzarwan conceded, silently cursing his carelessness.

They'd already released the hostages from their restraints when the attack started, and he hadn't wanted to risk his insurance policies getting damaged in an open gun battle. He should have left someone in there to keep an eye on them, but at the time it had seemed more important to have every gun available to repulse the unexpected attack.

With a locked board, the hostages' hands tied, and no weapons available, it had worked out all right. But it had still been sloppy, and if anyone else had made the decision he would have flayed the man alive.

"But they're gone now," he continued. "Come on—next stop is the bridge."

Two by two, the pirates slipped out into the passageway, some heading toward the Manticoran ambush site, the others creating a vanguard and heading forward.

"You weren't really going to give her the bomb's location, were you?" Eigen asked quietly.

"You heard that?" Guzarwan asked.

"The cockpit intercom was still on."

"Ah," Guzarwan said. "To answer your question, I might have. She fought well, and I appreciate that in an enemy. I might have given her back her husband as a reward."

"Ah," Eigen murmured. Pretending to believe his captor, just as he'd pretended to accept his captivity.

But Guzarwan wasn't fooled. So far, aside from the shuttle attempt just now, Eigen had behaved himself. He hadn't attempted to escape, not even when Guzarwan pretended to give him an opening.

But that was all illusion and a biding of time. The Manticoran had simply known better than to try anything aboard the confines of a shuttle or aboard a ship already firmly under enemy control. Here, with *Saintonge's* ownership still under some dispute, all bets were off. If Eigen found an opening, Guzarwan had no doubt he would go for it.

So he made sure to stay close to the hostages, where he could keep a close eye on them, as the group filed out of the shuttle and headed forward. Fortunately, the need for hostages would soon be past. The charade would be over, and he could relax.

Until then, he would make sure neither of his prisoners got away. He would make damn sure.

☆   ☆   ☆

Massingill's reflexive assumption, when she'd first noticed that Boysenko was no longer with the group, was that the young com officer had broken under the unaccustomed stress of combat and fled. Now, after the unexpected reestablishment of contact with *Guardian*, she recognized the far more palatable and honorable truth.

Boysenko was in the hijackers' shuttle, the one they'd entered *Saintonge* through, when Massingill and the others arrived. "I'm sorry—I shouldn't have come back here without telling you why," the young rating apologized as Massingill joined her in the cockpit. "I thought that if our own shuttle's com was out I could run a relay through here instead."

"It was a good idea," Massingill assured her, glancing at the controls. The shuttle was still on standby. Perfect. "I probably couldn't have heard you over the noise anyway. Get to the passageway with the others and get the hatch closed."

Out of the corner of her eye, she saw Boysenko's eyes narrow. "Shouldn't we have two of us for this?"

"You know how to fly this thing?" Massingill countered. "No? Then get out."

"But—"

"Get out or I'll shoot you," Massingill said, turning to look her straight in the eye. "I mean it. Go."

Boysenko nodded, a quick, guilty jerk of her chin. "Yes, Ma'am. Good...good luck, Ma'am."

Ninety seconds later, with the hatch closed and sealed, Massingill hit the thrusters and drove the shuttle hard away from *Saintonge*'s flank. Rolling over, she gave herself a long push outward, backing away as many kilometers as she could from the battlecruiser's flank. More distance would have been better, but she was pressed for time, and this was all she dared risk. Swiveling the shuttle into a corkscrew one-eighty, she headed up and over, firing a long blast from the thrusters to kill her outward momentum. A pair of tweaks from the starboard laterals turned her back around and lined her up with her target.

There in front of her, jutting thirty meters upward from the hull, was the aft dorsal radiator.

Massingill smiled tightly. *Good luck*, Boysenko had said. But she hadn't meant it. Or, rather, hadn't said it with any expectations that the words meant anything. She'd looked into Massingill's eyes, and she knew beyond a doubt what was about to happen.

Alvis Massingill was gone...and with that crushing loss, Jean Massingill no longer had anything to live for.

Throwing full power to the aft thrusters, Massingill sent the shuttle leaping toward the radiator. Forty seconds, she estimated, until impact.

"For Alvis," she murmured.

☆   ☆   ☆

On the status board, a set of amber lights went green. "Wedge is up, Ma'am," the helmsman reported.

"Thrusters off," Metzger ordered. "Increase speed of yaw to full; pitch positive twenty degrees. Missile Ops; bridge. Confirm missile readiness. TO; prepare to launch on my command."

Travis looked at the forward display, his pulse throbbing in his neck. *Saintonge* was nearly in range now, with *Guardian*'s rotation suddenly speeding up now that her wedge was driving the movement.

But *Saintonge*'s wedge was almost up, too, and the floor was currently between the two ships. In order for *Guardian* to get her shot, she was going to have to line up with the battlecruiser while simultaneously rising to get above the forward edge of *Saintonge*'s lower stress band.

And meanwhile, Massingill was doing...what?

Travis didn't know. No one aboard *Guardian* knew. *Saintonge*'s wedge was already strong enough to block all the destroyer's sensors: optics, radar, and lidar. For the moment, as far as *Saintonge* was concerned, *Guardian* was blind.

The next few seconds would tell the tale. Until then, there was nothing to do but wait.

☆   ☆   ☆

Wanderer's drift upward in its orbit—upward, and backward—had been slow. Sometimes infuriatingly slow.

But Jalla's patience had finally been rewarded. Over the rim of the planet's horizon, *Guardian* was finally in sight.

Actually, all the players were in sight. *Péridot* was closest, floating dead and quiet the way Guzarwan had left it, her remaining crew still unaware of the larger drama going on beyond her hull. Far beyond *Péridot* was *Guardian*, her wedge completely up now, her bow mostly turned away from *Wanderer* as she continued lining up for her shot on *Saintonge*. Just beyond *Guardian*, practically on top of her in fact, was *Saintonge*, her wedge angled upward like a fighter with his forearm raised to block his attacker's incoming fist.

Jalla took it all in, the way an experienced warrior took everything in. But really, he only had eyes for *Guardian*. For *Guardian*, and her stern turned so inviting and vulnerable toward him.

Larger warships had aft autocannon to protect them from up-the-kilt attacks. But compact destroyers like *Guardian* didn't have room for such things. Their only defense against an up-the-kilt attack was to make sure no enemy ever got behind them.

Wanderer's missile was a bit out of date, as such things went. Unlike modern missiles with their ten-thousand-gee sprint modes, Jalla's could only manage five thousand.

But five thousand gees would be enough. More than enough. At that acceleration, it would take a little over forty seconds to cross the forty-five thousand kilometers separating them.

Which meant that the Manticorans would see what was coming, and even have time to recognize and bitterly regret their folly. That, for Jalla, was the best part of all.

"Hatch door open," he ordered. "Target parameters ready to load. Stand by to ignite booster."

He grinned tightly. He'd always, *always* wanted to say this. "Prepare to fire."

☆　　☆　　☆

With barely twenty seconds left to impact, Massingill threw herself out the shuttle hatch.

She was going way too fast to stop, of course. Fortunately, she didn't have to. Kicking her thruster pack to full power, she drove straight up, directly away from *Saintonge*'s hull, clawing for distance up and over the huge radiator vanes rushing toward her. She made the necessary clearance with less than two seconds to spare, wincing as the sudden spike in heat from the now distant radiator nevertheless blazed through even the extra protection of her Marine vac suit and singed her skin. The heat continued to increase, peaking as she sailed over the top of the radiator. Directly below her, the shuttle slammed into its target—

And the entire center of the radiator disintegrated into a boiling cloud of superheated liquid metal.

Reflexively, Massingill flinched, despite the fact that sitting inside a suit traveling on a ballistic path made the value of flinching pretty much zero. For a heart-stopping couple of seconds she was afraid the expanding cloud of superheated liquid would overtake her and burn her alive. But she was still hurtling past at the shuttle's original impact speed, and the extra vertical momentum she'd given herself was still eating up meters, and the blazing light from the cloud was already fading as the metal droplets dumped their heat into the universe at large and began solidifying again. She watched the cloud another few seconds, just to make sure it was safely behind her, then turned her eyes to the vastness of space above.

The vastness of space . . . and the whole of the incredible starry host stretched out across the sky. A view she could see with perfect clarity, unimpeded by anything.

The gamble had worked. *Saintonge's* reactor had scrammed, and taken her wedge with it.

"There you go, Guzarwan," she said under her breath toward the ship pulling away beneath and behind her. "That's the kind of deal *I* make. Choke on it."

☆   ☆   ☆

The group was still only halfway to *Saintonge's* bridge when a wailing klaxon alarm erupted around them.

Cursing, Guzarwan grabbed a handhold as the alarm shifted from solid tone to a staccato three-one-three-one cadence. Spinning around in a half circle, his gun held ready, he darted quick looks both directions down the cramped passageway. But there was nothing. "What the hell is going on?" he bellowed over the siren. "Mota?"

The hacker was hunched in half a fetal position at the side of the passageway, working furiously on his tablet. "It's—my God, it's a *reactor scram*."

Guzarwan felt his eyes widen. "A *what*?"

"The reactor's shutting down," Mota said, his voice suddenly frantic. "Automatic safety—someone's got to override it or it'll just—oh, *God*."

There wasn't any time even to swear. "Get the bridge!" Guzarwan shouted. "Get the reactor room. All of you—go. Get the hell back there and—"

But it was too late. Abruptly, the passageway lights flickered and went out, the dimmer red glow of emergency lighting springing up to take its place.

And in that fraction of a heartbeat as the lights went briefly out something hard and unyielding slammed against his throat.

Reflexively, he let go of his gun and grabbed at the agony that his neck had become, trying desperately to dislodge the bar squeezing against it. But he was too late. The arm pressed against his throat—it was an arm, he realized now—had locked into the elbow of another arm, and the second arm's palm was pressed hard against the back of Guzarwan's head.

And with a wave of horror he realized that his life was being choked out of him.

He tried to shout to the rest of his men, milling uselessly around him, looking wildly in all the wrong directions for the ambush they obviously expected was imminent. But his voice was long gone. He tried to retrieve the gun he'd let go of when the attack first began, but the weapon was also long gone, plucked from the air by yet a third hand.

How? The word remained unspoken, because there was no air with which to speak it.

Perhaps his killer sensed the question anyway. Or perhaps he merely had need to gloat. "You shouldn't have left us alone in the shuttle cockpit," Eigen murmured in his ear, just loud enough to hear over the now distant alarm and the hammer of blood pounding through Guzarwan's head. "Or maybe you just didn't know that military cockpit med kits always include scissors."

Guzarwan almost smiled. But there was no air for even that. No air, and no time.

And then, there was no time for anything. Anything at all.

☆   ☆   ☆

"There she is," Gill said. It really wasn't necessary to point that out, he knew—everyone on *Péridot*'s bridge could see *Wanderer* coming up over the horizon. But the tension inside him was reaching the unbearable point, and he had to say *something*.

"There she is, indeed," Commodore Flanders agreed. Agreeing, or humoring. Gill wasn't sure which. "Are we ready, Captain?"

"We're ready." Captain Henderson smiled tightly at Flanders from his place in the command chair. "Under the circumstances, Commodore, I think it only fair that you give the order."

"I appreciate the offer, Captain," Flanders said. "But *Péridot* is your ship. The honor is yours."

Henderson inclined his head. "Thank you." He turned to the forward display and seemed to straighten up. "Tactical officer? Fire."

And with a violent discharge of plasma from its capacitors, the collimated pulse of X-ray energy lanced outward.

One shot was all *Péridot*'s capacitors could give it. One shot was all it needed. In the distance, *Wanderer*'s bow disintegrated before the unstoppable fury of the energy beam. The fury continued unabated, boiling through the forward impeller ring, the forward cargo bay, the center of the hab spin section, and into the reactor.

And then, for a few seconds, the trinary system had a fourth sun.

The blaze had faded into a fiery glow when the com officer lifted a finger. "Captain Henderson? Shuttle Control reports Marines are geared and packed and ready to fly."

"Order them to launch," Henderson said. "Then signal *Guardian* and tell them reinforcements are on their way. Whoever the Manticorans have aboard *Saintonge*, I imagine they can use a little help."

"Yes, Sir." The officer turned back to his board.

"In a way, it's almost too bad," Henderson continued, almost wistfully. "With *Wanderer* gone, so is our best chance of figuring out who they were and where they came from. Can't sift much evidence from an expanding cloud of dust."

"Oh, I'm sure there'll be a few survivors left after we retake *Saintonge*," Flanders soothed. "And Haven has some very good interrogation techniques. Whatever they know, we'll get it out of them."

"There's also the bomb your people found in *Péridot*'s reactor room," Gill reminded him. "There may be clues in the materials or design that'll point us in the right direction."

"The important thing is that we've kept Havenite military technology from being stolen," Flanders said. Deliberately, he turned his eyes on Gill. "Which reminds me, Massingill. You and I need to have a talk."

Gill frowned. There'd been something in the commodore's tone right then. "Yes, Sir," he said. "I'll look forward to it."

"Maybe," Flanders said. "Maybe not."

☆   ☆   ☆

Massingill had been planning to wait until she'd stabilized her position and relative velocity before calling anyone. Boysenko beat her to it. "Colonel Massingill?" the younger woman's tentative voice came through Massingill's helmet. "Are you there? We're picking up a thruster trail about thirty kilometers from *Saintonge*. Is that you?"

"That's an affirmative, PO," Massingill said. "Nice timing—I was just about out of maneuvering fuel. Where are you?"

"In the second Havenite shuttle, the one Guzarwan brought from *Péridot*," Boysenko said. The relief in her voice was so thick that Massingill couldn't decide whether to be amused or touched. "Thank God. I thought you were..." She trailed away.

"Planning to go out in a blaze of glory?" Massingill offered.

"Yes, Ma'am," Boysenko said, sounding embarrassed. "When you said *Guardian* didn't need to send another shuttle, we all thought... I'm sorry, Ma'am."

"That's okay," Massingill assured her. "I just meant that they didn't need to send another shuttle because we already had the one you're now riding in. No, I'm not ready to die just yet. Not while Guzarwan is still alive. I need to at least take a crack at killing him first. So who's flying the shuttle? Pohjola?"

"It's Holderlin, Ma'am," the sergeant's voice cut in. "Just relax— we'll be there in a few."

"Yes, thanks, I think I can manage that," Massingill said dryly.

"One other thing, Ma'am," Holderlin said. "Boysenko, you want to do the honors?"

"Thank you, Sir," Boysenko said. "Colonel, we've just heard from *Péridot*. Your husband is alive and well."

Massingill caught her breath, her vision suddenly blurring. "You're sure?"

"Very sure, Ma'am," Boysenko said. "Commander Metzger says he called and talked directly with her. And the crew found the bomb and disarmed it. There are also two shuttles on the way—Commodore Flanders is sending all of *Péridot*'s Marines here to assist."

"Really," Massingill said, blinking away the tears as best she could. "In that case, Sergeant, you'd better step on it so we can get back inside. Can't have the Havenites thinking we're lazing on the job."

"Certainly can't, Ma'am, not at all," Holderlin agreed. "Stepping on it now, Ma'am. Anything else you'd like to talk about? We *do* have a few more minutes."

"Just concentrate on your flying," Massingill said. "The last thing I need now is to get run over by some hotshot who isn't watching where he's going."

"Yes, Ma'am."

"Actually, yes, there is something," Massingill corrected herself as a thought suddenly occurred to her. "Boysenko, do you know whose crazy idea it was to ram a shuttle into the radiator?"

"I believe it was Commander Metzger who came up with the shuttle part, Ma'am," Boysenko said. "She was giving Commodore Flanders the details. The radiator idea itself... I'm not absolutely sure, but it sounded like that one was Gravitics Tech Long."

Mentally, Massingill threw Long a salute. Rule-stickler, crazy-idea Travis Uriah Long. Somehow, it seemed fitting and proper that he'd been the lunatic behind this. "Thank you," she said. "If you talk to *Guardian* before I get back, please congratulate the XO for me on a brilliantly successful scheme."

She smiled tightly. "And tell Long the chocolate-chip cookies are on me."

☆　☆　☆

"I trust," Commodore Flanders said soberly, "that you see the problem."

Massingill looked sideways at her husband. Alvis was sitting there quietly, his eyes holding Flanders's gaze.

His hand was on Massingill's lap, gently holding her hand.

It had been years since he'd held her hand in public. Whatever this problem was that Flanders was about to unload on them, that alone almost made it worth it.

"Or possibly you don't," Flanders continued into the silence. "Let me explain." His gaze locked onto Alvis. "You're a civilian, retired from your naval position, yet traveling aboard a Royal Navy ship. You came aboard *Péridot*, ostensibly as part of a friendship envoy, but with the actual goal of giving Havenite military hardware a good, hard look. The only two reasons for you to do that are, one, to see if our ships are worth purchase by the Star Kingdom; or, two, as actual military espionage."

"Yes, I can see how the situation could be interpreted that way," Alvis said mildly.

"Well, *I* can't," Massingill said, her heart suddenly thudding in her chest. *Espionage?* After all they'd done for Flanders, he was going to drop *espionage* charges on them? "And as long as we're talking interpretation, how does the RHN interpret the fact that we saved its butt here?"

"Jean," Alvis said, quietly soothing.

"No, I mean it," Massingill said, ignoring the warning. Just because Captain Eigen had given his permission for them to talk to Flanders didn't mean the commodore had carte blanche to do or say whatever he wanted. "Because on *that* charge it's pretty clear we're guilty."

"Please," Flanders said, raising a calming hand. "You misunderstand. I'm not saying Haven is interpreting your actions that way. I'm suggesting that Chancellor of the Exchequer Breakwater will probably do so."

Massingill felt her jaw drop. Of all the names Flanders might have dropped into the conversation—*"Breakwater?"*

"Captain Eigen and I had a long talk yesterday," Flanders said, his voice turning a bit sour. "It's his opinion that Breakwater's faction has a vendetta against the Royal Navy, and that they'll do pretty much anything they can to make you look bad."

"That's a pretty accurate assessment," Massingill murmured. The politics were a bit more complicated than that, she knew, but the end result was the same.

"And since there's really nothing else the Royal Navy did here that can be the least bit criticized," Flanders continued, "it's Captain Eigen's belief that they'll latch onto Mr. Massingill's presence and activities."

Massingill looked at her husband.

"Yes, it's insane," Alvis said. "But I think the captain is right."

Massingill grimaced. Unfortunately, she had to agree. Whether or not this incident ever made it to the general public, Parliament would certainly be told, and Breakwater would never allow it to go into the records untarnished. Even if he had to invent the tarnish and slap it on himself.

"Captain Eigen also told me," Flanders continued, "that you two aren't particularly happy where you are."

Massingill frowned at him. That was also true; but what in the world did that have to do with any of this?

"So let me lay out my cards," Flanders went on, his eyes steady on her face. "Our reports indicate that the RMN is currently in a state of build-down, with some of our analysts wondering if it may even cease to exist in another few years. Mr. Massingill has already accepted early retirement, and opportunities for you, Colonel, are going to be steadily shrinking.

"The Republic of Haven Navy, on the other hand, is *the* up-and-coming power in this sector. We need good people—which you've already proven yourselves to be—and you need a service that will give you the opportunity to achieve your goals." He gestured to Massingill. "Senior rank for you, Colonel—" he shifted the gesture to Alvis "—a challenging, high-level yard or ship design position for you."

He cocked an eyebrow.

"So. What do you say?"

It took Massingill a few seconds to find her voice. This was not the direction she'd expected this conversation to go. She looked at her husband... and only then belatedly realized that her own confusion was nowhere to be found on his face.

And then, finally, she got it.

"You two have already set this up, haven't you?" she asked.

Alvis shrugged, a little uncomfortably. "We've discussed it," he admitted. "But nothing's been decided."

"But it could be?"

"It could be," Alvis agreed. "But only if you're on board. If you don't want to go, we don't."

Massingill took a deep breath, exhaled it slowly. "And Captain Eigen's all right with this?"

"He doesn't like the thought of losing us, no," Alvis said. "But he understands our position, and freely admits that Haven can offer us more than Manticore can right now."

"What about the politics?" Massingill asked, a small part of her mind noting that worrying about Breakwater and his cronies was a ridiculous thing to be doing right now.

"The captain concedes that Breakwater can still pick on me," Alvis said. "But it's going to look exceedingly petty when I'm not there to defend myself. More to the point, he's going to have a hard time accusing us of spying on Haven when Haven's just hired us."

"I suppose," Massingill said. "And this is really what you want to do?"

"Haven is the cutting edge of ship design and construction, Jean. It's the sort of thing I wanted to do on Manticore. It's basically what they promised I could do. Only Parliament won't let the RMN do anything."

He squeezed her hand a little tighter.

"It's a big step," he said quietly. "I want to go—you already know that. But if you don't, we won't. We'll go back to Guardian, and I'll never say another word about it."

Massingill took a careful breath. Serving with the bright, shining star in this part of the galaxy. No more of Parliament's close-fisted, short-sighted stupidity. Alvis happy. Her happy.

Yard dog and ship designer Alvis Massingill. Brigadier Jean Massingill.

"One request," she said. "Marine Squad 303, part of the team that helped us take back the *Saintonge*? Once I have my command, I'd like them assigned to it."

"I can certainly put in the request," Flanders said, frowning. "But I'm obligated to point out—how shall I put this?—that 303 isn't exactly the best Haven has to offer."

"You're right, they're not." Massingill smiled tightly. "But they *will* be."

CHAPTER THIRTY-ONE

TRAVIS DIDN'T RECOGNIZE any of the vehicles parked along the street or in the drive of his mother's house. But that was hardly surprising, given how little of his mother's life he'd shared recently.

Or really, shared ever.

So why was he here?

For a long moment he sat in his rented air car, amid the small cracklings as the engine and body cooled down from the flight, listening to that question as it echoed through his brain. His mother probably wasn't expecting him to show up for her birthday party. She probably didn't even know he and *Guardian* were back from Secour. In fact, he would give long odds that she didn't even remember that he'd *gone* to Secour.

His mother wouldn't care. Most of the other guests wouldn't know who he was. Travis's half-brother Gavin probably would be here, but Travis couldn't decide if that was a vote for or against.

There was a tap on his passenger window. Travis frowned, peering out at the woman bent over at the waist looking in at him. Her face was sideways at that angle, but she did look rather familiar...

With a sudden rush of warmth, he jabbed at the switch and unlocked the door. She pulled it open—"Petty Officer Long," Commander Metzger said, nodding in greeting. "May I join you?"

"Of course, Ma'am," Travis said. "I'm sorry—I didn't recognize you in civilian clothing—" He winced, belatedly realizing how stupid that sounded.

Fortunately, Metzger was nothing if not gracious. "Don't worry about it," she assured him. "Faces out of context. Happens to everyone."

"Thank you, Ma'am," Travis said. "Ah...may I ask...?"

"What I'm doing in the neighborhood?" Metzger gave a little shrug. "The Massingills used to live nearby. I'm helping some of their friends pack up their things for shipment to Haven."

"Oh," Travis said, feeling a sense of the universe tilting around him. A senior officer helping with the mundane job of packing was a scenario he'd somehow never imagined before. "I thought... shouldn't there be people to do that?"

"Senior officers are people, too, you know," Metzger said dryly. "But you're right. If they were still in the service, some yeomen would have been assigned. As it is, they have to rely on friends."

"Yes, Ma'am," Travis said. He somehow hadn't imagined senior officers having friends, either. "Do they, uh, need any more help?"

"Thank you, but we've got it covered." She gestured out the window. "I was told you were coming here today. I'm glad I was able to catch you before you went inside."

"Actually, Ma'am, I'm not sure I *am* going in," Travis confessed. "The main reason I came..." He stopped.

"Was to tell your mother and brother about your citation?"

Travis sighed. "Yes, Ma'am," he admitted. "I mean...I heard about it yesterday, and Captain Eigen seemed to think it was going through. I didn't know until I got here a few minutes ago and checked my mail... I know, it's petty of me."

"It's petty, all right," Metzger said, a sudden hard edge to her tone. "But the pettiness isn't yours. Do you know why the First Lord denied Captain Eigen's request?"

Travis shrugged uncomfortably. "Probably because I didn't really *do* anything," he said. "I had a couple of ideas, but you and Lieutenant Donnelly and Colonel Massingill were the ones that made everything happen."

"True," Metzger agreed. "But everything starts with ideas, and whether you were officially part of the team or not, you went above and beyond. No, the reason you were passed over was because of politics."

"*Politics?*" Travis said, completely confused now. "But I never—did I break some regulation, Ma'am? Or offend someone?"

"You, break regs? Never," Metzger said with a wry smile. "Change *offend* to *drive people crazy*, and that one's a maybe. But I'm not talking about *your* politics. I'm talking about your brother's. Were you aware that he's part of Breakwater's anti-Navy coalition?"

"Uh..." Hurriedly, Travis searched his memory. Now that she mentioned it, he *had* heard Gavin's name mentioned in conjunction with the Exchequer's. "I didn't realize that he was *that* much against us."

"Well, he is," Metzger said sourly. "And the people most annoyed by that are also fully aware of your blood relationship to him. Apparently, those same people think that any honors or citations awarded to you will somehow bleed over onto him and raise his status even higher among his peers."

Travis stared at her. Being passed over because he hadn't done anything noteworthy was one thing. But *this*—"That doesn't even make sense," he protested. "I've seen him maybe three times since I enlisted. We don't meet regularly—I don't think he even particularly *likes* me."

"I agree, it's insane," Metzger said. "But that's one of the frustrating things about pride and politics. Once an idea gets anchored to either of those, it no longer *has* to make sense. It just is."

Travis looked away. He'd joined the Navy looking for order and stability for his life. It had never occurred to him back then that stability was a two-edged sword. "I see," he said.

For a moment there was silence. "So what are you going to do?" Metzger asked. "I don't mean whether you're going to your mother's party or not. What are you going to do about the Navy?"

Travis let his eyes drift around the street and the houses. The *civilian* street; the *civilian* houses.

He could come back to this life, he knew. There would be a circle or two of hell to pay if he quit the Navy now, but he could do it. If nothing else, Gavin could probably help push his resignation through the system. He owed Travis that much.

But if he quit, he'd be turning his back on some good people. A *lot* of good people, really. Good, competent people, who'd found a way to do their jobs inside of an imperfect system.

People, moreover, who apparently recognized his contributions even if the system itself didn't. Why else would Metzger have bothered to chase him down this way, if not to subtly let him know that she appreciated what he'd done? Captain Eigen did, too, and probably a few others. Maybe even Lieutenant Donnelly.

Maybe that was all he really needed. Maybe it was people like that who were the stability he'd always hungered for.

"I signed up for five T-years, Ma'am," he said. "I'll serve it out."

"That's good," Metzger said. Out of the corner of his eye, Travis saw her reach into a pocket. "Because the Navy has plans for you." She held out a data chip. "Here are your new orders."

"My orders?" Travis frowned as he gingerly took the chip. "I thought I was on R and R."

"You are," Metzger said. "It's just that when you report back for duty you won't be returning to *Guardian*. You'll be transferred to a shore command to start working on your college degree."

Travis felt his eyes widen. *"College?"*

"That's right, Gravitics Tech Long," Metzger confirmed, a tight and slightly wicked smile creasing her face. "You're going to college . . . because a college degree is pretty much a requirement for Navy officers."

It took Travis a moment to find his voice. "But . . . you want to make me an *officer*?"

"Indeed we do," Metzger said. "It'll be college, then OCS, then a commission. The Powers That Be may have cut you out of a citation, but even they can't be everywhere. Captain Eigen put in your application, I seconded it, and we even got a statement from Colonel Massingill before she and Gill headed off for Haven. You've been officially approved, so if you accept, there's not a damn thing anyone can do about it unless you flunk out. So don't."

"I won't, Ma'am," Travis said, his hand starting to shake a little. "I—thank you, Ma'am."

"No thanks needed," she assured him. "You earned it." She pointed at the chip in his hand. "In the meantime, there's a party to attend, and possibly a little bragging to be done. Have at it, and don't be modest."

Her smile faded. "Because you're going places, Petty Officer Long. I'm not sure where those places are, but you're going to go there. And I'm thinking that at the end, the Royal Manticoran Navy is going to be damn glad that you were along for the ride."

Travis swallowed hard. "Thank you, Ma'am. I'll try to live up to your expectations."

"Don't worry about *my* expectations," she said. "Just live up to your own."

She smiled dryly. "And stock up on your sleep. OCS isn't a resort camp like Casey-Rosewood."

"Yes, Ma'am," Travis said, smiling back. "I'll remember that."

☆   ☆   ☆

Prime Minister Burgundy looked up from the report and shook his head. "Incredible," he said. "Simply incredible."

"Isn't it?" Edward agreed, studying Burgundy's face. There was a darkness there that seemed to go beyond even the threat that the Star Kingdom—indeed, the entire region—had just avoided. "It's staggering to think of what might have happened had they succeeded. Even an old heavy cruiser is a formidable weapon; but a modern battlecruiser like *Saintonge*?" He gestured toward Burgundy's tablet. "I daresay even Breakwater may have to eat this morning's words."

"You mean his characterization of the Navy as a group of squealing pigs in a trough?" Burgundy said sourly. "Oh, yes, the Exchequer was in rare form today." He huffed out a sigh. "Only one flaw in your theory. Nothing in this report is going to change Breakwater's mind...because he's already seen it."

"He's *what*?"

"I don't know who leaked it to him," Burgundy said sourly. "But I know for a fact that he obtained a copy over the weekend. He knows exactly what happened at Secour."

"And he still insists that the Star Kingdom is overmilitarized?" Edward demanded. "That's insane."

Burgundy shrugged uncomfortably. "You have to look at it from his point of view. We have three battlecruisers in service. Even if Guzarwan had succeeded, he'd still only have had one. The man was incredibly bold, but he wasn't incredibly stupid."

"I'm sure the fact that the Star Kingdom would have been off his list would have been of great comfort to Casca, Zuckerman, or Ramon," Edward countered. "*Or* Ueshiba. Remember, Guzarwan was using *their* credentials. That might mean he'd already checked them out and seen something there he liked. And not just their fine mushroom dishes."

"Perhaps," Burgundy said. "Another possibility is that he had Ueshiban credentials because they're the ones who hired him."

"You're not serious," Edward said, frowning. "Wouldn't that be rather—I don't know. Obvious?"

"Obvious, or calculatedly audacious," Burgundy said. "They might have given him credentials on the assumption that everyone would dismiss them for exactly that reason." He made a face. "I'm almost sorry Captain Eigen had to kill him. It sounds like the prisoners the Marines collected had no idea who actually hired them."

"Haven's got good investigators," Edward said. "If the prisoners know anything, they'll get it out of them."

At the third point of their triangle, King Michael cleared his throat. "I think, gentlemen, you're both missing the point," he said. "As is our Lord Exchequer. Yes, Guzarwan didn't get the warships he went to Secour to steal. But who's to say those are the only ones he's gone after? Or that his other efforts haven't succeeded?"

A chill ran up Edward's back. His father was right. Somehow, he'd assumed this had been a one-off job, based on a once-in-a-lifetime set of interlocking opportunities. "Wouldn't we have heard if something like that had happened?"

"Would we?" the King asked. "If Guzarwan had succeeded at Secour, I hardly think Haven would have sent out a news release. I doubt any other victims would behave any differently."

"Ships disappear all the time," Burgundy muttered. "Not as often now as they used to, but they still occasionally just vanish into hyperspace."

"And it's much easier to blame forces of nature than admit you had a warship stolen," the King added.

"So what you're saying is that someone out there could already have a battle fleet?" Edward asked. "And that we have no idea who?"

"It's not quite *that* bad," the King soothed. "A destroyer or cruiser takes a certain level of infrastructure and money just to keep going, and a battlecruiser is even worse. If Guzarwan was representing a rogue system, it has to be one that has both spare cash and the expertise to train people to operate military-class equipment."

"So you don't think they were part of the pirate gang Casca thinks they've found?" Edward asked.

"The resources we're talking about should be well beyond a group of pirates," the King said. "Certainly any gang trying to survive on the sparse traffic around here. No, if it's an independent group, then I think we're looking at something more like the Free Brotherhood."

Edward winced. "What a lovely thought."

"It is, isn't it?" the King agreed. "Still, even a new Brotherhood will probably have a planetary base somewhere, and that base will still need that threshold of money and expertise. Those are the systems where we'll start our investigation."

"*Our* investigation?" Edward asked, frowning. "I thought we agreed that Haven would take point on this one."

"*Haven* agreed that Haven would take point," the King corrected. "That doesn't mean we can't poke around a little on our own. Admiral Locatelli's been pressing the Cabinet for years to authorize more hyperspace experience for his ships and crews. This might be a good time to give it to him."

"*If* you can get it past Breakwater," Edward growled.

"I know," the King agreed heavily. "But we have to try."

"We have to *try*?" Edward repeated, a sudden stirring of anger and frustration rippling through him. "With all due respect, Your Majesty, this has moved beyond politics. There's someone out there—someone maybe very close to Manticore—who's collecting or at least trying to collect a full set of capital warships."

"You're right, of course," the King agreed, his voice suddenly sounding old. "This has indeed moved beyond politics. The problem is, I haven't." He looked over at Burgundy. "And I don't think I ever can."

Edward stared at his father, his flash of anger gone. "I don't understand."

"I'm tired, Edward," Michael said quietly. "I've been at this for a long time. Longer than I expected. Much longer than I ever wanted." He waved a hand. "You create alliances in this job, some permanent, most temporary. Every one of those alliances and compromises creates a connection, some thickness of political thread that now runs between the two of you." He took a deep breath, exhaled it softly. "At some point, you find that all those threads have enmeshed you in a web from which there's no escape or even freedom of movement."

"The bottom line is that he can't push Parliament for the kind of reform and funding the Navy needs," Burgundy said softly. "It would trigger a massive governmental crisis, and if Breakwater played his cards right it could very well end in a complete gutting of the Navy."

"I have too many threads encircling me, Edward," Michael said. "I can't revive the Navy." He smiled faintly. "That task will be up to you."

Edward's breath caught in his throat. "*Me?*"

"Oh, not yet, of course," Michael hastened to assure him. "Not until you're king. But that day isn't far off. And when it arrives, in the pomp and bustle and uncertainty as everyone sizes up the new monarch, that will be the time for you two to strike."

Edward looked at Burgundy. "Us *two*?"

"Us two," Burgundy confirmed. He straightened up in his chair.

And suddenly, the weight of years and diffidence that Edward had assumed were a permanent part of his face seemed to crack like thick piecrust and fall away. The eyes gazing at him across the room were the eyes of the young Davis Harper, Duke Burgundy, eyes that blazed with hope and righteous fire and the future of the Star Kingdom. "Your father isn't a fighter, Edward," he said. His voice was still the older Burgundy's voice, but it too had a hint of old fire behind it. "Not in the way you want, or in the way the Navy needs. And up until now, there seemed no harm in just letting history drift along while we waited for the time to be right.

"But drifting is no longer an option. With this document, Parliament is going to get a wake-up call."

"And we're going to persuade them how?" Edward asked cautiously.

"Not by precipitating a crisis, if that's what you're worried about," Michael assured him. "It'll start slowly and carefully, with a gentle levering of one Lord at a time. It'll probably take a few years, but by the time you ascend the throne, the majority you need to revive the RMN will be there waiting for you."

"I see," Edward said, not really sure he did. "And how does this levering occur?"

"I told you I was trapped in this mass of political threads," the King said. "But those threads go both ways. There are favors that can be called in, desires that can be met, honors that can sway both hearts and votes."

"And if more is needed," Burgundy added darkly, "be assured that I've been in this business long enough to know where all the most interesting bodies are buried. The right word, the brandishing of a figurative shovel, and we'll have what we need."

Edward winced. That same figurative shovel would also undoubtedly make them a whole new set of enemies. He and Burgundy would have to think long and hard before they went that route.

"But that's for your future," Michael said. "Right now, you get to go back to your family, and from there back to your ship."

"Right," Edward said dryly. "Like I'm going to be able to relax *now*."

"You will," his father said. "Because on at least one issue, our Lord Exchequer is perfectly correct: we will never be anyone's primary target. Not with three battlecruisers on station and another five ready to reactivate."

"Wars, like all political conflicts, are fought for a reason," Burgundy added. "And while I love the Star Kingdom I also know that there's nothing on Manticore, Sphinx, or Gryphon that's worth that much trouble. To anyone."

☆　　☆　　☆

The best thing about working for Axelrod of Terra, Karen Wamocha had always maintained, was the pay. A star-spanning megacorporation like Axelrod could afford to hire the best, and could more than afford to write salaries commensurate with that quality.

The worst thing about working for them was the overall working environment. Specifically, the scenery.

There wasn't much you could do, after all, with a windowless office ten stories below Beowulf street level.

There was a projection wall, of course, that could dial in any view Wamocha wanted. But it was only visual, without the sounds and aromas that made the real world come alive to her, and she'd gotten bored with the toy after her first month. Now, she usually just set it to a nice dark blue. There was the row of potted plants across the front of her desk, and the giant fern in the corner, but aside from providing a little extra oxygen, there wasn't much point in them anymore, either.

She was staring at the plants, toying with the idea of simply saying screw it and escaping to the Tapestry Mountains for a few days of skiing, when there was a tap at her door.

She looked up to see Luther Luangpraseut standing in the opening, an oddly intense look on his face. "Chief, can I see you a moment?" he asked.

"Sure, Luther," Wamocha said, gesturing him in. Proper business etiquette recommended that managers address their subordinates by their job title or a deferential form of their last name. But *analyst* was such a vapid term, and having mangled Luther's name three times in his first day on the job, Wamocha had given up on that approach, as well. "What is it?"

"Maybe nothing." Luther stepped inside, pointedly closing the door behind him. "Maybe something big. I don't know if you remember, but one of the jobs I was hired for was to go through all the old astrogation data, consolidate it, and recode it into the new storage format."

"Yes, I remember," Wamocha said. She did, too, though she'd have been hard-pressed to pull up Luther's job description without that hint. "And?"

"I've been working on the Manticore system," he said, stepping around behind her desk and inserting a chip into her computer. "I may be crazy, but I think there may be something there."

Wamocha gazed at the data sheet that came up, the mountains, skiing, and even the inherent dreariness of windowless rooms abruptly forgotten. The data wasn't even close to being conclusive. But all the right hints were indeed there.

And if those hints weren't just data-smoothing constructs...

"The thing is, I'm wondering how to proceed," Luther continued. "I know our division has a contract with the League to hunt down wormhole junctions. But Manticore isn't *in* the League. So does that mean we don't need to tell them?"

Wamocha smiled tightly. There were some situations in which a manager had to make decisions on the fly, using his or her best judgment. But on this one, at least, company instructions were extremely specific. "That's exactly correct," she confirmed. "The contract explicitly states that the League only gets information about its own local wormholes." It wasn't all *that* explicit, she knew, having made a point of slogging through the whole damn thing a couple of years ago. But the concept was implicit enough in the fine print to stand up if there was ever a court challenge. "Where's your raw data?"

"Mine? It's right there," he said, pointing to the chip. "But really, all the background information is out there for the taking. Anyone who knows what to look for could dig it out with a little work."

Wamocha nodded. Fortunately, though, no one would. Manticore had been sitting out in the middle of nowhere for over a hundred years, with ships coming and going throughout that time. No one would ever find a wormhole in that system for the simple reason that no one would ever go looking for one. Only Axelrod, with its vast resources and huge bottom line, could afford the luxury of spending time and money on this kind of crapshoot.

Which was why, when one of those gambles paid off, Axelrod deserved the lion's share of the profit. Axelrod, and the Axelrod employees responsible.

And if there was indeed a Junction in the Manticore system, damn right there would be profit. There would be profit and to spare.

Luther was looking expectantly at her. "Well, they're all welcome to try," she told him, mentally pulling up the procedure listing she'd memorized so long ago in the hope that one of these long shots would someday come in. "But never mind them. Here's what we're going to do. As of right now, you're out of the research tank. Turn all your projects over to Carnahiba and Oehm—tell them I'll talk to them later about sharing out the load with the rest of the team. Then collect your computer, your files, and everything else you've got down there and report back up here. You know the visitor's office across from the conference room? That's yours until I can get someone reassigned and we can move you into something more permanent. What's your pay level?"

Luther's eyes had gone wide. "Uh—uh—Five," he managed.

"You're now at Seven," Wamocha told him. "What the hell—make it Eight. Take the rest of the day to relocate and then go home and have a nice, relaxing evening. Starting tomorrow, your one and only job will be to start pulling together everything you can find on the Manticore system. And I mean *everything*—astrogation records, merchant ship course adjustments and fuel usage, regional grav wave data, and anything else that might help nail this down. Pull it, consolidate it, graph it, normalize it, and otherwise just analyze the living hell out of it. Clear?"

"Y-yes, Ma'am," Luther stuttered, his face glowing now like a minor star.

"Good." She lifted a warning finger. "One other thing. As of this moment, this project is under the Black Dagger protocol. You understand what that means?"

"Yes, Ma'am," he said again, more confidently this time. "It stays between you, me, and the Board."

"Correct," Wamocha said. "Once you have your stuff in your new office come back here and I'll give you the encryption you'll use for everything from now on. I'll go ahead and re-encrypt this chip; you'll do the same for everything else on your computer. Questions?"

"No, Ma'am," he said.

"Then get to it." She smiled at him, something you *never* did with subordinates. "Welcome to management level, Luther."

"Thank you—" he braced himself "—Karen?"

"Karen it is," she confirmed. "Now get moving. Time is money."

"Yes, Ma—Karen." He flashed a smile of his own, and was gone.

Wamocha turned her attention back to the data, her smile fading a little. It still could be nothing, she reminded herself firmly. In which case the huge bonuses Axelrod offered in these instances would blow away in the wind.

And even if there *was* a wormhole it would likely take years to confirm and track down. They would have to send ships out there, probably more than one, packed with the kind of expensive and sophisticated instruments that hadn't even existed a few T-years ago. Even more important, the surveys would have to be kept utterly quiet, lest the Manticorans get wind of what was lurking in their system. Subtlety, like everything else of value, also cost time.

But if the wormhole was there—if it *was* there—the rewards would be astronomical. For her, for Luther, and for Axelrod.

She could but hope.

And speaking of Axelrod, it was time to share the cautious good news. Pulling up the Black Dagger encryption, she began composing the most important letter of her life.

AFTERWORD

IN THE AUTHORS' FOREWORD, we explained that there are really three authors for this book and mentioned something called BuNine in connection with how Tom Pope became involved with the Honorverse in the first place and this book in particular. Those of you who have read *House of Steel: the Honorverse Companion* will have recognized that name. Those of you who *haven't* read *House of Steel* (and I'm sure all of you had some sort of valid excuse) may not have recognized it, however.

So, we'd like to tell you that Bureau Nine (affectionately known to inhabitants of the Honorverse as BuNine, for short) originated as a group of Honorverse fans that originally coalesced around Ad Astra's *Saganami Island Tactical Simulator*. BuNine is not just a group of Honor Harrington fans, however. About half of them have some sort of connection to the US military, mostly the Navy, in either a civilian capacity or in uniform. The other members include artists, lawyers, computer specialists, and the like, all of them expert in their own fields (and all of them prepared to offer their skills to David . . . and to argue with him upon occasion, shocking though he knows his legions of devoted readers might find that to believe). They had a tremendous amount to do with *House of Steel*—indeed, they wrote (with David's oversight and checking) three hundred and eighty of its five hundred and sixty pages and produced the sixteen pages of full-color plates which illustrate that volume. A huge percentage of the content they contributed consisted of their applying their own expertise and historical knowledge to actually building portions of the Honor-verse which David had sketched out in his notes but never fully developed for the reader. When BuNine got done, the portions of the Honorverse covered in *House of Steel* had moved from elements which had been described in passing into strong, fully developed components of the Honorverse literary canon.

Speaking for himself, David has found all of BuNine's members immensely helpful, and they have moved from fans who read his books to people who collaborate with him in *improving* his books and who have become close personal friends, as well. BuNine's members in particular contributed to *A Call to Duty* by critiquing the manuscript and sharing their insights—always useful, frequently entertaining, and occasionally painful—into that mystic military rite of passage known as "boot camp." They offered us plenty of other insights, as well, and we'd like to specifically thank Barry Messina for sharing his memories and experience and serving as a window into "how this stuff *really* works" for people creating a fictitious Navy.

Thanks guys, you did good.

David Weber
Timothy Zahn
Thomas Pope